PRAISE FOR PIKE LEGAL THRILLER SERIES

"As a fan of William Bernhardt, I've been reading Ben Kincaid adventures for years. When the Daniel Pike books dropped, I became an instant fan due to the interesting themes, legal challenges and fascinating characters. Now, like peanut butter getting into chocolate, two great things have come together . . . . Bernhardt has elevated both characters into an Avengers level event that thriller fans will love!"

— RJ JOHNSON, AUTHOR OF *DREAMSLINGER* (FOR *PARTNERS IN CRIME*)

"A man on the run... a woman on the run... in a thriller that hits the ground running... then running faster... then absolutely flying. And you're flying, too, flying through the pages with one of the masters of the modern thriller at the controls. William Bernhardt knows when to soar and when to dive, when to make you sweat and when to let you breathe, when to throw this flying machine into a barrel roll that will absolutely shock you and when to bring you home safe and satisfied."

— WILLIAM MARTIN, *NEW YORK TIMES*-BESTSELLING AUTHOR OF *THE LINCOLN LETTER* AND *DECEMBER '41* (FOR *PLOT/COUNTERPLOT*)

"William Bernhardt returns with a stunning piece of fiction.... In a story that mixes fiction with the deadliest realities, Bernhardt provides readers with a novel unlike any I have read in a long while. With graphic depictions told in a highly realistic fashion, William Bernhardt proves why he is at the top of his game and eager to share his skills with readers!"

— *BOOK REVIEWS TO PONDER*, CANADAMATT (FOR *PLOT/COUNTERPLOT*

"*Exposed* has everything I love in a thriller: intricate plot twists, an ensemble of brilliant heroines, and jaw-dropping drama both in and out of the courtroom. William Bernhardt knows how to make the law come alive."

— TESS GERRITSEN, *NEW YORK TIMES*-BESTSELLING AUTHOR OF THE RIZZOLI & ISLES THRILLERS

"*Splitsville* is a winner—well-written, with fully developed characters and a narrative thrust that keeps you turning the pages."

— GARY BRAVER, BESTSELLING AUTHOR OF *TUNNEL VISION*

"*Final Verdict* is a must read with a brilliant main character and surprises and twists that keep you turning pages. One of the best novels I've read in a while."

— ALICIA DEAN, AWARD-WINNING AUTHOR OF *THE NORTHLAND CRIME CHRONICLES*

"*Judge and Jury* is a fast-paced, well-crafted story that challenges each major character to adapt to escalating attacks that threaten the very existence of their unique law firm."

— RICK LUDWIG, AUTHOR OF *SOUL OF A SLEUTH*

"I could not put *Trial by Blood* down. The plot is riveting....This book is special."

— NIKKI HANNA, AUTHOR OF *CAPTURE LIFE*

"Once started, it is hard to let [*The Last Chance Lawyer*] go, since the characters are inviting, engaging and complicated....You will enjoy it."

— *CHICAGO DAILY LAW BULLETIN*

"Thrillingly interwoven plots are Bernhardt's forte, a talent he once again demonstrates full-blown in his latest superb thriller."

— *BOOKLIST* (FOR *DARK JUSTICE*)

"William Bernhardt is a born stylist, and his writing through the years has aged like a fine wine...."

— STEVE BERRY, BESTSELLING AUTHOR OF *THE KAISER'S WEB*

"Bernhardt is the undisputed master of the courtroom drama."

— *LIBRARY JOURNAL*

JUSTICE FOR ALL

Copyright © 2024 by William Bernhardt

Cover design by Maria Novilla Saravia

Interior design by Lara Bernhardt

Illustrations by Ian Seo

All rights reserved.

No part of this book may be reproduced in any form or by any electronic or mechanical means, including information storage and retrieval systems, without written permission from the author, except for the use of brief quotations in a book review.

WILLIAM BERNHARDT

#1 NATIONAL BESTSELLING AUTHOR

JUSTICE FOR ALL

A
DANIEL
PIKE
NOVEL

BABYLON BOOKS

*This one's for the dreamers...
like Jerry Siegel, Joe Shuster, and Bill Finger*

"It's not so much do what you like
as it is that you like what you do."

— STEPHEN SONDHEIM, *SUNDAY IN THE PARK WITH GEORGE*

Part One
CHILDREN AND ART

CHAPTER ONE

MICKEY MOUSE MIGHT BE BELOVED BY CHILDREN ALL AROUND the world, but Lydia Franchini hated the rodent enough to kill him. Hack him into tiny gray bits. Serve him as pâté. Better yet, serve him to Pluto as pâté. In a dog dish. Then she could go to work on the damn duck. Roast mallard flambé with cherry jus and Lyonnaise potatoes. That sounded about right.

Lydia collapsed into a chair, one hand pressed against her forehead. Okay, when you started fantasizing about the grisly dismemberment of the world's most beloved characters, it might be time to take a breather.

This had been one of the toughest weeks of her life. On Tuesday, her idiotic husband lost his balance while making toast and fell face-first on the kitchen floor. Four stitches. Her oldest daughter went into the hospital with a perforated colon. Her taxes were twice what she expected them to be and the driver's-side window in her ancient Ford Expedition was lowered and stuck. In Florida. Where the sun shines all day every day. Unrelentingly. She couldn't protect herself from the sun with an executioner's hood. That window was an invitation to skin lesions.

Some days she regretted retiring. Granted, twenty-two years in Yonkers was long enough for anyone. Her parents were snowbirds, fleeing upstate New York for Kissimmee. It only made sense for her to follow. An only child should keep an eye on her elderly parents. Except she found her pension impossible to live on, even with a working spouse, leading to this miserable job in the Baggage Claim office for terminals A and B at Orlando International Airport.

Roger passed through the door with the hangdog expression he bore most of the time. "Brace yourself for the worst."

She briefly wondered what could be worse. When she thought of something, she immediately stopped thinking about it, because it was too terrifying to contemplate.

"I always do," she replied. "Something new happening?"

"Schedule change. Festival starts the twenty-seventh now."

"Food & Wine?"

"Except earlier."

Sadly, she knew exactly what he was talking about. Disney World. Because when you worked at MCO (Orlando International), it was all about the mouse. EPCOT's festivals were a major draw. Kids thought EPCOT was boring, but since opening day it had been the universal favorite of dads, since it had no roller coasters and allowed them to pretend the educational content justified the gigantic cost of the vacation. Time passed. EPCOT got a roller coaster, added characters, and lost most of the educational content. They replaced the science with food and liquor, which turned out to be a better draw.

Lydia stared stone-faced at the wall. "Mobs of tourists will pour in."

"Mobs of drunken tourists will pour out."

"Carrying more crap than they can shove into their bags. Creating more work for us. Damnable mouse."

"The mouse isn't the problem. It's the people who scalp him and put his ears on their heads."

"I think I may have reached the end of my tenure at this position, Roger."

"Say it ain't so. How would I get through the day without you?"

"You'd manage."

"Come on. There are worse jobs."

"Are there, though? America loses two million suitcases a year, and I think at least half of them arrive here. I babysit them till their owners sober up and realize they left the bag with their Collector's Edition Lego Cinderella's Castle with the TSA. If they don't show for three months, their bags get sent to Scottsboro for auction. The airline makes a bundle reselling other people's junk, Louis Vuitton bags and Prada shoes. Do we get a cut? Of course not. All we get is paperwork."

Roger snuffled. "I don't mind the paperwork."

Lydia didn't hear him. "Half the people who come in to complain haven't waited for the carousels to stop spinning. And when did everyone start packing like they had a private audience with the queen? Just stick a pair of jeans and some T-shirts in your carryon bag. You don't need the entire Sephora counter or overpriced dresses from Anthropologie to go to a theme park."

"Remember the lady who wanted to pack her desk? In pieces?"

"She was a writer. Claimed she couldn't work unless she sat at that very desk. With her writing blanket. And her writing cat."

"Did she pack the cat with the desk?"

"Probably. She was bonkers."

"She was a writer. They're all bonkers. Got any gummies?"

"Sorry, no. You're out?"

"Took my last one a little while ago. But I've got five hours till I can go home."

Lydia did have some, but her supply was low and she didn't

want to share. Took Florida forever to legalize cannabis. She wasn't going to give it away. Technically, it was for her anxiety, but she'd never get through the day without those chewy sugary mind-melters. "Need to stop by the store on the way home."

"Me too. After payday. They don't give those babies away."

Roger used too much. She did a little, the occasional microdose, just enough to take the edge off. Roger overindulged and she'd had to cover for him on more than one occasion. She knew her limits. If she took too much, her thinking got muddled. Foggy. And if she took far too much, she started imagining things, like dramatic confrontations with killer mice and . . . and . . .

How long had that suitcase been sitting by the door?

Did someone bring it in? Was she so tired or so busy that she missed a delivery?

After several years here, she could ID luggage the way NASCAR enthusiasts can ID cars or TCM fans can ID movie actresses. That was a blue hardshell Gonex bag, a savvy choice for someone who could travel light. Even overseas, that bag fit into overhead compartments. And it contained a compression packing cube that allowed people to squeeze in more clothes without wrinkling them. If she ever went anywhere, that's the bag she'd want.

She glanced at Roger. He was paying no attention, apparently focused on a wolf spider crawling across the ceiling. Marijuana. Wonderful drug.

Where did the blue bag come from? Normally, long after each carousel stopped spinning, one of the skycaps brought her the leftovers. Occasionally the airline or luggage handler made an error, but by far, the biggest cause of lost luggage was morons racing through the terminal after too many drinks. TSA PreCheck or CLEAR might be great for seasoned travelers, but some people didn't need to be rushing.

The blue bag remained at the side of the room, glaring at

her. Okay, maybe it wasn't glaring, since it didn't have eyes. But it was definitely in the room.

Taunting her. Laughing at her.

Daring her to come close.

"Roger?"

He didn't answer. The spider consumed all his attention.

It was a suitcase. She looked at them all day long.

But this one was different. She didn't know why. She had a feeling. Which sounded like the dumbest thing in the world. People don't get feelings about suitcases. Do they?

She took a step closer.

The suitcase stayed where it was.

She took another step.

She felt like an idiot. She was approaching this lost luggage like it was rampaging lion. But where had it come from? Something weird was going on.

When she was maybe two feet away, she detected the odor. She didn't recognize it, but she smelled it, insinuative and nauseating, strong and wrong. A sudden warmth permeated her body. Was she about to faint? She'd never hear the end of it from her husband if she had to get stitches too. She knelt, reached out to steady herself . . .

. . . and laid a hand on the suitcase. Which felt like every other suitcase she'd ever touched. What the hell did she expect? This was Orlando International, not a Stephen King novel.

She picked up the suitcase. It was light. Couldn't be much inside.

But there was something. She could hear it rolling around. It didn't come close to filling the bag, so it thudded from side to side.

What was it?

Roger couldn't care less, so she decided to find out for herself.

She crouched down. The suitcase wasn't locked. All she had

to do was pop the latches and the lid would spring open. It violated protocol and privacy, she felt it was justified in this instance. "I'm opening this."

"Should you scan it first?"

"No one's trying to get it on an airplane. You think terrorists want to bring down the Lost Luggage hegemony?"

Roger smiled slightly. "You know what my momma used to say?"

"How could I possibly know what your mother used to say?"

"Curiosity killed the cat."

Whatever. She used her thumb and forefinger to pop the latches.

The contents spilled out and rolled several feet across the floor, leaving a wet trail in its wake.

Lydia's scream was so frenzied that everyone within earshot froze like they'd been dipped in liquid nitrogen. The screaming went on so long that when it finally stopped, most people assumed the screamer had died.

CHAPTER TWO

Dan knew he should focus on the counterfeiting case, especially now, when the cross-examination of the primary opposing witness was imminent. But all he could think about were his sneakers.

Funny, he reflected, how some of life's biggest decisions are made gradually, as if you're feeling your way down a long hallway in the dark. Only later, when you recount the story in retrospect, does it become a coherent purposeful narrative in which you made intelligent steps toward a clear goal . . .

That seemed to be the story of his life. First he was a hotshot big-firm defense attorney for the city's pond scum. Then he joined the Last Chance Lawyer firm and defended needy clients who deserved representation. Then the LCL boss, Ben Kincaid, asked him to run the whole outfit, and he did for a time. Not very well.

Now he was back in the courtroom while his pregnant wife ran LCL. And if he couldn't impugn the integrity of the man on the witness stand, his client was going down hard. So he needed to stop thinking about his shoes . . .

For years, Dan had favored Air Jordans in the courtroom,

preferably black and black-soled kicks that could pass as dress shoes if no one looked too carefully. But now that he was launching Dan 2.0—actually, Dan 3.0—he felt it was time to evolve. Air Jordans are great sneakers, but they're not the only great sneakers. Sean Wotherspoon's Air Max sneaks and some of the Adidas lines were beautifully designed. He loved his latest, the AJ3 Off Noir. After deliberating for about half an hour this morning, he chose the Noir, but he still wasn't sure he'd made the right selection. What if one of the jurors didn't like them? What if the judge didn't like them? What if he should be thinking about his case rather than his sneakers?

His client, Adam Lopez, had been a part-time cashier at a local big-box lawn-and-garden store. He was arrested for violating the US federal code provision prohibiting the "uttering of counterfeit US currency" after fake hundreds appeared in the company safe—shortly after Adam started working there.

He sat at the defense table beside his client. "How are you feeling?"

Adam was a young, thin, quiet man. He'd graduated high school and was trying to make enough cash to go to college. He wanted to study environmental sciences and protect the planet from climate change and other existential threats. But he would never get the chance if his life was derailed by a ten-year prison sentence. "I'm feeling like I'd rather be anywhere else in the world."

"Have you figured out why Gordon Doyle is accusing you of something you didn't do?"

"No. I never did anything to him. But he's didn't like me. Not from the first day I worked there. Practically ran me down in his shiny new Dodge Charger outside the courthouse this morning."

"Doyle's been working in the same store for more than a decade. He'll probably be there for several more. You, by contrast, have a promising future ahead of you." He pondered a moment. "Tell me something about your boss that most people don't know."

Adam blinked several times rapidly. "By definition . . . if most people don't know it . . ."

"There must be something. You worked with him for several weeks."

Adam thought another moment. "He loves tabletop games."

A smile crossed Ben's face. That was his partner Jimmy's area. One of his many pop-culture interests. He sent Jimmy a text. "Any games in particular?"

"Catan. Settlers of Catan. He said that it's the greatest game of the modern era. But he also liked some of the older stuff."

Dan nodded. "That was what I needed."

"That's all? You should've told me before."

Dan knew he couldn't win every case, but he also knew Ben wouldn't have assigned this one to him if he didn't think Adam was innocent. There had to be some way to take this witness down and prove he was lying.

He peered at Doyle's face, trying to read between the wrinkles. He thought about this man's testimony on direct, plus the public statements he'd given. His certainty about Adam's guilt. He seemed adamant, more positive than most eyewitnesses . . .

Which convinced him Doyle was the real counterfeiter.

All he had to do was prove it.

"How long have you worked at Garden Depot?"

Gordon Doyle was a middle-sized man, pudgy, with a large nose and more cheek than mouth. He had strong arms, though, and his chest appeared bigger than it had the last time Dan saw him. He'd been pumping iron. Given the speedy results, Doyle must have a gym membership. Maybe a personal trainer.

"About twelve years."

"What's your position?"

"General floor manager."

"What are your duties?"

"Basically to make sure everything runs smoothly. I oversee the floor displays, the sales team, the stock team, the janitorial staff."

"And the safe?"

"Yes." Doyle shifted slightly in his seat. "I'm also in charge of transferring the money collected each day from cash registers to the safe, and later from the safe to the bank. A teller first spotted the counterfeits."

Dan withdrew an exhibit from his backpack. The bill was in a transparent plastic protector. He introduced it into evidence. "Would this be an example of the counterfeit bills the bank teller found?"

Doyle barely looked. "Yes."

"They're good forgeries. Was the teller surprised?"

"Objection." Dan's opponent was a new kid, a fresh hire named Brandon Stall. Dan knew the DA, Jazlyn Prentiss. If she assigned Baby Driver to this case, she didn't care about it too much.

Or she also suspected Adam might be innocent. And she wanted Dan to have the opportunity to prove it. At any rate, this was the kid's first objection of the day and he looked as if he was afraid the judge might scold him for speaking out loud.

Judge Joplin arched an eyebrow. "May I ask the basis for your objection?"

"This stuff . . . doesn't matter."

"Not relevant?"

"Yeah, that's it. Not relevant . . . whether a bank teller was surprised."

"I thought as much." Judge Joplin was Black, henna-haired, and smart as a whip. In her fifteen years on the bench, she'd probably seen it all. Nothing fazed her. She kept greasing the wheels and plowing forward, which in this case, meant basically doing the prosecutor's job for him. "Counsel, you do seem to have strayed from the topic of counterfeiting."

Dan cleared his throat. "It all ties together, your honor. Give me another minute and all will be clear."

The judge frowned. "Very well. Based on your assurance, I'll allow the witness to answer." She nodded at Doyle.

"Actually, he was the opposite of surprised. He was . . . unsurprised." Yes, that would be the opposite of "surprised." This guy needed to read more. Of course, if he read more, he might not have been working at Garden Depot.

"He was unsurprised to see a national chain store passing fake bills?"

"It's been going around."

"Counterfeiting?"

"That's what I was told. Lots of fake bills, mostly hundreds but some smaller. I've heard people talking about it. Apparently you can buy these fakes on Amazon."

Dan pivoted, glancing back at his partner Garrett Wainwright, who sat in the back row of the gallery. Garrett handled most of their research and had off-the-charts computer-hacking skills.

"Why would anyone buy these?"

"People use them for jokes and parties. Movies and TV."

Dan had been in LA recently, and he learned that movie studios typically used oversized bills that couldn't be confused for the real thing but photographed well enough to pass. But these bills looked like the real deal. Anyone who glanced at them would assume they were real. The only difference in appearance was that if he looked closely in the space where there should be a serial number, it instead read: PLAYMONEY.

The judge nodded. "It's thinner. Less friction. Like notebook paper."

"On the nose. Real currency is a weave of cotton and linen. No paper. As a result, it feels thicker."

"Your honor," Stall said, "this is fascinating background info on counterfeiting. But I don't care how thick the paper is. All that matters is that Adam Lopez passed fake bills."

"Except," Dan said, eyeing the judge, "how could he hope to pass something that felt so different? He knew someone would pick it up and transfer it to the safe and later to the bank."

Stall shrugged. "Not all criminals are Lex Luthor."

"No. This counterfeiter is more of a Kite Man. Or Condiment King."

And Jimmy thought Dan wasn't listening when he prattled on about comic books. Ha!

Judge Joplin, however, was puzzled. "You know . . . I missed the last twenty-seven Marvel movies. You may need to explain . . ."

"Sorry, your honor. Different company and medium. But my point is that this is an obvious frame-up. The witness incriminated the new kid, then discontinued the operation after pocketing the real money." He paused, then gave Doyle a sharp eye. "Which we'll probably find when we search his apartment."

"*What?*" Doyle clutched the sides of the stand. "When are people raiding my space?"

"Right after the court issues a subpoena. My associate Garrett is filling out the paperwork now, your honor. We want access to Mr. Doyle's Amazon account too." That sounded like the best way to phrase it, since Garrett had already hacked into the guy's account.

"You had a smart plan, in your own modest way," Dan continued. "The cashier is supposed to be the first layer of counterfeit protection—so you bypassed him altogether, swapping out the counterfeits with cash in the safe. Maybe put a few in Adam's cash drawer. So he would touch them. Once we know what you ordered from Amazon and when, you're toast. I bet we find most of the cash you stole, too. Hard to spend cash, these days." He paused for a moment. "But you might be able to pay your personal trainer in cash, right? Or to make a down payment at a sleazy used-car lot."

Dan paused, then allowed himself a small smile. "Where exactly did you buy that flashy new Dodge Charger?"

CHAPTER THREE

DAN WAITED PATIENTLY ON THE THIRD FLOOR OF THE courthouse as the marshals plowed through the forms needed to release his client from custody. After Garrett provided evidence that Doyle ordered the counterfeit bills, Stall folded.

Dan twiddled his thumbs and tried to remain patient. Even though this was a minor case, it felt good to be back in the courtroom. He kept thinking about a Perry Mason TV-movie he couldn't get out of his head. It was the first one, years after the series ended, where Mason resigns an appellate judgeship so he can defend the wrongly accused Della Street. How did he explain?

"Let's just say . . . I'm tired of writing opinions."

Rounding the courthouse corner came DA Jazlyn Prentiss, moving fast and obviously unhappy. "Damn it, Dan. What have you done this time?"

They'd known and opposed each other for years, so they could talk trash comfortably. "Whipped your baby boy's ass. Where did you find him? High school debate team?"

"You are insufferable." Jazlyn was a slender woman whose

only accommodations to age had been sensible shoes and eyeglasses. Probably her workload left her too busy to eat.

"You know what I think?" he asked.

"No one understands how you think."

"You had doubts about this defendant's guilt. You had to prosecute, given the evidence, but your instincts are good and you knew Adam wasn't the type. So you took a powder and let me prove it."

"I would never do that. I could be removed from office. Disbarred."

"Which explains why you aren't going to admit it."

"You're delusional, Dan. Always trying to enlist the rest of the world in your quixotic quest for justice."

"Did I just hear the district attorney say the pursuit of justice is quixotic?"

"Not on the record. I'm planning to run for reelection."

"You certainly have my support. And everyone in the 'Justice-is-a-Myth' lobby."

She took a tiny step closer. Many years before, they'd flirted with the possibility of a more intimate relationship, but that ship had long since sailed, especially now that he was living with Maria Morales, who was many months pregnant. "By the way, Esperanza says hello."

"Still doing well?"

"Are you kidding? She owns middle school." During an earlier case, Dan prevented a young Hispanic girl from being deported to a crime-lord family in El Salvador. But his even greater achievement was persuading Jaz to adopt her. "She's like an invisible streak on the soccer field. Team captain. Had the lead in the school play, too. All in all, a very happy little girl." She looked at him levelly. "And that's thanks to you."

"I think you had something to do with it."

"I wouldn't have even been in the picture if not for you. You didn't just improve *her* life. You made *my* life a thousand times remember Dan as the pimp-and-pusher man they tossed out of the firm. He would cling to the past.

Because he was jealous of Dan's present.

Adam bounced back. "Maria says I'm your new office assistant! And I'm starting college this semester!"

"Great news."

"Maria has already started picking my freshman courses."

That sounded like her.

"This is so exciting! I mean, a week ago, I was ready to off myself and now . . . this!" He grabbed Dan by the shoulders. "You saved my life, Mr. Pike!"

And then he turned and practically skipped down the hallway.

Okay, maybe this job did have a few perks.

Stoddard was still hanging around. "That . . . one of your clients?"

"Yes. And one of my employees, apparently."

"No need to feel embarrassed. We can't choose our clients, right? Bills to pay. Vacation homes to finance."

He looked back at Stoddard. This is what he could have become. Old school. Competitive. Resistant to change. Money-grubbing. But instead, he got lucky and found something much better.

"I'll let everyone back at the firm know that you've returned to the courtroom. You never said—why the change?"

Dan smiled. "Let's just say . . . I'm tired of writing opinions."

CHAPTER FOUR

Dan hated to admit it but he loved the Snell Isle mansion which, now that he'd rejoined the firm, was his place of business. How many people had a law office three times as big—and three times as valuable—as their home? Originally built to be a Brazilian importer's vacation palace, Ben seized it cheap and turned it into their office. Flying buttresses, three gables, Federal columns, wrought-iron fence, imported marble. Immaculately trimmed lawn. And he hadn't had to mow it once!

Ben knew how to get the lawyers he wanted. He made them offers they couldn't refuse.

He parked his Bentley and passed quietly through the front door. No one was in the living room (which they called their lobby) but he smelled something wafting its way from the kitchen.

He tiptoed in that general direction. Maria stood at the stove, oven mitt on one hand and spatula in the other. She stared intently at a frying pan. She appeared distraught, as if the pan held some strange lab specimen.

Which allowed him to creep behind her and squeeze her waist. "Gotcha!"

Maria almost dropped the spatula. "What are you doing?"

He snuggled in and kissed the back of her neck. "Just bringing some laughter into your life."

"Why do men think it's funny to sneak up on someone? Men are so twisted."

"And yet, here you are." He leaned closer. "By the way, you appear to be cooking."

"Is that a problem? I know cooking is supposed to be your thing."

"Absolutely not. It's good to acquire new skills. Expand your horizons." He took a closer look. "You're making an omelet?"

"Excellent detective work." Given the degree of concentration registered on her face, you'd think she was assembling an atomic bomb. Maria had never cooked, never even been interested in cooking—until now. She explained it as part of her new supervisory role. She wanted to reduce their overhead by preparing lunches instead of using DoorDash every day. Or it might have something to do with the fact that she was extremely pregnant. "I can't get the flip right. So I can cook the other side."

"It's hard for everyone at first. You'll get the hang of it. How are you feeling?"

"I'm fine. The doctor says everything is perfect."

In his experience, there was no such thing as perfect, but that sounded promising. "Iron? Folic acid?"

"Everything is okay, Dan. Stop fussing. You know I'm in excellent shape. From personal experience."

"Delightful experiences."

"And none of that is going to change because I have a small human parasite gestating inside my body."

"Gee, when you put it like that . . ."

"It's basically a tumor eating away at me, but you're a man so you're never going to know or understand this."

"You are not in the best mood ever."

"You think? I've been trying to make this omelet for an hour. While answering a flood of phone calls. You get to play around in the courtroom but who's got their hand on the tiller?"

"Or a better question, who needs a break?" He took the pan off the heat (the omelet was waaaay past done anyway), turned off the burner and led her to the sofa. "Busy day?"

"You wouldn't believe it. Ben opened another LCL office in Milwaukee. As if we didn't have enough to do. And I have to arrange Lamaze appointments and pick out wallpaper for the nursery and arrange for a diaper service—"

"Wait. Diapers?"

"You haven't heard of them? They come with babies."

"But why a service? Surely disposable diapers will—"

"Expand landfills to an unacceptable degree. We're already destroying this planet. While Earth is in jeopardy, we're not using disposable diapers."

"You're the boss." That'll last about a week, he predicted. "Have you considered . . . my proposal?"

"Remind me. What did you propose?"

Dan gave her a look. "What do men usually propose to their pregnant girlfriends? Do you want me to get down on bended knee?"

She waved him away. "Stop already. We don't have time."

"It might help you feel better—"

"If I conformed to the patriarchy? Let others tell me how to live my life? No thanks. I'm happy with things the way they are. I'm in a great relationship. I have a great job. I have a great kid coming. That's all I need."

He peered deeply into her eyes. *Really?* Or was there something he was missing?

"Let me tell you what happened in court. You won't believe this one."

"You always say that."

He grinned. "I do seem to get the best cases."

"A criminal case that involves comic books. A Jimmy Armstrong fantasy-come-true" He smiled. "Told you I get the best cases. I'll collect Jimmy."

Maria and Garrett exchanged a pointed look.

"What? He's in his office, right?"

Still no reply.

"What is it? Is something wrong?"

Maria tilted her head to one side. "No . . . nothing is wrong . . . Have you seen Jimmy lately?"

"I spoke to him on the phone this morning."

"Yeah. Not the same." Garrett's lips tightened. "It might be best if . . . you invited Jimmy to the meeting yourself. Since you've been away for a while."

"What are you two making such a fuss about? Was he in a horrible disfiguring accident?"

"No, nothing like that . . ."

Dan pushed himself off the sofa, giving Maria a tiny nudge. "I'll get him."

Maria bounced up. "Good idea. I'll dial Ben and put him on the screen." In the early days, Ben had spoken to them anonymously as the mysterious "Mr. K." Now they all knew who K was, but deep down he missed the romance of taking instructions from a mysterious offstage source. Had a Fu Manchu vibe that was kinda exciting.

Dan mounted the stairs and headed to Jimmy's private office, the far room at the end of the hallway.

The door was shut. He knocked.

"You don't need to knock, Dan. Come inside."

How did Jimmy know who it was? Did he have a distinctive shuffle? Did Jimmy recognize the squeak of high-quality sneaks?

He opened the door. "Mr. K is calling. And you'll want—"

He stopped short. Now he understood what Heckle & Jeckle had been side-eyeing about.

He could only see what was visible above the desk, but that was enough. Jimmy wore a dress, a lightweight sun dress, with a bright blue floral pattern. And pearls. And earrings. And a big bouffant wig. And unless it was a trick of the light—mascara.

"Jimmy?"

A brief silence, then the soft-spoken words: "Call me Jenny."

CHAPTER FIVE

WERE THEY GOING TO TALK ABOUT IT? IGNORE IT? DAN HAD NO idea which way to go. But ultimately, he felt that when your law partner suddenly started cross-dressing, you were permitted to inquire.

And to be fair, a sun dress was far more practical for this climate than a cardigan.

"Hey there . . . Jenny. Been a while."

"Yeah. Last time I saw you, you were just back from your big cross-country adventure."

Last time I saw you, Dan thought, you had a beard.

"Are you upset?" Jenny's voice seemed softer than usual, although it wasn't that she was deliberately speaking in a higher pitch. She seemed more . . . relaxed. "Is it too much?"

"Um . . ." There were so many possibilities.

"The wig. You're staring at my wig."

"It's a new look."

"I've been trying new things."

"You and Garrett both."

"Garrett bought a silly sweater because he has a crush on a

songwriter who could be his daughter. You think that's the same thing?"

To be fair, he'd known Jimmy was gay—and married—since the first moment they met and it had never bothered him in the slightest. Jimmy was easily the most fun person in the firm, spicing dreary legal discussions with lively references to movies and comics and games. He was a dark-skinned African-American, a generous person with generous proportions. Married to an ER doc named Leon. But Jimmy had always presented male in the past. Jenny, dressing in traditional female clothing, was new.

"Not remotely the same. Is there . . . more to this than meets the eye?"

"I don't know yet." Jenny rose and took a few steps from the desk—which allowed Dan to see the spike heels. "I think I'm . . . transitioning."

"To . . . ?"

"Not sure yet. Who knows where it might lead."

"Why Jenny? Other than the similarity to . . . you know."

"I have my reasons."

"DC comic book character?"

She pondered. "There's Jenny Sparks, former leader of Stormwatch, who I like very much. But no. That's not why I chose the name. Nothing to do with comics."

And since she said no more, he assumed she didn't care to explain. "Leon is on board with this?"

"Are you crazy?" A flash of the wild flickered behind her eyes. "He's loving it. Every single moment."

"You mean . . . ?"

"We haven't had this much fun in years." Jenny stopped, blinked. "I mean in the sack."

"I got that."

"We have a new friend."

His eyebrows knitted. "You and Leon have . . ."

"You still are," Ben replied. "But Batman turns out to be even cooler than you imagined."

"Batman is an old bald guy?" Jenny's eyes turned downward. "Nothing personal, but . . ."

Dan jumped in. "Let's cut to the chase, Ben. Who died this time?"

Ben's expression didn't change. "No one. I mean, that I know of."

Dan's forehead creased. "This isn't a murder case?"

"Nope. Change of pace. Don't want you to get stuck in a rut. No murders in the building."

"What is it, then? Jaywalking?"

"I was hoping for a good jewel theft," Jenny said. "Like in those old movies. Have you seen *Raffles*, with John Barrymore? I love that one."

"I'd like a juicy antitrust case," Garrett reflected. "Something we can really dig deep into. Years of motions and discovery practice. Millions of documents."

Ben coughed. "If something like that turns up, you'll be the first to know. But this case is all about comics. And movies. I know you wanted to return to the Florida courtroom with a big splash, Dan. I'm going to make it happen. But in civil court. Not criminal."

"Civil?" Dan's face puckered up like he'd bitten a lemon. "You mean . . . people suing each other?"

"Right."

"For money?"

"That is the usual goal."

"I don't do civil."

Maria cut in. "You do now. Dan 3.0."

"I never said—"

"And," she continued, "I'm hoping this will be safer than the criminal work."

Dan whirled. "This was your idea?"

"No. But I like it. You're about to be a father. You don't need to be chasing people down dark alleys or getting beaten up at the dock."

She had a point. Dan glanced around the room, but the expressions on the rest of the team's faces were inscrutable. "Is this . . . mandatory?"

"No. You can always decline. This or any other case I send your way." He shuffled some papers offscreen.

Damn. He didn't want to seem ungrateful. "But this is . . . *civil*. Money-grubbing. Ambulance chasing."

"You're saying this isn't as prestigious as representing accused murderers?"

"Usually, you give us deserving clients who are being strongarmed or framed or cheated or . . ." He glanced up. "And this is the same thing, isn't it?"

Ben nodded. "I'm not exaggerating when I say this might be the most deserving client and the most valuable case you've ever had. Or ever will. Billions at stake. Possibly tens of billions."

Gee, raise the stakes, why don't you?

"Tell you what, Dan. Before you decide, meet your client. He's got an interesting story."

"I suppose I could do that."

"What's the cause of action?" Maria asked. Leave it to the pregnant woman to ask the smart questions.

"Still undecided. You're going to draft the petition. But I assume it will involve several intellectual property claims. Copyright, trademark, plagiarism, breach of contract, possibly. Maybe a tort claim so you can pursue punitive damages."

"What happened?"

"I think I should let your client tell the story. But basically, he created a character that has become enormously popular and is now poised for a huge media breakout that could make the character the new James Bond."

Jenny started bouncing up and down on the sofa. "Is it a comic book character? Tell me it's a comic book character!"

"Yes. The first six issues were published here, but the most popular adventures came from Japan."

"Manga!"

"Correct. Huge splash in Asia. Then an anime series, available here on Netflix. Now a possible live-action feature-film deal with a projected two-hundred-million-dollar budget. But your client claims he created the character and he's been completely shut out. He writes under the moniker—"

Jenny's eyes spread like parachutes. "Monkey Punch!"

"Well...yes..."

"You're talking about King Kaiju!"

Ben touched his nose. "Ding ding ding."

"Ohmigosh. I love that show!"

"You're not alone."

Jenny leaned forward excitedly. "We'll be representing Monkey Punch?"

"Yes."

Jenny pressed her hands together. "Holy heartache! I wanna play! I wanna play!"

Ben smiled. "Maria is in charge of staffing..."

She cleared her throat. "Dan's taking the lead."

Jenny looked crestfallen.

"But you are definitely assigned to the case, Jenny. I don't want to list you as counsel, though, because . . . we might need you as an expert witness."

Dan covered his smile. Outside of *My Cousin Vinny*, lawyers didn't call friends to the stand as "experts." But if there was a great deal at stake, she wanted Dan to take the lead.

Yes, Maria was going to do well in this position. She was already aware of the subtleties.

Jenny settled back into the sofa. "That's all right. Just so I get to meet Monkey Punch."

"We didn't have any other friends so we hung out together. We both loved science fiction. *Star Wars. Star Trek. Doctor Who.* And comics. That was right after Jack Kirby and Stan Lee revolutionized traditional comics. I noticed that their most popular characters—before Spidey came along—were monsters. The Thing. The Hulk. So I started thinking about a monster of my own. We also loved Japanese movies and manga, when we could get it. Eventually we decided we were going to create one of our own."

"King Kaiju."

"Right. I'd read a book called *The New Apocalypse* that had scientists trying to create a super-powered creature to save the world from an impending apocalypse. I didn't love the plot but it got me thinking. What if there was a giant monster who was a good guy? Maybe a heroic figure with a tragic appearance. Except in addition to making him ugly, I made him huge. Too huge to ever have a personal life. I wrote an eight-page origin story, then got Joe to illustrate it."

"And you offered it to . . . Sidekick Comics?"

"I offered it to everyone. No one was interested. Not even Sidekick at first. Then they had an artist run late on a story for an anthology title, so they decided to give Kaiju a chance. Ran the origin. And it was a huge hit. Readers demanded more."

"And that led to the fabled first six issues. The mini-series!" Jenny said.

"Yeah. We prepped all six as one large story, but Sidekick only agreed to publish one issue. If it had tanked, you'd never have seen the rest."

"But it didn't tank. Far from it."

"Right. I was so proud when that first issue came out."

"I'll bet."

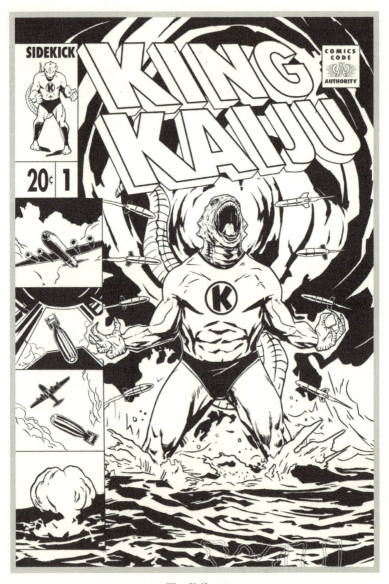

King Kaiju #1

"Sidekick gave me a check and later claimed that when I endorsed it, I gave up my rights to the character. They had some boilerplate trash stamped on the back of the check and said my endorsement made it a signed contract. I never even read that green-print nonsense. I was thrilled to see my character in print. But that was back in . . . back in . . ." He rubbed his hand across his forehead. "A long time ago."

More memory issues? It was late and he had been drinking. But still . . .

"And you probably know what happened after that. The first mini-series led to a continuing series. Then an overseas manga version that was even more popular. But the anime adaptation was a blockbuster. And now Headmark Studios wants to make a live-action King Kaiju picture, the first in a projected series of films designed to create a Kaijuverse. Like the Marvel Cinematic Universe. It could earn billions." He paused. "For someone."

"What have you been paid for the anime?"

"Nothing for being creator. I only got paid a pittance when they adapted a specific story that I'd written."

"What will you be paid if the rights sell to a studio?"

"Nothing. Welcome to the American Way of supporting the arts, which is give art to big corporations and put artists out with the trash. We were children, barely twenty-one, eager and ambitious. I'd been trying to sell the idea for so long without success. I would've agreed to anything. And I did."

"Neither you nor Joe got much."

"Only payment for specific stories we produced. No ownership percentage." His drinking hand began to shake. "I created King Kaiju. I even sketched out what he would look like. But they didn't care."

"What about Joe? Did he work with you to get a better deal?"

"Till Delia got involved." Wu frowned. "His wife."

"You said everyone thought he was gay."

"Probably bi," Jenny informed him. "Maybe he evolved, too."

"Nothing new about Delia," Wu explained. "They've been married more than twenty years. They have a son. Ernie. Wants to be an actor, I hear."

"But if you never made any serious money—"

"We got a little money at first. Did pretty well the first year. Then I got drafted. Could've fled to college or Canada, but that didn't feel right. Did two tours. Got the Bronze Star and some other fruit salad. But when I returned stateside . . . everything had changed."

"How so?"

"King Kaiju had been expanded by Sidekick Comics in my absence. Instead of one King Kaiju comic, there were six published every month. One was a twofer team-up mag. One was an Avengers-type group that Kaiju led. There was even a Kaiju romance book! But the one that really offended me was Baby Kaiju."

"I'm guessing he was smaller?"

"He was the same damn thing, except a little younger. This was an idea I'd suggested before I left and they told me it was stupid. Then look what happened! When I complained and asked for a cut, they told me this was a different character. I thought they must be joking. The cover literally said, 'The Adventures of King Kaiju when he was young.' How can that be a different character? They're saying it's the same character right on the cover! Ludicrous. And there were Kaiju toys and action figures and games everywhere."

Dan could see Wu was becoming agitated. They were reopening wounds, old and deep. "They took advantage of your absence to merchandise the character without your involvement."

"No kidding. I was at war. Joe was losing his sight. So they robbed us without remorse."

"How did you respond?"

"I sued. And won. I mean, there was really no question about the fact that Baby Kaiju was basically the same character as King Kaiju. Plus he was my idea. So they paid me a smidgeon for royalties owed." He took a deep breath. "And then they fired me."

Dan's head fell. "Now . . . what?"

"My contract could be terminated at will by either party. So they dumped me. And then, since they never acknowledged my role as creator and had an endorsed check saying they owned all the rights, they claimed they had no obligation to pay me anything. While they made millions off my character. We've sued repeatedly, without any success. A few years back, they gave me and Joe a small pension, just for PR. A tiny annuity. Barely enough to keep us alive."

"But now the US copyright law has changed," Dan said, "giving creators a chance to recoup their rights under some circumstances after the passage of many years. The point of our lawsuit would be to use the new law to re-establish your rights, since you're the creator of the character. Have you talked to Joe or Delia? Maybe you could work something out privately. Avoid a big costly lawsuit."

"I called. She's working on some deal of her own. She has money and lawyers. She calls me an 'undeserving leech.'"

"How can Joe prevail if you don't?"

"I don't know. He's executed agreements with Sidekick that I haven't. They're acting like they've done all they need to do."

The company was probably deliberately dividing Joe and Wu, assuming that would make them easier to trample. "I'll arrange for a meeting with Delia or her counsel. The sooner the better. If she's represented by anyone reasonable, they'll understand you have a legit claim and will be amenable to a less painful resolution."

Wu looked at him with tired eyes. "I have literally been listening to people say that to me for fifty years."

"But now we have laws that allow original creators to recover their rights after fifty years."

"As it should be." Jenny shook her head. "Could you contract away your child? No. This should be the same. If we want to have great art, we have to protect our artists. Even when they are not great businesspeople. Which would be most artists. If we continue to allow big business and big money to decide what art is produced, all we're going to have is corporate crap."

Dan didn't think he'd ever heard her give such an impassioned speech. Maybe she was transitioning in more ways than she realized.

"It's how the one percent remain the one percent," Wu said. "You know how much money DC Comics makes off Batman every year?"

"When they make a new movie?"

"Doesn't matter. Movies, TV, merch, toys. It's half a billion dollars a year."

Dan whistled.

"Superman does almost as well. And his creators never got much either. DC is owned by Warner Brothers. Disney bought Marvel and turned it into a hugely successful film franchise. Tens of billions of dollars a year." His teeth clenched together. "Need I say the obvious? Most of that money does not go to the creators."

Dan pressed his hands together. "Let's see if we can do better than that. Assuming you want to hire us."

"Do you have a lot of experience?"

"With the courtroom, yes. With intellectual property cases— no. But I have a flexible team and we will adapt. From a courtroom standpoint, it's not that different. We will fight for you."

Still no light in Wu's eyes, but he gave a curt nod.

"I'll draft a restraining order," Jenny said, pulling a small notepad out of her purse. "Prevent Delia from making any deals until . . . we know who controls what. If she's in a big hurry to get some cash, let her settle *with* us, not around us."

"Good." Wu paused. "I'm glad the fans have taken King Kaiju into their hearts. I love going to conventions and hearing them talk about my character like he was their best friend."

"Really?"

"Why do you think people love these superhero stories? There's nothing new about them. Westerns were mostly superhero stories, except the heroes had sixguns instead of powers. Buck Rogers. Tarzan. The Lone Ranger. The oldest surviving literary works are what? *Gilgamesh. Beowulf. The Iliad. The Odyssey. The Aeneid.* Stories about great heroes with great abilities who used them to help others. Superman is a symbol of hope. Batman is a case study in transforming tragedy into purpose. Spider-Man taught kids that everyone has problems—even heroes. Readers are inspired by these stories. Bettered by these stories."

Wu took another swig from his drink, then wiped his lips with his sleeve. "Stories heal the world. Don't let them take that away from us."

CHAPTER SEVEN

Although Dan had heard about the new Saltaire building and he'd seen the glittering exterior, he'd never been inside before. This was a towering skyscraper, thirty-five stories shooting 408 feet into the air. Primarily for condos, but some of the lower suites were offices, often for condo occupants.

The firm representing Delia Ulrich was from out-of-state, so it leased space for this meeting. In fact, it looked like they took the entire floor, which was completely unnecessary. A small conference room anywhere would do. But instead, they took several big rooms and had them stocked with a minibar and soft drinks and snacks. Plus, of course, a fancy coffeemaker.

They were spending considerably more money than was necessary.

They wanted to make an impression.

They wanted to impress Dan with what he was up against.

They wanted to scare Wu into submission.

Dan considered asking Wu to remain outside the conference room, but that impractical. They were likely to make a settlement offer. He needed to tell them what he would accept and what he would not.

They hesitated outside the conference room door. "Are we all ready to do this?" Dan asked.

Maria had come with him. He wasn't sure why, but technically, she was the boss now, so he didn't question it. Wu looked as if he'd rather be anywhere else in the world. He also looked as if he had stopped by Cap'n Bill's on the way to the Saltaire. Smelled that way, too.

"I don't understand why you need me here," Wu mumbled. "I never—never—wanted this." At times, it seemed to take him seconds to find the right word.

"If you want to fight this lawsuit, I'm afraid there are going to be some uncomfortable moments. Nothing I can do about that."

"That woman is in there."

"You can handle Delia."

"Says the man who hasn't met her."

"How much time have you spent with her?"

"Too much."

"She was rude to you during previous discussions?"

"She was rude to me at Joe's wedding. And every moment since."

Maria seemed to grasp the heart of the matter. "She came between you and your best friend."

"You don't have to forgive," Dan added. "Just remain flexible. Civil. If we can make some kind of mutually acceptable agreement today, you might never have to see her again. I have experience—"

"With criminal law," a voice interrupted, "where the defense has all the advantages. You're going to find civil court a lot harder. Your hackneyed courtroom tricks won't help you."

What?

Dan spun around. A woman had emerged from the elevator. Petite, brunette side-shave, well-dressed, supremely confident. And vaguely familiar.

Maria scowled. "Sorry. Do we know you?"

The woman pointed. "Your sweetie does. We met before on another case."

That's right. He recognized the face but he couldn't quite place the name. She'd come down when he was working on that final showdown with Conrad Sweeney...

He snapped his fingers. "Katie!"

"Close. Kenzi." She extended her hand. "Kenzi Rivera. Just in from Seattle. Let me tell you something, Danny Boy. You may be the Big Noise here in St. Pete. But the Big Dogs are in town now. And you're going down."

DAN STILL FELT OFF-BALANCE TEN MINUTES LATER WHEN THEY finally took their seats in the conference room. Once she said her name, he started to remember more about the esteemed Kenzi Rivera. She was a divorce lawyer, or at least started that way. And he remembered that she spent most of their encounter livestreaming, which tended to make him want to knock her cellphone out of her hand.

A quick Google search told him that Kenzi now ran her father's firm in Seattle. Since she became managing partner, they'd expanded, hired more people, took more pro bono work, and handled a wider range of cases. But why was she involved in this case?

He wasn't crazy about the guy representing Sidekick Comics, either. David Christopher, who looked like the prototype frat-boy corporate apparatchik. Slick suit. Blue shirt. Floral pocket square. With three completely unnecessary associates who carried his catalog cases and looked like clones.

Maria whispered into his ear. "Don't let all those guys intimidate you."

Dan shrugged. "They're Christmas ornaments."

"I'm not following."

"Decorative. But they don't do much. Kenzi will run the show."

Delia Ulrich sat in the corner. She was Black, a little heavier than she probably wished, and pensive. She didn't look old enough to be married to Wu's best friend. He hoped she felt some guilt about this situation. Not that she was going to gladly give away all that money. But a trace of guilt might make her more amenable to settlement.

She'd also brought her son, Ernie. Dan knew he was an actor, or wanted to be, which made him wonder if the kid was involved with the proposed movie deal. Or perhaps hoped to use it to get meetings with the right people. But Delia had not brought her husband—the man who arguably held a claim to the character. Apparently she felt his presence was not necessary.

Dan outstretched a hand toward the son. "Dan Pike. Good to meet you."

Ernie started to take his hand—but a sharp look from him mother stopped him. He retracted his hand and simply nodded.

"I'm sure this very hard for you," Dan said. "But I want you to understand that this lawsuit is about getting Wu's rights back from Sidekick. We are not out to get your father."

Delia snorted. "No. You just want to take all the money Joe should've had decades ago."

"Not true. I think we can come up with a solution that allows both artists to live comfortably for the rest of their lives. This time the corporation won't trample the creators. I've already got investigators turning over every rock and opening every file. We're going to get to the truth."

She could tell Delia didn't like him talking to her son. "We already know the truth. So did Wu's last lawyer. And you know what happened to him." Her eyes narrowed slightly. "Maybe you need to be a little more careful about what you do and say."

Dan didn't understand what she was suggesting. Was that some kind of threat?

"Shall we begin?" Christopher said. He did not smile. He had a sort of tired ennui about him, like someone who already knew how this was going to end but nonetheless had to go through the motions. "As I think you know, I'm David Christopher with Goldworm and Goldberg and today I have authority to represent both Sidekick Comics and Headmark Studios."

Dan cleared his throat. "We already know—

"Headmark is of course owned by Phantasmagoria Entertainment, which also owns a host of other companies in TV, film, publishing, and cloud computing. Phantasmagoria is owned by the Bannerman Group, a German multinational corporation."

"Is there a point to this or are we just supposed to be awestruck?"

"The point is, I'm not here to mess around, and my client does not plan to give an inch. We have a lot of ground to cover and I have a five o'clock flight back to LA."

Dan glanced at his watch. "You think we can wrap this up in three hours?"

"There's not that much to say."

Maria looked offended. "Are you kidding? This intellectual property is potentially worth—"

"But that's not what we're here to discuss today, is it?" Christopher said, interrupting her. Dan hated him already. "We're here to determine whether your client has any rights regarding this character. And sadly, he does not."

Dan looked bored. "You may be aware that we have a different opinion."

"Opinions are like assholes. Everyone's got one." Arrogant, vulgar, and trite. Good. Now Dan had a more objective reason for disliking this man. "Perhaps you're not aware of this, but with the help of my co-counsel, Kenzi Rivera, we've reached a tentative deal for Headmark to acquire all rights to King Kaiju so they can make a big-budget live-action film series. All we need is a judicial declaration that Delia owns the rights. She needs to hold clear title. Unencumbered."

"We're never going to give you that. Well, not unless you give us something in return."

"Shouldn't you consult your client before you tell me what you will and won't do?"

"You haven't made an offer."

He sighed. "Maybe . . . given your lack of experience with this kind of case . . ."

"I know the stakes," he replied. "Disney paid four billion for Star Wars. Four billion more for Marvel. This could be bigger than any of those M&As."

"No. My guess is, if we go to court, this case will take about four years to resolve."

"If you drag it out with motions and discovery."

"Thorough discovery is essential to good litigation."

"Thorough discovery is essential to billable hours. Don't we already know everything we need to know about this situation? Let's work together and come up with something fair everyone can live with."

"I'm afraid that's not an option we're considering at this time. Let's be frank. We have far more resources. I know you have that LCL thing with the Oklahoma whack-job, but you're going to have to staff up."

"Do we? My sister's a law student and she needs more to do." He glanced at Maria. "Also, I think we just hired a new office assistant . . ."

"You'll need more. Ten times more. Plus our PR team will be working full time, painting your client as a leech, a loser who wants what other people have. Defending that man will cost you a fortune."

"I'm filing in Florida. You and your clients are located in California. This case will cost you a lot more than it does us."

"We can afford it."

"If, as I suspect, you had an associate research me personally, then you already know I used to be with a big firm and I used the same tactics you're employing now. Except more skillfully. I've seen it all before and it's never fazed me, I don't like it, and it won't get you anywhere. So let's skip the threats and intimidation and start talking about actual issues. This isn't that complicated. You might still make your flight."

Delia was muttering again. "Only if we agree to give your client something he doesn't deserve."

He could see Wu fuming. "I created King Kaiju."

"Pfftt." She blew air through her teeth. "You signed away your rights. Being coupled with you in court can only hurt Joe's chances of recovery."

Wu did not reply.

"Furthermore, Kaiju would never have become popular but for the anime series. And you had nothing to do with that."

"Kaiju was popular from the first issue," Wu softly corrected. "By the time the second issue was released, it was a blockbuster. Many of the anime episodes adapted my stories."

Dan kept his eyes on Kenzi. He guessed she represented Delia in a prior divorce so Delia brought her in on this mess. Christopher might be talking, but Kenzi was in charge. He could tell from the way they related to one another. She could steamroller him. Probably already had.

He could see there was something on her mind, but she was keeping it to herself.

King Kaiju #2

"I can't change the facts," Christopher continued. "Wu signed the check. Years later, he signed an agreement to get a pension. He's given away his rights. Joe Ulrich has not. He and his wife deserve to profit now and do not deserve to be held back by someone who gave away his claim for peanuts."

"You don't know anything about character creation or contracts. You just want the character. And don't care what you have to say or do to get it."

Christopher ignored him. "Only out of respect for your friendship with Joe—"

Wu laughed out loud.

"—let me offer this. A one-time payment. Not a pension, not an annuity, but a cold hard hundred thousand dollars."

Dan and Kenzi exchanged a look.

"I know, that's ridiculously generous given that you have no case. But we want to get this wrapped up so we can make the studio deal."

"Then you should be offering us ten times that much," Maria commented.

"Would that we could. But money is tight these days."

"Headmark Studios is a Fortune 500 company."

"Doesn't mean we have a lot of cash floating around."

"I bet you have more cash than my client."

"Which is not relevant. Look, you are going to lose. Worse, you are going to be pounded into humiliating submission by the woeful clout of one of the largest and most successful law firms in the United States of America." Christopher raised his hands. "Why do that to yourselves? Take the money."

"It's not enough. Not even close."

"Wu could live a good long time on that amount of money." He glanced at the beaten-looking man. "Maybe for the rest of the ride. Make a smart business deal."

"This is about art."

"This is about a giant costumed dinosaur."

"Loved by millions."

"We're fighting over money. Are you saying your client doesn't want money?"

"We all have to eat." He paused. "But it's still art. And creators have rights. Just like businesspeople."

CHAPTER EIGHT

ONCE DAN MADE IT CLEAR THAT THIS WAS NOT A NUISANCE SUIT and they were not going to settle for chump change, Christopher proposed that they have a private meeting, just lawyers. Dan knew this would be a complete waste of time, but it was a hoop he had to jump through before he could get anywhere else. He didn't want Christopher suggesting to a judge that he had been uncooperative or thwarted early resolution.

He spoke privately to Maria. "I'm going to another room to listen to this blowhard not make a deal. Think you can hold down the fort?"

"Easy." Her eyes darted to the other side of the room. Her voice dropped. "When did you meet that arrogant chick?"

"Who?" He looked up. "Oh, the divorce lawyer?"

"Yes. The stunningly attractive divorce lawyer who may dress better than I do, so I hate her already. Would be even worse if she had some secret ex-thing with the father of my baby."

"There was no thing. Not even close to a thing."

"She looks like someone who isn't afraid to go after what she wants."

"Probably correct. But she's not my type."

"Then why do you know her? She's from Seattle, right?"

"I met her once because she had a divorce client who knew something helpful in a prior case. I'm sure I mentioned it at the time."

"No. Never."

"Well, it wasn't important, especially given that we were buried in the case of our lifetime."

"Aren't we always."

"She didn't make that big an impression on me. In my experience, when lawyers start swaggering it's not because they know their case is so strong. Just the opposite."

Maria gave him a stern look. "No starlets."

"Understood. I already have a well-dressed super-lawyer. Without a weird side-shave."

"And just in case you think this is something going around, you are not going to be the unicorn in a polyamorous relationship!"

He held up his hands. "I get it. I get it." He smiled, sort of. "I'll check back with you after I finish this waste-of-time meeting. You have fun in here with Kenzi and Company."

Ten minutes after Dan and Christopher left the conference room, no one had spoken. Not so much as a word. Not even once. Wu got up to take a call, Delia went for a smoke, and Ernie said he had to call his agent—leaving Maria and Kenzi alone.

Maria had always prided herself on her collegiality. She was a firm believer that lawyers could be strong professional adversaries in the courtroom and still treat each other like civilized human beings when court was not in session. And she especially felt that women need to stand up for one another. Present a united front. But this Kenzi woman was giving off a vibe she did not want in her workspace. At the moment, she was talking into her phone, doing some kind of livestream.

"Hey there, KenziKlan. I'm coming to you from sunny Florida where once again I've traveled to prevent another woman from being ripped off by men. *You shall not pass!* The KenziKlan has the magic staff and we're coming for you." Deep breath. "And by the way, ladies, read those damn contracts before you sign them..."

After Kenzi finished, Maria spoke. "So you and Dan met before?"

Kenzi glanced up from her phone. "Oh yeah. He didn't tell you? Funny, that." And her eyes returned to her phone.

Tramp. She knew exactly what she was doing. "During the Sweeney case?"

"Yeah. We did an info swap. Win-win scenario." Brief smile. "I'll say this. Your guy looks good in a swimsuit."

"You were swimming?"

"He was. What's that high-risk male-insecurity ocean thing he does?"

"Kite-surfing. And he's going to quit."

Kenzi chuckled. "Right. Glad to hear it."

"And you two only met once?"

"Is there a problem? I don't see a ring on that finger."

"I don't need one."

"It was just one of those things. You shouldn't give it a moment's thought," Kenzi said, thus guaranteeing that Maria would. "He does look good in that suit, though. Does he work out?"

Maria tried to contain her rising temperature. "That won't be important in the courtroom."

"True enough. I've mopped the floor with hunkier guys than Pike." Kenzi started pacing around the table, but neither the room nor the table were all that large, so mostly she was walking in circles. "I suppose you don't have to worry about getting clients like normal folk do. You get all your work handed to you on a silver platter."

"FYI, I'm running the LCL, not to mention our little branch of it. And I didn't inherit it from my daddy, either."

"Oooh. Burn." Kenzi grinned. "You get prefab clients. And now that Dan has stepped down, you're in the catbird seat, administrating instead of litigating. How sweet it is."

"FYI, I've been with this outfit longer than Dan. I've never liked being in the courtroom, and I'm not going to start now when I'm about to give birth. Administrating requires about sixteen times more patience and skill than the worst trial that ever was."

Kenzi arched an eyebrow. "Defensive much?"

"Not in the slightest." Maria pivoted and stared at her notes, though she was so angry she could barely read them. Who did this woman think she was?

"By the way, are you wearing Dolce & Gabbana?"

Maria's eyes narrowed. "Yes. Is that a problem?"

"No. I love D&G."

"Really? This isn't some sideways criticism?"

"Would a woman lie about something that important?" Kenzi leaned in closer. "But honey, you're much too old to wear those skinny jeans. You should've packed those away the day you turned thirty-five."

Maria felt her fists clenching.

She had been pleased when she realized Ben wasn't sending them another murder case.

But if she didn't get away from this woman soon, it was going to become one.

Dan spent the first half hour with Christopher trying to identify the issues. He suggested that Wu and Joe join forces and present a united front to Sidekick and Headmark. For the past several decades, he noted, Sidekick had dealt with the artists separately. A typical divide-and-conquer move. If they worked together, a jury might see the virtue of their claims.

He hated to be critical, but for all the confidence Christopher exuded in the main conference room, he seemed singularly ill-prepared for getting down to details. He was tossing around numbers like they had no connection to real life.

"I hear what you're saying, Danny. I don't think you've got a case. Your boy signed his rights away."

"It would be worth something to eliminate a remote possibility."

"Sure. That's why I offered a hundred grand."

"Not enough. Make it a million. I think I can sell that to Wu."

"A million? That's real money."

"Sidekick has made millions off King Kaiju. Billions, maybe. They will try to cut you out—"

"We have a tentative agreement, remember?" Christopher grinned. "As soon as we show them a judicial declaration of our rights. They will never make the same offer to Wu. He's too difficult, too uncooperative."

"They'd rather screw him over than give him a little money?"

"They prefer to work with the cooperative one."

To Dan's surprise, Christopher pulled a vape pen from his inside jacket pocket and took a long drag. "You tried this yet?"

"Definitely not."

"You should. It's relaxing."

"Smoking is smoking. It's a bad habit. It'll kill you."

"Is it worse than kite-surfing?"

"Exercise is good. Smoking is bad. But I'm not your daddy. Give me a million and you can go home and vape your lungs away."

"It is tempting." Christopher took another long draw. Did the pen relax him so much he was more likely to make a deal?

"You're gonna file for a declaratory judgment, right?"

"Right."

"First time I've seen one of those."

"It's not common. But I want an immediate judicial declaration of my client's rights, and I want it before you make the billion-dollar studio deal and shut him out."

Christopher tossed his head from one side to the other. "Makes a certain sense, I suppose. Wouldn't want to close the deal and then have you come along trying to re-open it."

"Which I would. Your work would be undone and you'd look like an idiot. Let's avoid that. Let's both come out looking like winners. Otherwise, I'm going to get a preliminary injunction to prevent you from making a deal involving King Kaiju without our consent. You'll lose your tentative deal and probably have to pay us damages."

"That does sound pointless."

"This dispute has been festering for more than fifty years. Let's put it to bed once and for all. Let everyone get on with their lives. We don't have to work out everything today. If we sign a letter agreement, a declaration of intent—"

"I don't know."

"C'mon, that is what we're supposed to be doing, isn't it? Resolving disputes? Rather than escalating them?"

Christopher took another long draw from his peppermint vape. "I bet they could scrape up the money. Maybe pay it out over time."

"I'm sure we could come up with a workable payment schedule. I can sketch out the main points in fifteen minutes. Do we have an agreement?"

Christopher smiled and extended his hand. "Well, sure, why not—"

"Hold your horses, boys."

Dan swiveled around. While he was arguing with Christopher, Kenzi Rivera had slipped into the room.

And their two clients, Wu and Delia, were only a few steps behind her.

"Let's not give up the farm quite yet, Christopher."

He sat up straight. "I wasn't giving away anything..."

"You were about to give away everything. This man is playing you like an Amati violin."

Dan's eyelids lifted. Amati violin? As in his last big case?

This woman *had* done her research.

"First he flatters and strokes you. Encourages you to be reasonable. Then he restates the case so there seems to be only one choice. Then he gets you to sign a letter agreement and we're stuck with your bad deal. You get bamboozled and we get cheated. Not happening." She glanced at Dan and winked. "This is why I'm here."

CHAPTER NINE

Dan couldn't help but be furious with Kenzi—even though everything she'd said was basically correct. He was seconds away from an agreement until she walked in. Could he criticize her? No, she was doing her job, protecting her client, while he was walking over Christopher like a doormat. Apparently Ken-doll looks do not mandate great lawyering skills.

Kenzi continued. "Step aside, Christopher. I'm in charge now."

Christopher slowly rose to his feet. "Wait a minute. I'm lead counsel."

"Not anymore. I've been recording this embarrassing convo during which you almost completely sold us out to this Florida snake oil salesman. Delia is appalled. You're toast."

"I've . . . heard nothing of this."

"Believe me, you will." Kenzi put her phone away. "But as of right now, I'm in charge of this, Dan, so all settlement negotiations have to go through me."

Dan tried to mask his sinking feeling. "A settlement would be good for everyone concerned."

"Bull. You want to take everything valuable and leave me with nothing but table scraps. It's the same story in every divorce. Women get the crappy leftovers." Kenzi raised her chin. "Not when I'm in the courtroom."

Wu seemed to shrink away from her. But then, given his age and demeanor, he wasn't sure if Wu was following this all.

"Perhaps," Dan said, "we should continue this conversation after the clients have been escorted back to the other room."

"Why?" Kenzi asked. "So the good ol' boys can make secret deals in smoke-filled rooms?"

"Men," Delia muttered. "Spare me from impotent overcompensating males."

"Joe trusted you," Wu said quietly. Despite the volume drop, his voice hushed everyone in the conference room. "He gave you everything he had."

Delia whirled on him. "And without me, his everything would've been nothing."

Wu's eyes narrowed. "You lied to him. You made him into something he never was."

She moved toward Wu. "You filthy slanty son-of-a—"

Dan slid between them. "Ok, there will be no fistfights at this settlement conference."

Kenzi's eyes rolled. "You're not going to cheat us out of potentially billions."

"All that money—and you can't give Wu a sliver?"

"I could. But as you know, I have to represent my client's best interests. And giving away money to someone with no viable claim is not in her best interests." Kenzi marched right up and got in his face. "You might be able to sell your bill of goods to Christopher—"

"Who is your partner."

"But we both know that a Ken doll is just a plastic head with nothing inside."

"I was trying to resolve the dispute expeditiously." He sighed. "Which I can see now is not going to happen."

"No, you're going to have to prevail the old-fashioned way. By winning in court." She stepped even closer, close enough to kiss. "I'm going to mop the floor with you, Pike."

He returned her steely glance. "Bring it."

A smile crossed her face. "I look forward to . . . locking horns with you."

"What the hell is this?"

They both turned. Maria stood in the doorway.

"I go to the bathroom just once, as pregnant women have been known to do, and when I return, you two are making out in the conference room."

Dan raised his hands, palms out. "We are definitely not making out. Exactly the opposite. I'm preparing to avulse her eyeballs."

"Yeah," Kenzi said, maybe too quickly. "He's disgusting. Can't stand him."

"A little while ago you were talking about how good he looks in a swimsuit."

"I was just trying to get your goat."

"It worked."

"Ten tactical points for me."

"And now you two are sucking each other's air."

"Because we hate one another so much," Dan assured her.

"Yeah," Kenzi echoed, waving her hands. "He's totally repulsoid. I don't even like being in the same room with him."

Maria raised a finger. "You better be telling the truth."

"I am. Your boyfriend is gross." She glanced at Dan. "Ick. I'm moving away. Can't stand to be near you."

Unfortunately, she backed in Delia. "Why is everyone acting as if I'm not really here?"

"Because you're not really here," Wu said quietly. "You are simply standing in the shoes of the man who should be here."

"I earned those shoes."

"Joe earned them. You are a liar and a gold digger."

Delia took a swing at him. And connected. Wu tumbled sideways until the table stopped his movement. Dan reached out to catch him but wasn't close enough. Kenzi jumped to get out of the way and collided with Maria. They both growled at each other as they tumbled sideways. Christopher looked as if he had no idea what was going on.

Dan ran to Wu's side. His client was on his knees, grasping the edge of the conference table. "Are you okay?" It wasn't a major spill, but Wu wasn't a young man, either.

"I'm . . . fine. Just . . . help me back to my seat."

Dan did. But he could feel the fragility. He wondered if there was more wrong with his client than mild cognitive diminishment.

Delia wasn't done. She grabbed the paper Maria used to make notes and ripped it into pieces. Maria shouted at her. Wu reached up to intervene, but Delia took another swing at him. Christopher shoved her back into her chair. Enraged, Delia grabbed an ashtray and threw it across the table. Wu ducked. The ashtray flew past him and clipped Dan on the side of the head.

"*Ow!*" He clasped his head. No blood, but it still hurt. "Okay, stop it! Right now! We are adults resolving a legal dispute. Not kindergarteners playing dodgeball."

Delia did not stop.

Why exactly did he want to start trying cases again? He was stuck in a room full of people who hated each other. And somehow, this group was going to reach an agreement on a property that could potentially be worth billions?

Someone fired off an earsplitting airhorn. He winced and clapped his hands against his ears. Kenzi whipped out her cellphone—totally violating the settlement conference rules—and acted as if she were going to start livestreaming this mess.

Nope. This case was not going to settle.

The case was going to trial.

Whether he had a snowball's chance of winning or not.

CHAPTER TEN

By the time Dan made it back to the Snell Isle office, after a brief stop downtown, Maria had already laid out a veggie-only charcuterie board, soft drinks, and a few less soft drinks. As usual, Maria could read the room. That had been a settlement meeting for the record books.

Garrett and Jenny joined them. Garrett brought his keyboard. Jenny sat at a table covered with books and paper. Apparently while he and Maria were gabbing futilely, Jenny had started researching and drafting pretrial motions.

"Can you believe Delia threw an ashtray?" Maria said.

"Threw?" Dan said. "She *hurled* it across the room. She is some kind of angry." He thought a moment. "Or desperate. And thinks our client is the only thing standing between her and a fortune."

"Christopher looked mortified."

"Or terrified. I don't think he's spent much time in Fight Club."

"Where did the airhorn come from?"

Dan shrugged. "Probably Wu. It's always the quiet ones."

Wu sat at the far edge of the sofa, mostly quiet. "Wasn't me. I wanted to be like Joe."

"In what way?"

"He wasn't there."

Dan caught an expression that triggered a thought. "I know why you called Delia a gold digger. But you also called her a liar."

"She's been lying to Joe since Day One. Inflating his expectations. How else would she get him to marry her? Like I said before—I'm not even sure he likes women."

"Is he ok? Health-wise, I mean."

"He's going blind."

Dan felt his heart sink. An artist losing his eyesight. A writer who might have dementia. King Kaiju had been more of a curse to them than a blessing. "How long has that been going on?"

"Since his twenties. He's always been extremely nearsighted and wore thick glasses. But he's getting worse. He can't drive. I'm not sure he can ride buses any more. Delia completely dominates him. He has no mind of his own. Or if he does, he's keeping it bottled up inside. Delia barely lets him leave the house." Wu's voice dropped. "Still might be better than living alone, though. Sometimes I get so confused . . ."

Dan and Maria exchanged a meaningful look.

"I don't like any of this," Jenny said. "Sounds like elder abuse."

"Delia will say she's struggling to care for her doddering old husband," Wu explained. "I've tried to get Social Services involved. Never got anywhere."

Maria laid a hand on Wu's shoulder. "That must be incredibly hard. Seeing your longtime friend end up controlled by a woman who's only interested because she thought he might have something valuable."

"And now, when she thinks it might finally pay off, we bring a lawsuit. Which makes her even angrier. She's losing the only reason she spent years with a man who . . . probably wasn't . . . well. You know."

"I've wondered why they didn't have more children."

"Probably because that would involve repeating an act that . . . neither had much interest in."

Jenny flipped her scarf around her neck. "You boys need to wake up and join the twenty-first century. Platonic relationships are totally common these days. Platonic life partners. People who enjoy one another's company without a sexual component to their relationship."

"What would be the point of that?" Garrett asked.

"I had a relationship like that, long ago," Maria murmured. "We slept in the same bed for nine years without so much as making out."

Dan's head whipped around. "What?"

"Of course, that was with my older sister. We shared a room when we were kids."

Jenny still looked irritated. "Many people are breaking away from so-called societal norms to create unique arrangements that make them happy. Even if it's not a conventional opposite-sex once-a-week relationship. Individuals have individual needs. Which you learn about by communicating rather than imitating."

"You don't want Delia to communicate," Wu said. "She criticized all Joe's work, all his friends. Never wanted him to go out or to see anyone. She was trying to isolate him. Which of course, would make him completely dependent upon her. She probably forbid him from attending the settlement conference. As if she had more right to be there than he did."

Dan could see how emotional Wu was becoming. This was more than a battle over a big pile of cash to him. In his mind, Joe was a victim. Of Delia, of lawyers, of corporate America. The world—and the law—had screwed them both over but good.

Even if he was the creator of the character—he still cared about his friend.

"Did Joe ever fight Delia? Object?"

"I doubt it. He's not the type. I think his work is all he cares about now. Well, that and their son. He would do anything for that boy."

"Ernie? The actor?"

"Wants to be. He's had a few small parts. Nothing major yet."

"You think he ever will?"

Wu smiled and spread his hands. "The odds are long. But no one bet on King Kaiju either, and now he's worth billions."

AFTER THE PRELIMINARY DISCUSSION CONCLUDED, MARIA MADE case assignments.

"Our main goal is a judicial declaration of rights. But in the event that our opponents file counterclaims, which is likely, we will respond with claims for copyright infringement, trademark infringement, trade dress, breach of contract, and tortious breach of contract. We will pursue complete control of the character, a lot of money, past royalties, and punitive damages, arguing that although Joe contributed to the early issues, Wu was the sole creator and thus should control the character."

"And control could lead to a fortune," Dan added. "The stakes are high. So we have to be ready. Garrett, you should—"

He was stopped by the alarmed expression in Garrett's eyes.

"We—need to—"

Jenny tilted her head toward Maria insistently.

Oh right. Damn. He wasn't the boss anymore.

"Like I was saying, Maria, I think you should ask Garrett to do . . . something, don't you?" He cleared his throat. "Go for it, Team Leader."

Maria's pressed lips became a thin smile. "My pleasure. Jenny, I think you've already got enough to do this week. After you file the petition, send out the initial discovery requests. Notice the obvious depositions."

Dan's brow creased. "We're taking depositions?"

"Yes, Dan. Here in civil court, you don't have to wait till someone's on the witness stand to ask questions on the record. You can notice a deposition and ask them in advance. Then use the transcript to impeach them if they change their story."

"Yes, thanks for the Civil Procedure rehash. My point was, just because we can take a deposition doesn't mean we should. You're tipping your hand."

"To make sure we don't get ambushed at trial."

"You can still get ambushed at trial. Maybe instead of depositions, we should—"

Maria cut him off. "Start the depos as soon as opposing counsel will allow, Jenny. Monday would not be too early."

Dan stood blank-faced and silent. Everyone was watching to see if he would throw a fuss about being interrupted and overruled. So he wouldn't give them the satisfaction. He should've kept his mouth shut. But it was a hard adjustment . . .

"Garrett," Maria continued, "I'd like you to look into this movie studio deal. Find out everything you can. There's lots of speculation on the internet, but few people from the boardroom are talking."

"On it."

"If we knew more about that, we might better understand what Delia is fighting for. And please give us thumbnails on the new copyright act, the Sonny Bono one, and all the amendments. And the subsequent case law. Any relevant precedents. We're going to need that to revive Wu's claim."

"Already on it."

"You should interview Bob Lydek."

"CEO of Headmark Studios?"

"Right. He's the man holding the big bag of money. Let's see what his take on this is."

"He's the CEO of a big corporation. His take is he wants to make money. And he won't volunteer anything."

"He won't have a chance once Jenny sends him a subpoena duces tecum."

"I'll start trial prep," Maria said. That was her usual function, since she hated speaking in court. "Try to map out a winning strategy. That's enough for now. Let's get our toes wet and then we'll see where we go next. We need to know more about the previous agreements and course of dealing in—"

The doorbell rang. Maria glanced at Dan. "Were you expecting someone?"

He held up his hands. "I'm not in charge of this meeting. Would you like me to go to the door?"

"If you wouldn't mind."

Dan swung the front door open—and almost immediately wished he hadn't.

Kenzi didn't wait to be invited. She marched past him into the living room. "Seriously? You people call this an office? Sheesh. The one percent do live differently."

Dan cleared his throat. "This is our office. We don't own—"

"I know all about it. You four are pampered little puppy dogs. You got your comfy padded beds, your Fancy Feast meals, everything provided on a silver platter. When was the last time you had to roll up your sleeves and work?"

"Never," Dan replied. "The fairy godmother drops by every day, waves her wand, and wins all our cases for us."

"Your fairy godmother lives in Oklahoma. Your team has a new leader. Because you quit."

"That's not even—"

"Dan!" Maria said. "Are you going to let this woman talk to us like that? I would think you'd have more self-respect."

"She's not bothering me." He knew exactly what Kenzi was

doing—because he'd done it so many times himself. Misbehave so opposing lawyers start to detest you. Because when people get angry, they don't think straight. They miss things. "Always nice to see you Kenzi, but—why are you here?"

"I've come to give notice. In person."

"You've decided to capitulate and give us the character rights? Sensible move. Will save a lot of time and energy."

"Hardly. But that's probably what would've happened if I'd been a little slower getting to that conference room. You practically had that dunderhead Christopher signing on the dotted line."

"I was able to persuade him to see things from my perspective."

"You wrapped that clown around your little finger. But that won't be happening again. Delia has issued her marching orders. In writing. I'm lead counsel now. Christopher is just hanging around to carry my catalog cases. And there will be no more settlement meetings." She poked Dan right in the chest. "This is your official notice. You and me? We're going to war. All-out war."

CHAPTER ELEVEN

"War?" Dan acted surprised. "I don't know what to say. This seems so sudden. Shouldn't we talk about this first? Maybe get some counseling...?"

She returned his smirk. "Don't be a smart ass. You thought this was going to be a cakewalk. Wrong. You have to deal with me. And I'm not giving anything away."

"Shouldn't we gather at the wigwam first? Parlay? Maybe pass around the peace pipe?"

"Your antiquated and racist metaphors are not going to change my mind. I'm telling you Delia and I will take no quarter."

"I believe that part," Jenny muttered.

"We are in it to win it. And I will. The facts are all on my side."

Dan shrugged. She wasn't entirely wrong there. "I like a good challenge. Even if you claim your guy was involved with King Kaiju—Wu was the creator."

"Wu sold his interest for a mess of pottage. Leaving us as sole claimant. Just so you know, I've already spoken to Bob

Lydek. Let me bottom-line it for you. The studio will back our IP claim—to the extent agreed upon—but will not accept yours."

"Their position will change if we get a judicial declaration of rights."

"Be that as it may, this is where we stand."

"So we have to take on all of you. Delia and the studio. In that order."

"And the comics company, which has held the rights for more than fifty years. They want to be added as a party-opponent to your lawsuit."

"So basically—it's us against everybody?"

"Yup. You vs. Everybody. And Everybody is represented by me."

"And Christopher is history."

"I might keep him around for appearances." Kenzi glanced at Maria. "He is pretty easy on the eyes, right?"

To Dan's surprise, Maria nodded. "No question."

Dan realized Kenzi was trying to intimidate them, but he actually preferred having a competent attorney on the other side, especially if they were going to trial. "I can live with you as lead counsel."

"That's nice. Since you have no say in the matter. But I'm gonna be your worst nightmare. You're going to wake up at night screaming."

"He already does that," Maria said quietly. "But it's because he sees dolphins, not you."

Kenzi squinted. "Dolphins? Who's afraid of dolphins?"

"No one," Dan said, knitting his eyebrows.

"Except him."

Dan drew in his breath. "They are kind of slimy. And those strange phallic noses..."

"This crew is even weirder than I realized," Kenzi murmured.

"Why does it have to be war?" Dan said. "Why don't we just

talk to each other like rational human beings? Seek mutual understanding and compromise?"

Kenzi's eyes seemed to turn inward. "Because the stakes are too high for all that touchy-feely crap. Way too high. For everyone involved. Including me."

"Now I understand why you traveled cross-country to get involved. Big money."

"I have no problem with making big money." She craned her neck awkwardly. "But the truth is always a little more complicated..."

SIX MONTHS BEFORE, BACK IN SEATTLE, KENZI ALMOST DECLINED to take Delia's case. Delia was considering divorce but wanted to know whether she would get some or all of Joe's claim to King Kaiju in the divorce settlement. Given that Kenzi was a lawyer, not a fortune teller, she said she couldn't make any promises. But since the claim predated the marriage, and it was an inchoate claim at best, she was not optimistic. Plus . . .

"I'm transitioning out of divorce work."

"Why?" her assistant Sharon asked. She stood by Sharon's station on the fifth floor of their law firm, just outside her private office, watching her open the morning mail. "That's how you made your name. And a ton of money for this firm."

"I think I can do more."

"Delia doesn't care about the divorce. She just wants that dinosaur."

Kenzi pondered. "Which could mean a lawsuit. It might be good for the firm if I branched out into civil work."

"You already run one of the best firms in the city."

"I want *the* best firm in the city. And then the state. I want to be the Mayo Clinic of law firms. The one everybody wants but only the best can afford." She sighed. "Delia is probably not a good fit for us."

She heard a familiar voice behind her. "Have you read the memo I sent yet?"

Emma. Her younger sister drafted a memo on intellectual property law she probably should read. But it was so long and boring and had so many footnotes and citations . . . "Her husband has no money. She's been supporting him. There's no cheese down that tunnel, li'l sis."

"I grant you, it will entail a fight. Her husband has lost in court before." Emma was showcasing her usual Goth Girl style, mostly black with some blue glittery eyeliner. Wednesday Addams could take style tips from her. "But the potential reward makes it worth the trouble."

"You and Dad. Always talking about the long term. But I need to generate money now, before the quarterly reports come in. Otherwise, the old fogeys will try to oust me."

"Not as long as your father supports you. He's still on the board, even if he isn't managing partner. They'll toe the line."

"Maybe. I want to give him something to brag about."

Emma pushed a copy of the memo closer to her. "And this is how you do it. If you handle this right, the woman who came to you for a divorce could end up a billionaire. And this firm could get a huge contingency fee."

"I still don't like it. Intellectual property. Sounds so nerdy." Kenzi glanced at her phone. Her daughter Hailie had left five texts with increasingly large quantities of emoji. She needed a trip to Target. Probably wanted more supplies for her murder board.

Why were there so few hours in the day when there was so much she needed to do? "What's your take on Delia?"

Sharon shrugged. "She's a sister, and I like that, but she doesn't make a bundle and her husband makes nothing. She can't afford you."

"Unless she gets a piece of this IP claim."

"Exactly," Emma said. "You take a stake in the outcome of the litigation. Which, so long as it's reasonable and handled properly, is not forbidden by the Rules of Professional Conduct."

"Sure. Like I said." Her hand reached for the file. "Who's this dude?"

"Co-counsel. David Christopher. Reps Headmark Studios. They're overseeing this since it could impact the ownership of the rights to a character they very much want to licence. This case will get a lot of media coverage."

"Is that a good thing?"

"It is for you. You thrive on attention."

Kenzi didn't reply. Since everyone knew it was true.

"But it ain't gonna be easy," Sharon continued. "The husband had a partner who also claims rights. He's sued before, lost, and signed an interim agreement to get a pension. Sidekick Comics says they own the rights and they've published the comics in the US and sold the rights in Japan for comics—"

"Manga," Emma corrected.

"Fine, thanks, whatever. You're no doubt an expert."

Short pause. "I do rather like King Kaiju. Particularly the Dark Griffin series. And that Baby Kaiju is just adorable."

"Sidekick says neither of the creators are entitled to anything and has been screwing them over for decades."

"So," Kenzi said, "my success depends upon not only succeeding with a claim that has failed for decades, but also dealing with the opposing claims of a similarly screwed creative partner. Sounds high risk and super-time-consuming." She picked up a black-and-white glossy headshot. "Is this the Headmark lawyer? Since when do lawyers put their glamour shots in the file?"

Emma shrugged. "First they started putting photos on business cards. Then email signature blocks. Soon we won't even bother writing briefs. We'll just send in photos and the judge can decide based upon who she likes the looks of best."

"Which, some say, is how it works now."

"That photo was at the bottom of his email," Emma said. "I printed it and enlarged it. I thought you would like to know what you're going up against. It might . . . incentivize you."

She pulled the photo closer. David Christopher had a chiseled jaw the likes of which had not been seen since Dick Tracy. He had all kinds of hair and his chest and arms suggested that he spent a lot of time in the gym.

"This pretty boy is what I'm up against?"

"Kind of a hunk, huh?"

"For a lawyer. I mean, he's wearing the traditional blue suit, but still . . ." She whistled. "Not entirely disgusting."

Sharon laughed. "He's gorgeous and you know it. You probably don't even fantasize about guys who look that good."

"I assume you've already researched him. How is he as a lawyer?"

Emma's eyes darted. "No one gets everything."

"Understood."

"But that could be good for you. You'll swim circles around him."

"I like the sound of that." She thought another moment. "And if I take this case, I'll be working closely with him?"

"Daily. Just the two of you. Hours and hours." She paused. "How long has it been for you? Two years? Three?"

"*Excuse me?*"

"I'm not counting vibrator activity. I mean the real deal."

Kenzi tossed down the file. "I can't believe you two! You're more sexist than men! You're using sex to lure me into a case. Because of course all any woman really wants is a good man to take care of her."

"Maybe for an evening," Sharon murmured.

"Correction," Emma said. "I want you to take this case

because I think it could make us a lot of money, give the firm enhanced credibility, and establish an important precedent. I'm using sex to achieve an important goal. It's a completely different thing."

Kenzi put her arms akimbo. "I am a serious feminist lawyer businesswoman. I am the managing partner in a major Seattle firm. I don't chase after men. And I don't need a man to motivate me."

"Of course. Absolutely true."

Kenzi gazed at the photo. "Conservative?"

"Probably, given his job, but that doesn't mean he's nuts."

"Hair product?"

"Sure. But to be fair, it works for him."

"Green bubble or blue?"

"Are you kidding? He probably has the three-thousand-dollar Hermes iPhone."

Kenzi took a deep breath. "Ok. I'll consider it. But just to be clear, I'm not doing this because of that dewy-eyed, floppy-haired thirst trap. I'm taking the firm in a bold new direction."

Sharon nodded. "Right."

"Taking one for the team, basically."

Emma agreed. "That's your story and you're sticking to it."

Kenzi snatched the file and sauntered into her office. "The sacrifices I make for this firm . . ."

"I DON'T CARE HOW COMPLICATED THE TRUTH TURNS OUT TO BE," Dan said. "There's no good reason to continue visiting pain. These people have been mistreated long enough."

Kenzi ignored him. "We're going to bury you. Your client's claim has never been worth anything. Now a court is going to declare that it's worthless once and for all."

"Perhaps. But I think your client wants the money more. My client has no wife and no heirs. He just wants credit for his own work. We could work something out."

"Sorry. Already told you. All-out war."

"Why? Because Delia is your path to getting a major Hollywood studio on your client list?"

"Aren't you the mind reader. You know what I think? I think you're not sure you can handle having me on the other side of the courtroom."

"I like working with you. Have since the day we first met at the beach." He glanced over his shoulder toward Maria. "Which I was totally unprepared for, unimpressed by, and uninterested in. Just a business meeting." Kenzi grinned. "But if I win, will you put that swimsuit back on?"

"Hey!" Maria said. "This is totally inappropriate."

Dan, however, couldn't resist a challenge. Especially when he thought this petite spitfire was trying to intimidate him. "Challenge accepted." He raised a finger. "But what if I win?"

"You'll get a lot of money."

"No, if I lose, I'll wear the suit. But if you lose . . . you have to live without your cellphone for an entire week."

Kenzi's eyes widened like balloons. "What kind of monster are you?"

"Those are my terms. Don't tell me you're chickening out. A minute ago, you seemed supremely confident. Was that all bluster?"

Kenzi's eyebrows knitted. "That's . . . not . . . I don't . . . bluster."

He held out his hand. "Then we have a bet?"

Kenzi's teeth were clenched. But she extended her hand. "You're going down, Kite Man."

He shook vigorously. "We shall see."

CHAPTER TWELVE

THREE HOURS LATER, MOST OF THE TEAM STILL SAT IN THE LIVING room, alternating between working and commiserating. Now that they knew early settlement was off the table and Kenzi had financial support from a deep-pocket movie studio, everything had changed.

Just before dinnertime, Dan's sister Dinah bounced through the front door, as usual full of twenty-something energy and enthusiasm. She sported a white crop-top tee and a ponytail which he suspected made her very popular down at the court clerk's office.

She took one look at the team. "Wow. Did we lose a trillion-dollar case while I was out?"

Dan looked up, a half-smile playing on his lips. "No. We're strategizing about our new case. So we can lose a trillion dollars."

"You're exaggerating."

"Not by much," Jenny said. "The Marvel movies made about thirty billion in the first phase. And as you've probably noticed, they haven't stopped."

Dinah pulled a face. "Eh, Marvel movies are so yesterday. Strictly for parents."

Jenny looked alarmed. "What about DC?"

"All those white middle-class heroes are lame. King Kaiju is cool."

"He's a monster."

"He's a cool monster. He wasn't created by a nuclear explosion, like Godzilla. That was a metaphor for postwar Japan. King Kaiju is a child of the seventies. He was created by pollution. He battles global warming. Much more contemporary. And important. And hot."

"He's kinda scaly . . ."

"He's adorable. Like the prince in Beauty and the Beast. Or Quasimodo. Or ET. Or—"

"Also, he destroys cities just by walking across them."

"Only when fighting crime. That makes him a good guy."

Dan couldn't help but smile. Dinah had brought so much joy to his world. He'd only learned he had a half-sister late in life, but they'd made up for lost time. He couldn't believe the enormity of her spirit, especially given all she'd been through. And now she was a law student! "I see you know as much about this character as Jenny."

Dinah crossed to the kitchen. "No one knows more about comic book characters than Jenny. But you should understand that you're fighting over a Gen Z superstar. Kaiju is for us like *Scooby Doo* or *Star Trek* are for Boomers."

"But he was created in the seventies."

"And is coming into his own now. I have a near-mint copy of King Kaiju #3."

Jenny's head whirled around. "The one where he's taking down enemy ships in Golden Gate Harbor?"

"That's the one."

Jenny gave her a stern look. "Girl, we need to talk about a trade."

King Kaiju #3

"What, for some Aquaman thing? Pass."

"I got early Wonder Woman."

"She's the one with the lasso, right? Nah, too S&M for me."

"Batgirl. Batwoman. Madame Xanadu."

"No thanks."

"Power Girl. Complete set. You know, you kinda look like her."

"Are you joking? No one looks like the women in comics. She's drool-bait for emotionally arrested adolescents."

"Thanks. I'm keeping my Kaiju."

Maria cleared her throat. "I hate to interrupt this scintillating comic auction, but is anyone hungry?"

"Always." Dinah grabbed some cold pizza from the day before.

"I've ordered dinner," Maria said. "I meant to cook, but time got away from me. DoorDash is bringing Mexican."

Dinah clapped her hands. "Excellent. I'm starving."

Maria frowned. "How do you stay so skinny?"

Dinah shrugged. "Good genes."

Dan added: "Young age." He entered the kitchen and grabbed a slice, hoping Maria wouldn't notice. But she did.

His phone buzzed. The ID at the top of his iPhone read KAKAZU. "Yeah?"

"Dan? Jake." His friend Jake Kakazu was now chief of the SPPD homicide department. "We have troubles."

"I don't know if you've heard, but I'm not handling murders. At least not at the moment."

"Are you repping a guy named . . ." Pause. Shuffling of paper. "Apologies if I mispronounce this. Kazuhiko Wu?"

Dan felt a chill tingle down his neck. "Yeah. But it's not murder. It's—"

"And before you came along, he sued something called Sidekick Comics?"

"Probably. I just filed a more recent—"

"Let me cut to the chase. I've got a corpse. A bloody, hideous, headless corpse."

"*Headless?*"

"You heard me right."

Dan recalled what Maria told him before. "You might find the head at Lost Luggage . . ."

"Thanks, genius. Already matched the two. ID'd him through fingerprints. No criminal record, but he sat for the bar exam, which as you know means being printed."

"He's a lawyer?"

"Kevin Lieber, who court records indicate represented your client in an earlier suit."

"I'm sorry to hear this . . ."

"Dan, let's have a talk."

"If you insist. I suppose you're worried Wu could be in danger."

Long pause on the phone. "This killer doesn't seem to have a problem with your client. This killer goes after his lawyers."

DAN DROVE SOUTH TO KISSIMMEE AT LEAST ONCE A MONTH, especially when tides were low and surfing was in its doldrums. Sometimes he went out on Lake Toho, but his favorite stop was Kissimmee Waterfront Park, which had walking paths, playgrounds, and a pier. But today he and Jenny were headed toward Old Town. Like so many would-be destinations, Kissimmee had rejuvenated its downtown by making it touristy, with brick pedestrian lanes, a Ferris wheel, the world's only year-round haunted house—and lots of shopping.

Jake sent a uniformed officer to escort them past the crime-scene tape. They were behind the Old Town Main Stage. Apparently, an hour before, local performers had put on a Disney-themed musical revue. But now, the mood was definitely not "Be My Guest."

He spotted Jake on the other end of the roped-off area. He was barking orders at forensic teams. Trying to collect evidence in an open area with tourists stomping around had to be a challenge.

He greeted Jake. "Thanks for calling."

Jake nodded. "I didn't do it to help you. I called because I need information I suspect you might have."

"If I can help, I will." He glanced behind them, where two officers from the medical examiner's office were lifting the headless corpse onto a gurney. A large pool of blood on the concrete was dark and congealed. He'd been there for a while. And he had not improved with age. Dan didn't know how the head had been removed, but the corpse's neck was jagged and black. Exposed bone was visible.

Dan had seen a lot in his time, but this was butchery. He had no idea what the motive might have been, but whatever it was, it didn't justify this.

"Dog found him," Jake explained. "Body was sorta shoved under the edge of the stage. Probably late at night when the joint was closed. I found a hole in the fence. Coroner hasn't given me a number yet, but he's been there for days."

"I don't know this guy. Never even heard his name."

"Your client must. Ask him why someone would want to kill his old mouthpiece."

He would. But the answer seemed obvious. He'd been killed because he had some connection to this IP rights battle. But what was the connection? What did he know? Many people with conflicting interests were involved, and the amount of money on the line made murder a definite possibility. But why the lawyer?

Didn't make any sense. And also established a rather unpleasant precedent.

"Why cut off his head?"

"Yes, that is the million-dollar question. Or in this case, the billion-dollar question."

"But you don't know the answer?"

"When I know why he was decapitated, I'll know who killed him."

Flawlessly logical, as Spock used to say.

"I will say this," Jake added. "I don't think it was planned, at least not well in advance. The removal of the head was . . . rough." He took a deep breath. "I doubt the killer had the proper tools."

"So it was a spontaneous decision to decapitate?"

Jake swore under his breath. "The investigation is still in progress."

"Anything in his pockets?"

"Keys. Change. Nothing that told us anything we didn't already know."

"Cellphone?"

"Didn't have one."

"How can that be?"

"He must be a time traveler from a different century."

"You've got someone checking his credit cards?"

"Of course. But I doubt he was killed because he spent too much at Walmart."

"Friends, family, co-workers?"

"We're just getting started. But he had a solo practice, has a cousin in Arizona, and has never been married."

"Not many people to interview."

"The Maytag repairman had more friends."

Maybe he should give Jake something. So he wouldn't regret inviting Dan and would be more likely to do it again in the future. "I know you've barely started investigating, but I can't think of any reason why this friendless IP lawyer would be at this park by himself . . . unless someone invited him."

Jake nodded. "I don't think he was murdered here. I can tell the body was moved after death. And decapitation."

"That suggests the murder happened somewhere around here."

"Which makes sense, since the victim lived nearby. And the head was found not too far away. I understand needing to get rid of a body. But I don't know why he cut off his head first."

"Watch your pronouns. You can't assume the killer was male."

"This would require enormous upper-body strength."

"You still can't be sexist. Maria has convinced me that toxic masculinity is ruining civilization."

"That sentence should've been in the past tense."

Down the boardwalk, Dan spotted some jugglers and, in another area, a guy doing magic tricks on a unicycle. Visitors were giggling and eating popcorn.

"So can you contribute anything to this mystery?" Jake asked.

"Sorry. But we're going into discovery mode. If I learn anything that might help you figure this mess out, I'll let you know."

"Appreciated. You don't have to do that."

"You didn't have to call me today and I find it hard to believe you thought I knew anything relevant. You were trying to help me."

"Don't be absurd."

"You think if this guy killed one lawyer, he might kill another. And you're worried about me. And Maria and the rest of the team. That's why you called."

"I'm the homicide chief. I can't play favorites and I definitely can't buddy up to a lawyer. Especially not a defense lawyer."

"Uh-huh."

"But I can be . . . thorough in my investigations. Interviewing the parties who might have relevant information." He flashed a quick grin. "Especially the parties who introduced me to my beautiful wife."

Dan nodded. "Give her my best."

"I will." He raised a finger. "I could tell you not to leave town. But you wouldn't listen."

A biting reference to Dan's previous case.

The medical examiner's interns covered the body, then carried it to a waiting ambulance. Even with the sheet, Dan felt he could see every line and curve of the headless corpse's body. And he could definitely smell it. Could practically taste it.

"But I will say this. You are in danger. You, your client, your team. Even your sister. Everyone. We have no idea what's going on here. All we know for sure is that it relates to you, or your client, or your case. So as far as I'm concerned, every one of you has a target painted on your back." He swallowed hard. "So be careful."

Part Two
EAST IS EAST AND WEST IS WEST

CHAPTER THIRTEEN

Lydia Franchini couldn't believe she was sitting in a therapist's office. There was no shame in it. Many people benefitted from talk therapy. Her perpetually jealous older sister, for one. Her co-worker Roger. He was in worse shape than she was. According to Dr. Quinlan, Lydia suffered from PTSD. Roger was practically catatonic. Apparently gummies and severed heads don't mix well.

"How is your anxiety?" Dr. Quinlan asked. She sat about five feet away in a much more comfortable chair, but that was fair, since she probably sat in it all day long. Here on the loveseat, Lydia had the option of lying down. Did anyone actually do that?

"Fine. No change really."

"Sorry. Medication isn't helping?"

"I tried half a Xanax one morning and put myself into such a fog I couldn't sort the lost luggage from the coffee machine."

"Hmm." The doctor made a few notes. "Maybe we should switch up your meds. Still having nightmares?"

"Yes. I see it over and over, again and again, like it's on some nonstop film loop. In the third person. I see myself, standing there, opening that damned Samsonite bag and . . . and . . ." She covered her face. "It rolls out."

Dr. Quinlan nodded. "The head."

"Yes. The bloody head with bone and viscera sticking out. Dripping."

"I can't even imagine."

"You don't want to. Trust me."

"I understand the victim has been identified."

"Yes." Lydia leaned slightly forward, her lips dry. "That's the most bizarre thing. I knew the guy."

"The lawyer?"

"Yes. My husband works at the local courthouse. They worked on some case together. I met him once when he joined us for lunch."

"Nice guy?"

"Seemed okay. I didn't leave wanting to hack his head off."

"But no normal person would. Forgive me, Lydia, we haven't known each other that long. But I have good eyes. I think you're holding something back. And that's why you're not recovering, not even slowly. Because you've got something trapped inside and it's tearing you apart."

Her lips were pursed. It was a long time before she answered. "You're right."

"Let it go, Lydia."

"I can't."

"It's the only way you'll ever heal."

Although the silence only lasted about thirty seconds, it seemed an eternity.

And finally, after weighing all the possible consequences, she spoke.

"When that head thudded onto the floor, I lost it. I mean, totally lost it. Screamed like a whipped dog." Her hands gripped the sofa cushion, as if that might somehow anchor her. "Didn't even think rationally. They say I cried for three minutes."

"No one is judging you. That was a horrifying experience."

"But even in the midst of all this panic and chaos . . . I noticed something."

"Something . . . about the head? Are you a trained CSI?"

"No. But I'm an experienced cook."

Dr. Quinlan appeared puzzled. "Have you told the police about this?"

"Of course not. They might come after me! They're already suspicious. 'If you have so much insight, maybe you're the killer. Which would explain why you found the head.'" She pressed her fingers against her forehead. "I've dealt with police before. I've had to deal with them nonstop since this hideous drama began. I'm not volunteering for more."

DELIA REMOVED THE BLACK FILE FOLDER FROM THE BATHROOM cabinet. Hiding it under a stack of towels might've seemed adequate before. But no longer.

Maybe this was the time she finally parted with this paperwork.

But there was always the possibility she might need to prove who was what one day. She didn't want to screw anything up, especially not now, when she was on the verge of getting some real money. If Wu knew the truth, he would never give her anything. And if her husband found out . . .

Well. That would ruin everything.

Her friend Imogene who works at the courthouse told her the last time this Daniel Pike shyster had someone on the witness stand, it ended with the police searching his home. She couldn't prevent that from happening. So she made sure there was nothing to find if and when they came. Although she couldn't be certain, she thought most cops were smart enough to look under the towels.

Just before she went in search of a new hiding place, she opened the file once more.

She hadn't looked at this in years.

She closed her eyes. What a mess. But it worked out. She got what she wanted. She had zero regrets. About any of it. But she couldn't let Joe know. Or Ernie. They would not react well . . .

She slid the file into her purse and left her hotel room. She considered a bank stop, but the police would likely find any safe deposit box in her name as well. She had to dig deeper.

Literally.

She climbed into her car with a smile on her face. Did she enjoy this? Not one bit. But the ends were going to justify the means.

IN HIS BURBANK OFFICE ON THE HEADMARK LOT, BOB LYDEK sprawled across the sofa and grabbed a cigarette. He was only wearing a button-down shirt with a loosened tie. "If there's anything more cliché than a studio exec having sex on the couch, it would surely be smoking a cigarette afterward."

Marion Hast, his new assistant, lay beneath him, draped languorously across the cushions. "This isn't a casting couch," she said sleepily.

"It's my couch." He checked his watch, then grabbed his shorts from the floor.

"But I'm not a starlet and I don't want a part." A mischievous grin crossed her face. She blew a strand of chocolate brown hair out of her face. "Except maybe a part of you."

"Again?"

She pulled him close and pressed herself against him. "A girl's got needs."

"No doubt. But you can probably make it till bedtime. Maybe you should get back to your station. Your coffee break is over."

"And I didn't even get any coffee." She pulled him tighter. "I want you, Bob."

"I don't doubt that you want something. But I have work to do."

He tried to push off the sofa, but she grabbed his hand and pulled him down again. "I have something for you."

"I think you already gave it to me. Shall I get out my whoopee cushion?"

"I hate that juvenile prankster crap. How about something much better?" She placed a long-nailed finger against his lips.

"Will this involve sex toys?"

"No, silly." She gave him a playful shove. "It's about King Kaiju."

He blinked several times, clearing his head. "This is an unexpected topic switch."

She took his head in her hands. "I could be so good for you, Bob. I really could. I could help you in ways . . . you can't even imagine."

"You said something about King Kaiju."

She laughed and said in a singsong manner: "I know something you don't know . . ."

"Spill. That deal is still tentative. Are you saying we shouldn't finalize?"

She shook her head, playfully brushing her nose against his. An excellent performance, but he'd seen it too many times before to be fooled. She didn't care about him. She wanted a better job and knew he could make that happen. Women had a hellacious time breaking into this industry, so even if this wasn't exactly the Harvard Business School approach, he couldn't fault her for trying.

"Just the opposite. I'm saying you should do it, and do it fast, no matter what it costs."

"My neck will be in the noose if the investment doesn't pan out."

"That won't happen." She laughed, high-pitched and brittle. "Take the hint from Gen Z, Bob. That dino is all over BookTok. Today's kids don't know Superman, they don't know The Lone Ranger, they don't know Tarzan, they barely know Star Wars. But they all know King Kaiju. That one little IP could be the tentpole you use to prop up this failing studio for the next ten years. You should do anything it takes to get that property. Anything at all."

CURTIS SWART, VP OF MARKETING FOR SIDEKICK COMICS, WAS IN the morgue.

That was what they called it, borrowing from the newspaper world. The morgue was where they stored all the back issues. These days, most of that was digitized, stored on computer files, so keeping mounds of curling pulp paper was no longer necessary.

Except here. Since this company was founded, back in 1935, they'd stored two copies of every comic they published in the morgue. For archival purposes. His predecessors had no way of knowing, back then, that old comic books would become collectible and astronomically valuable. Today, the comics in this archive were worth over seventy million dollars.

To be sure, they had over 40,000 comics, many predating World War II, all in excellent condition. They had early superhero comics, romance comics, monster comics from the fifties inspired by Godzilla, and of course, monster comics from the seventies inspired by King Kaiju. Today, some of these early Kaiju comics were more valuable on the secondary market than much older prewar comics. He was in the top tier, with Superman and Spider-Man. Batman and Captain America. The first six issues alone were worth around 1.2 million bucks, especially the origin story issue and #4, the one that introduced She-Shogun, his arch-nemesis.

DC sacrificed some of their early archive copies to make expensive omnibus collections in the days before digitalization. Marvel didn't really start till the sixties, so this was probably the most valuable comic collection anywhere in the world. And here he was, bathing in it like Uncle Scrooge in his money bin. What would he have given for this forty years ago, when he was a skinny kid in Amarillo getting picked on every day, only finding solace in these magical four-color stories.

They still used library shelves and book boxes to store the comics upright so they wouldn't develop curled spines. Each issue was individually bagged in mylar. He pulled out the one that contained the earliest issues of King Kaiju, then removed the first six and spread them across the table.

There it was. Big as life and twice as ugly, as they used to say back in Texas.

Stone-cold proof.

He took a few snaps with his phone, no flash.

He had never felt so powerful in his life. He had a secret worth millions. Possibly billions. And he might be the only one who knew, other than the cover artist himself, Neal O'Neill. And that chump already had a foot and a half in the grave.

His eyes glistened. Life hadn't always been easy after he got his degree from Duke. Archivists were not in high demand. He'd wanted the Huntington Library, but instead ended up with comic books. But they were damn cool comics. Even if the pay wasn't what he wanted, he was working with books he loved.

King Kaiju #4

That love had produced a potential cash cow. He could practically feel the power emanating from his fingertips. (Okay, maybe he'd read too many comic books.)

Would he use his power for good, or for evil?

Would he write a scholarly paper to inform the world of his discovery?

Or would he sell it to the highest bidder? There was a lot of money at stake. Even here at Sidekick, he could probably improve his standing dramatically. Just by whispering a few words.

What should he do?

He carefully placed the comics back in the box, then left the archive.

Some questions were so obvious they didn't need to be answered. He picked up the phone and asked his assistant to call Megan Sanderson, the literary agent.

This was going to be a memorable conversation. Because what he knew changed everything.

IN A DARKENED BASEMENT, SOMEONE DRESSED IN BLACK descended the wooden steps. They creaked with each footfall, and that eerie squeal filled the basement.

Carefully, a gloved hand laid a cellphone on the worktable.

And a moment later, that same hand took a hammer from a nearby toolbox.

The hand used the hammer to smash the phone into oblivion.

In fact, the hand kept smashing the phone long past there was any chance that anything on it could be recovered. The glass shattered, the metal crumpled. It started to look like a small ashtray that needed to be emptied.

That ends it, the brain behind the hammer thought. Desperate measures, sure. Crazy, some might say. But now I'm safe. Now there's no chance anyone will ever find out.

This dangling thread had been snipped. No one would ever understand why the lawyer was killed. And that was just as well.

Because Leiber might not be the last to die before this adventure ended.

DAN CHOSE TO WALK BACK TO THE BUNGALOW HE SHARED WITH Maria. The walk was only a few miles and he needed to stretch his legs and suck in some sea air. Sometimes, when he was wrapped up in a case, he forgot what was genuinely important. What he loved.

He grinned. Who was he kidding? He loved practicing law. He loved Maria. Water sports were a pleasant diversion. But he had to stay in shape if he was going to see this case through.

His phone buzzed. Jake Kakazu.

"How's my favorite Chief of Police?"

"Very concerned. Can you come to headquarters? I want to show you something."

"I suppose. But—"

"Are you somewhere safe?"

"Am I ever? Why?"

"Your favorite opposing party just reported her gun was stolen."

"Delia? That woman has a gun?"

"Had. And if I were you—"

Dan never heard the end of the sentence. Instead, he heard the unmistakable sound of a bullet whizzing past. Didn't hit him, but came close enough to sound like an earsplitting parasite.

He ducked, accidentally dropping the phone. He crouched and looked around. He saw nothing.

Another gunshot rang out. It didn't sound like a rifle. Something smaller.

And closer.

He scrambled around a street corner, but it was hard to effectively take evasive action when you weren't sure where the shooter was.

Up ahead, he spotted a Shell station. If he could get to it, he'd probably be safe.

If he could get to it.

Sweat dripped down the sides of his face. His hands were slick. Was he just thinking that he loved practicing law? What an insane idea that was.

Another shot rang out, this one so close he felt a spray of brick pellets spatter his face. He wouldn't remain lucky forever.

He hunkered down like a track star and ran.

Two more reports of the gun rang out, but he kept racing forward. A few seconds later he was inside the station. He moved away from the glass doors.

Maybe he'd just wait in here a while. Make sure no one followed him. Maybe call Garrett to pick him up.

The clerk behind the cash register glanced up. "Can I help you?"

"No." He looked at his hands and saw they were bleeding. Must've scraped himself while he was crouching and hiding. "On second thought, maybe some iodine. And Band-Aids."

"Sure thing. Anything else?"

"I don't know." He felt his heart rate slowly returning to normal. "Keep any bulletproof vests back there?"

CHAPTER FOURTEEN

"I STILL THINK THIS IS A BAD IDEA."

"Give it a chance. You might warm to it."

"This is not something lawyers do."

"I've brought lawyers in here before. During homicide cases."

"This is not a homicide case!" Dan ran his fingers through his hair. "At least . . . it wasn't supposed to be."

He stared at the letters stenciled onto the translucent glass in the door. CAROLINE CREST and below that MEDICAL EXAMINER.

"You seriously think I should be around for the autopsy?"

Jake Kakazu, standing beside Dan, smirked. "You'll survive. You're a big boy."

"But . . . why?"

"I'm just trying to help. You might learn something of value."

"It's not a homicide case!"

"Obviously. If it were, I couldn't do this. But today I can since, for once, nobody thinks your client committed the murder."

"Look, this is a tragedy. But it's a sideshow. It has nothing to do with our civil suit."

"You really believe that? One lawyer is dead and someone's taking potshots at you."

Dan glanced away. "I can't allow myself to be distracted. We don't have much time before trial."

"All the more reason for you to step inside." Jake knocked gently on the door. There was no reply, but he still entered.

Dr. Crest was hunched over a table, mask across her mouth, tools in her hands. She looked early forties, though it was hard to be certain when her face was partially covered. She wore standard-issue scrubs and a focused expression.

Dan glanced down at the table, then quickly looked away. The head was there, artfully placed above the body to which it was no longer attached. Most of the blood was gone, but the exposed bone and viscera were not anything anyone wanted to see this early in the morning. The body seemed gray and chalky. Not all that much time had passed, but he had to assume the decapitation altered the body's natural pattern of decomposition.

"Dr. Crest? This is Daniel Pike."

Crest's golden hair was held in place by a scrubs hairnet. Her hands were inside the corpse's abdomen scraping something. He wasn't sure what, but then, he didn't really want to know.

She did not look up. "You'll pardon me if we don't shake hands."

"Just this once." Dan executed a perfect maneuver whereby he appeared to be leaning forward, as if observing the doctor's work, but in reality, he diverted his eyesight and thought about baseball. "Anything interesting?"

She spoke with the detached timbre of a scientist, but at the same time, he detected a tinge of excitement. "Everything about this corpse is interesting."

"See?" Jake said. "Told you this would be useful."

"Don't get ahead of yourself." He turned back toward the

doctor. "I read the prelim report. No fingerprints or bite marks or any other potentially useful trace evidence?"

"This is all preliminary," the doctor explained, "but based upon what I've seen so far, taking into account the toxicology and tissue sample reports—I don't think the killer touched the victim."

"Gunshot?"

"No evidence of any foreign object, not a bullet, not a knife. Not poison."

"Except he's missing his head."

"Nothing gets by you, does it?" The doctor reached for her silver equipment tray. "I'm about to use a craniotome. If that's going to bother you, you might want to step outside."

"I'm fine." But what he was actually thinking was, What's a craniotome?

Jake for the win. "I hate those skull saws. What a racket they make. Bone fragments fly everywhere."

Crest stiffened a bit. "I'd like to think I have a bit more skill with the drill."

"Why is this necessary?" Dan said, hoping the pained tone in his voice wasn't too telling.

"I want to know how long the brain was oxygen-deprived so I can lock down time of death. Decapitation is a traumatic event."

"I would imagine," Dan murmured.

"So all my readings are whacked." She paused. "That's a technical term in the medical community."

"Of course."

"Might be evidence of more trauma. Brain damage even."

Dan swallowed. He was a tough guy and loved extreme sports and all that—but this was messing up his stomach to an extreme degree.

How had he missed the smell when he entered the room?

Now it seemed omnipresent and overwhelming. The smell of death. Nothing else like it. Thank God.

He took a long slow breath. If he could just get through the next five minutes without embarrassing himself by vomiting all over the tile floor...

"Was the head cut off before or after he was murdered?"

"Neither."

Dan squinted. "How is that possible?"

"Because the decapitation was the cause of death." She activated the craniotome. The high-pitched whirring was not as ominous as he expected it to be. "At least that's my working hypothesis."

"Someone did this . . . while he was still alive? Like . . . an execution?"

"He might've been unconscious. Asleep. Or physically restrained. That's what I'm trying to discern."

"Cutting off someone's head—" Dan pressed his fingers against his temples. "—must require a lot of strength."

"All depends on how it was done." She chuckled. "Some people are smarter than others." She started whistling.

For real? The coroner whistled while she worked?

"Most common way of decapitating someone would be with a sharp blade. An axe or machete."

"Or bone saw?" Dan suggested.

"Possible, but that doesn't come up too often. Paucity of maniacal killers who went to medical school. But there is something odd about this. The brutality might suggest a lack of planning. I talked to that poor woman at the airport who found the head. Lydia Something. She was so hysterical I couldn't even understand what she was saying. I hear she's getting therapy."

"I bet she needs it. Can you imagine?" He shivered. "Horrible."

The coroner turned. "Have you people learned anything

about this guy? Any reliable environmental data could be helpful."

"Not much," Jake answered. To his credit, he seemed to have no trouble staring at the head or corpse for extended periods of time. He was probably used to it by now. Or he was better at faking his indifference. "He's a lawyer. He handled mostly intellectual property cases. He represented Dan's current client in a previous civil suit. He lived near the Orlando airport. And someone disliked him so much they took his head off."

Dan's eyes narrowed. "The motive was not necessarily hatred."

"Do people normally butcher folks they like?"

"Not often." Dan's voice dropped. "But it has happened."

"Our background checks have not produced anything suspicious," Jake said. "There are no signs that he was connected to the mob, or deep in debt, or hooked on drugs. No red flags."

"Doesn't mean he's completely innocent."

"Obviously. He wasn't killed by accident. What I'm saying is, we have no idea why he was murdered."

Dan continued thinking. "Any prints on the luggage? A luggage ID tag?"

Dr. Crest answered. "No such luck."

"Why dump the head at the airport?"

"I'm a doctor, not a detective. But a suitcase seems like an obvious choice for carting a head around. And if you've already got it in a suitcase . . ."

"Why not leave it at the airport?"

"Take a look at this." Jake crossed to a table that bore several sealed evidence baggies. "This is what we got from the body, the head, and the suitcase. Labeled and processed." He picked up a small evidence glassy. "We found this in his pants pocket."

Dan took a closer look. "Receipt?"

"Yeah. Ticket stub."

"He went to the movies."

"He went to a Fathom Events screening of the final double-length episode of the King Kaiju anime series."

Dan's lips parted. "He liked King Kaiju?"

"Or he was updating his knowledge of King Kaiju. And an hour or so later—he's dead."

Dan tapped a finger against his lips. "Have you found his cellphone?"

Jake shook his head.

"Are we sure he had one?"

"His assistant says he did. What's more, he had Find My Phone activated so she could locate him if an unscheduled hearing or other emergency arose."

"And she can't find his phone?"

"Not even a blip. I don't think it exists anymore."

"Someone destroyed it."

He noted that the good doctor was returning her attention to the craniotome. Which seemed like a good reason for him to leave. "Thanks again for the invite, Jake, but I have a ton of work to do."

"Understood. Thank you, doctor."

She nodded, not looking up.

Jake walked him out to the parking lot. "Do you have an appointment now?"

"Where do you want to take me next? A haunted house? A crematorium?"

"I was hungry and thought you might want to grab lunch."

"Oh." He stepped outside into the warm Florida sun. The air smelled of the sea, not death, and the horizon was bright, not bleak. "I may walk back to the office. Clear my head. But thanks. Say hi to your sweetie for me."

"Will do." He stopped walking for a moment. "And Dan..."

The sudden change of expression—to grim seriousness—was worrisome. "Yes?"

"Be careful. I mean, I know I've said that before, but . . . this time I really mean it."

"Appreciate your concern. I'll be fine."

Jake took a step closer. "I know how much Maria means to you. And you have a child coming. You should not be taking risks."

"Jake—this is a civil case. This should be the safest work I've had in my career."

"That's what concerns me. You're off your guard. You think you're safe. So you might not see it coming."

"See what?"

Jake slipped on his sunglasses. "The bullet with your name on it."

CHAPTER FIFTEEN

Dan watched Jenny carefully as she exited the second-floor elevator. Normally, he would take the stairs, since the courthouse had the slowest elevators known to humanity. Maria would take the stairs because she had to get in her steps to please her Fitbit. Jenny simply murmured that, "A lady rides," and that was the end of it.

Dan wasn't completely sure what that was about, but he suspected those heels Jenny wore had something to do with it. Why any woman would inflict that kind of pain on her feet when she could be wearing sneakers, he could not imagine.

And that wasn't the heart of the problem. Even back when Jenny was Jimmy, she didn't come to the courtroom that often. Since her job was primarily drafting the innumerable documents required by modern litigation, her physical presence was rarely required. But Jenny was coming today, and this would be her first appearance since she started . . . dressing differently.

To his relief, no one said a word to her. If anyone noticed, they had the sense to play it cool. He had to give credit where due—Jenny was learning to put herself together.

Maria whirled around a corner. She'd stopped in to see the

DA and was now running a trifle late. "Got everything ready to go?"

Jenny nodded.

"I got the docket sheet and anything else the clerk was willing to share. Which wasn't much."

Jenny made a *tsk*-ing sound. "Hasn't been the same since Shawna left."

"No joke. I don't think her replacement likes his job. Or maybe he just doesn't like me. At any rate, we already knew there was a motion to suppress coming."

"There will be more," Dan said quietly.

"You know this for a fact?"

He nodded toward the end of the hallway. "I know who's on the other side. We're at war, remember?"

Kenzi bounced out of the stairwell, talking to the phone she held at arm's length.

"Remember, KenziKlan, never trust a handshake. Get it in writing. Should you make an exception for your love interest? Hell no. You should get it notarized if it's a love interest. Consider a cashier's check. Those are the people you have to be most careful about." She spotted her opponents in the hallway, signed off, and dropped the phone into her Louis Vuitton purse.

"Are you trying cases online now?" Dan asked.

"No. I'm an influencer. I help people."

"Come on. You're promoting your business."

"The two are not mutually exclusive."

Kenzi ignored him and spoke to Maria, which Dan thought somewhat ironic, because although Maria believed Kenzi was a worthy opponent, she couldn't stand to be in the same room with her. "Have you got this boyfriend of yours ready for trial? Told him what to say?"

Maria tried to resist, but a small smile broke out just the same. "I try, but he doesn't listen."

"Life in the patriarchy." She turned to Jenny. "Oooh. I like those pearls."

Jenny brightened. "I picked them out myself."

"Akoya PurePearls?"

"Absolutely. Just as good as Tiffany's." Her voice dropped. "At half the price."

Kenzi raised a hand and Jenny high-fived her. "My kind of girl! Woo-hoo!"

Maria looked as if she hadn't been invited to a party. "I helped pick them out..."

Kenzi swung around. "Woo-hoo to you too then, girl!" They slapped hands.

Dan watched with grudging admiration. Kenzi was a very good attorney. In more ways than one.

Kenzi sidled toward him, hand still raised. "I got one for you too, big boy."

"Pass. I'm representing my client and you're on the other side."

"Don't be such a stuffed shirt. We're just having fun. The trial hasn't started yet."

"The trial started the second you rounded that corner. And this is your attempt to cozy up to my staff."

"My staff," Maria corrected.

"If you seem friendly and unthreatening, they'll be less worried. And consequently, less cautious."

"This is a trial, not a chess match."

"They are much alike. You're trying to put us off our guard."

Kenzi pressed a hand to her chest. "Li'l ol' me?"

"Then once we're unsuspecting, you'll spring the big surprise."

"I think you have a negative impression of me, Dan."

"To the contrary, I have an excellent opinion of you." He paused, and his voice dropped. "As a lawyer."

"All right, have it your way." She wiggled her fingers. "See you crew inside."

They watched as she and her Dolce & Gabbana's entered the courtroom.

Jenny whistled. "Should we be worried?"

"Oh yes," Dan said.

Maria's voice had a scornful tone. "You're gonna let that flashy little nobody get to you?"

Dan thought carefully before answering. "She's planning something. I can see it in her eyes. It's that sparkle, the extra burst of confidence. She knows something we don't."

"And that is?"

He shook his head. "If I could answer that question, it wouldn't be something we don't know, would it? But if we don't figure it out soon—Wu is going down in flames."

Dan slid into his seat at the plaintiff's table beside Wu. He wasn't sure, but as he approached, he thought Wu was muttering to himself.

"Did you say something?"

Wu looked up abruptly. "No, no. Just thinking."

"Practicing your testimony?"

"God no. I don't even want to think about it. I get confused..."

Dan felt another chill. "We're a long way from you taking the stand. And when you do, all you have to do is tell the jury what happened. Easy."

"Not so easy." His voice seemed thin and unsure. Wobbly. "This happened decades ago. I can barely remember yesterday's breakfast."

There it was again. The possibility of memory loss. Dementia. Wu spoke in complete sentences and in most cases, when they talked, he sounded intelligent and was responsive to questions. But at times Wu was halting, hesitant, tired easily, and Dan could see him struggling for the right word.

He hadn't talked about it much, but he knew that if his client couldn't tell his story on the witness stand, they had no chance of success.

"You'll be fine. Today is just boring motions. You didn't even have to come."

"I like knowing what's going on."

And normally, since this was a civil case, that would not be a problem. But if the judge got the idea that he was not competent to testify, the ramifications could be terrible.

The bailiff entered and instructed them to rise for the Honorable Judge Cheridan Parkwood. She was in her mid-thirties and had only been on the bench about two years. Since she sat on the civil side, Dan had not been in her court before, but everything his friends said about her was positive. She was attentive, fair, and sometimes even a little fun.

The judge took her seat at the bench. Her black hair was cut short with bangs across the top. "This is a change of pace," she said, as she stacked the papers before her. "Intellectual property. Comic books. Monsters." She rubbed her hands together. "I can't wait."

Dan arched an eyebrow. That was something he didn't often see from the bench. Enthusiasm.

The judge sorted through her documents. "We have some prelim motions, right? Normally, I'm content to take those things up at the pretrial, but—"

"It couldn't wait, your honor," Kenzi interjected.

Dan bit his lower lip. Interrupting the judge? Maybe they did things differently in Seattle. Or maybe Kenzi wasn't as smart as he thought.

"I submitted a brief, your honor. Relating to this business

with the poor man and the severed head and . . . I don't even want to think about."

"Good. I would also prefer not to think about it."

"So let's take that off the table, ok? The police say there might be some tangential connection to our case, but no one knows what that would be, and I don't see how it can possibly impact the rights to art created decades before."

"But it might," Dan added.

"At any rate, it's more prejudicial than probative, so we're moving to exclude all the evidence relating to this murder," Kenzi continued. "It's a sideshow, and . . . it's murder, you know? It's a lot sexier than intellectual property. It could be a diversion that prevents the jury from focusing on the key facts of the actual case."

"Unless," Dan said, "it turns out this murder is one of the key facts of the actual case."

"You don't know that."

"Yet. This motion is premature, your honor. Let the police investigate. Let us investigate. Once we've seen the big picture, we can make a determination about relevancy. Perhaps at the pretrial."

"That will be too late. The press is all over this case. The damage will be done." Kenzi took a few steps closer and held out her hands, almost as if praying, imploring the judge to grant her boon. "If my esteemed colleague's client had a good case, all he would need are the facts. But as we know, he has tried to gain control of this character before and failed."

Dan felt himself becoming impatient. "The law has changed."

"And how will the new law be impacted by this murder? Answer: it won't."

Judge Parkwood turned to Dan. "Can you prove a connection? Or at least make a reasonable inference?"

"Not today. I don't—"

Kenzi raised a finger. "Don't let him stall for time, your honor."

"I am not—"

Kenzi held her hand on one side of her mouth and dropped her voice. "He has a rep for that sort of thing. Courtroom shenanigans. As you probably know."

Dan glared. "Wait just a minute!"

"Only telling the truth, your honor."

"You wouldn't know the truth if—"

"Stop." Judge Parkwood did not raise her voice but did raise a hand. Dan expected chastisement to follow. But instead, a huge grin spread across her face. "I like this case. It's exciting!"

"Your honor..."

"I don't need to hear any more. I read your briefs. I'm granting the motion. I think this murder case is an unwanted distraction. Even if it turns out to have some vague connection to one of the people involved, no one thinks this local lawyer was involved in the creation of the fictional character whose disputed ownership forms the gravamen of this case. I'm also concerned about jury contamination."

Dan couldn't believe it. "But your honor—"

"It's over, counsel. Motion granted. I know, given your background, you might be more comfortable talking about murder." She gave him a sharp look. "But I don't want to hear about it during this trial. Moving on. There was something else to discuss, wasn't there?"

"Yes, your honor," Kenzi said. "I'm afraid it's me again. I apologize for being such a high-maintenance gal."

Dan rolled his eyes. Kenzi was playing this judge like a violin.

If this was all-out war, he was beginning to worry that he wasn't the smartest general in the field.

"No worries, counsel," the judge said. "I know it's hard to juggle so many balls at once."

Dan raised a hand, like he was in the second grade. "Your honor? If I may, before we move on—"

The judge looked at him sternly. "I've ruled, counsel."

"I know. That motion is over. But since the court is concerned about jury contamination . . ." He turned to pivot toward Kenzi. "I move for a gag order. From now till the end of trial."

Kenzi looked at him as if he were speaking Urdu. "You want to prevent my clients from talking about the case?"

"Not the clients. You."

A stricken expression crossed Kenzi's face.

"Your honor, as you may know, my worthy opponent is a noted internet, uh, poster . . . person . . ."

"Influencer," Kenzi said, rolling her eyes.

"She talks about legal cases and offers her opinions. Offers advice."

"To women," Kenzi added. "So they don't get trampled by the unjust male-dominated judicial system like they have been for the previous five-thousand years."

"Yeah. That's the tone. And she has thousands of people who watch or listen to her on a regular basis."

The judge nodded. "And you don't want her to talk about this case."

"Yes, but that's not enough. Even if she doesn't specifically mention this case, people will know what she's talking about. She's already mentioned this case twice in her broadcasts last week." He glanced at Kenzi. "So with considerable regret, I move for a gag order prohibiting all KenziKlan livestreams and posts during the pendency of this case."

Kenzi's lips parted, forming a round soundless O. The horror in her eyes defied description. "No."

"Fair's fair," Dan said. "I can't talk about the murder that I believe is relevant to this case. And she can't babble on about why her client deserves to win even though she's in league with a soulless corporation sucking creators dry to feed their inexhaustible need for profit. Sidekick Comics has made more than seventeen billion dollars off this character, and my client, the man who created him, is living with assistance in a one-room—"

"Stop." Judge Parkwood raised her hand again. "We are not going to try the case today."

"Apologies, you honor."

"But I do see your point."

"Your honor." Kenzi looked pleadingly at the bench. "Don't do this. It's not necessary. I never discuss the evidence in a case."

"But she offers her opinions," Dan added.

"I have a constitutional right—"

"—to pollute the jury pool? I don't think so."

"Judge, he is just doing this out of spite because I won the first motion."

The judge nodded. "Yes, I grasped that. You won, so he went after the thing you love most."

"That's what men do." A short pause. "Hey, wait. I love my daughter most. And my sister. And my friends and—"

"And the KenziKlan," Dan said quietly.

"Regardless of his motivation," the judge continued, "your opponent does have a point. A livestream with a large following gives you the ability to taint the jury pool in unprecedented numbers."

"I'm hardly the only influencer out there. I'm not even the only legal influencer. There's Legal Eagle and—"

"So here's what we're going to do." Dan was starting to like this judge. Despite her relative inexperience, she kept pushing forward and didn't let the lawyers slow her down. "I will allow you to continue your livestreams, Ms. Rivera. But you may not mention this case. Even indirectly. Even discussing general principles of law. Don't come close."

"Got it, your honor. That won't be a problem."

The judge took a deep breath. "But I want you to blackout Florida listeners from all your posts and streams. Until this case is over."

Kenzi's eyes ballooned. "What? I don't even know if that's possible."

"It is," Dan murmured. "Garrett can show you how."

"But your honor! I'm not going to talk about this case."

"You could still influence the outcome. This measure will prevent that. We don't know who the jurors are yet, but we do know they will be Floridians."

"But—"

"You heard my ruling, right?"

Kenzi sucked air. "Yes."

"Do you understand it?"

She chewed her lip. "Yes."

"Very good."

Kenzi glared at Dan. "Happy now?"

He shrugged. "All's fair in love and . . . war."

CHAPTER SIXTEEN

The judge shuffled her papers, then glanced at her watch. "Wasn't there something else you wanted to take up today?"

Dan didn't need clairvoyance to know Kenzi was seething. He could see the wheels grinding inside her head, trying to think of some way to obtain quick and petty revenge. She couldn't stand someone getting the best of her in court.

"Yes," Kenzi said, her voice dripping with venom. "Yes. There. Is." She glanced at Dan, then continued. "We have received reports that my distinguished colleague's client is suffering from severe dementia."

"Reports from whom?" Dan asked. "Delia? Your corporate masters?"

"No. A trained medical diagnostician who came to the settlement meeting with me, sat outside the conference room, and watched. Sadly, Wu barely knows where he is and his memory is worse. And since this case revolves around events that occurred long ago..."

Dan's expression of disbelief was even bigger than the one Kenzi had worn a few moments before. "You're trying to weaponize dementia?"

"All's fair, right?" She faced the judge. "You can see the gravity of the situation. If his client isn't able to tell the jury what happened reliably..." She shrugged. "What's the point?"

The judge didn't seem moved. "It's the jury's job to determine the credibility or reliability of a witness. Not mine."

"But your honor. Will the jurors be trained observers? Are they qualified to discern when someone is speaking reliably and when they're fantasizing? Delusional? Isn't that asking too much?"

"I can't believe I'm even hearing this." Dan looked back at his table. Wu appeared mortified, as he supposed anyone would be, hearing others talk in open court about whether he's lost his marbles. "How can you keep a named party from testifying in his own case? If he can't testify, we'd have to fold."

"And sadly," Kenzi said, a sad expression plastered on her face, "that might be the best result. Neither of us wants to waste the court's time with a meritless case. Or to embarrass an elderly man."

"Your honor, this is more than a motion to suppress. This is a backdoor motion to dismiss."

The judge nodded. "Got that already, counsel, but thanks for pointing out the obvious."

"We can't dismiss the case before my client has a chance to speak."

"I agree with that. So this is what we're going to do. I'll hold the motion in abeyance to allow you both to gather evidence and medical records, hire psychiatric witnesses, whatever. They'll want to spend time with your client. Once you have the results, submit them in supplemental briefs. Then I'll set a hearing date. Or maybe, if we keep moving forward at a steady pace, we can just deal with it at the pretrial. That would be more fun, don't you think?"

Probably not the word he would've chosen.

Dan heard a rustling behind him. To his surprise, he saw Wu

rise on shaky legs. His gaunt appearance made him seem even older than he was.

"Judge," Wu said. His voice trembled. Jenny was muttering for him to sit down, but he ignored her. "May I speak?"

The judge was not unfriendly, but she was firm. "Sadly, the answer I have to give you at this time is . . . no. You're represented by counsel. You'll be heard through him."

"But . . ." He pointed toward Kenzi. "She's talking like . . . I'm crazy or something."

"As I said, we will address this issue at a later time."

"But—But—this—" A pained expression crossed Wu's face, as if decades of frustration were finally rising to the surface. "This is what they've been doing to me for . . . fifty years. They always find some way to twist things around. Only people with money get justice."

Dan winced. He was almost proud of Wu for standing up for himself, but wished he'd left off the last part.

"I understand your concern, sir." He was impressed by how gentle the judge was. Most would've said nothing, except maybe to tell him to sit down and shut up. "And you will have a chance to speak. Just not today. Okay?"

Wu nodded.

"Furthermore, let me assure you that in this courtroom, justice is for everyone. Just like you used to say in the Pledge of Allegiance. Justice for all."

The judge looked back at the lawyers. "So, just to recap, the score stands one to one, with one undecided. The motion to suppress evidence relating to the murder is granted. The motion for a gag order suppressing the"—she glanced at her notes—"KenziKlan livestreams is granted in part. And the motion questioning whether the plaintiff is competent to testify will be held in abeyance until a later evidentiary hearing. Are we good?"

Again, not the word he would've chosen.

"Very well." The judge looked at both lawyers for a moment. "I can see that this is going to be a thrilling case. Two superstars in a cage match worth billions of dollars. We could sell tickets. But instead, let's just make sure we get the job done right, okay?" She smiled. "Court dismissed."

CHAPTER SEVENTEEN

Garrett was not ashamed of the fact that, despite living in St. Petersburg for years, he'd never been to the Universal theme park in Orlando, barely ninety minutes away. He'd only been to Disney World once, and that was for a case. Jenny constantly tried to get him to go with her, but he never would. Not a Disney Adult, he grumped. Too many shiny happy people for his taste. He preferred it when employees acted as grumpy as they felt. And why did people assume that "the most magical place on earth" was a good thing? Maybe it was black magic. That would explain so much...

And yet, here he was, riding the escalators, passing through the gates and entering City Walk, which appeared to be another pedestrian mall full of shopping and eating, with brighter colors and extremely high prices. He spotted many familiar chains—Margaritaville, Hard Rock—but also some he'd never noticed before like The Toothsome Chocolate Emporium & Savory Feast Kitchen. Appeared to have a steampunk theme and meet-and-greets with their own characters, a robot and some woman who, he presumed, made chocolate.

It was still morning and the weather was cloudy but the City

Walk was packed. He didn't understand what people saw in this. The food was adequate, unhealthy, and certainly not deserving of these prices. The shopping was no different from the junk all over town, and not nearly as good as the International Premium Outlets Mall, where he went once a year to buy sneakers for Dan's Christmas present. But there was a festive atmosphere. It was almost as if, simply because they were amusement park-adjacent, people were required to find it amusing.

Garrett knew he was the most conservative member of the LCL team, and he didn't mind that. After spending years in the prosecutor's office, he rather enjoyed hanging with people who had a different point of view, even if he didn't always agree with them. He genuinely liked Dan, but he also knew Dan had a tendency to risk everything on some dangerous crusade. He was worried about this new case. He wasn't at all sure Dan had grasped the differences between a criminal case and a civil one.

He was especially concerned about discovery. Dan was accustomed to being given everything. In criminal law cases, prosecutors are required to turn over any evidence they intend to use at trial, plus anything potentially exculpatory. Defense lawyers, on the other hand, didn't have to turn over anything. When he was a prosecutor, many a time he'd gone into the courtroom with no clue what the defense would be until they started putting it on. Defense lawyers always griped that the courtroom was the prosecutor's playground, but in fact, they knew everything the prosecution was going to do well in advance, while prosecutors had to listen carefully at trial and wing it. Seemed more like a defendant's playground to him.

Dan was already fielding motions and prepping for trial, so he agreed to handle some of the witness interviews. He'd considered noticing depositions. Depositions allowed you to question a witness in a less imposing environment and to learn what they knew in advance of trial. Then, if the witness tried to change their story at trial, you could whip out the deposition transcript and use it to impeach them. But in truth, that happened infrequently. Yes, you could ask questions at a deposition, but there was always a lawyer sitting right next to the witness, interrupting or coaching whenever they thought you might get something useful. He preferred to talk to people without interference. And since Bob Lydek was not a party or represented by counsel, he was free to do that.

He strolled down the main drag, admiring the huge Universal globe and dodging Zillenials who'd lingered too long at the tiki bar. He was supposed to be looking for a young man named Elliott Gomez, apparently some assistant to Lydek. Probably one of many. Probably the newest of many, since he drew the unpleasant duty of escorting Garrett.

Off in the distance, upstairs, he saw someone waving near Pat O'Brien's, a spinoff of the famous New Orleans landmark. He heard the tinkling of piano keys. He wished he had time to step inside and enjoy the dueling virtuosos. He had enormous admiration for these performers who could spontaneously play almost any song scribbled on a napkin.

Gomez met him at the foot of the steps. He was holding a King Kaiju comic book, a reproduction of the famous fourth issue, the one he had been reliably informed introduced King Kaiju's arch-nemesis.

The kid was maybe twenty-five, if that. He had long hair and lots of teeth. "I thought this would get your attention."

Garrett nodded. "Although I notice many people here are wearing Kaiju tees and ball caps."

"I know. The bootleg merchandising has begun while the parties-of-interest fight over the rights. This could be the biggest IP battle since Universal outbid Disney for Harry Potter." He pointed. "Follow me, please."

"I was surprised Mr. Lydek was in town. He offices in Burbank, doesn't he?"

"This case is commanding his attention at the moment. Zoom allows him to keep in touch with everything else."

They hiked in the general direction of the park entrance. "What's your role in this business?"

"Pretty simple. I do what Mr. Lydek tells me to do."

"Such as?"

"I've spent the last three days digging through the Kaiju Archive."

"And what exactly is that?"

"All the files we got from Delia. Or from Sidekick. And some other sources. Exercising due diligence, before the big acquisition."

"Good stuff?"

"Mostly trash. Fifty years of trash. But you never know. There might be something in there." He pointed off to the left, dodging a kid with a balloon bigger than the kid. "Bob's on the porch."

Garrett followed his finger. "Margaritaville?"

"Yeah."

"I miss Jimmy Buffett too."

"I think Bob is more attached to the Blackberry Moonshine Margarita. Most of the kids in there don't know who Jimmy Buffett was. They just like tequila."

As he neared the porch, he spotted a silver-haired man wearing a blue jacket over an open-collar dress shirt with khakis. He had a golden tan and looks that made Garrett wonder why he wasn't in front of the camera instead of behind it.

Lydek extended his hand. "Thanks for indulging me by meeting here."

Garrett shook his hand. And the hand, with the attached arm, came out.

Garrett jumped, startled.

Lydek cackled. "I love that gag. Works every time." His real arm slid down the sleeve, replacing the fake arm now lying on the ground. He slapped Garrett on the back. "Sorry. I'm kind of a practical joker."

Garrett forced a smile. "I've . . . never really understood the . . . appeal of practical jokes."

"Aww, loosen up. Here, shake my hand for real this time."

Garrett did. And got a jolt of electricity strong enough to make his ulna tremble.

Lydek laughed hysterically. "Gotcha!" He slapped his knee. "The joy buzzer. It's a classic. Never gets old."

That, of course, was a matter of opinion. But getting mad would not improve this interview, so he kept his thoughts to himself.

Lydek monologued. "I used to work in the magic shop at Disneyland when I was a kid. Back when it was actually a magic shop that sold magic tricks. I learned to perform. But I always got a bigger response when I pulled gags."

"Was that your first job?"

"Oh no. I started scooping ice cream at the Crystal Palace. Had to work my way up to magic. Then I went to Knott's Berry Farm and did their stage show. That led to a mailroom job at Headmark and . . . well. Now I run a whole damn studio."

Garrett got it. Perhaps when you were running something as huge and risk-prone as a movie studio, you had to do wacky stuff from time to time just to keep your head together. "Thank you for meeting me. I thought I'd have to take a redeye out to California."

"Nah. I got friends here. Headmark has always been tight with Universal. I can't function in hotel rooms. I need space. Open space. And privacy from snooping eyes when . . . you know. Opportunity presents itself."

Was Lydek talking about bedding females or masking social anxieties? He couldn't be sure, but he suspected the former.

"And I had some business here. They're about to open their

third park, you know, the Epic Universe park. And we want King Kaiju to be a part of it."

"Big new park?"

"Biggest. It's the Disney-killer. Universal has been ahead with teens and young adults for some time. This will drive the final stake into the heart of that corporate tyrant."

"The Mouse House?"

"Take it from me. Most ruthless business people on earth. Bob Iger has more enemies than Vladimir Putin. He's like Lucifer in a button-down shirt."

Sure. "I had no idea."

"Mind if we walk as we talk?"

Garrett didn't, so they took a slow stroll around the enormous loop that connected the City Walk. Shopping kiosks, endless supplies of Harry Potter merch, none of which interested him much. That minigolf course looked innovative, but he doubted he could lure Lydek into a nine-hole game at Invaders from Planet Putt.

"I guess you know what I want to talk about."

Lydek seemed almost like a walking solar battery. That Florida sunshine gave the rest of the world lesions and cancer, but it made him glow. At least for now. "Delia. What a mess. Always was, always will be."

"You know Delia? The woman who has . . ."

Lydek grinned. "Yes, that's the billion-dollar question, isn't it? What exactly does she have? What does her husband have? Tune in next week. Same Bat-time, same Bat-channel." He laughed. "Yeah, I know her. Know her son, too. He's auditioned for a few parts at the studio. She used to work for me."

This was news. "Delia worked for . . . Headmark Studios?"

"Under me. She was a low-level script reader."

"Meaning?"

"She read scripts submitted by legit agents. Prepared a report. Coverage. In most cases, we've already made our decision before we assign the script to the reader. But the report gives us something to put in the file."

"This seems very convoluted..."

"Everything in Hollywood is convoluted. Scripts have to be handled with kid gloves to avoid plagiarism suits. And that's barely the tip of the iceberg. Why does it take two-hundred-million bucks and three years to make a movie? Hell, we're not inventing quantum mechanics here. It's a *movie*. And yet, most war-appropriation budgets get passed faster than we can approve one film."

"Must be frustrating."

Lydek waved at some suit passing. "I'm used to it."

"Was Delia good at her job?"

"Terrible."

"So you fired her?"

"Nah. I didn't care that much. But I never fooled myself into thinking she was at that desk because she wanted to help me. The only person Delia ever wanted to help was Delia."

This was not the take he expected from someone technically on Delia and Joe's side of the case. "Is this how she found out about King Kaiju?"

"Probably."

"Is that why she married Joe?"

"I don't know. But savvy people understood the copyright law was going to change, so . . . who knows?" He winked. "Maybe she had some other plan for exploiting him. She's all about the bottom line."

"Delia married Joe when he didn't have a penny."

"But he had potential. Which she is now successfully milking."

This seemed harsh, even coming from a corporate tool who wanted to improve his M&A profile. "You think her only interest was the IP?"

"She didn't know what King Kaiju was till she came to the

studio. He wasn't that well known around here. I got a recent lesson on how valuable King Kaiju is myself. Pleasant and instructive. Anyway, Delia learned how much Kaiju might be worth. And she's been controlling Joe ever since. Part of the reason the movie deal didn't happen sooner was the uncertainty about the rights. Sidekick keeps saying they own the character and always have, but those Joe and Wu are going to comic book conventions and appearing on camera every chance they get to whine about how they were ripped off."

"Maybe their claims are justified."

"From my standpoint, it doesn't matter. I don't care who gets paid, just so I get the rights. But Delia was always . . . sneaky. I didn't trust her."

He wondered if that related to the color of Delia's skin. "Did she do anything else suspicious?"

"On several occasions I came up behind her and noted what was on her laptop screen. Suffice to say, she was not working, even though she was on the clock. She was doing some . . . independent research."

"Do you recall what she was researching?"

He thought for a moment. "Offshore bank accounts, on one occasion. Marijuana laws. Surrogacy. LinkedIn. I think she was looking for side hustles."

"Did she need them? What did you pay her?"

Lydek squirmed. "I can see where she might want a side hustle. Or three."

"When did Delia quit her job?"

"As soon as she had everything she wanted. To her credit, she got her stake. God knows Joe didn't have the fight in him to make his claims pay off. Maybe she will. Or if not her, her son."

"You said Ernie auditioned for you. Did he work at the studio?"

"No, never. He used to come around and hang with her some days. I don't think he was in school and I don't think he had a job. He kept hinting that he'd like a studio position. Like I can hand out jobs to any uneducated boob who appears on the lot." Lydek paused. "Well, I probably could. But that would not be sound business practice."

"You didn't care for Ernie?"

"No more than I would any other pervert."

Garrett's eyes widened. He wasn't particularly impressed by the kid either, but that was harsh. "And why . . ."

"I spotted him going into one of those adult toy shops."

"Sex toys?"

"Right. Not far from my gym in Malibu. Called Joanna's."

"Does using sex toys make one a pervert?"

"Have you ever needed sex toys? Or wanted them?"

"Well . . . no."

"You know, today, with AI and computer chips and stuff . . . some of those sex toys do amazing things."

"I'll take your word for it. But getting back to the case— what's your stake in this mess?"

"I just want the rights. They could make my rep as a CEO. Permanently. People are saying the Disney four-billion-dollar acquisition of Marvel Comics may be the best M&A play in the history of corporations. For that matter, the Lucasfilm/Star Wars four-billion-dollar acquisition paid for itself in three movies. That's business. You go for it, move the needle, run the flag up the pole and see who salutes."

"I hear you have a tentative agreement with Delia. Or Joe, technically?"

"We've signed a letter agreement. I've commissioned a screenplay based on the initial issue 5, you know the trippy one where the space aliens try to control his brain. But it's all contingent upon Delia securing the rights. Our first-look deal with Sidekick requires them to deliver clear title."

"I think I just have one more question. Why are you helping me?"

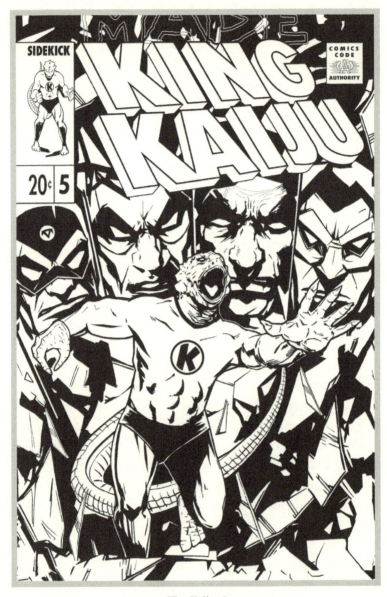
King Kaiju #5

Lydek beamed. "I'm a helpful person. Pride myself on it. And of course, if your client ends up with the rights . . . we may do business together sometime in the future."

"So you're playing both ends against the middle?"

Lydek sighed. He spread his arms out expansively. "I want *this*."

Garrett took a shot. "A theme park?"

Lydek's eyelids closed. "Universal is nice but it's basically for teenagers. Kids. Who's serving the so-called Disney Adults?"

As if he would know. "Just to take a guess . . . Disney?"

"But they aren't. I'll give Walt Disney credit where due. That man was a genius. Theme parks were a genius-level idea. But he's gone now and creatively, no one has taken his place. So the parks stagnate. EPCOT, Hollywood Studios . . . who cares? Animal Kingdom is just a big zoo, like you can find in every city on earth."

"So you want to build . . . HeadmarkLand?"

"In time. We might need a different name. But that's the general idea. We'll start in Universal's new park and use that foundation to build a park of our own design. No more roller coasters. How many times can you scream about doing the exact same thing over and over again? 'I'm moving fast, woohoo, flip me around and make my head hurt.' No. I want King Kaiju in a park. I want to create new, genuinely original experiences. I want an immersive storytelling adventure that incorporates AI and VR to make grownups believe they are there, immersed 360 degrees in a virtual world. And free to explore. Nothing like this has ever been done. And it will make us a mint. If we have the right IP."

It was not a bad idea, Garrett had to admit. But the devil was in the details, and creating a new entertainment experience was likely to be more difficult to execute than to devise.

Lydek continued. "We've only begun to discover what we can do merging tech and imagination. I want to be on the forefront of the new wave. King Kaiju is gonna be my Mickey Mouse!"

At least they were agreed on one point: King Kaiju was worth fighting for. He'd seen cases where people committed murder over a child's car seat. Imagine what might happen with billions of dollars in play.

"If you can help me get my mouse, I'll do anything for you. In secret. I wouldn't want the other side to hear about it."

Garrett understood. "Thank you for your help. Please let me know if you think of anything else."

"I will." Garrett turned, but Lydek stopped him. "Watch Delia carefully. She doesn't care about the law. Or Joe. She thinks she's earned this. Personally." He took a handkerchief from his pocket and wiped his forehead. "That woman will do anything to get those rights. Absolutely anything. And she won't let lawyers like you get in her way."

"I'll keep my eye on her."

"Which eye?" An instant later, a stream of water gushed from the apparently fake flower on Lydek's lapel.

Cackling ensued.

Garrett smiled, shook Lydek's hand, and left.

He was handsomely compensated for his work with the LCL.

But after this interview, he thought, as he wiped water from his face, he was entitled to a raise.

CHAPTER EIGHTEEN

"So remember, KenziKlan, the internet has no screening system. No bouncers. It admits all types. There are good reasonable people like you and me . . . and then there are others. Toxic people, and fyi, there's toxic masculinity *and* toxic femininity. Don't put up with any of it. You see them coming, walk the other way. They post to your social media, delete it. Or delete them. But do not get caught up in a big posting war. Ignore them. Follow your own dream."

She finished her livestream without once making reference to the case occupying most of her attention. And Dan's partner Garrett Wainwright had indeed managed to temporarily block her streams from Florida residents. So she was in compliance with the judge's gag order.

Which made her even angrier. If this had been all-out war before, it was a revenge play now. And she intended to draw first blood.

While she had her phone out, she thought it would be a good time to call her fifteen-year-old daughter. Hailee was smart, tough, and uncomplaining (usually), but she was also mostly wheelchair-bound and Kenzi couldn't help but worry. Her sister

Emma, who Hailee adored, stayed with her when Kenzi was out of town. But she still worried.

Hailee was home from school. And she picked up on the first ring. "Holy smokes, Mom. You found me another murder!"

Her smile faded. "It was not meant as a personal favor."

"No doubt. But ohmigosh. A dead lawyer!"

"I don't recall so much excitement when I left for Florida."

"Back then it was an IP case. Booooooo-ring. But a murder! That's different. I've already started a new murder board. Kelly thinks we should start a podcast."

Now she really felt like a bad mother. Her daughter was obsessing over murder. And she had no idea who Kelly was. Boy or girl? Who knew?

"I think the podcast could take off. Murder mommies love that stuff."

"Murder mommies?"

"Yeah. Like you."

"I don't have time to listen to podcasts."

"But you'll listen to ours, right? I was thinking you could be our first guest."

Hard to know whether to be flattered or despondent. What happened to the little girl who crocheted scarves and talked about going to medical school? "I don't want you to neglect—"

"—my schoolwork. I won't. Okay, you've done your token responsible-parent bit. Want to FaceTime so you can see my board?"

"I wouldn't appreciate it, honey. I'll be working late into the night."

"Problems?"

"Mmm." She flipped her side-shave. "Tricky case. Formidable opponent."

"You'll trounce him."

"Sure of that?"

"Yup. No one's as tough as my badass mommy."

She couldn't help but smile. "I hope you're right. Let me know if you need anything."

"I will." Pause. "Especially if it's something I can add to my murder board!"

KENZI REGRETTED HER DECISION TO COME TO FLORIDA, NOT FOR the first time since this case began. She wanted to gather everyone for a team meeting—but she didn't have a team. She missed working with Sharon and Emma. She'd considered flying them out for this, but Emma had cases of her own and Sharon was in a new relationship and didn't want to travel.

Heck, even Hailee would be more useful than her lunkhead co-counsel. Christopher was easy on the eyes but hard on the head. Delia was also here in her room with her son, Ernie, who she had specifically asked to be present. She thought Delia might be somewhat more manageable if her son was in the room.

"Maybe Pike will just call his client to the stand and quit," Kenzi mused. "I think that's what I'd do. Assuming the judge allows Wu to testify. Which she probably will. Everyone deserves their day in court and all that rot, yadda yadda yadda."

Christopher appeared incredulous. "With a billion bucks on the line? You'd call one witness then quit?"

She shrugged. "Who else knows anything? If the jury believes Wu, they win. If the jury doesn't, they lose. So I'm going to focus on Wu's cross-examination, the one we have to win."

"I think you need to be hands-on with everyone, if you're going to be lead counsel. You have to spread yourself wider. And I'm here to help, anytime you need me."

Yeah, she probably wouldn't rush into that, unless he was talking about a different kind of "need." Actually, she wasn't sure she was even interested in that anymore. Smart is sexy. Stupid is not. "Have you found all our witnesses and subpoenaed them?"

"Not yet. But I will."

Yes, she'd like to think he was capable of handling simple secretarial tasks. But she didn't want to risk her client's case on it.

She'd taken up temporary space at a local extended-stay hotel, but she didn't like it. Not a good work environment. No desk, poor lighting. Like trying to do serious work from a Motel 6. She was accustomed to better.

Although maybe what really bothered her was knowing her opponent was officing in a Snell Isle mansion.

Delia leaped into the convo. "I'm concerned about Wu. That man is inscrutable."

Criticism? Or racism?

"He's always been difficult. And he's always been a liar."

"No worries, Delia. If he performs badly at the evidentiary hearing, he might not be allowed on the stand. But even if he is, it shouldn't be hard to tear him apart, if he's genuinely cognitively impaired."

A sly smile spread across Delia's face. "I'm thinking a smart girl like you can make him look idiotic on the stand, no matter what."

"Like how?"

"I don't know. That's your job, isn't it?"

And that was another problem with this case. Was this irritating woman entitled to billions just because she married the guy who created a popular character?

But entitlement had nothing to do with this. She accepted the case. Her job now was to win it.

"Leave her alone, Mother." Ernie, this time. She liked him better than she did her client, but she could tell they were related. "She knows how to do her job."

"Thank you, though—"

"But what the hell is this business about letting Wu testify? Are you a lawyer or a first-year student?"

Kenzi clenched her teeth. This chump wasn't paying her. Couldn't afford her if he wanted to. So she didn't really have to put up with his crapola. "I argued the motion thoroughly. The judge disagreed with me. For now."

"Then you should've made a different argument."

"That's not how it works. You—"

"I'm not interested in excuses. I'm interested in results."

Said the boy whose entire lifetime had not yet resulted in . . . any results. She wasn't sure if he was really upset or putting on a show to impress his mother. He was an actor, after all. "The truth is, although I argue extremely well, and my brief was much better than my opponent's, the law simply was not on my side."

He jutted his arm out, pointing at her face. "That's a loser attitude."

She took a deep breath. Temper, temper. "That's a realistic attitude. You don't win cases if you can't make an intelligent appraisal of what you've got and what you've not got. No one wins every motion. No case is perfect. But if you can identify your problems—sometimes you can solve them. In advance. So I'm not going to wring my hands over a motion that probably will make little to no difference."

"That guy was killed for a reason. The decapitation was bizarre. And the victim was a man who worked for Wu in the past."

"Doesn't mean the murder is related to this case."

"You don't know that."

"No, *you* don't know that, because you have no courtroom experience. I know it very well, which is why I'm going to ignore everything you just said."

"Wait just a—"

"I'm going to focus on the direct and cross-examinations that might matter. Because that's how you win cases. That's how I got my awesome win-loss record."

Delia spoke, perhaps to rescue her son. "I wish you'd turn your expertise to the internet. I'm getting some ugly posts."

No kidding. That's why Kenzi had made post-shaming the topic of today's KenziKlan livestream. The internet had been exploding. Of course, the connection to King Kaiju guaranteed the fan press would be all over this, but the mainstream media was flogging it too. The hearing was widely reported along the lines of "GREEDY WIFE WANTS RIGHTS OF IMPOVERISHED CREATOR." This morning, she'd hired a team of professional "internet scrapers" to see if they could make more progress—without making it worse. The Streisand Effect was always a concern. The more you want people to forget about something, the more likely they are to remember. "I'm working on it."

"I'm not paying you to work on it. I'm paying you to get it done. Eradicate it. Wipe it from the face of the earth. Do I need to remind you how much money is at stake?"

"No. But we don't want to cover it up. We want to turn it to our favor. Eyes still watching, but in a different way. After all, these IP rights have been disputed for decades. We need to play up all the reasons you're entitled to this. You kept fighting after they'd given up. You're the one who read about the new copyright act and—"

"I don't care about all that weak sister stuff. Just get me my money and I'll never go on Instagram again."

"We should paint them as racists," Ernie said.

She didn't expect that one. "What?"

"We're Black. They're white. All the studio heads. Same at the comic book company. This is a bunch of rich white guys pulling up the ladder because they don't want any Black folk joining the club."

"Wu is Asian-American. Joe is Jewish."

"Not the same. The powers that be have it in for Black people."

Kenzi bit her tongue. "I'm not sure that's our best case theory."

"Then get a lot of Black people on that jury."

"I don't get to hand-pick the jury. Given the local demographics, we're more likely to draw Hispanic jurors."

The kid pulled a face. "I guess that explains why we hired you. But I'd still prefer it if the jurors were Black."

She put that in the same mental file folder with Delia's suggestions. In other words, she ignored it.

Delia pulled out her phone. "I'm not going to sit around doing nothing. I'm fighting back."

"With angry posts? That's a mistake."

"It's my mistake to make." Delia typed assiduously on her phone. Given the speed of her fingers, Kenzi guessed she was a frequent poster.

Then she glanced over Delia's shoulder. "Wait just a damn minute!"

Delia barely glanced up. "Yeah?"

"You're posting about the judge's staff. And the judge!"

"I don't like the way that clerk looks at me. She's biased. And the judge has already ruled against me. I want it to stop."

Kenzi yanked the phone out of her hands. Delia grabbed for it. Kenzi held it at arm's length.

"No. You do not get this back till you promise me you can use it responsibly."

"Who do you think you are?"

"The person who's going to win your case. If you don't screw it up before I get a chance."

"We have to fight back."

"All this post will get you is a gag order." Without even

asking, she deleted the message. "The judge will not forgive an attack on her own staff. She'll be your enemy on Day One."

"What about the First Amendment? Aren't I allowed to say what I think about the judge?"

"The question isn't whether you have the right. The question is whether it would be smart."

"The jury, not the judge, delivers the verdict."

"Unless the court takes matters into its own hands and grants summary judgment. Or a directed verdict. Or dismisses the case. Or dismisses a claim. Or excludes useful evidence. Or one of the hundred other things a judge can do to destroy you. Does it make sense to anger the judge?"

"We need a new judge."

"You don't get that just because someone ruled against you."

Delia waved her hands in the air. "Fine. Have it your way. I won't post. May I have my phone back?"

Kenzi wasn't sure she should return it. But she did. Even though she knew Delia would probably send that post or one like it as soon as she got out of eyesight.

Every case had its challenges. But how was she going to handle a case where her worst problem wasn't the opposition—but her own team?

CHAPTER NINETEEN

As Garrett approached the Tradewinds Hotel, he wondered what exactly people did at a writers conference. Did they sit around a table and type together? Did they exchange typing tips? He envisioned mystery writers chatting about guns and romance writers chatting about sex positions.

Probably not what really happened. But he enjoyed the daydream.

He'd learned that this hotel annually hosted the Novelists Ink conference, a gathering of professional writers. Emphasis on the word "professional." Authors had to rise to a high level of sales before they would even be considered for membership. But happily, the person he came to see was a literary agent, not an author, so she didn't have to be a member. She'd been invited to speak, some kind of lecture about navigating the chaotic modern book marketplace.

He found his quarry outside on a large patio area not far from the beach. She sat at a table beneath a wide white umbrella, her phone in one hand and a cigarette in the other.

Megan Sanderson cut an imposing figure. She was large, not heavy but big-boned, broad-shouldered. Her voice was loud and a trifle nasal. East Coast. Her conversation appeared to be a one-way monologue composed of endless run-on sentences.

"I'm telling you, it was metal as hell." She waved her cigarette arm back and forth as she spoke in a loud, animated fashion that the people at neighboring tables did not enjoy. "It's the most exciting thing I've done in my life. I've never felt like that before. Never!"

Garrett was not an eavesdropper by nature. But on this occasion, he had to admit, he was curious.

He held up a business card. She saw the name and nodded.

"Suzie, gotta ring off. Promised this guy I'd talk to him. Won't take long. Then I've got a two o'clock." Her thumb tapped the big red button and she put away her phone. "You're the lawyer, right? You've got eight minutes."

Garrett drank Sanderson in at one gulp. She had big hair, probably to match the rest of her figure. She was professionally dressed in upscale clothes, but a bit awkward. For some reason, she made him think of Julia Child.

He started. "Did you ride the VelociCoaster?"

"Haven't had the chance yet. You?"

No, but when he'd been at Universal he'd seen signs for this massive roller coaster. "Sorry. I just heard you mention excitement so I assumed..."

"Roller coaster?" She laughed. "I'm about twenty years too late for roller coasters. But I am in my sexual prime."

Garrett blinked. "Do tell."

Her eyelids lowered. "Are you into erotic hypnosis, handsome?"

"Uh... no. At least... I don't think so."

"You'd know." She gave him that look again. "I think you'd like it. If you had proper instruction."

He recalled his conversation with Bob Lydek about Delia's son. "Does it involve sex toys?"

"Oh, hell no. I hate that stuff. Toys are for children."

"Some people disagree."

"What I like is when mind-meets-mind. That's sexy."

"So you're at this writers conference looking for smart people?"

"No." She blew a perfect smoke ring. "I'm looking for prosperous clients. But I wouldn't mind taking you back to my room for a hypnotic session."

He pulled out a chair at her table and took a seat. Even if this conversation creeped him out, she did appear to be warming to him. "Does this involve staring deeply into one another's eyes?"

"Nah. That gets boring fast. Have you heard of the Bambi Files?"

"I saw the movie when I was a kid. Really messed me up."

"This is different. Posted anonymously online in 2017. A collection of hypnosis recordings that will change your life. Made a new woman of me. Literally created a better and healthier persona."

"And . . . this relates to sex?"

"It's a form of sex play. Hypnotherapy has been around for ages, of course, but this is new. People undergo hypnosis and get into trance states in pursuit of sexual gratification. Soothing background noises. Ticking metronomes. Messages added with a high-pitched text-to-voice generator."

"Sounds delightful."

"Better than that, if you stick with it. The messages become more complex, more confrontational. It's a form of therapy, really. Peering inside yourself."

"I'd rather watch a Rays game."

"The online community is huge. Over twenty-thousand members on Reddit alone. Of course, some spoilsports want to ban it."

"Because it's a fraud?"

"Because it works too well. It's too powerful. Too dangerous. Really messes with some people's minds. Some think it creates a whole new personality, like programmed dissociative identity disorder. Some call it brainwashing."

He wondered if she had to undergo this therapy just to deal with Delia. "Why would anyone want that?"

"It was perfect for me. Just the prep I needed. Before, you know. The next big step."

His eyebrows danced. As long as he acted interested and kept her talking, his chances of getting something useful improved. "And then?"

"My boyfriend took me to a brothel."

"A—" He tried not to appear mystified. "Where? Deadwood? Dodge City?"

"Not far from Reno. I think it's legal there. Like the Chicken Ranch."

"And you went with your boyfriend?"

"Of course."

"But—if you already had a boyfriend..."

"Why did I need a brothel?"

"I was wondering..."

"To get a willing third party."

Ah. Here we go again. "You wanted a unicorn for your polyamorous relationship?"

Sanderson's eyes fairly bulged. "You're a little hipper than you let on, big boy."

He opted not to explain about Jenny. "I'm open to new experiences."

"I wouldn't mind seeing you in the lineup."

"What's that?"

"What happens at the brothel. First we go into this charming place made all old-timey. You know, red lacy frills. Lampshades. Piano player with an armband. I was so nervous. I'd never done any kind of threesome before. Always fantasized about it, but never had the guts to make it happen. My boyfriend pushed me over the edge." She smiled, big and wide. "For my birthday."

"What a sweetheart."

"It was run by this woman called the 'house manager.' She wore a three-piece business suit and looked just as no-nonsense as I do. Formidable, you know? She had all the working women line up in front of the fireplace. So we could review our options and decide who we wanted in our room." She beamed again. "Harold let me pick."

"Such a gentleman."

"I chose Delores. Dark hair. Fishnet hose and thong. Flirty and happy. Did a little shimmy on my lap and I was in love." She covered her face with her hand. "I think it's the first time I've felt truly sexual in my entire life."

Garrett nodded, while also glancing at a clock on the wall. He wondered if she was sufficiently warmed up that he could address the actual reason for the visit. "I can see now why you're excited."

"Over the moon."

"This work conference must be a buzzkill."

"Just the opposite. Look around you, boy." He did, and for the most part, he saw a lobby filled with well-dressed businesslike women. Their success was self-evident.

"Romance writers," she continued. "In the main. That's the most popular genre by far, and also the most profitable. I have friends who make a million bucks a year self-publishing their romances, pricing them cheaply, producing a consistent, frequent product and reaping the benefits." She paused. "Hard work, of course. Some of these people write a novel a month."

Garrett was impressed. "Is that possible?"

"If you don't have a private life. And don't revise. There are other popular genres. Horror is on an upswing. But the most popular books today are the so-called romantasy titles. Romance and fantasy. We have some crime writers too. But romance is king." She paused. "Romance is queen? Whatever.

You know what the boom segment of the romance market is right now?"

"No clue."

That wobbly smile crossed her face again. "Spicy romance." She said it again, this time drawing it out. "Spiiiiiiicy romance. Dark romance. Sugarkink." She took another deep breath. "Tentacles."

"What?"

"It's a manga thing. Have you not done your homework? Your case is all about manga."

At last. The case. Since she mentioned it, he assumed it would be okay for him to follow up. "I've seen the King Kaiju manga. You signed on as Joe Ulrich's agent, right?"

"Yes, thanks to his wife. If I'd been around when King Kaiju started we wouldn't be having a lawsuit today. I always get my clients a fair contract. If I sell something or make a deal, I get ten percent off the top. Of course, now everything is contingent on the outcome of your lawsuit. I can't license his rights till the court tells us what he owns."

Behind her, he saw people crowding into meeting rooms. Looked like the next breakout sessions were about to begin. "You're on the opposition witness list. They must think you know something of value." The question was whether she would want to talk about it. Kenzi had almost certainly told her to keep quiet.

"I think I'm a background witness."

"Meaning . . . ?"

"Someone to explain the contemporary publishing world to the jury. It's not what people think it is. I also have a legal background, so I can help with some of the copyright law issues. So much depends upon common course of business, worker expectations, subsidiary rights, blah blah blah . . ."

"Is it that complicated? I thought writers wrote stuff, publishers published it, and everyone shared in the profits."

Sandstrom laughed out loud. "The old school New York publisher-to-bookstore chain has completely broken down. New York doesn't have nearly the dominance it once did. Because bookstores don't. Only a small percentage of books sell in stores these days. It varies, but it's always a one-digit number. Online is where most books are sold. Amazon, obviously, but other venues as well. And writers don't necessarily need New York. They can publish themselves. Just upload the files to Amazon and you're off to the races."

"The ability to self-publish your own work has been a gamechanger?"

"People have always been able to publish their own work. They just had no place to sell it afterward. Now they do. Some are better at selling than others, just as some are better at writing than others, but anyone can do it. No more gatekeepers. Seventy percent slice of the profits. Little to no overhead."

"What sparked the transformation?"

"Digital books. eBooks, if you will. They'd been around a while and no one cared, so we agents didn't pay much attention to that contract clause. Then Amazon brings out the Kindle, Apple brings out the iPad, and suddenly everyone wants eBooks. But the clauses in authors' contracts either didn't mention eBooks or gave authors very little for them. So . . . chaos. Suddenly even successful authors weren't making nearly as much money and everyone down the food chain was in the same situation. If authors don't make money, agents don't make money. If print books aren't selling, publishers and bookstores don't make money. The people you see in this room are the Titans. The ones who survived the Purge. Or emerged afterward in this Brave New World of Writing."

"But that all happened long after King Kaiju, right?"

"Yes. But people need to understand the environment. The context. Back then, if you wanted to work in comics, you had to sign a contract giving up ownership over your creations. Things have changed in recent years so much that many don't realize what it was like back then. Wu and Joe did more than create a character. They created an empire—then got shafted by it. And they weren't the only ones. By far."

"Given your attitude, I'm surprised you're not more sympathetic to Wu."

"I agree that creators should never lose the rights to their creations. But who am I to say who the actual creator was? I personally wouldn't object to giving your client a sliver. Congress passed the most recent copyright acts and amendments to make the law more favorable to creators, including a provision that gives them and their heirs the right to terminate copyright grants executed prior to the new law."

As if he didn't already know. "Basically, a law protecting people from their past mistakes."

"Everyone knows artists are terrible businesspeople. They walk around with their heads in the clouds. That's what makes them geniuses."

"And targets." He wanted to know more about her arrangement with Delia and Joe. And possibly any side agreements with the movie studio. He had a sense that she knew more. But wasn't going to volunteer it. "Thank you for talking with me."

"Hey!" She grabbed his hand and squeezed it. "Not so fast. Have you forgotten what I said about . . . you know. A little spicy romance?"

"Flattering. But your boyfriend probably wouldn't like it."

"Are you kidding? He got totally turned on when he saw me making out with Delores."

"Well . . . I'm not Delores."

"I know. I don't know how he'll feel about a male unicorn." She winked. "But there's only one way to find out."

He winked right back at her. "Totally tempting. But you know the rules. You're on the other side."

"You're not allowed to have sex with people on the other side of a lawsuit?"

"Completely forbidden. I could be disbarred."

"Well. We don't want that." She paused. "Have you tried polyphasic sleep? It'll take those wrinkles off your face in no time."

He smiled. "I like my wrinkles. I earned them. Enjoy your conference."

CHAPTER TWENTY

Dan had handled mental acuity hearings before, but always in a different context. Typically, in criminal cases, the issue of sanity arose to determine whether a person could be convicted of a certain crime. Most serious offenses require that the alleged criminal have some understanding of the nature and consequences of their actions. If they don't, the jury can find them not guilty by reason of insanity.

Today the issue was being raised for an entirely different purpose—to prevent a witness from taking the stand. Most judges required at least minimal mental competence from their witnesses. The question was whether the witness' testimony was sufficiently reliable that it would help the jury achieve justice rather than hamper them.

Unlike sanity, competence to stand trial was a minimal standard. Dan didn't think Kenzi was likely to succeed in blocking Wu's testimony. It would effectively be a dismissal of the case. But she could do a lot of damage to him. If she impugned the integrity of the witness before the trial began . . . it would hurt their case with the judge, and perhaps damage Wu's confidence.

Of course, both sides hired psychiatric witnesses to take the stand. Both met with Wu in advance of trial. They also considered Wu's social and psychiatric history. Then they generated a written report explaining their opinion and conclusions.

Predictably, Dan's witness said Wu was just as quick as the day he turned twenty. Kenzi's witness said he showed signs of delusional thinking, time-space displacement, long-term memory loss, and personality disorders.

There was never a moment when Dan felt either witness escaped the label of "paid witness" to become "impartial expert." Even though compensated witnesses tended to be the least persuasive to juries, lawyers put on experts because they didn't want some appeal court deciding that they didn't provide adequate assistance at trial.

Both experts focused on whether Wu understood the nature and consequences of these legal proceedings. Each had spent several hours administering tests. It seemed obvious that Wu was competent. He'd never had any trouble explaining himself or answering questions . . . eventually. But Kenzi's expert said he was "living a fantasy construct" and had a child's "fairy-tale view of the world" and expected the judge to be his "fairy godmother."

Even if they couldn't completely exclude him, they were working overtime to impugn his credibility.

Dan's expert had a more positive view, naturally. He found that Wu was elderly and suffered from occasional memory gaps, as all people do after a certain number of years, but understood the court process well enough and knew exactly what he was doing. He understood who the judge was, who Dan was, who Kenzi was, and what their roles in this proceeding would be.

Dan thought his expert performed well, but for that matter, so did Kenzi's. He might not believe her witness, but it wasn't because he performed poorly on the stand. Dan didn't bother to cross-examine her expert and she didn't cross his. What was the point?

It was all going to come down to how Wu performed on the stand. But Kenzi couldn't get into the facts of the case, except to the extent that they related to his mental competence. Kenzi called Wu as a rebuttal witness and a "hostile witness," meaning one with relevant information who would not be friendly to her position. The judge approved. This allowed Kenzi to "lead the witness" and to engage in other brutal questioning approaches normally only available on cross.

Dan tried to keep Wu calm. "Nothing to worry about," he said, patting his client on the shoulder. "You got this. You've told your story a hundred times."

His shoulders were hunched. He seemed locked up, closed in. Tight. "I don't like . . . that woman."

"Call her Ms. Rivera, not 'that woman.' And don't let her get to you. She puts on an aggressive front, but she's not bad at heart. All show."

"I read up on her. She has a killer rep."

"You'll be fine. Stick to your guns."

"She looks like Pennywise without the clown makeup."

"Stay calm and answer her questions. She wants to get you flustered, confused. Take a deep breath and don't play her game. You have nothing to worry about."

He didn't believe that any more than Wu did. But that was his job, right? Tell the clients what they needed to hear. And be ready to spring into action when it proves untrue.

DAN WATCHED KENZI AS SHE COZIED UP TO WU WITH A FEW softball questions. She asked Wu to identify himself. Name and address. But after a few minutes, he realized Kenzi had a tell. Of course she would never telegraph a trap with a facial expression. But she held a pen in her left hand for some reason. And when she felt she was on the brink of getting something good, that hand clenched the pen, tensed up like a woman on the verge of . . . well, a different kind of explosion.

Now he could see her coming. Which probably wouldn't help much. But it was something.

"Mr. Wu, you don't dispute the fact that you signed a contract giving Sidekick Comics all rights to King Kaiju. Correct?"

"I endorsed a check. I needed food. That was the only way the comic would get published."

"And you were paid, correct?"

"A pittance."

"And you subsequently received payment for your work. You lived on that for some time, didn't you?"

"As long as I could."

"And then you got other jobs."

"At first. Till they turned on me. Couldn't get back into the comics industry. Sidekick blackballed me. Anyone wanted to work for them, you had to toe—"

"Objection," Kenzi said. "Lack of foundation. Probable hearsay."

Judge Parkwood nodded. "Sustained." So far, the judge appeared to listen attentively. She wasn't just going through the motions. She was taking this hearing seriously. Was it possible she might exclude Wu's testimony?

This could be the first time in history he lost a case during a preliminary evidentiary hearing.

Wu cleared his throat. "I work as a delivery boy, when work is available. I do not make minimum wage. When I was young, I was never able to afford college. Then, after King Kaiju, I thought I didn't need college. Now it's too late for college."

"Oh, it's never too late." Dan knew what she was doing. Lulling him into complacency with sympathy and encouragement. Then she would pounce.

"I do not wish to learn another profession in my seventies. I wish to write the character I created."

The pouncing came sooner than he expected. Kenzi abruptly whirled around, glaring. "Mr. Wu, where are you right now?"

He was startled. His head jerked back. "What? How—"

"Pretty simple query. Where are you?"

Wu's eyes shuttered. He seemed confused, thrown. "I'm—I'm—It's obvious. You're here, too."

"Where?" She smirked, which just made it all the worse.

Wu lowered his head as he concentrated. Dan could see he had the word in his head. He just couldn't quite land it.

"C-Courtroom," he stuttered. "Courthouse. Downtown, St. Pete." He glanced awkwardly at the judge. "Don't you hate that? When there's a name on the tip of your tongue but all you can remember is the first letter?"

The judge did not smile. "Please address your comments to the lawyer asking the questions. If the court feels the need to intervene, it will."

Dan jumped up. "Your honor, it's obvious he feels pressured. Maybe we could do this in a less stressful environment?"

The judge did not agree. "How would that tell us whether he can assist the jury? Nothing is more stressful than testifying in an actual trial. This is a cake walk by comparison."

The judge did have a point. He reluctantly sat down.

"Mr. Wu," Kenzi continued, "what year was it when you first sold the rights to King Kaiju to Sidekick Comics?"

Dan was back on his feet. "Your honor. Give me a break. That was more than fifty years ago. What is this, Final Jeopardy?"

The judge looked down at him. "Is that an objection?"

"Yes. Objection. Relevance."

"Overruled. Proceed."

Wu fumbled a bit. "That was so long ago. Early seventies."

"Don't you mean sixties?"

"Right. Sixties."

Kenzi glanced at the judge. "Actually, it *was* the seventies."

Dan rose. "Your honor. This is offensive. She's playing tricks, trying to trick him. The character was created in the late sixties and published in the early seventies. If opposing counsel wants to impeach his testimony, fine. But a memory quiz over ancient history is ridiculous. Anyone would be confused. It doesn't prove anything."

The judge nodded. "Was that an objection?"

This was not going well. "Objection. Relevance. Argumentative."

"Overruled. Proceed."

Now he was worried. The judge didn't seem to like a single thing he said.

Kenzi plowed forward. "Was Joe Ulrich present? When you endorsed that check?"

"Uhh . . . yes. Joe was definitely there."

"He says he wasn't."

Wu's head jerked up. "Really? When?"

"About fifteen minutes ago. In the hallway."

He paused. Wu glanced at Dan, then back at Kenzi. "What did he say?"

"He said he wasn't there. He says it was all your fault. And indeed, you're the only one who endorsed the check, right?"

"It was made out to me. But I split the money with him."

"Did Joe sign the check? Did he consent to you signing it?"

"I—I—" He ran his hand through thinning hair. "It's been so long. Sometimes it's hard to bring it all back. Particularly late in the day . . ."

Dan peered at the judge, who had a concerned expression on her face.

"And by the way, if you want to doubt someone's sanity," Wu said, "forgive me, but it should be Joe."

Dan's head snapped around. He wasn't expecting that. Wu had never said anything like that before.

Kenzi was equally surprised—but pleased. "You're saying your partner is crazy?"

"I wouldn't use that ugly word. But I can tell he's slipped a few steps. He's almost eighty, you know."

"The same age as you."

"But Joe has had it tougher. Living with . . . his family environment. His . . . wife."

"Now you're saying his wife made him crazy." Kenzi glanced up at the judge. "This is the most sexist line of attack I've heard in a long time."

"I don't mean it that way. It's just . . . a fact." Wu sat up straight. "You people are so two-faced. You treat us like garbage for fifty years. Joe couldn't support his family. I couldn't afford to have one. We've been living in poverty for longer than I can remember. For a while, Joe was eating cat food. Yes, I know that's a cliché, but it's true. He was eating cat food because that was the only protein he could afford. Which, okay, if he was some loser who never did anything with his life, fine. But the man who drew the first issues of one of the most beloved fictional characters of all time should do better."

Dan could only gape as he watched Wu rise to unsteady feet. "You people ripped us off, kicked us to the curb, and now you want to say I'm not competent to claim my own work because you've done such an effective job of destroying us, mentally, physically, and economically." He looked at the judge again. "Are you going to let them get away with this? Is this justice?"

Dan couldn't think of a way to stop it. He normally did not have to object to the words of his own client. Plus, if he interrupted to save Wu from himself, it was almost like admitting Wu was incompetent.

The judge cut off the rant, pounding her gavel until he

stopped. "Let me remind you that your role today is to answer questions. Nothing else."

Judge Parkwood turned to Kenzi. "Are you done with this witness?"

Which was a pretty good indication that the judge thought she should be done with this witness. "Okay."

"Any more witnesses?"

Kenzi shrugged. "This is the only one that matters."

"I agree. So you rest?"

Kenzi was not stupid. She knew when to go with the judge's flow. "Sure."

"Good. Anything more from you, Mr. Pike?"

"No."

"Great. Diverging from usual practice, the court will rule from the bench."

Dan scooted forward. Was it that obvious? Had Kenzi shut them down already?

"The motion is denied. Although the court finds that the motion is not entirely devoid of merit, it will not prevent the plaintiff from taking the stand, a drastic remedy that would effectively end the case. The court will be monitoring carefully, and if it detects any signs of a lack of competence, we can revisit this motion. But the court is also aware that the plaintiff is elderly and has not always had access to the best medical care or nutrition, and all of those factors impact mental performance. Some slowing with age is natural. The court is not going to say the statute of limitations has run just because the plaintiff is not young. Especially since some of the factors leading to his current issues may stem from his treatment by the parties to the lawsuit."

The court slammed the gavel again. "Trial begins first thing Monday morning. See you then."

Dan could see Wu was relieved—but it left him even more worried about what might happen when this trial began. Garrett was flying to NYC, but he would ask Jenny to spend the weekend with Wu and a tall stack of flash cards, drilling him on the key points to his story. It was a delicate balance, improving your client's recollection without coaching or telling him what to say. But Jenny had a soft touch and could usually help people see how they could improve—not what they said, but how they said it.

He waved at Kenzi. "Sure you don't want to fold?"

Kenzi folded her arms defiantly across her chest. "I didn't lose."

Dan's eyes narrowed. "Maybe you should ask the court reporter to read back the court's ruling."

"I heard what she said. I never expected to win."

"Then why file the motion?"

"To remind the judge what she's dealing with. A bitter old man who's told his story a million times but really doesn't remember what happened. And that's what she saw on that witness stand. Sure, she's not going to preclude him from speaking on his own behalf. That would in effect be granting summary judgment." Kenzi smiled, big and broad, then added: "But she will remember. When it matters."

CHAPTER TWENTY-ONE

GARRETT HATED NEW YORK. ALWAYS HAD, EVEN WHEN HE WAS with the Solicitor General's Office. No quantity of "I Heart NY" commercials would ever change his mind. It was dirty, crowded, disorganized, and a prime example of what happened when you shoved too many people into too small a place. As he strolled through Times Square, he recalled how the area used to stink of human waste. Times change. Now all he could smell was secondhand marijuana fumes. Was that an improvement?

They should've sent Jenny. She would at least enjoy the Broadway shows. He hated musicals. Normal people suddenly start singing and dancing for no apparent reason? Does this make sense?

Jenny and the rest of the crew were busy with trial prep, so he flew to the Big Apple to visit Sidekick Comics, with offices just across the way from the Marriott Marquis. He was impressed. He expected a comic book company to be a smaller outfit. He suspected some kind of takeover was in the offing. DC Comics was owned by Warner Brothers. Marvel Comics was owned by Disney. A corporate acquisition was supremely possible—especially if this King Kaiju project went into production.

Security inside was tight, and he supposed it probably should be, not so much because of street crime as corporate espionage. His preliminary research informed him that there was too much competition in this field, plus too much talent swiping, idea swiping, and money. Comics had been transformed from a harmless reading pleasure for kids to a major industry generating billions of dollars every year—not from the comics themselves, but from merchandising the characters.

Which did not explain why Jeanette Zimmerman had been so agreeable about meeting with him. She'd been a major player in Sidekick's ongoing negotiations with Headmark Studios, as he learned during his interview with that insane practical joker. So from her standpoint, this lawsuit was an obstruction to her landing a huge sum of money for her company and probably a fat raise for herself.

His security escort took him to her office. She rose, all smiles, and greeted him with an outstretched hand. She appeared to be about his age and wore a two-piece business suit that made her look professional and attractive, accenting the curves and diminishing the hips. Striking.

He mentally scolded himself. He should be devising some means to extract the truth, not thinking about her appearance. He hadn't been on a date for years, for good reason, and he didn't need to start now with an opposing New York witness—any more than he needed a threesome with a romance writer.

"Thank you for meeting me."

"No worries." She gestured toward a chair.

Outside the window, he could observe the hustle and bustle of Broadway, taxis whizzing by at unsafe speeds, a huge marquis for the musical version of *Back to the Future*. Tourists were taking pictures with performers dressed in cheapass Disney character costumes. Street vendors were selling Rolexes for twenty-five bucks (sure). The rest of the view was blocked by the largest Margaritaville he'd ever seen in his life, even bigger than the one at Universal. Was Margaritaville everywhere? Would Jimmy Buffett be the one who brought us all together to form one world? "You have a great view."

"Thanks. But it's still New York."

"Not a fan?"

She shrugged. "DC and Marvel have both moved west. So they can be near Hollywood. We need to do the same." Her desk seemed like the usual unruly mess of paper and file folders. The only exception was a fuzzy brown teddy bear resting on the credenza behind her.

"I assume that will happen if the deal with Headmark goes through."

"It might." She grinned. "Fingers crossed. I love some aspects of New York. But I could probably give up the noise for palm trees and Disneyland."

He nodded. "Not a fan of the noise?"

"I live in a high-rise not far from here. Near The Dakota, but not so pricey or notorious. Nice enough. But still, constant noise. And since I used to have insomnia, it didn't help."

He gave her another quick onceover. "You look healthy. Did you get over it?"

"I did."

"I have trouble sleeping sometimes. Mind if I ask how you managed it?"

She waved a hand dismissively. "The usual way. By paying a therapist more than I pay for my apartment."

He smiled. "But it worked?" He learned a long time ago that interviews went better if they were preceded by a little casual conversation on one of the witness' favorite subjects. And most people's favorite subject was themselves. "Freud triumphs?"

"Oh, no one listens to Freud anymore. But therapy is alive and well. I was having troubles. Not just sleeping."

"Divorce?"

She looked up. "How did you know?"

"Been there, done that."

"I'm sorry."

"Not at all. Long time ago."

"Painful?"

"Is there another kind of divorce?" They both chuckled, but there was no merriment in it. "Caught me by total surprise. I thought we were happy. And one day I come home from a work trip and she's packed up all her stuff, split the marital property, and loaded her share into her SUV."

"With no warning."

"None that I detected. I probably missed the signs. I did work long hours. Prosecutors usually do. So I came home and she hit me over the head with a large metaphorical hammer. Shook my hand, can you believe it? We'd been together for six years and she shakes my hand. And leaves."

"That must've been hard."

"I just . . . I felt like a failure. School was easy. Breezed through law school. Got a great job. Good marriage, I thought. Talked about having kids. Then everything I thought I had, everything I thought was going to happen, evaporated in a puff of smoke. I had nothing and looked forward to nothing. I was completely . . ."

"Lost?"

"Destroyed. Devastated. I remember it being about three in the morning and I walked out to the reflecting pool on the national mall and . . . I really planned to keep walking. Or falling. Face first. And staying there."

"What brought you back?"

"Maria Morales."

"A new love interest."

"Oh no. I wouldn't've even paid attention to that, I was so sure I was a complete loser. No, she's a lawyer I work with. And she offered me a new job. At the exact moment that I needed one." He paused. "I don't think I've ever said this to her. But she basically saved my life."

"Did she know you? How did she come to be there?"

"She was sent by her boss. The head of the Last Chance Lawyers network." He grinned again. "Mr. K. Said they needed someone to handle research at their small firm. So I moved to Florida and . . . eventually learned how to sleep again."

"That was a lucky break."

His eyes darted. "It had nothing to do with luck. But I didn't mean to gas on about myself. What turned the trick for your insomnia?"

She drew in a deep breath. "I started therapy because of my divorce, but what we uncovered were memories. Bad ones. From long ago. Like . . . sexual assault. When I was five. This neighborhood boy. Lived across the street. He played football so my parents thought he was all that and a bag of chips. They didn't know he was luring little girls into the woods. He told me he wanted to show me something and then he held me down and started . . . fingering me. You know, a free pelvic exam before I was old enough to know what that was. Made suggestive comments. Of course, I never said a word about it to anyone. Even after the third time."

His eyelids fell. "I'm so sorry."

"Even as an adult, I kept acting like I was over it and it was no big deal, but of course I was just repressing. My therapist told me it *was* a big deal. And that's when she suggested that I sleep with a teddy bear."

He blinked. "Did I miss a step?"

She chuckled. "I didn't get it either. I didn't even sleep with teddy bears when I was a kid. But she said hugging this plush toy would help me become more present in my own body, and then I might be able to face my past trauma. Of course I told him I was an adult professional college graduate and I wouldn't be doing that." She paused. "Until I did."

He nodded toward the bear he'd noticed before. "That your pal?"

"Yeah. I bring him to work with me. Makes me happy. Kind of a therapy bear. My doc says a beloved object can become a psychological representation of yourself. Over time."

"Is that a good thing?"

"It helps you develop self-love. Self-respect. Self-reverence. When I nourished Bear-Bear—yes, that's what I call him and I'm not taking any grief about it—he helped me start nurturing myself. Increasing my sense of self-worth. And I started sleeping better. I think we'd all be better off if we worried less about being grownups and focused more on experiencing joy and loving ourselves. And others." She wiped a hand across her forehead. "Whew! I feel better just for talking about that."

"Me too." He stared at the bear. He hadn't been sleeping well lately either...

She leaned across her desk. "Look, you seem like a nice person. I can see the pain behind those smiling eyes. But there's nothing I can do for you."

Were they still talking about teddy bears? Or had they segued to gigantic reptilian comic-book monsters? "Not sure what you mean."

"You want to talk about the King Kaiju case. But I don't know that much about it. I'm not a lawyer. I know the position of this company has always been that we have full control of King Kaiju and we have marketed it accordingly."

"Even after the Copyright Act of 1976?"

"As you probably know better than me, that law gave creators the ability to revoke a license of intellectual property rights. But there are many hoops you have to jump through to qualify. And apparently your client signed some kind of interim agreement, well after the initial check endorsement."

"According to your company."

"And everyone else involved. Do the boys deny this?"

"They were young and stupid. They're entitled to a share of the royalties. Even during past periods when they weren't being paid at all. Which would lead to a huge settlement."

"Right. That's what Jerry Siegel's heirs did. You know, the teenager who co-created Superman back in the 30s. He got squeezed out and died poor, living off a measly thirty-thousand-dollar pension, while DC/Warner made billions. And DC only started that puny pension because they didn't want bad publicity to screw up their big Superman movie. After this new copyright law and its amendments were passed, Jerry was gone, but his wife—the original Lois Lane—was able to sue. And when she passed, their daughter continued the fight. Now the family gets a flat annual payment. It's not nearly as large as it should be. But it's something. Meanwhile, the artist who co-created Superman, Joe Shuster, died poor and his heirs have not recovered anything, because he signed a later agreement not forgiven by the new act. Not unlike your client."

"I can't agree with that assessment."

"Doesn't matter to me. We've come a long way in recognizing the rights of creators. But we've still got a long way to go."

"Do you have copies of the agreements involved?"

"Of course. But they won't help you."

"We'll see. And you sold the rights to the anime company?"

"Yes. I handled that personally. Not that much money involved initially, but at that time, King Kaiju was a largely unknown character from a relatively small company. When the anime blew up, everything changed."

"Fancy Times Square offices."

"And now this deal with Headmark Studios. If it happens."

He pondered a moment. This woman had no reason to help him. So why were they having this voluntary conversation?

Perhaps sleeping with Bear-Bear had made her a kinder person. But he suspected there was more. "How much is potentially at stake?"

"I'm not allowed to reveal the terms of the deal. But . . ."

"Big?"

"Bigger than Marvel. Bigger than Lucasfilm. This might be the most expensive and also the most profitable IP grab in the history of corporate acquisitions."

"Enough to kill for?"

She seemed startled. "I . . . suppose."

"Did you know the lawyer who was murdered? And decapitated."

She looked appalled. "No. Sorry. Was he working on this case?"

"Not exactly."

"We have had threats. Warnings. Angry Reddit threads. I had a personal threat against me from some rabid Kaiju fan. They all predictably think we should surrender the rights to the character. What they don't consider is, we're the ones who made King Kaiju popular. We're the ones who took the financial gamble, who spent hundreds of thousands of dollars printing and promoting the character. Sure, creators should get something. They did. And I'm sorry they didn't negotiate better. But you can't expect corporations to give up valuable properties just to be nice. Corporations don't exist to be nice. They exist to make profits."

"And you're okay with that?"

Zimmerman took a long moment before replying. "I am . . . sympathetic to the creators. Seeing your creations co-opted by others . . . it must feel like . . ." She glanced back at Bear-Bear. "Like having your teddy bear ripped away from you."

"Is that why we're having this meeting?"

She pushed a thick brown expanding file across the desk. "Here's everything I could find relating to this case. Everything.

No, I am not supposed to give you this. And no, I don't know if it will help you." She exhaled heavily. "But I think you're entitled to have it."

He took the file and slid it into his briefcase. "Thank you. I really appreciate this."

She nodded. "You know, I always expected to be in a Big Five publishing house. Dining with bigshots and going to cocktail parties with Gore Vidal and Truman Capote. I only got into comics when I couldn't find anything else. But . . . I kinda like it here. Comics may not save the world . . . but they do make the world a happier place. And these superhero stories have an . . . *ethos,* for want of a better world. Right versus wrong. Good versus evil. Trying to help others whenever possible. Making sacrifices for a greater cause. These are good values. Important values. So I'm proud to work in comics and I'm glad to see manga taking off like a rocket. Those illustrated stories may not change the world . . . but then again, you never know."

CHAPTER TWENTY-TWO

OVER THE YEARS, DAN HAD LEARNED TO LOAD HIS TRIAL backpack strategically. He never intended this, but his backpack had become "a thing," as the kids liked to say. Everyone else in town was carrying briefcases, which perversely seemed to get more expensive as they became slimmer, like less space was somehow more valuable. Regardless of the size, eventually they became heavy and pulled your shoulder out of whack. Associates got stuck hauling hernia-inducing catalog cases, often filled to the brim with paper.

Dan didn't see the point. Virtually all the paperwork, including exhibits, could be scanned and loaded onto a computer. He didn't need actual paper unless there was something he wanted to place in a witness' hand.

That did not mean packing had become easy. Before he left for the courthouse, he wanted everything in exactly the right place so he could find it in a hurry if he needed it. In the main section, a legal pad, an iPad, a MacBook Pro, and his trial notebook. Side pockets held pens, business cards, paper clips, and Post-It notes, which had won cases for him on more than one occasion. The pack would be balanced on his back, nothing distended to one side or the other. He'd seen old school lawyers develop back problems in their fifties. He was not going to be one of them.

"Ready to rock and roll?" Maria asked. Maybe it was his imagination, but she was starting to look more pregnant every day.

"I think I've got everything." He hoisted it onto his shoulder, making a small grunting sound as he did.

"Want me to help with that?"

"No chance I'm letting an expectant mother carry my bag."

"I can handle it. I'm a tough mommy."

He brushed against her cheek. "That I know very well."

"Heard from Garrett?"

"He called. Won't be back in time for trial."

"Anything useful?"

"He says he got some leads and a ton of documents to review. But nothing that's going to help us today."

"Shall we depart?"

"I guess." He shrugged. "Still doesn't feel like a Daniel Pike case, though."

"Even with a headless corpse?"

"I'm not sure that has anything to do with this. Certainly has nothing to do with the case we're putting on in court. We can't even mention it."

Jenny came downstairs carrying a stack of notebooks. "I've got the trial plan in here. Maria helped me with it."

Maria shook her head. "Jenny did all the heavy lifting."

"Bull. I did all the fast typing. You did all the thinking. You have a strategic mind. I have a mind that would rather be reading comic books."

Maria laughed. "Well, both have value. Especially in this case." She grabbed her Gucci tote and headed toward the front door.

"Have you seen the news?" Jenny asked.

Dan pivoted slowly. "Something relating to this case?"

"Oh yeah. Quite a scene at the courthouse, I hear. Protesters."

"Do they think a politician is going on trial?" Dan glanced at his watch. "The courthouse won't even open for another half hour."

Jenny followed Maria out the door. "King Kaiju doesn't punch a time clock."

JENNY UNDERESTIMATED THE SCENE WAITING AT THE courthouse. Police had to block off the street due to the congestion. By the time Dan arrived, the entire city block had been barricaded, which meant Dan couldn't park in his usual spot, which meant it took even longer to get to the building. Which was packed with people.

Some were protesters with placards taking one side of the case or the other. Some were pro-Joe. Some were pro-Wu. Some were pro-Sidekick. The Sidekick fans were better dressed, which made him wonder if they were ringers sent by the company. Some were even dressed like King Kaiju or other characters from the series. He had no idea how cosplay was going to help anything, but it certainly gave this case a different look.

The police formed a barricade across the main entrance to the courthouse, but Dan knew that wasn't the only way in. He wondered if all the other entrances were guarded, or if SPPD was assuming no one really wanted inside. The media was present with at least four live-remote trucks. Someone stood on top of one with a bullhorn, but he didn't appear to be affiliated with the station. Others were scrambling to get him down.

He met Wu at the foot of the steps. "Can you believe this?"

Despite the chaos, it had to be fun, seeing all these people showing their love for his creation. "People dig your work, Wu. You should be proud. How are you holding up?"

"I'll feel better when we go inside. I don't like crowds."

Dan couldn't blame him.

"Do you think I'll testify today?"

"The judge sets the pace. We have to pick a jury first."

"Do you think Joe will be here?"

"He's a likely witness. But he doesn't have to be present the rest of the time."

Despite this being a case about a comic book character, the people on the street seemed to be taking it very seriously. He didn't even know what some of these people were saying. King Kaiju had "rizz?" Was that a good thing? Someone else said someone on the opposite side was having a "menty b." He wasn't sure of the translation, but he doubted it was a compliment.

Maria leaned close. "Feeling the ick?"

"Stop already. You're barely younger than I am."

"You wish. I'm a three full months younger."

"Guess you can start calling me Grandpa."

Dan scanned the crowd. Far in the distance, behind the blockades, he spotted Delia exiting a black limousine. Arrogant and tasteless, he thought. Or in other words, totally on brand. Joe followed behind her, looking as lost and shambling as ever. Their son trailed a few steps behind.

He turned away and almost missed it—but the limo wasn't empty. Bob Lydek crawled out of the middle section, facing the other way. Which suggested they'd been facing each other, probably talking during the ride. A few moments later, he saw Lydek's assistant, Elliott Gomez, emerge. Why was he here? Maybe Lydek made him drive the limo. For his sake, he hoped Lydek gave up the practical jokes when someone was driving.

As they mounted the steps, the crowd erupted. Deafening

shouts, cheers, and jeers filled the square. Delia held her fist over her head and pumped it up and down, egging them on.

Were they cheering for her? He'd assumed Wu would be perceived as the sympathetic party here, the underdog, the little guy. Didn't that make him the heroic figure in this drama?

"In case you're wondering, they hate you."

He turned and saw Kenzi behind him. She didn't carry a briefcase either, but that was because she, of course, was holding her phone. Christopher stood a few steps behind her carrying three different heavy-looking bags.

Glad she'd found a use for him. Other than the obvious.

"Why would they hate Wu?" he asked, but his voice was almost entirely drowned out by the noise. "I would think King Kaiju fans would honor and respect the creator of their hero."

"You'd think, wouldn't you?" She winked. "And maybe a few of them do. But most don't. What they want is a King Kaiju movie. And why isn't that movie-of-their-dreams in production?" She pointed a long-nailed finger. "You. Opposing Delia."

"You exaggerate." And just as he said it, something flew past his head, missing him by inches. It smacked into a column and splattered, sending what looked like blood—but was likely red paint—everywhere.

"Still certain about that, Danny Boy?"

"Surely no one wants a movie made without the input of the creator."

"Stop kidding yourself. They don't care. What they want is a movie they can watch over and over again and dissect and post about and maybe do a Master's thesis on. Then they can watch the director's cut. Then the 4K Blu-Ray DVD set with extras." She pointed again. "See the guy with the big white camera? He works for Headmark. This is probably all going to be footage for a DVD extra about how they battled the villains—you—so they could bring King Kaiju to the big screen."

"Is there no loyalty to the men who gave this character life?"

"You know the creators of Superman were robbed, right?"

"I've heard about the—"

"Has that ever prevented anyone from seeing a Superman movie? Or watching *Smallville*? Or reading the hundreds of Superman comics published without identifying the creators? Bill Finger was robbed too. Has that stopped people from reading Batman? Hell no. These fans are consumers, not activists. They want to be entertained."

"Seems like an active fanbase could organize some kind of boycott."

"But that would mean they'd have to give something up. Not read the next action-packed manga. So basically, that is never going to happen."

Dan gave her a long look. "Did you organize this protest? Create a flash mob? With your . . . KenziKlan thingy?"

"'Thingy?' How old are you?"

"But did you—"

She grinned. "I'll never tell."

"Then would you please remind me what we're fighting for here?"

"According to you, creators' rights. Problem is, there's a dispute about where those rights are now."

Maria appeared beside them. "Is this a private conference, Dan? Or can the mother of your child participate?"

He winced. "Kenzi was explaining why she's going to stomp us in court."

"We have justice on our side."

"Yes, but she has the King Kaiju fans."

Dan watched as Delia strode up the steps leading to the Federal-style columns flanking the entrance to the courthouse. The others followed. He had to admire her determination. The woman had never run a business, hadn't even been to college. But here she was, leading the charge with a Hollywood CEO and other flunkies trailing in her wake.

The steps were packed with people, but Delia managed to forge a path for herself, like Moses parting the Red Sea. She cleared an area at the top of the steps, where the press had their microphones mounted. Physically, her son walked a foot or so behind. Psychologically, he wasn't even in the picture.

Delia cleared her throat, but the tumult did not diminish. She wanted to give some kind of statement. Come to think of it, the judge never did issue a gag order pertaining to Delia, did she?

Ernie bellowed at the top of his lungs. Eventually, people got the idea that Delia wanted to address the crowd. Dan was amazed at how quickly the press assembled. Barely five seconds later, Delia had a bouquet of minicams in her face.

"I just want to say a few words," Delia said. The volume was too loud. The microphones squealed, making everyone wince.

She tried again. "We begin this trial today. I hope it will not take long."

A faint smattering of applause. They were listening, but Delia wasn't who they came for.

"This is what I wanted to say," Delia continued. "Regardless of what happens, regardless of what you may have read on the internet, I want you to understand that . . ." She took a deep breath. "We're doing this for you!" She thrust her arms out. "For you! The fans! You're the ones who *really* made King Kaiju. And we are going to make sure you get the movie you want and deserve!"

The response was thunderous. The sound was so loud he

almost staggered. Even the crowd seemed to shake as if they were in an earthquake. Or a Taylor Swift concert.

He knew there was no point in responding. No one would hear it. Better to get on with his work. He didn't like trying cases in the press, and he couldn't possibly compete with Kenzi's endless livestreams. He started up the steps...

The next few seconds seemed to pass in such an action-packed blur that no one was entirely sure what happened, who did what and where or when or why. All Dan knew was that he heard something that sounded like a gunshot, then someone collided into him, sending him tumbling sideways. If it hadn't been for the density of the crowd, he probably would've ended up with a concussion. Instead, he ended up in a stranger's arms —and someone with a high-pitched voice screamed into his eardrum.

"What? What?" He struggled to get to his feet. Could this be the same person who took shots at him before? He felt a sudden flash of terror. Where was Maria? He felt short of breath. If this was a free-for-all on lawyers, she was in danger, too.

The shrill sound of another gunshot reverberated through the open area.

Dan's eyes widened. *Maria? Where was Maria?*

Somewhere ahead, he heard another voice, lower, male.

Joe. Despite having been described as weak, he seemed perfectly strong now, mentally and physically. He held a gun level and aimed it toward Bob Lydek, the Headmark CEO.

"You think you can take what we made? You think you can hire lawyers and steal our lives? Our work?"

Everyone was scrambling, but no one seemed to be able to get to Lydek in time. Delia looked stricken, but her path was blocked.

"This court won't stop the steal any more than the others did." He raised the pistol. "You took everything from me. Now I'm going to take everything from you."

The gun fired. Screams split the air. People ran, shoved, panicked.

Dan scanned the crowd for Maria. He knew she was tough and could handle herself. But still...

Bob Lydek was not on the ground. Apparently Joe missed.

"I killed that bastard lawyer who tried to steal from me. And you're next, Lydek."

Another shot. Everyone ducked, not quickly enough.

Lydek's assistant, Elliott, crumbled to the ground.

Police surged up the steps. Someone blew a whistle. They wanted to disarm Joe, but he still held the gun and they couldn't get to him without potentially getting shot.

The expression on Joe's aged face was indescribable. His hands shook. Sweat dripped down his cheeks. His eyes burned red. The desperation in his eyes suggested he had given up long before he pulled the trigger.

He was massively outnumbered. The police would get him eventually.

The only question was how many police officers would die before they did.

On the left, he saw a uniformed officer creeping around the side, hoping to slip behind Joe. This was about to get nasty fast.

"Stay away!" Joe screamed, with his thin, brittle voice. "Stay away from me!"

The officers slowed, but no one stopped. No one backed down.

Dan watched in horror as Joe slowly turned the gun around and pointed it at his right temple.

"*Nooooo!*" Dan screamed. He lurched forward. He was barely a foot away when the gun fired. Blood and brain tissue splattered everywhere, all over Dan, all over the steps. What was left of Joe's head became a messy puddle on the marble steps.

The crowd backed away, leaving him standing in the middle

of everything, a bloody body on one side, another bloody body on the concrete before him. Panic and chaos. People scrambling in abject terror—some of them in dino costumes.

And the smell of death permeating the air.

Yes. This definitely seemed like a Daniel Pike case now.

Part Three
COURT OF MANY COLORS

CHAPTER TWENTY-THREE

Delia could not believe how long incompetent cops could drag out the obvious. It was as if they thought this was some kind of special skill. Thoroughness to a mind-numbing degree. What the hell? It's not as if *she* shot anybody! When she married, everyone accused her of being a gold digger. They might be more sympathetic now. She'd always suspected he was mentally unwell. Now Joe had proved he had a violent streak. It was always there, lurking just beneath the surface.

She was questioned four different times, even though all she did was stand and watch the murders happen. No, she had no idea her husband was planning to kill anyone. No, she didn't know he had a gun, and even if she had, she wouldn't have thought he had the guts to fire it. Okay, he might've been weaselly enough to shoot himself, but not another person.

The police couldn't let it go. Why did he kill the decapitated lawyer? Why go after Lydek? Gomez died, but they assumed his boss, Bob Lydek, was the target. In how many languages could she possible say: I don't know anything!

The worst of it was, she had blood on her blouse. Her late husband's blood. Not that much. But enough to creep her out and it wasn't something she could take off, at least not until they let her go home. She felt as if she carried a wet, dripping piece of his flesh on her body. Even though she knew this was mostly in her imagination, she still couldn't stand it.

The trial had been delayed, given the chaos following the shootings. The police cordon surrounding the courthouse thickened, and police were all over the building, collecting evidence and looking for witnesses. Everyone involved was so traumatized that Judge Parkwood rescheduled—but only till Wednesday.

If this was Joe's way of getting a continuance, he did a poor job.

But that wasn't why he did it.

It was long past dark before the cops let her leave, and even then, she feared they might be watching. She stayed in until well past three in the morning, long after any nosy busybodies might be watching. Then she quietly got into her rental car and drove, careful not to attract attention, not even using headlights if she could avoid it.

Until she found the spot. She parked the car and raced into the scrub trees not far from the dirt road . . .

It was gone. Even though it took almost half an hour to dig that hole, it wasn't deep enough. Someone dug it up.

After she went to so much trouble. She pounded her fists against her forehead. Idiot! Why didn't you put it in a safe deposit box?

Of course, if she'd done that, the police would already have it.

And if the police had it, they would not have let her go.

She pressed her hand against her chest, as if that might still the pounding of her heart. Stay calm, she told herself. Don't assume the worst. You don't know what happened.

A chill wind blew through the tree branches. She felt a shiver run up her spine. She'd planned everything so carefully, worked so hard to make it happen, and now . . .

She felt goosebumps spread. Her whole body tingled.

Don't fly off the handle, she told herself.

But you'd better be careful, just the same.

She was finally on the brink of having everything she wanted. Everything she needed.

She took a few more slow deep breaths. She could do this. She was still in the game. More complicated now, with blood on the courthouse steps and her forced to play a grieving widow for the looky-loos. She just had to keep her head together.

But someone dug up her buried treasure for a reason. Either to destroy her case . . .

Or to destroy her.

"His eyes. That was what creeped me out the most."

Lydia blurted it, all at once. Judge me if you like, she was saying. But there it was. She'd been seeing this therapist long enough that they could skip past the usual baloney about her parents and talk about something that mattered.

"His eyes?" Of course, the therapist gave no visible reaction, but Lydia could imagine what she was suppressing. "A decapitated head flops out of a suitcase, and what bothered you most was the eyes?"

"They were staring at me." She covered her own eyes. "Unblinking."

"Dead men don't blink."

"They don't normally stare at you, either!" She leaned forward, an almost demonic expression on her face. "Don't people close their eyes when they die? That's how it happens in the movies."

The therapist laid down her notepad. "Perhaps the rules are different when the head has been hacked off."

Lydia's left eye twitched. "Are you making fun of me?"

"I'm suggesting that . . . perhaps that isn't the aspect of this bizarre situation that's causing your extended emotional reaction."

"A head fell at my feet!"

"And you're suffering from PTSD. But it isn't because of the eyes."

She wished she'd never opened her mouth. Whose idea was therapy, anyway? She was sick of talking about herself. Same damn thing, over and over again.

"I tried to close the eyes. After I called security. You know, just used two fingers to tug down the eyelids." She snapped her fingers. "That's when I noticed."

"That you knew the man?"

"No, not that."

A puzzled expression crossed the therapist's face. "I'm confused."

"On his head. Neck, really. Bone. Look, I don't need any more weird in my life. This is my post-retirement job, and I plan to retire soon. Get a place in Key West. Sip piña coladas all day."

"And you will. You can push through this. Might take a while. But you can."

Lydia hoped her therapist was right. But she wasn't sure. Especially since the police kept calling. And the lawyers. And she had no idea what any of it meant.

But someone out there did. Someone who might be worrying what she knew.

And contemplating what to do about it.

Jeanette Zimmerman stared at her face in the mirror behind the bar. All the lovely multi-colored bottles made it look so classy. Grey Goose had the best bottles in all of alcoholism, didn't it? Though Skyy had her favorite color. She wanted to redecorate her kitchen in Skyy blue...

She sighed. She'd spent waaaaaay too much time in this bar...

Normally she'd go for a beer, but tonight she needed something more serious. Like a vodka martini, easy on the vermouth. And she didn't give a damn about the lemon peel.

She downed her third then ordered her fifth. The bartender give her a look. He would probably cut her off after that.

And she'd have to pull herself together and walk a straight line... to another bar.

Could this be the reason she was single, childless, and alone? Except for Bear-Bear. She was trapped in a profession that barely still existed and wouldn't much longer, at least not in its current state. She needed a new direction. She needed a gym membership. She needed to give up sweets.

She knew something few if any others did about this King Kaiju mess. What she knew could blow it wide open. Which was why she'd been generous with the lawyer. But she could do more. The question was whether she should. All well and good to talk about morals and ethics, but a girl still had to eat. She was getting a little long in the tooth for standing in bread lines...

Bear-Bear would forgive her, in any case. This was business. She had no choice.

But she might have to hug him a little tighter tonight.

After she had another drink.

Wu sat on the curb outside JZ's Comics & Games, a nicer-than-average comic store that survived the digital storm by embracing gaming, arcade machines, and microwaved junk food. Judging from what he'd seen the past half hour, more people came to play Magic: The Gathering or Scythe than to buy the colorful adventures of heroes in capes. Or manga monsters.

This store had been around almost as long as he had. He bought his first comic here, not long after it opened, just after the direct sales comics market started to emerge. It was a Jimmy Olsen story that involved the young cub reporter going back in time to prevent the destruction of Krypton. Not the best story ever, but back then, it set his mind on fire. He wanted to know more about the whole Superman mythos, the five kinds of kryptonite, the bottle city of Kandor, the tragic death of baby Kal-El's parents. He became a story junkie. And the stories he loved best were told with pictures.

It was inevitable that he would try to join the industry he loved most. And thanks to talent and a lot of luck, he managed to make his mark.

Only to lose it. And his love of comics with it. Maybe it was best that you didn't let your vocations get too close to your avocations. You might end up losing both. Or simply not caring any longer.

A young man approached him silently, glanced down, then sat on the curb beside him, maybe a foot away.

"Hell of a mess, isn't it?" It was Ernie, Joe's son. All things considered, he was amazed the boy could even think straight right now.

"That it is. Did you know your father had a gun?"

"I know for a fact he did not have a gun. He hated guns."

"That's what I thought." Wu shook his head. "If your daddy and I had any idea what we were getting into when we started working together..."

"You would've done the exact same thing."

"Yeah. But I wouldn't've signed the check."

They both laughed a moment. Then silence fell.

Wu broke it. "I'm sorry about your dad. I loved him. Even after his marriage and everything. I'm sure you did too."

The kid seemed astonished. "I thought you two were enemies. You... loved him?"

"Like the brother I never had."

"But the lawsuits—"

Wu waved a hand in the air. "Lawyer crap. Joe was my best friend. Only real friend I ever had. I didn't know what a friend was till I met him." He shook his head. "I would've done anything for him. And what do we end up with? Nobody happy. And nobody benefitting from our work except rich bigwig CEOs."

"Yeah." Ernie sat another moment. "You... asked me to meet you here?"

"This is where my love for comics began. This began the journey that led to King Kaiju. Maybe some kid is in there now dreaming up the next King Kaiju. I don't know. I hope so."

The kid looked uncomfortable. "If there wasn't anything you wanted or needed..."

Wu laid a hand on his sleeve. "I wanted to tell you something. I wanted you to know that... no matter how this lawsuit comes out, your father will receive credit for his work."

"Huh?"

"Delia wins, you're her heir. But even if I win—I'm giving your father credit. On all future King Kaiju projects."

"Why would you do that?"

"Because Joe played a big role in the genesis of King Kaiju.

Sure, he was my idea, but Joe was there right from the start and I want him to be recognized. Seen."

"That's—just—I don't know what to say."

"No need to say anything. Just wanted you to know. Your daddy and I were always tight. Delia caused the split. Delia wanted to replace me. And she did. I knew she was only after the money, but if she made Joe happy, I thought, who cares? Not the first time someone married for reasons other than true love. But . . ." He sighed. "Now people are dead. And no one is happy."

"You've come too far to turn back. We all have."

"I'm not so sure."

"I am." Ernie turned and looked deeply into Wu's eyes. "I wish you had told me this before . . . ."

CHAPTER TWENTY-FOUR

Usually the chaos began at the courthouse, but not today, not this bright and early Wednesday morning. Dan stood in the center of the lobby/living room of the Snell Isle office/mansion, trying to get a fix on a bonkers case rapidly spiraling out of control.

Jenny might be the one who looked most confused or distraught, but that was in part because she was running around in circles fretting about revising the witness outlines in light of the tragedy. A minute before, Maria had looked worse, but given her delicate condition, he put considerable effort into calming her. If she weren't pregnant, he'd give her a tranquilizer.

Yes, they'd confronted difficult cases before. But this was their first civil IP case that mutated into a triple-murder, and somehow that seemed to change everything. The police wanted access to all their witnesses and evidence. The district attorney —his pal Jazlyn—had left six messages. Jake Kakazu left three.

The shooting had been one of the most gruesome experiences in a career that was, at times, all too gruesome. The police focused on the crowd, since it was obvious that both Elliott

Gomez and Joe Ulrich were very dead. He'd hoped for the best, but from a foot away he could see Joe had blown away the majority of his face. There was no way he was coming back from that. And given his confession prior to pulling the trigger, there didn't seem much need for an extensive investigation.

The news media had already declared it a "mass shooting," attributing all three deaths to Joe and his despondency over the loss of King Kaiju. So the only real question was what impact the deaths would have on the case. They were expected in court in an hour, and they'd spent most of the past two days dealing with law enforcement. He was glad Jenny prepared outlines. Because after all this intervening trouble, he had a hard time remembering what the case was supposed to be about.

Jenny paused in front of him, covering her cell with one hand. "I got the judge's clerk on the line. No more delays, no more continuances. We're pushing ahead."

"There will probably be a bigger mob scene than we had on Monday."

"But fewer murders, we hope. The police will have every available officer on hand to secure the building. They're going to block off the surrounding streets. They even have people watching for snipers. We will be given a security escort to courtroom two."

"Well, that's special."

Maria entered through the front door. "Two more broken windows. And paint on the west wall."

"What?"

"Vandalism. Started Monday. Apparently fandom has learned where we live."

"Swell." He paused. "Did you say *paint*?"

Maria showed him a photo on her phone. In sloppy red spray paint, the west wall read: FREE KAIJU!

"I'll call Ben. He'll hire security."

"Already done. Just informing you."

Right. Because he wasn't running LCL anymore. He was never going to get used to this...

"You need to take this seriously, Dan. Someone threw something at you on the courthouse steps."

"Delia threw an ashtray at me during a settlement meeting. I'm getting used to it."

"It could've been a bullet. Or a bomb." She grabbed him by the lapels. "I know you've been in danger before. So have I. But this... feels different."

Because she's pregnant? "I'll be careful. I promise."

"You'll do more than that. You'll stay safe. You'll stick with your security detail instead of trying to evade them."

"Okay."

She put her face right up to his, but not in a romantic way. "Make sure you do. Daddy."

He held up his hand in a Boy Scout salute. "Promise."

"Jake has interviewed and released everyone associated with this trial, though he says he might need to talk to them again in the future. He sees no reason to believe this is anything other than what it appears to be—a despondent elderly man killing people he believed stole from him, then killing himself. He'd been defeated too many times. He couldn't make himself believe this lawsuit would end any differently than all the others."

Garrett had been noodling on his keyboard, but stopped. "Jazlyn called. Said she couldn't get through to you. Thought you were dodging her calls."

"No comment."

"She's not even thinking about bringing charges. Everyone wants to consider this a closed case, even if we don't know everything. She wanted you to know that she's not going to detain Wu. She understands that..." He paused a moment. "He gets confused sometimes."

Right. Especially late in the day, Dan had noticed. So he

would make a point of putting Wu on the stand in the morning, while he was still at his best.

"She does want to talk to him more, though. About Lieber."

"The decapitated lawyer? Why? Joe confessed."

"Guess she just wants to understand what went down."

Seemed strange, but he knew and trusted Jazlyn, so he wouldn't interfere. Ironic though, that he could be a police witness when it was still uncertain whether he would be allowed to take the stand and testify on his own behalf.

He heard a pounding on the front door. Three fast, decisive raps.

"Kenzi Rivera," Pike muttered under his breath.

Maria pulled a face. "How can you tell?"

"She has a distinctive knock."

"She didn't need to knock. There's a doorbell."

"Exactly."

Dan opened the front door. Kenzi did not wait for an invitation. As before, she strolled past him and took a central position in the room so she could address everyone. "Shouldn't you people be getting to the courthouse?"

Dan smiled. "As should you. To what do we owe the joy of this visit?"

She pressed her hands against her chest. "You find joy in my visits?"

Maria mumbled. "He's speaking for himself."

Kenzi was as direct as usual. "Let me get straight to the point. I think we should settle."

Dan's chin dropped. "Are you kidding? You weren't interested before. Unless we wanted to give it away. All-out war, remember?"

Kenzi's face lost some of its vigor. "I remember. I started a war. And now there are dead bodies on the battlefield. Maybe it's time we consider a gentler approach."

"And when you say 'we,' you actually mean 'you.'"

Kenzi approached Dan. Perhaps she thought he would make the ultimate decision. If she had more sense, she'd be trying to convince Maria. Although that would be much harder. "Look, here's how I see it. We've got this case. Your guy can't remember what he had for breakfast, and Joe is sadly gone. So who's going to explain to the jury what happened? Only my witnesses. And you know how that will end."

"Wu will do fine. All your attempts to make him look senile when he obviously isn't are agist and mean-spirited. If we have any jurors over forty, which we will, they'll see exactly what you're doing."

"Which is why I would never do that. But if your man stumbles on the stand, your case is over and you know it as well as I do."

"My witnesses don't stumble. They come to court prepared."

"Rehearsed?"

"Prepared. And there's no doubt about the fact that Wu created the character. I don't like exploiting tragedy, but when Joe shot himself, you lost your best witness. Probably your only witness of any import."

"You might be surprised."

"We'll see. I know this jurisdiction better than you do. Here in Florida, the judiciary is more conservative than what you get in Seattle. I don't believe the judge will—"

"Five million dollars."

Dan blinked. "Now . . . what?"

"That's what I'm offering you. Full and complete settlement, including fees and costs. Payable as soon as we get paid by Headmark."

"But—But—" He glanced around the room. No one else was speaking. Was he hearing her correctly? "Your last offer was, what? A hundred thousand bucks?"

"This has become too grim. People are dying." Her eyes

moved downward, as if she didn't want him to see her face. "It's not fun anymore."

He stared at her. "No, there's something you're not telling." He peered into her eyes. "Of course. Joe's will. Now that he's dead, his estate goes into probate. Let me guess—Delia doesn't get everything."

The corner of Kenzi's mouth turned upward. "I guess your connect-the-dots superpower isn't entirely fictional."

"Not entirely."

"Ok, so you're right. Delia gets a third of the estate, but his will, which he drafted himself from a form he bought at Staples, says the majority goes to his children."

"Meaning Ernie."

"He didn't have any others."

"So that's why you're making this offer. Delia is seeing her share shrink. Shouldn't she be trying to buy out her son?"

Kenzi looked away. "I can't discuss confidential matters . . ."

"She's already trying to buy out her son. Because he's broke and probably can't afford to wait until probate is complete. Especially if Delia causes probate to be dragged out for years."

"He's young. He can live off ramen and play the long game. Delia wants to buy her Florida vacation home and yacht while she's still young enough to enjoy it."

Delia wanted the good life and she wanted it now. "You're offering five mil. But if your deal with Headmark goes through, you could be looking at ten times that much in the first decade. Maybe more."

"Paid out over time."

"Still. Your widow gets the cookie and the creator gets the crumbs."

"Dan, would you be reasonable for one minute? I know it's hard for a seasoned pro like you to accept but—you do not have a winning hand here. Your dude signed away his rights. And later signed another agreement with Sidekick."

"I'll play it as best I can, just the same."

"Listen to yourself! Dan, I know you're good in the courtroom. But this time you have no reliable witnesses. Only a doddering old man. You have no evidence. No collaboration or conspiracy." Her voice dropped lower. "You are going to lose."

"Well, I've lost before."

"Have you lost five million before?"

A sobering thought. "Why are you being so generous all of a sudden?"

"Because things have changed, dunderhead. People have died. No one wants this case to continue. Delia—"

"—didn't give a damn about Joe."

"She's wearing black. She'll be wearing black in the courtroom. Sitting next to her son who just lost his father."

He knew what she was saying. Juror sympathy would be with Delia. How could it not be after these dramatic events?

"The judge doesn't need this case. The courthouse staff definitely wishes it would go away. The police have better things to do than guard a courthouse. And I'm sick of being groped in the elevator by middle-aged men dressed like Godzilla. Be reasonable, Dan. A settlement would benefit everyone."

She might be right about that. But he couldn't throw in the towel. Even for a decent offer. Not when there was still a chance Wu might get what he wanted most.

"Will the money come with the restoration of credits on the comics? Wu wants to be acknowledged as King Kaiju's creator. As he should be."

"Don't push it, Dan. You're getting a fortune. Take the money and run."

He drew in his breath. "I will take your offer to my client, who I expect to see shortly. But I know Wu will decline."

"Unless you persuade him otherwise."

"He'll think you're trying to buy him off."

"If the price is right—who cares?" Kenzi's frustration was

evident. "Dan, we've both tried big cases . . . but we may be in over our heads this time."

"I wouldn't have been assigned this case unless—"

Kenzi's voice was so loud it made him physically take a step back. *"Ben Kincaid is not always right!"*

Her words reverberated like a thunderbolt. All eyes in the room looked at one another.

Truth was, they did, always, take it on faith that any case Ben assigned was worthwhile. But that didn't mean it was winnable.

"I'm not a gambler," Dan said quietly. "So I don't play by the odds. I believe we have a worthwhile case and we're fighting for an important principle."

"You're going to get creamed. And people are going to get hurt."

"Do you mean that? Or is this another KenziKlan tactic?"

"Look around you. The witnesses in this case are dropping like flies. Who's next? Your client? Mine? Me? Delia is certain someone has been following her. Someone's taking potshots at you."

"There's no reason for anyone to go after lawyers."

"We have a dead lawyer already! I don't know how I can say this any more clearly. Dan—wake the hell up! And settle!"

He cleared his throat. He felt as if every eyeball in the room was upon him. "I will take your offer to Wu. But I don't think he cares about the money. He has no heirs. He's too far along to do much with it. What he wants is credit acknowledging him as the creator of King Kaiju."

Kenzi's face fell. "So he won't take it."

"I can't predict the future."

"Sadly, I can." She started to leave, then stopped and spoke to Dan one last time. "This is something we need to do. For everyone's benefit." She paused before adding, while glancing at Maria, "For everyone's safety."

CHAPTER TWENTY-FIVE

ULTIMATELY, IT ONLY TOOK DAN AND HIS TEAM ABOUT TWENTY minutes to get up the courthouse steps, but it seemed much longer. Even more people mobbed the courthouse than had been around two days before. He supposed some of these people were King Kaiju activists, but the rest were regular folk who showed up just in case violence erupted again. Who knows? They might become a witness to history! Or at least something dramatic they could talk about at parties for years.

This little IP case had become the trial of the century. Although, Dan mused, those seem to come along about every four or five years...

In his daydreams, these people turned out to embrace him with cheers and accolades. But no. It was a crowd of unemployed people with nothing better to do. And regardless of which side they favored, they would hurl the same trite lawyer-hating epithets you could hear at an AMA meeting or on a morning talk show.

He ignored all the questions and comments pertaining to the murders or the pending investigations. He was here to do one job. And dealing with reporters wasn't it.

He met Wu inside, near the rotunda. He was strangely alone. Given the throng outside, he expected more attention to be paid to the man who started it all. But for some reason, he seemed to fly under the radar. King Kaiju made for better headlines than a destitute Asian-American comics writer.

"Ready to start this thing?" Dan asked Wu. People scurried past them on both sides, but no one took much notice.

"You asked me . . . the same question . . . what day was it? Monday."

"Circumstances have changed."

"The entire world has changed." Wu's lips pressed together.

To his surprise, Jenny rested her hand on Wu's elbow. "You miss him, don't you?"

Wu looked up at her, his eyes wide. "Like I would miss my leg."

Jenny swallowed him in a hug. "Let it go, Wu. Let it go."

And he did. Despite the hustle and bustle surrounding them, the elderly man streamed tears. "He was my first friend. My only friend. I—I—" He wiped his craggy face clear. "We knew each other for more than fifty years. Can you believe that? Fifty years."

Jenny patted his shoulder. "Let it all spill out."

"He was my partner. My only partner. Never had another. Never wanted another." He buried his face in her shoulder.

Dan stared at this sad spectacle, and it brought home once more why he did what he did. This was a creative soul whose entire life had been stolen by suits who cared more about money than people. They sucked away what he had and for decades no one would do anything about it.

Turns out, criminal courts aren't the only places where people got railroaded.

Now he understood why Ben Kincaid sent him this case.

DAN ENTERED COURTROOM TWO AND DRANK IT IN.

The gallery was packed. He was told the bailiffs held a lottery to see who got the available gallery seats for the King Kaiju battle royale. Bailiffs were posted on either side of the double doors, but there was a third in front of the door leading to chambers. That meant the Chief Judge had loaned one to Judge Parkwood, which was a fairly brave thing to do given the situation outside. He also noticed officers in the hallway wearing dark suits and earplugs. Unless he missed his guess, Jake sent them. Undercover to minimize the disruption, but there just in case they were needed.

No one wanted to take unnecessary chances. Hadn't been that long since someone held a courtroom in this building hostage.

Kenzi appeared to be hard at work, shuffling paper and barking commands to Christopher. Although he had not yet formally rejected her settlement offer, he decided to leave her alone. Let her run her own battle camp.

Delia sat beside her, wearing black as promised. Hypocritical, but he got it. If this jury suspected that she'd only married Joe to get his Kaiju rights, her claim would be seriously impacted. Ernie sat beside her, looking miserable.

Bob Lydek from Headmark, Jeanette Zimmerman and Curtis Swart from Sidekick, and that literary agent Garrett interviewed were all in the gallery, but he supposed that was probably because they could be called as witnesses.

Judge Parkwood entered the courtroom with little fuss and no reference whatsoever to the dramatic events of two days before. Probably for the best. No one could have processed those events yet. Better to leave it alone and proceed with business as usual.

She called the case, offered a few preliminary greetings, and read some pro forma statements into the record.

"I have also reviewed all submissions from the parties. The court will not grant the motion to exclude testimony from a named party-opponent at this time. The court will, however, be listening."

The judge continued. "The court will also, *sua sponte*, expand the previous ruling pertaining to the homicide involving Mr. Lieber. There was to be no mention of that man or his demise during the trial and the court now expands that ruling to include the two men who died on Monday. Counsel and witnesses are advised to make no reference to those deaths or the circumstances surrounding them. At this time, the court sees no direct connection between these events and the contractual dealings between the parties that form the basis of this suit. The parties are welcome to re-visit this issue should circumstances demand it, but for now, that is the court's ruling."

Dan expected this, and also expected that it wouldn't matter. Everyone in the jury pool already knew what had happened. And unless the judge sequestered the jury, an extreme and expensive process, they would continue to get news updates every day the trial proceeded.

"And finally," the judge added, "there will be no additional gag orders."

At this point, Kenzi rose. "Your honor, may I suggest a limited order? Not a complete blackout, but maybe a restriction on threats against witnesses or parties. There have been some. In fact, there are people making threats right now outside the courtroom."

Judge Parkwood glanced at Dan. "Objection?"

Dan shrugged. "Do we need this? Is someone running for president?"

The judge almost smiled. "The court will modify its ruling as suggested by Ms. Rivera. No threats or defamatory comments about court staff, personnel, witnesses, jurors, or parties. Or their families. And I'll add lawyers to the list. Which includes judges. Anyone have a problem with that?"

No one did.

After a few more preliminary matters and instructions, the bailiff called the first eighteen names to the jury box. They only needed twelve, but the judge indicated that she wanted six alternates. That might seem like overkill, but given how high profile this case had become, he wasn't surprised. In all likelihood, they would call three times this many jurors to the box before they settled on a jury. He hoped they were finished today, but he was not optimistic. He tended not to screw around with this much, but some lawyers took forever.

Maria had suggested a different approach to jury selection. In the past, she'd shunned anything that required her to speak out loud in a courtroom, but this time she was volunteering. She would ask the jurors the questions, leaving Dan free to simply . . . watch.

He was good at reading faces and often saw things in the eyes that he could never get from a verbal answer. Jenny didn't feel comfortable sitting at the same table with them, despite Dan's protestations, but she would be watching, too. And Dinah had promised to monitor from her computer back at the office. Jenny texted her the names and Dinah scoured social media and the rest of the internet.

By the time Dan had to start making decisions, they knew more about the people sitting in the box than he knew about his next-door neighbor. Or wanted to know. But the slightest clue could be invaluable. The only questions the judge permitted were so obvious as to be virtually useless. No one would admit to being prejudiced against Asians like Wu or Jewish guys like Joe. No one would admit they had prejudices against the elderly or those suffering from cognitive issues. And no one copped to having any pre-existing opinions on the King Kaiju rights.

But that didn't mean they didn't exist.

He ran the usual rules through his head, even the ones he didn't believe, just to remind himself. Strong middle-aged women (what Maria called "potential Karens") were dangerous. Especially when you wanted money. "Why should he get a lot of punitive damages just because he made a bad business deal?" Dan wanted people who could be generous, given the proper facts and circumstances. No punishers. No bitter old battleaxes who couldn't stand to see a man succeed. And so forth...

Dan preferred questions like, Are you a dog person or cat person? Boxers or briefs? Granted, they were less specific, but as a result, less threatening. Which meant people tended to open up and tell the truth, much more so than if you asked a question that might get them removed from the jury. In this case, he wanted the jurors to feel sympathy for the little guy, someone who stayed at home all day and wrote. So he wanted cat people. Briefs, not boxers. A juror who would look into Wu's sad eyes and offer him a billion bucks.

Which would probably require more than a hangdog expression.

Knowing your jurors was invaluable, but at the end of the day, it was not possible to perfectly predict how a person would react to the witnesses and evidence. He looked for generous souls, mothers, people who still had a bright light behind their eyes. People who cared less about bottom lines and more about artists trying to survive in a hostile world that did not appear to care about the creators who make life so much better than it would be otherwise...

He could persuade a fiscally conservative person to be generous—if he made the right argument. He could persuade a liberal person to be tight-fisted—if he made the right argument. So to him, this exercise wasn't so much about picking the right people as it was about discerning the smartest arguments to persuade them to find in favor of his client. And it was perhaps more important in this case than in any he'd had before. The fact was, Wu did endorse that check. The Copyright Act gave them a day in court but it didn't guarantee a win.

THEY SKIPPED LUNCH AND THE JURY WAS FINALLY SELECTED JUST before one in the afternoon. Dan was relieved. He'd been in cases where it went on for days, but Judge Parkwood was taking a hands-on no-nonsense attitude that he hoped continued throughout the case.

Since they worked through lunch, the judge gave them a half-hour break before they continued.

"Think we got a good one?" Garrett asked. He was heading back to the office.

"No telling. But they all seem to be paying attention. That's all I need."

Maria and Jenny headed downstairs for sandwiches. Which meant they would be vegan, probably lettuce with cucumbers or something equally unpalatable. But he would survive. Wu wandered off aimlessly. Dan had no idea what was going on in that man's mind. You'd think he'd be excited, or nervous, or . . . *something*, after waiting so long to get to this day. But he only seemed despondent as he shuffled down the hallway. Dan did not sense that he wanted company.

Before he even realized she was near, Kenzi appeared at his side, just below his shoulder. Was that part of her strategy? Ninja in the courtroom?

"And so it begins," she said quietly.

"Yup. All-out war."

"Let's have a brief armistice. Ten-minute break from all-out war."

"What would we talk about?"

"Settlement."

"Your offer has been formally rejected."

Kenzi's lips turned up at the corner. "Haveyou considered the Plinko Bounce?"

"Is this a new Gen Z term? Or are you going delulu on me?"

She tilted her head. "You know what, Pike? I could learn to like you. If you weren't so Joe Cool all the time."

"Sorry. Attitude came with the Air Jordans. You were saying something about a bounce?"

"Yeah. Ever play pachinko?"

"Sure. I spent a month in Japan on a case several years back. What's Plinko?"

"That's a made-up word for pachinko they use on *The Price is Right*. Which I'm going to guess you've never watched in your entire life."

"I think I saw a few minutes of it in the waiting room at a doctor's office once."

She rolled her eyes. "Anyway, they drop the ball down this giant pachinko, but because of all the geometrically arranged pegs, it's impossible to know for certain where the ball will land. You might be able to say, two times out of five the contestant will win the big money. But you can never be sure."

"And you're bringing this up because..."

"It's the perfect metaphor for the courtroom. We can prepare, line up our witnesses, review the evidence, and everything else, but once the trial starts..."

"Plinko Bounce."

"Right. The ball hits the peg and we can't know what will happen next. We can take our best guess. But we can never know for sure. And after that, each successive bounce becomes increasingly unpredictable." She paused. "I mean, sure, I can look at the Big Picture and say, it's me against Pike, so ninety-eight times out of a hundred I'm going to win."

"Ninety-eight?"

"But how can I be sure this isn't one of the rare exceptions? I can't. That's the Plinko Bounce conundrum."

"Noted." He couldn't help but smile, even though he thought warming up to opposing counsel was the stupidest thing he could possibly do. Especially when the mother of his child couldn't stand her. "That's a good analogy, actually."

"I aim to please." She gave him a small salute. "Except not any more, my friend. You rejected our settlement offer. So once opening statements begin, we're back to all-out war."

CHAPTER TWENTY-SIX

DAN DECIDED TO TAKE A CHRONOLOGICAL APPROACH TO HIS opening statement, an approach he normally found pedestrian and dull. Prosecutors often began with "On March fifteenth, in the dead of night, while the Conway family slept quietly in their beds . . ." Etc., etc., etc.

But today he saw the advantages of the strategy. Regardless of how much pretrial publicity the jury had read—and at this point, he had to assume most had seen a lot—they didn't understand the complete story. He knew journalism on legal matters in the mainstream press was often woefully inadequate. Anchorpeople announced court rulings as if they were laws handed down by legislators, rarely providing much insight into how a case came before the court or how the decision was reached.

In this case, it was important that the jury understood Wu's story. If Dan was going to succeed at portraying Wu as an underdog, as a sympathetic character, then the jury had to understand how he came to be the penniless, washed-up relic they saw in the courtroom today.

Of course, Maria had bought him a new suit and tried to

make him look presentable. But his lids still hung low and his wrinkles dug deep. No necktie on earth could disguise the fact that this man had led a hard life, a despondent life, and that he held little hope that this courtroom proceeding was going to change anything.

"Ladies and gentlemen of the jury. Thank you for giving up your time to help the court resolve this dispute. We know it's a sacrifice and we appreciate it." Okay, enough, don't get smarmy. "This is a dispute between several parties revolving around a comic book character called King Kaiju." He smiled a little. "Kind of a cross between Godzilla and Barney, with a little Superman in the mix. But you probably already know that. Let me tell you something you may not know. I usually work in the criminal courts, so I'm accustomed to talking about justice. Not money. As it turns out—this case involves both. But at its core, this is not a business dispute. This is about right and wrong. This is about fundamental principles. Do we protect our artists, the people who enrich our lives and show us the light? Or do we allow business tycoons to reap all the benefits? There's a reason why 'starving artist' is a cliché. It's not because artists don't make important contributions. It's because our capitalistic society doesn't protect them. The pursuit of gross revenue is not the same as the pursuit of beauty or artistic truth."

He turned slowly to face them. "This is nothing new. This is the way it's always been. Until now. Perhaps. Now, you folks on this jury, whether you like it or want it, have the power to change that. And I'm hoping this will be the case that ignites a wildfire."

He reached inside his jacket pocket and pulled out some eyeglasses. He didn't need them. He was only mildly near-sighted. But Maria thought they made him look smart. He was going into professorial mode. So he needed to look smart.

"In the summer of 1969, comic books were exploding. Superman had launched the superhero genre in 1938. Other characters like Batman and Wonder Woman soon followed. Marvel started its new universe of characters in 1961 and gave us Spider-Man in 1962. In 1966, Superman was on Broadway and Adam West's Batman came to TV." He pointed at one of the older jurors. "I saw that grin. Yeah, I loved that show too. Stupid beyond belief, but cracked me up every time." He wiped his forehead. "Point is, comics were hot. And in this heady environment, two boys, one Asian, one Jewish, both ostracized by their peers, became friends. Friends who loved comics. In time, Wu created his own character. King Kaiju, the good-guy monster who fought the bad-guy villains. Brilliant, in its own way. Wu created the character, wrote the stories, and asked Joe to draw the pictures. There had been nothing like this. Marvel had a Godzilla comic for a while, but it made little impact. How long can you read about a hulking monster who doesn't even talk?"

He continued. "But Wu fixed all that. King Kaiju is a hero who likes humanity and wants to save it from its own worst impulses. He tackled all the most prominent issues of the time—pollution, overpopulation, bigotry, and much more. Even got to climate change. Turned out King Kaiju's origins weren't radioactive like Godzilla's. He was incubated by increasing temperatures in the Marianas Trench due to global warming. Nonetheless, he loved people and saved millions."

He glanced at Kenzi's table. "No, the bad guys weren't covered in scales. They were covered in suits."

He turned back to the jury. "The sad thing is, the facts here aren't even much in dispute. The evidence will show that Wu spent two years trying to sell his creation without success. The market is saturated, people said. Monster comics are yesterday. No one will believe it. They tried revamping it as a comic strip. Still no takers. Tried distributing it themselves, but they had no money and the industry did not want new competitors. Eventually, Sidekick Comics took a chance on it, not because they loved it so much but because they need a lead feature for

Astounding Adventures #28 and time was running out. So they bought it and ran it.

"You know what happened. Huge sensation. Fewer than six months later Kaiju had his own book. The first six issues, all conceived at the same time as parts of a larger overarching story, are considered classics. In eighteen months Kaiju had four books plus a team-up mag. Then they licensed an overseas manga series. Money poured in. But there was a problem—as often occurs when huge sums of money are involved. The evidence will show that when Sidekick supposedly acquired the rights, it was by means of a standardized contract stamped on the back of the payment check. If the payee endorses the check, they've signed the contract. Which is exactly what happened. Wu signed. He got about $1250 and an offer to write future issues."

Dan paused, letting the words sink in. "But he did not own the character. According to Sidekick, he signed that over when he endorsed the check. And subsequent courts backed Sidekick. So while Sidekick made millions—tens of millions—off the character, his creator received a low-level payment when he turned in a new story. No salary. No control. And no credit. That lasted a few years, then there was another dispute over who owned Baby Kaiju, the adventures of King Kaiju when he was young. Sidekick said it was an original creation, but Wu said it was obviously based on King Kaiju and that he had pitched a Baby Kaiju book that they turned down. And then they did it behind his back while he served in Vietnam. Two tours, thrice decorated. Wu won that lawsuit, got a little money—and they never let him work on his own character again. In fact, they banned him from even visiting the Kaiju offices."

He leaned close to the jury to make sure they heard what he was saying. "That's what this lawsuit is about. Not just money, but also about what constitutes fair business practices. Right and wrong."

He drew himself up, signaling that he was approaching the end. He knew the worst thing you could ever do when you were trying to persuade was to talk too long.

"I won't go into chapter and verse on all the details. You'll hear about it later from my client, the creator. After the American comic and the manga came the cartoons. American animators thought it was too Asian, but the same company that made *Cowboy Bebop* picked it up in Asia and made a killer series that ran for twelve seasons. One of the highest-grossing animated series ever. And now Headmark Studios, the MGM of the modern era, wants to make a big screen live-action film. They see this movie as launching a potential franchise—a universe, really. The Kaijuverse! A tentpole they can count on for decades. Valuation estimates go as high as three or four billion annually. So you can see what we're fighting about. There's a lot of dough involved."

He let his voice become quiet. "Maybe some of you don't consider comic books great art, but that doesn't matter. When a creative soul creates something that sparks the imagination of millions—who should benefit? Corporate America? The one percent? People who can buy anything they want because they have more money? Is that who should control art? Entertainment? All the things that make life beautiful?"

He gave them a stern look. "Those rights should belong to the genius who created the art that corporations exploit. I hope you will also favor the creatives, not those who habitually take advantage of them."

Kenzi came on like a firestorm. That was her style, but Dan suspected she was also preventing the jury from dwelling on anything he'd said. Dan's approach had been somewhat lowkey (at least for him). He didn't want them to feel they were being lectured. Just . . . guided.

Kenzi, by contrast, did not act as if choice existed. The jurors needed to do what she told them, and she was not giving them any wiggle room.

"Is the sob story over?" she said. "Can we start acting like grownups now?"

She introduced herself and explained her function. "I represent Delia Ulrich, widow of Joe Ulrich, and she wants to make a deal with Headmark Studios. When you're offered several million and you don't have to do anything except sign a piece of paper, most would consider it a blessing. Does that make her evil? Or does that make her the one with the intelligence to see that they had something of value after several decades of botching it at every turn? They needed help. She provided it. She's still providing. And that's why we're here today."

The juror balance was 8-4, more female than male, and one of the males was likely trans, though of course Dan did not ask about that during jury selection. He was concerned that all those women would be more likely to sympathize with Delia, which was clearly what Kenzi was campaigning for.

"You just heard my distinguished colleague admit that his client signed a contract giving Sidekick the right to King Kaiju, including subsidiary rights like movie and television. That should be the end of the lawsuit. Game over! But instead, he wants you to forget what happened and nullify the contract. Just to be nice. In other words, he's saying, my client made a stupid mistake, but instead of forcing him to accept the consequences of his own actions, let's forget he ever did it." She folded her arms across her chest. "I don't think so."

She sashayed from one end of the jury rail to the other. "Let's give a little more thought to that sob story you just heard. Did anyone make Wu sign the check? No. He did it freely and of his own accord, and he got more money than he'd ever seen in his life. Did it last forever? No, money never does, which he should've realized in advance. Could he have made King Kaiju a success without Sidekick? No. Wu couldn't afford to take King Kaiju big and distribute comics all across the country. So he got a business partner who could. Did he negotiate the best possible deal with that partner? Probably not. Is it our job to save people from their own lack of business acumen? Definitely not."

She pressed her hands together, almost as if in prayer. "My opponent keeps acting as if all corporations are evil. What exactly did Headmark do wrong? They want to make a film fans are clamoring for. What did Sidekick do wrong? They made a smart and profitable deal. Isn't that what corporations are supposed to do? Was anyone cheated? No. Robbed? No. No wrongdoing whatsoever, but there's a new copyright law in town and they want to use it to undo the deal these parties made voluntarily. Sidekick agreed to give Wu and Joe a pension several years ago. Why didn't opposing counsel mention that? Those two get thirty thousand a year for nothing. Basically Sidekick is paying them just to be nice. Which is a rather generous act for a soulless corporation filled with heartless suits, right?

"If you ask me," Kenzi continued, "these boys got more than most. Talent isn't that uncommon. That's why 'unfulfilled talent' is a cliché. Most people come up with their King Kaiju and it goes nowhere because they don't know how or can't afford to produce and distribute it. These boys didn't have to figure the market out. Someone else did it for them. And now they can go to their rest knowing they did the unthinkable. They created a character that has endured for decades. Will likely endure for more decades. How is that a rip-off? I'd call it a gift."

She rubbed her hands together. Was that her "wrapping up" tell? Was she wiping her hands of the plaintiff's disgusting case?

"This is a court of law. Not a charity. I wish they were the same thing. But they are not. And never will be. You do not award a judgment to someone because you feel sorry for them. This man handled his business affairs poorly, then made several failed legal attempts to recover what he lost, which should bar further claims. When does it end? Wu lost his partner two days ago and I'm sorry about that. But it doesn't alter the fact that more resourceful individuals could've figured out a way. Or created a new character. Or parlayed it into work at Marvel or DC. Or anything other than sitting around wringing their hands and whining all the time.

"You can only award a judgment to a plaintiff if they've proved their case by a preponderance of the evidence. The witnesses and testimony will demonstrate that they can't meet that burden. Can't even come close. If they had a case, this would've happened fifty years ago. It's not going to happen now. This is a spiteful final thrust from an embittered aging man who..."

She chose her words deliberately, in a way that made it clear she was holding something back. "... who ... may not be at his best, at this point in life's journey. You may be wondering why this trial is happening after so much time and so many other failed attempts. Let me suggest two possibilities. The first is, as I said, age. Sometimes when people get older, they get crotchety and ... don't always make the smartest choices. Maybe some of you have grandparents like that." She paused. "Or I don't know. Maybe you are the grandparent like that!"

She smiled briefly, then proceeded. "Of course, we should be kind. To all elderly persons. But ... these problems that arise late in life might be the whole reason we're having this trial and ... well, possibly wasting your time." She took a deep breath. "That's a decision for you to make. But there's another possibility here. Another reason for this lawsuit."

Dan felt an anxious sensation creep up his spine. Danger, Will Robinson...

"As you've already noted, Delia is Black. Is that part of the equation?"

Dan pressed his hands firmly against the table. Objection? Seemed early to play the race card, though he knew it was coming eventually. An objection would give Kenzi a chance to argue and whine more in the presence of the jury, so he decided against it.

"Looks to me," Kenzi said, "like Wu accepted the fact that he might never gain control of King Kaiju. But when he saw that his old best friend's Black wife might end up with everything"—she jerked her thumb toward Dan—"that's when she called in the bigshot lawyer with the flashy Air Jordans. Does that prove justice is on his side?"

She shook her head as she stepped back. "Doesn't look that way to me. I think contracts should be honored, not erased when convenient. My client inherited her late husband's rights to this character. Sidekick popularized the character. Headmark is positioned to make him bigger than ever before. Don't let them get sidetracked by a bunch of emotional blather. Respect the law."

CHAPTER TWENTY-SEVEN

Everything about this case felt wrong, Dan realized, as the judge gestured toward him. Everything. For starters, he was contemplating putting his most important witness on the stand first. Who does that? All lawyers—for that matter, even people who aren't lawyers but watch them on television—know you save the best for last. Warm up with some less important stuff, then go out with a bang.

Except this time, he didn't have much bang. If the complaining witness is less than perfect (and they almost always are), maybe it was best to put that up front. He might garner more sympathy if they didn't try to build him up, but instead acted as if he were an Everyman. It was making a statement, in a way. No tricks. No games. Our story is simple. It's the thieves who need endless witnesses and documents and lawyers. He liked the feel of that. Jenny had basically made it the central theme of her trial notebook.

But how to say it? When he was a kid, the OJ Simpson trial was on television most afternoons after school. He remembered how frustrating it was that OJ never took the stand. Not long ago, the world watched the Johnny Depp/Amber Heard showdown. That was a civil case, just like the one he was in now. When Depp testified, critics commented that he was so slow and halting that he almost seemed like the drugs had left him with permanent brain damage. But he didn't seem rehearsed. He seemed real. Amber Heard went for a more energetic, full-out drama-queen approach—and no one believed her.

Maybe Wu's quiet stillness would work to their advantage. He hoped.

"Mr. Wu, is the document previously marked as Exhibit 14 the cancelled check you mentioned?"

"Yes, it is."

"And that's your signature on the back?"

"I believe so."

"Did you read the endorsement before you signed it?"

"No. Does anyone? If you want to cash a check, you have to endorse it. Nobody ever said they were giving me a contract."

No, that would've defeated the whole purpose.

Wu walked them through the story Dan outlined during his opening statement, competently, if unexcitingly. He was fuzzy on some of the details, but that was to be expected after the passage of so much time. He paused frequently and had a soft, somewhat high-pitched voice. But one critical fact was coming across that the jury couldn't possibly miss. This man invented King Kaiju. He was inspired by the work of Toho and Godzilla and others, but this was a unique take that readers, and later viewers, loved. All his frustrations—growing up as a minority kid in a white neighborhood, never fitting in, feeling powerless—he took all that pain and turned it into a character readers could root for. Joe brought the idea to life with his drawings without any outside input, not from Sidekick Comics or anyone else.

The character sprung from his brain. How could it legally belong to someone else?

"Was there any prior discussion of the legal impact of you endorsing that check?"

"Never."

"Did they offer any other contract?"

"No."

"Did you ask for one?"

"No."

"Did they talk about your future with the company?"

"Yes. With great enthusiasm. Talked about what a fine writer I was. They wanted me to work on other characters. Create other characters. At one point they were talking about forming an entire Kaiju imprint." He paused. "Which they eventually did. But without me."

"So they offered you a job?" Of course they did. Probably after they saw the initial sales figures. They distracted him with petty cash so he'd take his eyes off the prize.

"Indeed. On a contract labor basis."

"And you didn't realize that you'd signed away the rights to your creation."

"Not till they told me." Though Wu spoke excellent English without a trace of an accent, he tended to speak in simple terms, without emotion or elaboration. Which should be the preferred approach in anything called a court of law. But today the law was whatever the twelve people in the jury box said it was. And Wu still tended to stutter and occasionally had to think a few moments to come up with the right word.

"How did you react?"

"I was devastated. I—I couldn't believe it. I would never do that. I mean, I needed money badly. And I wanted to see my work in print. But to steal my character? That's just criminal. They stole my baby. They—"

"Objection." Kenzi rose to her feet. "Repetitive and conclusory."

Judge Parkwood nodded. "Sustained. Please wait for the next question, then answer it. Nothing more."

Wu winced. He didn't like being scolded.

"So you continued to work for Sidekick, right? After they claimed sole control of King Kaiju."

"I had to eat. Nothing else was selling. New York is expensive."

"I can imagine. How long did you work for them?"

"About two years. I helped build the Kaijuverse. I created Willie Wong. Doctor Arcadia. Captain Ultimatum. All of which Sidekick now owns. But Kaiju is the Big Kahuna. I also made personal appearances. Gave interviews. Did PR for the company."

"When did your employment end?"

"When I saw this." Wu pulled out Exhibit 27, which was a large black-and-white drawing, penciled and inked, of a draft cover for *Baby Kaiju #1*. What he called 'trashcan editions' because they were generated well in advance of publication to reserve the name for copyright and trademark purposes.

"Why did that upset you?"

"First, I was supposedly in charge of the Kaijuverse, but this new comic was about to go to press without my involvement."

"They'd been keeping it from you deliberately."

"Obviously."

"While you were serving your country. And you didn't like that they went behind your back."

"In the past, they'd paid me a small percentage of all Kajiu-based profits. Plus, I had proposed a prequel comic based on Kaiju's earlier adventures. They told me it was a bad idea. And then, while I was gone, they did it. Without crediting me."

"What did they give you for Baby Kaiju?"

"Nothing. Get this—they claimed this new character had nothing to do with my creation."

"You must be kidding."

"No! The cover has Baby Kaiju at the top, and beneath it, in slightly smaller black block letters: THE ADVENTURES OF KING KAIJU WHEN HE WAS YOUNG." He shook his head. "Different character? Their own cover admitted that it was not a completely different character. They didn't even draw him differently. Just a little younger."

"So what happened?"

"A lawsuit. I won. I got a small settlement for back pay." He drew in his breath. "And the next day, they fired me."

A retaliatory firing, to be sure, but back then there were no laws against it.

"I had no work and no one would hire me. Sidekick put the word out. I was a pariah. Anyone in this industry hired me, they'd never work in comics again. Kaiju was worth millions and Sidekick was playing hardball." He pressed his hand against his face. For the first time, a trace of the emotion he'd been suppressing emerged. "I—didn't know what to do. I had some savings, but not enough to last forever. I couldn't afford any more lawyers. Joe was losing his eyesight. He couldn't draw any more." Wu's voice choked. "They took the best thing we ever did and left us to die."

Dan thought this would be a good time to pause and allow the jury to absorb. He wouldn't stare but he took furtive glances into the jury box. He didn't detect any outright scorn. But that didn't mean they were sympathetic.

"Have you had any contact with Sidekick more recently?"

"Constant. They can't leave me alone."

Probably because he kept going to conventions and whipping fans into a frenzy with his sad stories about being ripped off. He'd heard Sidekick complain about his constant efforts to regain his creation. "When was the last time you were contacted by someone at Sidekick? Other than a lawyer?"

"Just after Joe's marriage. They called up. Offered me some petty cash."

"Did you accept?"

"No."

"Didn't you need the money?"

"Why would they offer money for rights they claimed they already owned? There was more than they were saying."

Wu had good instincts. The reason for the call was Headmark Studios. They wanted to make a big-budget deal, but a condition of the deal was a clear and unencumbered declaration of IP ownership. Obviously they didn't want to spend two hundred million bucks making a movie only to learn that they didn't have the rights.

"But you did accept a pension."

"Thirty thou a year."

"But you took it."

"That was a PR gesture with no strings attached. They originally required me to sign another document surrendering all claims. I refused. Ultimately, they just started paying the pension so they could tell the press they did."

"But you never agreed to anything."

"No. After they saw they wouldn't get anywhere with me, they went after Joe."

Unfortunately. But he'd deal with that later, if Delia got into it. He wanted to mention it, so the jury wouldn't think he was hiding anything. But he'd let Kenzi do the heavy lifting.

"And since that time have you had any contact with Sidekick Comics or King Kaiju?"

"None. I'm not allowed. I came by their offices the last time I was in New York. The CEO's assistant came downstairs to hassle me. He tried to quietly slip me a twenty and told me to scram. Like he thought I was there for a handout. It never occurred to him that maybe he should be treating me better, since this whole building and his entire life wouldn't exist if it hadn't been for me!"

Wu's eyes flared and his body tensed like a piece of steel. Dan wasn't sure whether to milk it or bury it.

He decided on the latter. He didn't want Wu to go so far he made the jury uncomfortable. He'd hit every legal point and he didn't seem mentally sketchy. He hadn't touched the jury emotionally, but that was probably not going to happen with this witness.

Later. During Kenzi's response. If he wanted a big judgment, he had to make this about more than a mere contract dispute.

"Pass the witness, your honor."

He turned to Kenzi and, with a magnanimous gesture, pointed her toward the witness stand.

CHAPTER TWENTY-EIGHT

As Dan anticipated, Kenzi plunged in headfirst. She didn't introduce herself and she didn't ask any softball questions.

"Did your mommy ever tell you that if you make a promise you should keep it?"

Dan was on his feet in a heartbeat. "Your honor! Objection."

Judge Packwood looked more bored than shocked. "Really, Ms. Rivera. I thought we were going to play well together and get this done in an expeditious manner."

Kenzi appeared clueless. "I'm sorry, your honor. I was just establishing a foundational principle for my cross."

"No, you were insulting the witness, and that was clear from the moment you said 'mommy.' So cut it out. In this courtroom, everyone will be treated with respect."

Dan loved it, though he knew it would make little difference to the case at the end of the day. The judge was bending over backwards to treat everyone fairly.

Kenzi took a deep breath with a bug-eyed expression, like she'd just come back from the vice principal's office. "Let me try again. You do not dispute that you signed that check."

"Correct."

"But did not read it. Do you think that's a smart thing to do? Signing contracts without reading them?"

"It was just a check."

"With a contract stamped on the back."

"No one mentioned that to me."

"You were an adult, weren't you?"

"Barely."

"Does a grown adult need to be told to read a contract before signing it?"

"They deliberately disguised the contract so they could steal the goodies."

"Did they tell you not to read the contract?"

"Of course not. Nor did they mention that I should. Nor did we ever have a discussion, much less an agreement, regarding ownership of rights. They hid what they were doing until it was too late for me to stop it."

She took several rapid steps forward. "Excuse me, but if you're going to accuse my client of a crime, you better have the goods. Where's your proof that someone at Sidekick deliberately hid the contract?"

Wu shrugged. "They sure didn't tell me about it."

"And you think you can meet your burden of proof with your speculation? That must be nice. So much simpler than dealing with witnesses and evidence."

Dan considered objecting, but decided to let her sarcasm stand. It didn't get her anywhere, and with luck, she would piss off someone on the jury.

"No one knowingly would give away King Kaiju for pennies."

"Not today. But this was a long time ago, right? At that time, the value of King Kaiju was zero. Did you take it to other publishers?"

"Yes."

"How many were interested?"

"None."

"So the truth is, without this company that you've spent years castigating, no one would've ever heard of your character."

"We would've found someone else. Someone with better ethics."

"Can you prove that? Or are you just inventing a fantasy company that doesn't like money?"

"I was there. You weren't. I know what it was like."

"How much did it cost to print and distribute the first issue of King Kaiju?"

"I don't know."

"Thousands?"

"Tens of thousands."

"Did you have that kind of money?"

"No."

"So once again, without this company, there would be no King Kaiju."

"The King would've survived. And thrived. Somewhere else."

"After you won the Baby Kaiju lawsuit, you were paid for Baby Kaiju."

"A little. Not enough. I had no bargaining power."

"And now you're back for more."

"My understanding is that the new law allows this. Many years have passed."

"You're trying to tell this jury that you're some sad sack who got cheated by the Big Bad Businessman in the Big Blue Suit. But in fact, you made money off this character, didn't you?"

"Some. Not enough. Not even one-tenth of one percent of what Sidekick made."

"By my records, you made more than a hundred thousand in royalties the first two years after the initial publication."

"And nothing since."

"Your pension."

"A pension is not a royalty. That's why they did it that way. They didn't want to admit I was entitled to royalties."

"But you have received payments. Repeatedly. You're not here because you never got nothing. You're here because you want more."

Wu stared at her coldly. "What I want is credit for my work. I created King Kaiju."

"Did you though? Didn't you take the idea from a book?" She glanced at her notes. "*The New Apocalypse?*"

"As I have acknowledged many times, I read that book and drew inspiration from it. But King Kaiju was my idea."

Kenzi continued. "I'm reading from page forty-seven of the book. It specifically talks about how ocean pollution could create undersea monsters."

"Does it mention a dinosaur in a skintight costume and cape? I don't think so."

"Should you share your royalties with the author of the book?"

"I do not get royalties and never have."

"But if you did—"

"I knew the author, John Wyndfield. I was with him when he died. Penniless, like the rest of us. He supported my efforts to reclaim my character and never once stood in my way. He was proud of the role he had played in the life of this media superstar."

"But you never offered to share your royalties."

"I never got any. And now, given that he's dead and left no heirs, I don't know where I would send the check."

"And what about Joe? Would you share with him? Or his heirs?"

"I loved Joe and would happily share with him, were he still with us. But he is not entitled to creator rights."

"Didn't he design the costume?"

"No."

"But he drew it."

"True."

"And isn't it traditional today for writer and artist to share creator credit for new comic characters?"

"Today? Yes, when the two work together to create something new. But that was not how Joe and I worked. I created the character. He drew what I asked him to draw."

Kenzi looked skeptical, but dropped the topic. "We'll circle back to that later. What about the 1981 negotiations? Sidekick wanted to renew the Baby Kaiju agreement, correct?"

"That was my understanding. I did not sign it. I never even read it."

"But Joe did." She held up what had previously been marked Exhibit 42.

"I did not consent to that."

"Joe says—"

This time, Dan objected. Fast. "Hearsay. And before she says it, the fact that the alleged declarant is unavailable"—given the judge's prior ruling, he couldn't explain why—"does not make this acceptable, since it's coming from a lawyer, not a witness."

The judge tilted her head to one side. "The jury knows who's speaking. I'm going to allow it. Overruled."

Kenzi continued. "I have an affidavit in which your former partner states that he discussed the 1981 amendment with you and subsequently signed on your behalf."

"I don't believe it. Joe wouldn't lie."

Kenzi pressed a hand against her bodice. "Are you accusing *me* of lying?"

Wu stared at the document. "I worked with Joe for a long time. I do not believe he would sign this. And it does not look like Joe's handwriting. It looks like Delia's handwriting. His widow. The woman sitting beside you."

That produced a murmur from the crowd. Wu basically

accused Delia of forgery in public. He knew the two didn't like each other, but he didn't expect this.

"Can you prove this isn't your partner's signature? Or is that just something convenient to say now? Since he can't set you straight."

Dan glanced at the jurors. This remark confused no one. Gag order or not, they all knew what had happened a few days before.

"I know Delia married Joe to get a stake in this fight." Wu looked down at his lap. "He knew it too. But he went along with it. Better love of money than no love at all."

Kenzi made some kind of noise but he didn't even know what it was. She was trying to undercut what Wu had said. Which told him Kenzi also perceived this weakness in her case. If the jury thought Delia was a manipulative gold digging forger, they wouldn't be generous, even if they did find in her favor.

"But the document is signed. And although only one signature appears, the line beneath reads Joe Ulrich, signing for himself and you."

"I did not write that. Or sign it."

"But you authorized Joe to sign it."

"Not true."

"What's more, Delia heard the whole thing."

Did she now? That solved one mystery. How to prove your case when your primary witness just shot himself. Answer: get his wife to testify about what he allegedly would've said.

Dan objected. "Since Ms. Ulrich is in the courtroom today, why don't we let her explain what she did and did not hear?"

The judge agreed.

Wu continued. "I worked for years on King Kaiju before he was published. I worked out his origin story, his MO, his genre, his world, his sidekick, his secret identity. Hard work. Creative work. It was as if I took everything I'd ever seen or done, everything I'd experienced, and put it into this character. I poured my heart onto the page. He would be a hero, not a washout no one wanted to be with. And people responded. Enthusiastically. It was as if this was the work I was always meant to do."

He drew in his breath. "I earned the right to profit from this character. I'm willing to acknowledge that others made contributions to the overall success story. But I do not accept that the original creator can be cut out. Ever. Under any circumstances."

"You want the jury to let you weasel out of both agreements."

"I never signed the second agreement. Forty years have passed since the original."

"Forty?" Kenzi blinked. "You mean fifty?"

"Twenty—Twenty—thirty—" He froze, momentarily confused. "Right, right, yeah. Fifty years. Since the first agreement."

"Sir, do you remember what year you signed the check that gave Sidekick the rights?"

"Of course I do. I'm just—"

"What year was it?"

Wu looked angry. "What—What is this—some stupid memory quiz? What d-d-difference does it make?"

Kenzi looked at him levelly, not letting him off the hook. "What year was it?"

"I—I don't remember, okay? Is that such a sin?"

"When was the second agreement?"

"That was . . . later."

"When?"

"I don't recall. It's on the documents."

"When did Joe marry Delia? When was his son born? Where were you when Sidekick sold the anime rights?"

"I don't know!" Wu's voice intensified, not that loudly, but compared to his previous testimony, he was shouting at the top of his lungs. "So my memory isn't perfect any more. I know what I'm talking about. I was there, damn it. Unlike you. Unlike your witnesses. I was there!"

Kenzi paused, letting it all settle into the jurors' minds. "Wu . . . what year is it now?"

Dan rose. "Your honor, he's not taking the SAT. This is not relevant."

The judge pursed her lips. "The witness will answer."

But he could not.

CHAPTER TWENTY-NINE

Ten minutes later, following the conclusion of cross and a short break, Dan returned to the courtroom. He'd done some heavy thinking. Every single member of his team disagreed with him. But he was going to do it anyway.

"Mr. Pike, you may call your next witness."

"We're done, your honor. The plaintiff rests."

He got a long look through the judge's cheaters. "For real?"

"Yes, your honor. No more witnesses."

Kenzi was rubbernecking from her table, just as surprised as the judge. All his teammates looked disgusted, because they knew this was coming and couldn't talk him out of it. But the truth was, Wu was the witness that mattered. He'd made his case. He was in no danger of getting a directed verdict against him. The burden was now on Kenzi to tear his case apart. Wu hadn't been spectacular, but he hadn't crumbled and, although he might seem elderly and a bit forgetful, he did not show true signs of dementia. He'd held up about as well as could be expected given his age. Kenzi could theoretically call him back to the stand as part of her case, but it would have to be to discuss something that hadn't been raised before.

"You're sure about this, counsel?"

"One hundred and ten percent," he said. "We've made our case and the defense can't alter the facts. In an effort to aid the court, however, I believe that at this time we can narrow the issues to be submitted to the jury."

Judges tended to favor anything that made their jobs easier or a trial shorter. "Proceed."

"Your honor, since this case falls within the purview of the 1976 Copyright Act and its subsequent amendments, and the instructions to be given to the jury will likely derive from them, I would ask at this time that the court consider a slate of stipulations."

He had submitted them in advance, so Judge Packwood knew what he was talking about. "Proceed."

"The stipulations couldn't be clearer. One. My client endorsed a check which a later court found transferred the rights to King Kaiju to Sidekick Comics."

"Agreed," Kenzi said. She wouldn't slow things down by objecting to matters that weren't in dispute.

"Two. That agreement and the publication resulting from it took place more than thirty-five years ago so, as in *Scorpio Music v. Willis*, the new Copyright Act applies."

"Agreed," Kenzi said, either firm or bored, depending upon your take.

"Three. My client therefore has the legal ability to sue for termination of a rights license granted more than thirty-five years before."

"Agreed."

"The original creator can sue for termination when, and here I quote, 'the value of the original work was not apparent at the time of creation.'" Which was an understatement.

Kenzi couldn't hold back any longer. "But that's not the only requirement. There's a notice provision—"

"And my client did it. In writing. Two years before the expiration of the notice period."

"Plus the Act doesn't apply to work-for-hire agreements."

"Which this clearly was not. Witness Exhibit 14. I'm not claiming there are no more fact issues, your honor. I'm just trying to frame and limit the issues."

Judge Packwood nodded. "Understood."

"So there are only a few questions left for the jury. Even if the original agreement constituted a valid meeting of minds, can Wu now terminate that license? And if so, going forward, how will the royalties be split amongst my client, his late colleague's wife, and the comic book company. Pretty simple, really."

Judge Packwood turned to the other side of the courtroom. "You agree, Ms. Rivera?"

"Believe it or not, your honor, for once, I actually do." Kenzi looked as surprised as everyone else. Maybe some of what she said back at Dan's office was true. "But we're not going to let the plaintiff weasel out of his agreement by claiming that a young man was too stupid to read the contract any more than we're going to let him ignore the agreement signed by his partner primarily for his benefit. His partner is barely cold in his grave and yet here Wu is, selling the man out for thirty pieces of silver—"

"Objection!"

"Sustained." Judge Packwood peered at Kenzi. "Really, Ms. Rivera. Maybe that sort of dramaturgy flies in Seattle, but here in the South, we like to keep things a little more down to earth. Does the court gather correctly that you accept the proffered stipulations?"

"We do, your honor. One hundred and ten percent."

"There's no such thing."

"Well, we're all in."

"Thank you. That will make the trial flow much more expeditiously. And will simplify drafting the jury instructions as well. We'll take a short break and I'll deal with the usual motions and procedural matters. I need to dispense with an emergency motion in another case. And then, if there's nothing more"—her head switched from one side of the courtroom to the other—"Ms. Rivera, you may call your first witness."

AT LEAST DELIA DIDN'T WEAR A VEIL. OR ARMBAND. SHE DIDN'T go so far that it might seem hypocritical. Wearing black was more like a form of identification. She was part of the family whose rights stemmed from Joe. If you focused on that part in isolation, dressing in black seemed like a simple gesture of respect.

"We've heard all about the original endorsed check," Kenzi said. "Tell us about the later agreement. If you know."

"I know what my beloved husband told me." Delia sniffled a bit but held back the tears. "Wu was zoned out and my husband, Joe, was dragging his heels. I never thought there was any chance they would recover the rights to the character. They just didn't have the chutzpah, you know what I mean?"

"I do indeed. So who initiated the agreement?"

"I did. We needed money. Bad. Like, we were about to be kicked out of a one-room apartment so pitiful most people couldn't be paid to live in it. But that was our existence. And we had a young son."

"That must've been . . . difficult."

"I saw the Sidekick CEO on the street one day. Curtis Swart. He was wearing Gucci loafers and a Burberry overcoat. I was wearing a tattered sweatshirt and getting three slices of pizza for our dinner because that's all we could afford."

"So you decided to do something about it."

"Someone needed to do something. We have a son and I could barely feed him a proper meal. So I tracked down a lawyer friend to see if we could get something going."

"Did you involve Wu in this?"

"I tried. He's . . . you know." She pointed a finger and drew circles around her temple. "Not so quick these days. I know he pulled it together long enough to testify . . . somewhat . . . but . . ." She shrugged. "You know. Good days and bad."

"Are you suggesting the plaintiff is suffering from dementia?"

"Objection." Dan was trying to remain low-key and not irritate the jurors, who tended to dislike lawyers who perpetually interrupted and prevented them from hearing the best parts. But he couldn't let that pass. "This witness is not a medical expert. She is not trained to offer a diagnosis."

"She's seen Wu off and on for more than twenty years," Kenzi replied.

"She's not a doctor."

Judge Parkwood cut in. "I will sustain the objection, since you asked if the plaintiff has a specific medical condition. But every witness is entitled to describe what they've seen and heard. Especially when it involves a party-opponent."

Dan had never been less happy to win an objection. The judge basically explained to Kenzi how to get around his objection. Was this turning into a Girls Club thing? He didn't want to be sexist, but he was detecting an ongoing theme of women taking charge and doing a much better job than men.

Kenzi rephrased her question. "What have you observed over the years regarding Wu's behavior?"

"He's getting older. I mean, we all are, but the years are weighing on him worse than most. I think the constant fighting wore him down. Crushed his spirit. He used to compare himself to Walt Disney. Can you imagine? He'd say, 'Disney creates a mouse and he gets an empire. I create the greatest kaiju character in comics, and I get bupkis.'" She paused. "What he doesn't grasp is, Walt Disney wasn't an idiot."

What she doesn't grasp, Dan thought, is that Walt had a brother who looked after him and handled the legal and financial matters. Wu didn't.

"How did that affect your negotiations?"

"Wu can't remember anything reliably. He forgets the details and wants to take full credit for everything. He's Sidekick's Stan Lee. Joe remembered much more clearly."

"Was Sidekick interested in renegotiating the agreement?"

"I'm sure Sidekick wished we would dry up and disappear, but we didn't, and they preferred to pay a little rather than risk losing a lot. A simple dollars-and-cents evaluation. There was too much at stake to completely ignore us, but they didn't feel our claim was strong enough to spend a lot of money on."

"They didn't believe the Copyright Act altered your position."

"It wasn't that exactly. They knew they could out-lawyer us. They were a big corporation. We were poor people with erratic income. Not much of a contest, really. We were lucky to get what we did."

"But you did sign the agreement."

"Joe did."

"And he signed on behalf of both himself and Wu."

"Yes. That's spelled out in the agreement. Sidekick wouldn't agree unless both of them were involved."

"How did he obtain Wu's consent?"

Dan stayed on his toes. She wasn't in hearsay territory yet, but she'd be there soon.

"He called. They talked several times."

"On the phone?"

"Right. Landlines, remember those? Wu was hesitant but he eventually agreed."

There it was. "Objection. Hearsay."

Kenzi shrugged dismissively. "Your honor, one of the two people in the conversation is dead, and the other is a party-opponent. That's two different applicable hearsay exceptions."

"Except," Dan said, "that she isn't testifying about what she heard. She wasn't on the phone conversation. She didn't even hear the hearsay. She's repeating what she heard from someone else who heard the hearsay."

Kenzi looked as if she'd never heard a stupider argument. "They talked about it later, your honor."

The judge tilted her head. "It's still double hearsay, Ms. Rivera. Possibly triple, in places."

"Very well. Let me waste everyone's time for several minutes telling them things they already know, just to appease my opponent. Then we can proceed with the trial."

Ouch. The Lady from Seattle did not like to lose objections.

She returned her attention to Delia. "Did you and Joe discuss those conversations with Sidekick after they occurred?"

"Yes."

"Do you recall what Joe said about them?"

"Yes."

"Did he say it near to the time of the original conversation?"

"Immediately after."

"Good." She snarled in Dan's general direction. "What did he say?"

"He said Wu agreed but he was too ill and too poor to come to the New York offices. So he asked Joe to sign on his behalf."

If Wu consented to that agreement, he might be barred from making future claims. He had to kill that agreement. And that was going to be a problem, since it was signed, executed, acted upon, appeared to include Wu, and hadn't been contested since it was signed.

"And did Joe sign?"

"Yes. On behalf of both."

"Thank you." Kenzi went through the motions to have the

document entered into evidence. "You mentioned there was some discussion about executing the agreement. What was the discussion about?"

Delia took a deep breath, then leaned back in her chair. Dan felt a clutching in his gut. He'd seen that movement pattern before, with other witnesses. Then he looked at Kenzi. She was squeezing her pen as tight as a gear shift.

They were about to deliver something important.

"The problem then, earlier, and now," Delia continued, "is that Wu continually insists that he created King Kaiju. But he didn't. Joe did. Solo. From the get-go. He didn't co-create the character. He created King Kaiju and later asked Wu to help with the scripts. And Wu knows it. Even as bad as his memory is now. Joe allowed Wu his delusions while alive, but now he's gone. It's time for my beloved late husband to get the recognition he so richly deserves."

CHAPTER THIRTY

To say that this testimonial revelation produced a reaction would be a gross understatement. Dan was astounded by how much interest those seated in the gallery showed. He noted that the audience was largely Gen Z or younger. A few even wore costumes.

The courtroom had become Comic Con East.

Dan focused on Wu, still seated at their table, looking as if he'd been slapped in the face. Dan didn't need superpowers to read those eyes.

I only have one thing in my life, his eyes said. *And she wants to take it from me.*

Kenzi pretended to be as shocked as everyone else in the courtroom, though Dan rather doubted she was. "Are you saying your late husband, Joe Ulrich, was the sole creator of King Kaiju?"

"Yes. And everyone knew it, back then. It's true that Wu wrote many of the early stories. But his role in the creation of the character was zero."

"Both names are credited in the early stories. Before the credits were discontinued."

"And that was appropriate, when Wu wrote the story. But those credits didn't indicate who created the character. They simply indicated who wrote and drew that particular story."

"If Joe was the sole creator, why did you ask for Wu's consent to the later agreement? Seems to me that by including him, you acknowledged that he had a claim."

"All we acknowledged was that Sidekick wanted a global settlement. With two names on it. To settle this mess once and for all."

"But you maintain the character was Joe's creation."

"It's not just me. A lot of the old timers know the truth. Talk to—"

"Objection. Nonresponsive." He hated to object. The jurors would think he was trying to shroud potential witnesses. Which he was. He didn't care about the names. He disliked the credence it gave her revisionist tale of King Kaiju's genesis.

The judge cleared her throat. "I will sustain the objection based on lack of responsiveness to the question posed."

Kenzi tried again. "You don't need to list the names. I'm sure there are many and the jurors might not know the names of the most prominent people in the comics industry."

Dan swore under his breath. That Kenzi was sneaky. But also, he had to admit, a good lawyer.

"Is this something you heard Joe claim?"

"Many times. He created the character, his backstory, his personality, his costume. And he storyboarded the first adventure. All Wu did was fill in the word balloons. Based on notes Joe left on the art boards."

Kenzi raised her hands. "Ok, we've covered a lot of ground in a little time, so let me make sure I've got this correct. Your husband, Joseph Ulrich, was the sole creator of King Kaiju."

"True."

"And Wu consented to the most recent agreement with Sidekick Comics."

"Also true."

Kenzi held out her hands and looked at the judge. "Then he doesn't have much to complain about, does he?" She shrugged and walked away.

Dan rose but he moved slowly. He needed time to think. He could feel Wu's eyes burning, begging him to eradicate these fresh lies. But how? He should've knew Kenzi had something up her sleeve. he wished he'd figured it out sooner.

He doubted he was going to poke many holes in this story. Delia and Kenzi had clearly planned this out and prepped it to the max.

But he had to try. "Ms. Ulrich, first of all, let me offer my condolences on your loss."

She nodded grudgingly. "Thanks."

"When you first met Joe, many years ago, I'm sure you were very much in love." He was trying keep his voice level and not sound sarcastic. Planting the suggestion was enough. "When did you find out he had a claim to King Kaiju?"

"Look, if you're trying to insinuate that I married him for his money, may I point out that he didn't have any money?"

"He had a claim."

"Which had failed in court—how many times?"

"Nonetheless . . . you knew there was gold in them there hills. Right?"

Delia pursed her lips. He sensed she was losing patience. He could use that. "You want to stop playing infantile games? I knew there was potential, true. I knew there was a possible claim no one was pursuing. If I'd been around when this started, I would never have let that company screw Joe over. But I wasn't, and these two children were easily duped and manipulated, so I had to work long after the fact to get what we deserved. Yes, the Sidekick agreement was my idea. My son was hungry. Can you blame me?"

Back in the gallery, seated just behind Kenzi, Ernie glanced up, knocking back a shock of thick floppy hair. The hungry years didn't appear to have hurt him much. He had the androgynous good looks that seemed to define television these days.

"So you took charge of the Kaiju claim."

"Someone had to! If much more time elapsed, no law on earth could've helped him. I—I—" She pressed the back of her hand against her mouth. "I did the best I could. All my life, I never had enough money and never had any way of getting any. And here comes this guy who invented a multi-million-dollar property but still lived in poverty. Someone needed to take charge. It wasn't so much a marriage as an adoption. I took that little boy and gave him a fighting chance. If we can win this case—"

"You'll qualify for Wife of the Year?"

"I'll be able to leave something to my son." Her voice choked. "Who at this point, is the only thing I have left."

"You realize that agreement is the biggest impediment to our claim under the current Copyright Act?"

"I didn't know it then. All I knew was that my son needed food."

Delia was nimble and quick. Probably a result of being well-prepared by her lawyer. He felt like he was treading water—on the surface of something with depth, but not quite plunging into it.

"And now, in court, for the first time ever, you're asserting that Joe created this character on his own. With no input from Wu."

"Because he did."

"Were you present when this happened?"

"You know I wasn't. Joe told me about it. I've already said that."

"Then in your future answers, I'll ask you to differentiate

between when you're testifying from actual knowledge and when you're relating the hearsay statements of others."

He could see Kenzi steaming, but she stayed in her seat.

"Do you know anything about the creation of this character that is not based on statements from your late husband?"

"I know Wu is never identified as creator. Anywhere. In any of the early documents."

"Is Joe?"

"Well..."

"Wu has been describing himself as the creator of this character for decades. And never once have I seen or read about any instance when Joe denied that."

Delia shrugged her shoulders, and a crooked smile trickled across her face. "They were friends."

"That's not a reason to give up a billion-dollar claim."

"Except—" Delia shook her head, almost as if the words surprised even her. "Except it was. To him. To Joe. Wu was his oldest friend. His only friend. He knew Wu had a rough childhood and he wanted to help his buddy. Who wouldn't? And of course, when you think you're going to make a fortune, splitting the fortune doesn't seem all that much of a sacrifice." She smiled wryly. "Most people could live off a half a billion."

"One problem with this story you're telling the jury which you have never stated before at any time—"

"It was Joe's story to tell. But now he can't. So I will speak for him. I had no way of knowing—of knowing—"

And then she launched back into grieving-widow mode. He cursed himself for falling into the trap.

"—knowing his desperate soul had taken all that he could bear."

"If you loved Joe so much, why were you planning to divorce him?"

He expected to get an objection to that one, but Kenzi

remained silent. Which told him she already knew what Delia would say and she wasn't worried about it. Which told him this was probably a wasted question.

"It was what we both agreed upon."

Dan gave her a long look. "Are you seriously suggesting that Joe wanted you to divorce him?"

She took another meaningful pause before answering. "Are you familiar with the community property laws in California?"

Probably not as familiar as the divorce lawyer from Seattle. "Why do you ask?"

"California inheritance tax takes a bigger cut from married couples. Particularly with property or claims acquired before the marriage."

"That makes no sense."

"Tell William Shatner. You know, the *Star Trek* guy? We're friends. He divorced his wife—but they still live together and love one another. The divorce was strictly for estate-planning purposes."

"You're saying you were divorcing Joe to help him get his estate in order?"

"Yes. I was trying my hardest, but at the end of the day, this wasn't my claim. People weren't going to talk to me until it was my claim. So I figured out a way to make it my claim."

Dan took a step back. "Are you suggesting . . . that Joe gave you the claim? Before he died? So you could recoup the rights?"

"Now you understand the situation. I knew you'd get there eventually."

Dan didn't stagger, but only because he was conscious of not looking thrown in the jurors' eyes. But he was thrown. And Wu's chances of success became more complicated. If this was true, Delia wasn't after someone else's claim. She was pursuing her own claim.

Now he not only had to prove Wu had a claim—against an

aggressive living counterclaimant—but also had to prove he was a creator. And they had to prove the Sidekick agreement didn't kill the claim.

Every word Delia had spoken went against them.

And Dan had done absolutely nothing to prevent it.

CHAPTER THIRTY-ONE

DAN COULDN'T SHAKE THE FEELING THAT HE HAD BOTCHED Delia's cross. Sure, Kenzi had surprise revelations and he had to react on his feet—but he should've done better. He didn't dent Delia's story in any meaningful way.

Maybe because there were no dents to be made. Because she was telling the truth. Certainly looked as if she was.

But Wu was his client. He needed to turn this case around. Somehow.

BOB LYDEK SEEMED LIKE AN UNCONTROVERSIAL WITNESS. Everyone knew he had a pocket agreement with Delia, ready to whip out the instant he saw a judicial declaration that she held the rights. He couldn't pretend to be disinterested in the outcome, since his studio stood to make billions from the transaction.

But none of that was in dispute. The only reason to put this man on the witness stand was to talk about Delia's agreement with Sidekick, by and through which Sidekick and Headmark jointly secured the rights to King Kaiju, Baby Kaiju, and the complete Kaijuverse. If Joe's signature was found to have been done with Wu's full knowledge and consent, the agreement would be enforced. They would pay Delia an annual stipend, as agreed, though she would have no voice in the business.

Dan was surprised Kenzi had not started with a rep from Sidekick. But the original sale was not being disputed now that the stipulations were in place. So much time had passed that there was no executive currently at Sidekick who had been there when the original deal was executed. So they started with the man from Headmark Studios.

Lydek was all smiles, wearing a slick suit that probably cost ten grand. He also had a flower in his lapel. Given what Garrett had told him, he made a point of staying away from it.

After introducing him and explaining his involvement, Kenzi asked, "How did the so-called 1981 agreement come into being?"

Lydek nodded. "The manga series adapting the original stories was doing huge numbers. Almost unprecedented. Bigger than *The Last Airbender*! We reached out to Sidekick. At that point, there was some question about the ownership of the rights and some concern that when the thirty-five-year period specified in the new copyright act expired, we would be negotiating from scratch."

"So you decided to make a preemptive move."

"Exactly. Settle the matter once and for all, give Joe and Wu something to live on, and let us take this property to the next level."

"Makes sense. How did it go?"

"At first, fine. As you know, Delia took an active role, so that part was easy. I had a much harder time communicating with Wu. He didn't have an email address. He didn't take my calls."

"Was Joe talking to him?"

"Yes. Both Joe and Delia communicated with him. More than once. They told us what he wanted. He was represented in the negotiations."

"Was an agreement reached?"

"Yes. That's Exhibit 45."

Kenzi had it admitted into evidence. "This agreement says that both Joe and Wu will be paid an annuity for the rest of their natural lives."

"True. In exchange, the two parties agreed that the subsidiary rights, including movie/TV rights, would go to us."

"Was that agreement executed? Signed?"

"And notarized."

"Were you present when this happened?"

"I was."

"Was there any disagreement? Any objection?"

"None whatsoever. We have operated under this agreement for many years now."

"Thank you. No more questions."

Dan rose. He was careful not to suggest to the jury that this was going to be a thrill-packed cross. He had work to do, but the case wasn't going to be won in the next fifteen minutes. This was a corporate exec, not a fact witness.

"Let's be honest about this. What you're calling the 1981 agreement was your attempt to steal a property you knew to be valuable for a song. You took advantage of Joe and Wu's vulnerable economic situation to steal the Hope Diamond of Comics."

To his surprise, Lydek did not argue. He did not even blink. The prankster was not messing around today.

"Look, I'm a businessman," Lydek said simply. "In my personal life, I like to mess around. Have some fun. But my role here is CEO of a publicly traded corporation. I have stockholders depending upon me to make their shares more valuable. And that means no bleeding heart nonsense and no soft-soap giveaways. My job is to get the best deal for the company possible. There's nothing wrong with that."

Not exactly Gordon Gecko in *Wall Street*, but he was making his point. "You never personally spoke to my client."

"Not at that time."

"So you don't know whether he agreed to this amendment or not."

"I know what I was told."

"Joe did not have the right to sell someone else's share."

"Except—maybe he did." Lydek sat up straight, an eagerness in his eyes. He had something good and he knew it. "Joe acted as authorized representative for both on many occasions."

If there was a course of dealing in which Joe repeatedly held himself out as representing both, if there was a legal agency relationship, the court could find that Lydek was not derelict in dealing with only one of them. Most partnerships only send a single rep, usually the managing partner, to a settlement meeting. Too many cooks spoil the broth.

"Will you admit you took advantage of their economic situation?"

Lydek shook his head. "I'll admit I knew they were in distressed financial conditions. The intelligent businessman does his research before the meeting begins. When you know the other party needs money badly, you make a lowball offer. Standard common sense practice."

Dan worried that Lydek was making far too much sense. His plan was to appall the jury with the man's money-grubbing ways. Not to win him an award for savvy negotiating.

"These two men lived in abject poverty. You used that."

"At the time that we negotiated, I understood Delia supported her family. I believe her son had some intermittent acting work. Were they rich? Probably not. But they weren't starving. I'm sorry Joe was not able to find work during his later years due to his vision problems. But he had Delia. That marriage wasn't the cynical one-sided exercise in greed you suggested. If it hadn't been for Delia, Joe would've been dead a long time ago."

"You never once spoke to Wu while negotiating this agreement."

"True. But I specifically asked about authority and I was told that Joe represented both of them."

"You bought them off as cheaply as you could. You stole their future."

Lydek raised a finger. "See, that's where I disagree with you. Sure, Sidekick bought the character and we bought the film rights from them. But what was the future if we hadn't? That original novel Wu read sold fewer than a thousand copies. Even after they recreated the character in comic format, they spent years unable to sell it. Sure, it was a good idea, but they did not have the resources or the business acumen to turn it into a hit. We did."

"You could've shared the profits."

"And they could've negotiated a better deal. But they didn't. I don't have the power to rewrite history or to make people smarter. Fair or unfair, sometimes you have to live with your life choices."

Dan drew in his breath. This was getting him nowhere. He wouldn't win this case by making Wu an object of pity. The jury had to feel he'd been cheated.

"At this point in time," Dan said, "you have a signed agreement to produce a series of live-action films based upon King Kaiju, right?"

"Can you define live action? We're trying to get Andy Serkis to wear a motion-capture suit for the lead role. CGI."

"Whatever. And the agreement commits Wu?"

"You can argue all you want about authority prior to the agreement, but the 1981 agreement, paragraph three, plainly states that Joe had the authority to bind both parties."

"Just because it says—"

"Joe gave Delia power of attorney over all claims pertaining to his creative work. So done and done. Any way you slice it, Delia has the rights and she sold them to us. And given that Wu had nothing to do with the creation of the character anyway—"

"Wait a minute. That's a question of fact for the jury. Which has not yet rendered a verdict." He wanted to make the jurors feel as if Kenzi was shoving her arguments down their throats.

"I talked to Joe before he died. He was unequivocal. He created King Kaiju. By himself." Lydek took one of the exhibits and pointed to some pencil notes in the margin of an art board. "See that scribbling? I know it's hard to read, but that's Joe's handwriting. Joe. The artist. He mapped out the story and drew it, then he left notes about what needed to go in the word balloons. It's called the Marvel Way, because it's what Stan Lee and Jack Kirby did in the sixties. Wu may have written some of those word balloons, but that's hardly the same as creating the character."

Dan removed a long art board from his backpack. "Do you recognize this?"

"Sure. This is the original art. First penciled, then inked, then lettered, then sent out for coloring and printing. These days, most of the coloring is done with computers." He held it up at arm's length. "This is the first story, isn't it? The origin. King Kaiju is created in the depths of the Pacific."

"Look at the last two panels."

He did. The first showed some military type telling King Kaiju to destroy the laser-powered pterodactyl. "I know I'm asking a lot. But the world needs a hero." And in the next panel, a close-up of the two shaking, hand to paw, with Kaiju saying, "I'm your huckleberry."

Dan put the panels on the overhead monitor. "Look familiar?"

"To me and every King Kaiju fan on earth."

Dan pulled another art board out of his backpack. "Recognize this one?"

Lydek's brow furrowed. "Not right off the bat . . ."

"This is a story Wu wrote two years before Kaiju. It's a superhero story involving a sentient computer that solves crimes. But look at the bottom two panels."

Dan put those two panels up on the overhead screen. The art was different. The "world needs a hero" panel was an outer space illustration showing the entire planet. The second panel focused on a purple squid creature's determined grin.

But the dialogue in both panels was almost word for word the same. Right down to the 'huckleberry.'

Lydek kept looking back and forth.

"Quite the coincidence, huh?" Dan said.

"Or a startling lack of originality," Lydek murmured.

"There's no question about the fact that Wu wrote the first one."

"Anyone could've done it."

"Seriously? Were a lot of comic writers at that time using the term 'huckleberry?' Had they all just seen *Tombstone*? Or listened to 'Moon River?'"

"I'll admit it's odd. But sometimes odd things happen."

"Isn't it more likely that the man who wrote it the first time used it again a couple of years later? Underpaid and pressed for time, it probably seemed like the smart thing to do."

"So what? You want me to pay him twice because he re-used the same lame dialogue?"

"No," Dan said, putting both art boards on the screen and enlarging them so the jury could compare them side-by-side. "I want you to admit what you already know. Wu adapted some of his earlier work and wrote this story, and this story provided the origin, the supporting cast, the love interest, the costume—almost everything readers associate with King Kaiju. Which proves that Wu created, or at the very least co-created, Kaiju."

"Anyone could've stolen from that old story."

"So now you're saying Joe was a thief? Of his best friend's work?"

"I didn't say that."

"What it demonstrates to me is an evolving talent. You can tell the later King Kaiju story is better written. The characters are richer, there's genuine suspense. But all writers have patterns, techniques. Instinctive ways of getting in and out of scenes. And if you read these panels—if you read these pages, even—it is immediately apparent that they were written by the same person. Wouldn't you agree?"

Lydek didn't speak. But he didn't argue, either.

CHAPTER THIRTY-TWO

Kenzi stared at the cocktail glass on the conference room table. What exactly was a negroni, anyway? Not her new favorite. She'd only been in Florida for a few weeks, but she missed home. And her daughter. And normal drinks with Sharon at Sherman's Ferry.

She'd considered leaving Seattle, back when she was fresh out of law school. Her father was already a major name in the legal community. If she wanted to make a mark, she worried that she would have to go elsewhere. But in the end, parental pressure and inertia set in and she ended up staying put.

No point in regrets, right? And now that she was basically running her father's firm, no one could say she hadn't made her mark.

And yet...

She couldn't shake the lingering feeling that she wasn't living up to her potential. That there was more she could do. Maybe much more. She just hadn't figured out what it was yet.

Christopher was still lurking around. That was technically his job as co-counsel. But pretty though he might be, she was accustomed to working with a higher quality staff. She had to work through three drafts of documents Sharon could've generated without being asked or supervised. She had to hire PI firms for background checks Emma could've done much better.

And Hailee undoubtedly had upgraded her murder board since the shootings on the courthouse steps. What it must look like now . . .

She missed Hailee. And worried about her. She was a superstar daughter, but her condition was not improving. Kenzi had to acknowledge that there could come a time when she might not be able to stand or walk at all. Might not even be able to eat unassisted. The thought of that Italian-loving girl not able to lift her own za . . .

She shook her head rapidly, dismissing those thoughts. She had work to do.

And speaking of pizza, why didn't they have any?

"Did you order food?" she asked Christopher.

"No. I was hoping we might go out for dinner."

"During a trial?" She looked at him incredulously. "Who does that?"

"Well . . ."

"Order a pizza. I got work to do. We might get through three, maybe even four, witnesses tomorrow."

"The literary agent? Or the comics guy?"

She didn't answer. Truth was—she didn't know. Not because she hadn't thought about it. Because she hadn't decided. This was an important strategic decision. Possibly a critical one.

"Don't agonize so much," Christopher said. "You're winning."

"It's a mistake to get overconfident."

"You left that Florida showboat choking in your dust."

"I had the facts on my side today. And a confident, assertive witness. That won't always be true. Dan is a gifted trial attorney and we need to be vigilant until the last bang of the gavel."

"I think Pike is overrated."

"He's a superstar."

"Was."

Delia had done as expected, nothing more, nothing less. Lydek managed to contain his practical-joker psychosis and deliver more-or-less credible testimony.

But Dan was floating like a bumblebee. She needed to anticipate his moves before he stung like a bee. "Did you ever track down that cover artist? The one who drew the first covers?"

"Not yet. Given how much time has passed, he's probably worm food."

Kenzi tried not to clench her teeth. She knew he was not only alive, but also planning to make an appearance at a Florida convention soon.

"You have the case in the bag, Kenzi. Live a little." Christopher nodded toward the bottle. "Maybe another drink. Might get you in the mood."

She didn't ask what mood he meant. He might answer.

"I need to keep my head clear. But Joe specifically mentioned that artist to me. Before he . . . you know."

"Why?"

"There was something he wanted me to know or understand or . . . something. At the time, I had more pressing matters and assumed we'd talk about it later. Now he's dead and it's too late. I'm making rookie mistakes. And I don't like it." She paused a moment. "Something is off. I need to figure out what it is. Before it rears its ugly head and bites me in the butt."

"Speaking of your butt." Christopher sidled toward her. "You do have a saucy little rear, you know it?"

"So I've been told."

"By the many men in your life?"

"Mostly by my daughter. There's some kind of sneaker she wants me to buy that will supposedly make my butt look better. I don't really understand it."

"But you bought the sneakers?"

"I did not. As I told her, I'm the leader of the KenziKlan. We are pro-women 24/7 and we believe women have value that extends beyond their physical appearance."

"Outside of frat houses, is there anyone who thinks differently?"

"I dress for success. Appearances matter. But I dress to improve my client's case. Not to impress men."

He shrugged. "If you say so."

She checked her Bulgari "Women in Pink" watch. Almost midnight. Where had the night gone? She was hungry. She had work to do. She was stuck with this wannabe molester. She'd made Delia a promise and she would stick by it, but . . .

She placed an order on her phone. "Pizza will be here soon. I'll put these witness outlines back in the binder and review them again in the morning. It'll probably be okay."

He slapped her on the back. Too hard. "There's the spirit!"

"Let me do a Google search. See if I can get a line on the cover artist. Then I'll be able to call the PI firm and—"

Christopher grabbed her arm and swung her around. "None of that needs to be done. But if you insist—you can do it later."

She looked into his eyes, which all of a sudden seemed extremely close to her own. "I . . . suppose I could."

"We've been working all night."

"True."

"Men and women have needs. We must practice self-care."

"Wait a minute . . ."

"You can't exercise the brain but forget the body."

"I wouldn't put it quite that way . . ."

"Now we're gonna have some fun." He pulled her tight. "Lots of fun."

Are we, though? "Look, I make it a rule to never get involved with other people in my lawsuits. At least not until the lawsuit is over."

"We're on the same side." She could feel his breath on her face. "So there's no conflict of interest."

"It's still not a good idea."

"Such a stickler for rules. You know what I think is more important than rules?"

She suspected she did, but allowed him to answer his own question. "What would that be?"

"Romance."

"Civil suits are not very romantic." Or so she thought, but maybe she was wrong. His hands were roaming and she didn't seem to be doing anything about it . . .

CHAPTER THIRTY-THREE

DAN HAD FEW SCRUPLES ABOUT CROSS-EXAMINATION OR, AS SOME called it, the Search for the Big Gotcha. It was his job, and an important part of his job, whether he enjoyed it or not. Cross was about trying to trip witnesses up, catch them in a lie, or at the very least, make them look foolish and forgetful. But Kenzi's industry witnesses were important. He wanted to use them to establish his own theme—that creators and distributors could work together honorably without ripping artists off. If these parties had simply agreed to split profits in a fair way up front, they might've avoided decades of litigation and mistrust.

Kenzi's next witness turned out to be Megan Sanderson, the literary agent. Which raised another ethics issue, since Garrett had informed him about her fondness for brothels and sex hypnosis. Should he bring that up on cross? It wasn't relevant, but it might impact her credibility. Tarnish her professional image. It wasn't as if they'd unearthed dark skeletons buried in an underground crypt. For reasons he didn't understand, she freely volunteered the info to Garrett.

Sanderson looked very New York, very professional, and very uncomfortable. She said the climate here was too hot and she didn't like to get sticky, so a move to Florida was probably not going to happen for her any time soon. But she seemed uncomfortable on the stand, more so than most.

Sanderson explained that she represented first Joe, now Delia, in the negotiations with Sidekick Comics and Headmark Studios. Unsurprisingly, she drank Delia's Kool-Aid, meaning she claimed Joe was the sole creator of King Kaiju—something she neglected to mention to Garrett during their interview. Of course, as Joe's agent, it was in her interest to say he held the rights.

Dan knew that was the critical issue, so that was where he began his cross. "Ms. Sanderson, you were not present at the time of the initial license to Sidekick Comics, were you?"

"Was I present?" Sanderson laughed. "Mister, I wasn't even alive."

"So you have no personal knowledge of what happened."

"I disagree."

"Do you have a crystal ball?" He smiled slightly. "Did you attend a seance?"

"No. But I've been dealing with these people for years. Joe and Delia were always generous to Wu, if you ask me, but they did it out of kindness, not obligation."

Behind him, at the table, he could see Wu's fists tighten. Must be painful to hear people deny your role in your greatest creation, over and over again. But it was going to get worse before it got better. "You represented Joe, but you never represented Wu, did you?"

"No. That would've presented a conflict of interest."

He agreed, but that wasn't his point. "So you have no relationship with Wu."

"I've never even spoken a complete sentence to him. Just greetings in the hallway here and there."

"You will not benefit if Wu receives some . . . or all . . . of the King Kaiju rights."

"I won't receive a commission on his royalties, no, of course not. I don't represent him."

"In fact, your commissions will be greater if my client loses this lawsuit, right?"

"I don't know." She couldn't resist a small smile. "I don't have a crystal ball."

"But you know this deal is potentially worth billions."

"So I keep hearing. Haven't seen any money yet, though. And if you're suggesting that I might lie or alter my story to get more money—forget it. I like money. Who doesn't? But I'm not going to lie for it. I like Delia, but she's not my only client. My reputation comes first. When one of my people is owed something, I will fight for them like a bull terrier. But I won't pretend I have a colorable claim when I don't. Life's too short."

"With too many bills to pay."

"Which is why people should practice self-care. Meditation. Even hypnosis." She smiled again. "Like it or not, life sucks. It's always hard and it's never enough. Money helps, but it's not worth ruining the one life you've been given."

Rarely in his career had he been thwarted so thoroughly by a witness. And she wasn't even particularly hostile. Just smart. He was never going to convince this jury she was lying out of greed. Time to try something different.

"You were involved in this case before now, right?"

"Yes."

"And you assisted the lawyer who previously represented Wu. Kevin Lieber. Before he came to an unfortunate end."

"Yes, I remember Kevin."

And you were in contact with Joe's previous lawyer, too, right?"

"Yes. I remember him too."

"You should." He took a deep breath. He was about to take a big swing. "Since you paid the man's legal bills."

All at once, the courtroom fell quiet. In Dan's experience,

this meant he'd managed to land a surprise. In one of the storage boxes from the previous litigation, Jenny found a photocopy of a cancelled check from this witness. He didn't know what it was for and there were several possibilities...

But what the hell. He went for it. Judging from her expression, he was right, so he plowed ahead. "How much did you pay Joe's lawyer?"

Her face seemed frozen. He could tell her mind was racing, trying to work out how best to play this. "I... don't... recall."

"Why did you pay him?"

He could see Kenzi contemplating an objection. But she was smart enough to know where this was going. She wouldn't be able to prevent it. All she could do was draw more attention to it.

The exhalation that preceded Sanderson's words suggested that she wasn't so much speaking as resigning. "Fine. Joe had no money. Delia had no money. That's how companies like Sidekick get away with this kind of crap. They out-money everyone else. On his own, Joe would've been a smear on the pavement. I gave him a shot."

Though not a shot that was successful, ultimately. "You financed the litigation. And in exchange..." His eyes narrowed. Her percentage was not enough to justify an investment like this. "They gave you a bigger piece of the pie."

The agent looked even more uncomfortable than she had before. That was encouraging. This might be the first time he'd said anything that caused her concern. "How much did that slice cost you?"

"I don't know. It wasn't a round sum."

"Which came to...?"

She sighed again. "About sixty thousand, before it ended."

"Is there a promissory note?"

After another long pause, she answered. "Yes. I drew it up myself. I agreed to pay his fees."

"And in exchange..."

"He agreed to give me an additional twenty-three percent of any funds I extracted from Sidekick or the movie studio. Over and above my usual commission."

Dan took a few steps back, as if staggering. "You have a direct financial interest in the outcome of this lawsuit."

"More indirect, really..."

"And you did not disclose it to the jury." He whipped around to glare at Kenzi, but he could see from the expression on her face that she was as surprised as everyone else. "What else haven't you revealed?"

Sanderson cleared her throat. "Joe didn't have any cash, but Delia had some bearer bonds."

Dan blinked. Seriously? Bearer bonds? In this day and age? Hard to put those in your E*Trade account. "And she gave them to you?"

"As security. She knew I'd have to do a lot of work and the deal wouldn't pay off for years. That was just... to tide me over. To hold in reserve."

Delia was constantly pleading poverty, but she was sitting on a bag of bearer bonds? Why wouldn't she have cashed them in herself, if she was so desperate to feed her son? "And you didn't think the jury would want to hear about this?"

The agent did not know what to say next. "I answered all your questions..."

"Did you receive a subpoena?"

"Yes."

"Did that *subpoena duces tecum* instruct you to produce any and all relevant documents pertaining to this lawsuit?"

"I don't think this directly relates to the lawsuit."

"That's not a decision for you to make. You should've produced the note. And I'm now making an oral motion that the missing document be supplied."

Kenzi rose. "This is the first I've heard about it, your honor.

But if there's a relevant note out there in this witness' possession, we will find it and produce it."

"Nice to hear, but it doesn't help me now." He turned back to the witness. "You deliberately withheld relevant evidence. Why?"

"The note isn't relevant. This lawsuit is over IP character rights. My little side deal doesn't affect that in any way."

"The jury is entitled to know if witnesses have a financial stake in the outcome before they start giving testimony. You presented yourself as an impartial witness, but the truth is, you're just as profit-oriented as the people you're testifying for. Maybe more so."

Kenzi rose. "Your honor, Mr. Pike is giving lectures, not asking questions."

True enough. "I move to strike all the testimony presented today by this witness. It was delivered under false pretenses. She is, in effect, a party opponent and failed to reveal her financial relationship to the litigation. Plus she apparently has relevant documents that have not been produced."

"We oppose," Kenzi replied. "We will produce that document as soon as I can lay my hands on it, but it won't speak to who is legally entitled under the relevant statutes to hold these IP rights."

Dan started to speak again, but the judge raised her hand to stop him. She took a few more moments, gathering her thoughts, before she spoke.

"First, let me assure all parties that the court takes this matter very seriously. It does appear that . . . important information may have been withheld, and we all know that fair and thorough discovery is a critical element of any fair trial." She frowned. "Then again, it has come out, so there's no permanent damage, assuming the note is produced expediently."

"It will be," Kenzi said quickly, though she was looking at the witness.

"The jury will be given the usual instructions at the conclusion of the trial informing them that, among other things, they can consider a witness' credibility, including their failure to be forthcoming, as they evaluate the case. And I think that covers the matter adequately. I would rather let the jury consider the witness' testimony than strike it from the record, which wouldn't strike it from the jurors' minds. Indeed, it might cause them to give it undue emphasis. So the motion is denied." She looked at Kenzi. "But I will expect to see that document. Tomorrow. Start of trial." She turned to Dan. "Any more questions?"

"Just a few." He would've been happy to go out on a big win. But if the judge wasn't granting his motion, he might as well continue. "It seems clear you were more involved with Headmark and Sidekick than we previously realized. Who have you spoken with at Sidekick?"

"No one."

"Not Jeanette Zimmerman? Curtis Swart?"

"No one."

"You made a deal with Sidekick without speaking to them?"

"There were lawyers involved."

"So your testimony before this jury, that very much wants to know if you can be trusted, is that you've never spoken to anyone at Sidekick?"

She craned her neck. He could see she felt the pressure. He had basically called her a liar and dared her to prove she wasn't still lying. "I . . . talked to a cover artist once."

"What was his name?"

"Neal O'Neill."

Seriously? He would've remembered if he'd heard that name before. But he noticed that Kenzi did not seem surprised at all. "And what was the reason for this chat?"

"Joe told me that O'Neill drew the early King Kaiju covers.

The first six issues, the original miniseries. I was trying to get some insight on what happened. So I could help Joe."

Something wasn't right. She's investigating a claim, so she visits one guy who isn't even in management. Why?

Looked like Garrett was getting another assignment.

Sanderson spoke again. "He's a nice man. Neal, I mean. Old school. Knows where all the bodies are buried." She laughed nervously.

Surely she didn't mean that literally . . .

"Did he know about your secret agreement with Joe?"

"Yes. That's why he wanted to talk to me."

Dan blinked. "Wait. He called you?"

"Right. Joe wasn't thrilled."

"Did you learn anything?"

"He just wanted to talk about the old days, the old covers. He's very proud of his work. He wanted covers that stood on their own, but also looked nice when grouped together, because they were meant to be released in rapid succession. He would've loved the modern comic world, where even mediocre comics get eighteen variant covers." She looked up and smiled. "Back then, it wasn't all about cash. It was a bunch of young comics-loving kids who just wanted to play in the sandbox, you know? And then you add big money, lawyers, publishers. And agents. And what started as a little bit of art and a lot of fun turns into . . ." She waved her hand around the courtroom. "This."

CHAPTER THIRTY-FOUR

Ultimately, Dan decided not to mention the brothels and hypnosis and such during his cross. He never favored that kind of tactic, so he wasn't going to use it when it wasn't necessary. This witness had already been impugned by her own secrecy far worse than he could do with sexy nonsense.

Dan waited patiently as Kenzi filled the morning with a long series of B-List witnesses. Maybe C-List. He wasn't criticizing her. She had to prove her case, which sometimes meant putting a witness on the stand to say something that's patently obvious. You have to get it on the record.

And so he listened. First up was another so-called expert, in this case a law professor who explained the recent Copyright Act and amendments and why Delia now had a chance to seize the rights to King Kaiju—though only if there was a finding that Joe had created or co-created the character. He also provided a brief history of the comics industry, plus a little about Hollywood, and how both had historically screwed writers at every possible opportunity.

He was not surprised when the next witness, Curtis Swart, claimed that the initial contract with Wu was a work-for-hire agreement—which would mean the copyright law revisions wouldn't apply and thus couldn't help him. He had reviewed all the files, brought the documents he planned to use, and seemed to be acting as a surrogate archivist.

Dan hoped he could use that during his cross.

"That's what we did in those days. There wasn't much money in this work, unless you owned Superman. Everyone else just got by. Even then, if anyone made money, it was the suits, not the artists." Swart shrugged. "Maybe that's wrong, I don't know. But that's how it was."

Dan nodded. "You've seen the endorsed check?"

"That's how it was done back then," Waits explained. "The rights contract was stamped on the back of the check. When you endorsed the check, you signed the contract."

"Did both of them sign the check?"

"No. Just Wu. My understanding is that he then gave half the money to Joe."

"And you later paid Wu for his stories."

"On a work-for-hire basis. He turned in a script, he got a check."

"And you didn't think you needed his signature on an employment agreement or anything?"

"Not particularly."

"So you claim it was a work-for hire arrangement, but you never executed a work-for-hire agreement. And you treated Wu like a creator or co-creator."

"As a favor to Joe. He and Joe had been friends for a long time and Joe agreed to give him credit. But there was never any legal entitlement. Joe has been generous. But we don't owe Wu anything."

"Are you being paid to testify today?"

"No. I'm being paid by Sidekick Comics as part of my usual compensation package. Nothing special for testifying."

"And coincidentally, you're promoting the official position of Sidekick Comics."

Swart smiled. "We own this character lock, stock, and barrel. We always have. Joe was the sole creator and he relinquished his rights, more than once, so we can license this character to a movie studio. But bottom line—we don't really care who created the character, and if we have to pay someone a little something to get this movie made, it's worth it. We just need the court to tell us who to pay."

"How much could this King Kaiju feature film be worth?"

He shrugged. "That's a big guessing game."

"Given the interest, there's no way you're going to lose money, right? Even if it's a terrible movie you'll make hundreds of millions. Like the Sonic the Hedgehog movies. Or the Mario Bros. flick."

"I would tend to agree with that statement."

"And if it's a good movie, the kind of thing fans watch over and over again, you could be looking at billions. You could beat out the Avengers for a new world's record."

He grinned. "We plan on it."

"So given that this is a low-risk, high-potential project... why not just give Wu his due?"

"I'm not the top decision-maker. But my understanding is that this is about precedent. And as a lawyer, you understand the importance of that."

"Would it be so bad? Allowing creators to share in the profits made from their creations?"

"Look, I acknowledge that the creator played an important role—but that's not the only important role. I think Sidekick is just as entitled as anyone else to profits."

"*All* the profits?'

"No one made Wu endorse that check."

"If he hadn't, you wouldn't have published their work."

"True. It's a devil's bargain. But Wu made it. And now he has to live with the fallout."

"Of course, you don't know what Wu was told when he endorsed that check. Because you weren't there."

"My father was."

Dan blinked. What?

"My dad was the original CEO of this company. He was the genius who took one look at King Kaiju and said, 'We're doing this.'"

"And screwed over the creators."

"My father was a good businessman and there's nothing wrong with that. Our entire family has benefitted from his financial acumen. He did what you're supposed to do. Find an asset you can buy cheap and build into something others are willing to pay for."

"Is that why Sidekick sent you to court today? The familial connection?"

Swart shrugged. "Maybe."

"Why not Neal O'Neill?"

It was a random shot. But he detected an almost immediate reaction when he said the name.

Swart cleared his throat. "Mr. Neill is no longer with the company. He retired some years ago. He'd been with the company... I don't know. A long time."

But he was present when King Kaiju debuted, right? Because he drew the covers for the first six issues."

"True."

Dan peered into his eyes, trying to pry out whatever was in there. "Was there some kind of dispute between O'Neill and Sidekick?"

"There was a... minor controversy. About the retention of original art. As you probably know, back in the day, comic companies retained those and threw them away or gave them away or whatever. No one thought they were valuable. Then we got comic book collectors and comic book conventions and suddenly artists were selling these art pages for top dollar. That changed everything. Huge fight in the '70s when Marvel wouldn't return Jack Kirby's art. He left Marvel for DC. Though they eventually reached an accommodation."

But let's talk about this case. "Sidekick wouldn't let O'Neill keep his original art?"

"Not from the seventies. He wanted stuff that went back decades and is now considered quite valuable."

"King Kaiju stuff?"

"Yes. The art boards for the first six issues, which today would be virtually priceless. My favorite was #6. You know, that's the one with the spunky kid kaiju who turns out to be his half-brother. Famous now, in comics circles."

"You couldn't come to agreement about the art boards. So you fired him."

"It wasn't about that."

"What was it about?"

Kenzi stood. He wasn't surprised. By her standards, she'd been patient. "Objection, your honor. Relevance. Fascinating for comic book collectors, I'm sure. But we're diving down a deep rabbit hole and I don't see that it relates to the issue of who has the rights to the character."

The judge nodded. "I tend to agree, Mr. Pike. Unless there's something more you haven't told us yet."

"This artist he's talking about is a potential witness, your honor. He's perhaps the only still-living non-party who was present when the original deal was made. But they haven't invited him to court. Wouldn't that make you suspicious?"

The judge tucked in her chin. "That's not the test. The test is whether the current testimony is relevant."

"The termination of a potential eyewitness is inherently suspect."

King Kaiju #6

"He wasn't terminated," Kenzi insisted. "He was . . . retired. And it was years ago. And it had nothing to do with the IP rights."

"According to her," Dan murmured.

The judge pondered another moment. "Mr. Pike, I'll let you continue. But don't drag it out. I want to see the connection. Soon."

"Understood." He turned back to the witness. "It wasn't mere retirement." He hoped. "Sidekick released O'Neill. Why?"

Swart frowned. It was evident he didn't want to proceed, but he had little choice. "It was believed . . ." Dan's head snapped to attention. When witnesses retreated to passive voice, they were always hiding something. " . . . that he had stolen art from the company archives."

"Like what?"

"Everything missing was his art."

"He took what you would not give him?"

"So we believed."

"Was there a police investigation?"

"No. We didn't report it."

"Didn't you say that art was valuable?"

"We wanted to avoid scandal. Bad PR could scuttle the movie deal. We chose to let him go and thus made sure it never happened again."

Awfully generous. And unlikely. Why not prosecute?

The light dawned a second later.

Because they didn't want to give him a megaphone. They were more likely to give him some cash and an NDA.

And if that were true, it led directly to another inescapable question.

What were they afraid he might say?

CHAPTER THIRTY-FIVE

As far as he could tell from the pretrial order—which Kenzi had already deviated from at least a dozen times—Ernie Ulrich was the last witness she planned to call. And that was worrisome. Because he knew a seasoned lawyer like kenzi would want to go out with a bang, not a whimper. So this testimony must be a potential blockbuster.

But how? As far as he could see, this kid had nothing to offer. He obviously wasn't around when the initial deal was made. He wasn't even around during the later negotiations. He undoubtedly loved his father and wanted to inherit from his mother, but that was no reason to put him on the witness stand. More like a reason to not put him on the witness stand. He was another obviously interested party.

And yet, there he was, looking a little nervous, but also sitting up straight, as if he wanted to make a good impression.

"Any idea why she's calling him?" he whispered quietly to Wu.

"None. That poor kid has nothing to do with this."

"Does he like you?"

"He should. Hell, I went to the hospital when he was born."

"Really?"

"It was a big deal. To them, anyway. They'd been trying to have kids for a long time."

"He must know something about the rights issue."

Kenzi started her direct with the usual questions, introducing Ernie to the jury in the gentlest possible way, skipping quickly over his history of brawling and his spotty employment record. She talked about his relationship with his father. She established that when he wasn't working, he indulged his hobbies, like reading and hunting. And, predictably, collecting comic books, especially those drawn by his father. She did note that he was not present during any of the legal negotiations, saving Dan the trouble. Or precluding Dan from scoring points by establishing that on cross.

"When did you first become aware of King Kaiju?"

"Oh, gosh. I don't know. That big masked dino has always been in my life. I used to have King Kaiju bedsheets." Ernie grinned. "When I was ten, my father gave me reprints of the first six issues of the original King Kaiju comic book. You know, the ones with coordinating covers?"

"By Neal O'Neill?"

"Exactly. Still considered the best in the series. Those are worth thousands of dollars today."

"Who chose the cover artist?"

"My dad. He thought the best comics had a guest cover artist. Gave it more energy, he thought, more originality. Different take on the same subject."

"Have you talked to Mr. O'Neill recently?"

"No. I understand he's made some kind of deal with Sidekick, so he's not talking to anyone."

"Did your father talk about King Kaiju?"

"Often."

"Ernie, I know your memory isn't perfect. You were young when much of this occurred. But I think it would be fair to give the jury some idea how your father felt about the matter, since . . . unfortunate recent events have precluded him from testifying on his own behalf." She stared at Dan as she said this, basically daring him to object.

"He felt he'd been robbed, first by Sidekick, then by the manga company." He looked up slightly. "And then by his oldest friend in the world."

"Did he ever show you anything relating to the early days of King Kaiju?"

Dan couldn't help but admire Kenzi. She was playing it safe —and smart. No reason to take big risks when you appear to be winning. She was doing her best to draw from Ernie's actual experiences, not hearsay, even though it might be admissible.

"He showed me the interior art pages for the early stories."

"What was the occasion?"

"He had just received some art from Sidekick after fighting for it for years. He wanted me to understand that this wonderful character embraced by millions was created by him. Him alone. And he wanted me to understand how much it hurt when Sidekick stole Kaiju from him."

"Him." She paused. "Just him?"

"My father always maintained that he was the sole creator of King Kaiju, in public and private."

"Did he ever talk about Wu's contribution?"

"Yes, and if you ask me, he was generous."

"How so?"

Ernie pondered a moment. "Like those original art pages I mentioned. He showed me the empty word balloons he drew, then explained that Wu would write the dialogue." He pauses. "Based upon the clearly visible notes my dad left for him in the margins."

"But the question today is not who wrote the dialogue. The question is who created the character."

"And the answer is, my dad. But way back when, it didn't

matter. I don't remember this being an issue until the copyright laws changed. I mean, neither of them was getting any money from Sidekick, so what did it matter? But of course, there was more to it than just King Kaiju."

Dan's head jerked up. Now what?

"What do you mean?" Kenzi asked.

"Well, you know . . . Wu dated my mother. For a time."

Kenzi arched an eyebrow. "Was this around the time you were born?"

"No, so don't get any soap opera ideas about Wu being my real father. He isn't. They dated long before. He wanted a splash page for the first issue with a beautiful scantily clad woman screaming in terror. So he hired a model who ended up being my mother, many years later."

Kenzi put a reproduction of the inside splash from the first issue of King Kaiju on the overhead screen. "Is this the illustration you referenced?"

"Yes. Can't you see the resemblance?"

The woman in the drawing did in fact resemble a younger Delia.

"So your dad drew her, but Wu dated her?"

"A bit. Back when she was working at Headmark. Didn't go far. I think he was more interested than she was. He carried a torch for her for a long time. May still, for all I know."

Dan could see what they were doing and he didn't like it a bit. Of course, he never liked anything he thought had been deliberately withheld during discovery.

"When did your father connect with her?"

"Years later. And that's important. She dated Wu when he was flush with King Kaiju cash. She dated my father when he was penniless. Didn't matter to her. She loved him. And she became the advocate he needed. The fighter who took on Big Comics to get the rights he deserved."

"You don't have any doubts about your father's claim?"

"None whatsoever. I've seen—I've—seen—" Ernie's voice choked. He paused and took several deep breaths. "I've seen how much that character meant to my dad. I've seen him, late at night, wracked with despair, crying. He was always so hard on himself!" Tears tumbled forth. "He was a wonderful man, a gentle soul, but if you talked to him long, you realized he had a very negative self-image. He felt that he'd only created two things of value in his entire life—King Kaiju and me—and these bastards stole Kaiju from him."

The judge pounded her gavel and admonished him for his language. Though quietly and without much gusto.

"When you use . . . that term, you're referring to the comics and movie companies, right?"

"Yes." Ernie looked up, tears still dripping from his face. "But mostly I mean Wu. My father treated him like a friend, cut him in on a potential bonanza—and he rewarded my father by trying to steal everything. First Wu tried to steal his future wife. Then his life's work. Wu was always so competitive. So jealous. He couldn't stand seeing my dad having any success, public or private. One thing to have corporate suits against you. An artist expects that. But you don't expect to be thrown to the wolves by your best friend. The person you've helped most."

He pressed his hand against his forehead. "My father suffered from clinical depression. He took medication and had it under control. But this Benedict Arnold was more than he could bear." He inhaled deeply, trying to steady his voice. "This former friend was the one who pushed him over the edge. Wu might as well have held the pistol and pulled the trigger." To everyone's surprise, Ernie rose to his feet, stretched out an arm and pointed. "He's the one who really killed my father! He's the murderer!"

Part Four
CHILDREN WILL LISTEN

CHAPTER THIRTY-SIX

Dan was grateful for a short break after the explosive climax of Ernie's testimony. He needed time to think. He was not at all sure cross-examination was advisable or that there was anything he could accomplish. A son loved his father and turned him into a saint. Sweet, though not unexpected. He was basically taking his mother's position, but with a vigor that might look grasping if it came from her. The jury would surely understand that this testimony was more based on a son's love for his father than any actual knowledge of the subject.

But if this was Kenzi's swing for the fences, he couldn't let it go unquestioned. And there was one aspect of this Big Surprise that particularly intrigued him.

"You say my client, Wu, dated your mother?" He'd asked Wu about it during the break.

"That's correct. Does he deny it?"

"No. He just doesn't think it has anything to do with this case. And neither do I."

Kenzi rose. "Objection. This is not closing argument. Much as we all wish it were."

The judge smirked. "Sustained."

"Let me restate that in the form of a question. Have you ever heard my client express any enmity toward your father?"

"I've barely spoken to him."

"So your answer is no."

"I guess."

"Did you ever hear your father suggest Wu was out to get him?"

Ernie shrugged. "Not in so many words. But he often talked about how he won my mom and Wu never got over it."

"Are you suggesting that . . . this whole lawsuit is about vengeance? A grudge match between two men who loved the same woman?"

"It's a grudge match between a man who created a character and won the woman, versus a bitter disgruntled man who did neither."

The kid wasn't budging. He decided to try a different angle.

"You're a comic book fan, right?"

"Not so much when I was a kid. Too much of it around, you know? I love King Kaiju because my daddy did. But I needed to find my own space. That's why I went into the theater."

"And later?"

"After I moved to LA, a lot of my adult friends were reading graphic novels, including some featuring King Kaiju. I thought that was all kid stuff. Boy, was I wrong. That's when I started collecting. I know an English Ph.D. whose doctoral thesis was a Derridean deconstructionist analysis of the King Kaiju origin and its relationship to postwar industrial Japan."

"How did that make you feel?"

"Proud. At first, I didn't tell anyone I had a connection to the character. Then I told one person. Next day, everyone on campus knew. I was suddenly a celebrity. Heck, I think it helped me get better parts in the plays we were doing."

"And King Kaiju still helps you attract attention."

"Occasionally."

"And you don't want to see that gravy train disappear, do you?"

Ernie pursed his lips. "You know, my mother is still relatively young. I won't inherit anything for decades." He smiled. "If anything is left. You're barking up the wrong tree."

"But you are an interested party."

"Remotely. You can play the long game. I have other plans for my life. Did I tell you I got a commercial?"

"I read about it. Local hardware store?"

"I'm a working actor."

"Right. Tell me, when you were re-discovering comic books, did you by chance hear of a character called Batman?"

Ernie pulled a face. "Of course I've heard of Batman. What do you take me for? He's one of the most successful characters in the history of comics."

"And for decades, this most valued character was credited to one man, right?"

"Bob Kane. I met him once. At a convention. Before he passed. He was pals with my dad."

"About eighty years of Batman comics credited Bob Kane as sole creator. Kane's father had a lawyer, so unlike your father and Wu, he was better protected."

"Wish my dad had his lawyer."

"I do too. But my point is, for decades, until his original agreement expired, Kane always got sole credit. When people talked about Batman, they said he was created by Bob Kane." Dan held his breath for a dramatic pause. "But he wasn't."

Ernie appeared puzzled. "He wasn't?"

"Kane may have come up with the name and concept of a man who dressed like a bat to fight crime, but the original writer, Bill Finger, played a huge role in the creation. Some would say the primary role. He designed the costume, the gadgets, came up with the tragic backstory, wrote the adventures. But he didn't get credit. For decades. DC acknowledges this omission, which is why every Batman comic now contains the credit: Batman created by Bob Kane with Bill Finger."

"And your point is?"

"For a long time, comics primarily gave credit to artists, rarely writers. The creators of Superman, Siegel and Shuster, are a notable exception. But there was a tendency to focus on the artist."

"Until Stan Lee came along."

"Exactly. My point is—the fact that Wu didn't always get credit in the comics or from other people in the business does not prove he didn't create the character, does it?"

"I guess not."

"There's only one person here who was present at the time of the creation and is still alive." He glanced back at his client. "And I think it's about time we talked to him again." He headed back to his table. "Your honor, I—"

"He threatened to kill my father." Ernie cut him off midsentence.

Dan pivoted slowly. The standard play would be to move to strike, then sit down. But the jurors had heard it. They would not be happy if they didn't get to learn more. "Could you be more specific?"

"Wu. Him." He pointed again. "The man who tried to take my father's greatest achievement from him. And also tried to steal his wife. And when he couldn't get her voluntarily . . . he showed up with a gun."

Dan glanced back at his client. Wu appeared just as confused as he.

"When was this?"

"Just a few weeks ago. The 15th. I'll never forget it. He looked insane."

Wu? "Your mother didn't mention this during her testimony."

"She wasn't there. I was. And he had murder in his eyes. He

left when I showed up. But if I hadn't been there, he'd have shot my father dead. I'm certain of it."

"Your honor—"

"Instead he threw down the gun and walked away, cursing as he went. That man is not right in the head. He's not just losing it. He's becoming dangerous. That's where my father got the gun he used on the courthouse steps. And you want to reward Wu? For destroying a good man's life?" Once more, Ernie rose to his feet. "I will stand up for my father. I will not allow his legacy to be stolen by some demented loser who's still stinging because he didn't get the girl. Who knows—maybe he'll go after my mother next!"

CHAPTER THIRTY-SEVEN

AFTER THAT OUTBURST, THE JUDGE THOUGHT IT WOULD BE BEST IF they took another short break. Dan had no problem with that. Hard as he'd tried to break Ernie, he hadn't, and he'd opened the door to a dramatic tirade that might well have impacted some of the jurors. Jury members were notoriously difficult to read because sometimes, like contestants just before their Final Jeopardy answer is revealed, they make a deliberate effort to remain stone-faced.

He stepped outside and placed a quick call to Garrett, who confirmed that the police had still not been able to trace the gun Joe used on the courthouse steps. He asked Garrett to do something else. Much as he hated to go down an unmistakably sleazy avenue, at this point, he had no choice.

While he contemplated whether he needed another jolt of the courthouse's notoriously bad coffee, Kenzi emerged from the courtroom. She had a big grin on her face, the surest indicator that she thought she was winning.

She walked right up to him. "How you feeling, esteemed opponent?"

"Not as happy as you."

"I have every reason to be happy."

"I assume that means you've finally lip-locked with your co-counsel."

"Excuse me. That would be totally unprofessional." She paused. "Course, there's a lot you can do without actually lip-locking. But my current delight is related to the case. Which I just won."

"Ernie wasn't as devastating as you seem to think. He doesn't know anything about the IP issues. And he's obviously interested in seeing his mom win the Kaiju rights."

"Yeah, but he put passion into this mess, not just dollars and cents. Not just whining about the sins of the past. He cares. He wants to preserve his father's legacy. The jury will remember that." She looked at him levelly. "Just surrender. Acknowledge that Joe is the sole creator. It'll will be less painful for you."

"If I just give you everything? Yes, I suppose that would be simpler than . . . you know . . . being a lawyer. I don't think you've already won. I'm calling Wu back as a rebuttal witness. He's the only witness who matters. Because he's the only one who was there when the deal was made."

"I don't think the jury likes your guy. He seemed wimpy. Like he has a chip on his shoulder. And he was out to get his old friend."

She wasn't totally wrong. "There's bad blood on all sides. That's all the more reason to end this. They might patch things up. Wu and Delia and Ernie could go on a King Kaiju Farewell Tour. Get interviewed on Good Morning America. Party with Taylor Swift. Garrett could wear his cardigan."

"I don't see that happening."

"This might be just what Ernie needs to give some impetus to his acting career."

"Now you really sound desperate."

Dan glanced up and down the long hallways. The rest of his team and Wu appeared to be elsewhere. People in suits carrying briefcases crisscrossed the hallways, everyone busy, everyone trying their best to take care of their charges. So many lives, so many crises.

Maybe there were more important things in the world than who got rich off a cartoon dinosaur.

Dan raised his chin. "In my mind . . . we do what we do . . . because we're trying to help people. That's why I became a lawyer. So I could help those who can't help themselves."

"And now you're losing your fervor."

"Now I'm realizing . . . we're not helping anyone here. These people were like a family. And we're tearing the family apart. Even worse than this nasty capitalistic world has already done. Friends. Parents. Sons. The longer this goes on, the greater the pain."

"All the more reason to push to a verdict."

"Which will resolve nothing." Dan slid his backpack off his shoulders and tossed it on a bench. "This bag is full of research on copyright law and let me tell you, it is far from cut and dried. Even after the 1981 overhaul the Act needed an overhaul. And then another one. It doesn't matter who wins this stage of the litigation. The other party will appeal. And then appeal to a higher court. And then when Congress changes the law again, we'll all come back. I mean—when does it end?"

"When one party gives up or runs out of money."

"That's not the way it should be. All-out war is not always the best approach."

"Hey, I tried to get you to settle."

"By offering a deal you knew we couldn't take. Wu will never relinquish the rights to his character."

"We feel the same way. I've been instructed by Delia that from this point forward, I am to reject any offer that gives Joe anything less than one-hundred-percent creator credit." She paused. "Though I might be able to talk her into a small . . . subsidy. In exchange for not contesting."

"If we continue like this, everyone will be hurt."

Kenzi pivoted. He assumed she was off to the vending machines to score some Cheetos. "I'll ask her. But don't get your hopes up. And we will not agree to a continuance under any circumstance, if that's what you were thinking. Not today, not ever. No delay of game."

"Not what I wanted at all."

"Good. Are you ready to let Ernie off the stand?"

"No. I want a few more words. Which I really wish I could avoid."

Kenzi winked. "Sucks to suck." She waved a little and headed down the hallway.

Dan wanted to be mad at her, but he wasn't. He knew in her situation he would probably behave the same way. You don't settle when you think you're winning. Unless someone offers a pot of gold. Which he hadn't.

But there was much more going on here than they realized, so much more at play than a fictional character. He was certain of it.

But how? It was like he was staring at all the right dots, but he couldn't quite make the connections.

And sadly, he didn't have time to go all cryptic crossword on it, because the bailiff was waving at him from the courtroom doors.

Time to get back to work.

CHAPTER THIRTY-EIGHT

GARRETT TEXTED DAN EVERYTHING HE NEEDED AND HE PRINTED it in the judge's chambers (with permission), so he was ready to roll when Ernie retook the witness stand.

"Do you recall a previous occasion when you spoke to Bob Lydek?"

"Yeah. He was okay. I liked him."

"Do you remember the . . . more unusual part of the discussion?"

"When he offered me the pepper-flavored chewing gum?"

"No. When you talked about sex toys."

For the first second, the courtroom fell dead silent. But during the second second, Kenzi erupted. "Objection! Relevance!"

"Sadly, it is relevant, your honor. I can assure you I wouldn't go there otherwise."

The judge waived them up to the bench so they could argue outside the hearing of the jury. She covered her microphone with her hand.

Judge Parkwood looked at him sternly. "I don't mind a little spice in my trials. But this seems beyond the pale."

"I agree," Kenzi said. "Your honor, I'm bringing an oral motion, pursuant to Rule 3.8 of the Rules of Professional Conduct. Counsel is deliberately trying to humiliate the witness by introducing irrelevant matters."

"I'm not," Dan replied. "I hope the court knows I would never do that. If you'll give me three minutes, the relevance will be apparent."

The judge frowned, rapping her nails on the bench. "I don't like this at all. Even if it is relevant, it sounds sleazy."

"Because it is sleazy," Kenzi echoed.

"Don't defame your own witness. He's the one frequenting Joanne's Adult Toy Shop."

"See?" Kenzi leaned across the bench. "See what he's going to do?"

Judge Parkwood raised a hand. "I will hold the objection in abeyance. And the motion. And give Mr. Pike his three minutes." This time, she raised a pencil. "But if you haven't convinced me this is relevant by then, I will come down on you with the harshest possible sanctions."

"Understood." He knew he was on thin ice. And was starting to think the judge did not care for him too much.

He returned to the witness. "Ernie, isn't it true that you frequent a place on Lakeshore Drive called Joanne's Adult Toy Shop?"

His face immediately reddened. He glanced at Kenzi, but she shrugged. Yes, you have to answer the damn question.

"Sure. I've seen it."

"And you've bought . . . toys there, right?"

"Mmm . . . maybe."

"Yes or no?"

"Fine. Yes. Nothing wrong with that."

Then why was his face redder than a strawberry? "And on August first, you purchased . . ." He glanced at the receipt. "The Svakom Slime Eye."

He saw the judge wince.

Ernie's voice was so muffled as to be almost undetectable. "Yes."

"I'm not sure if the court is familiar with that particular product. Could you explain what it is?"

"I... don't know exactly how to describe it."

"I do. It's a"—he glanced down at his notes—"a dildo with an integrated camera so you can take and stream video while..." He cleared his throat. "... while it is in use." He looked up, clearing his throat. "Does that sound accurate?"

"I guess."

The judge looked supremely uncomfortable, and Kenzi looked as if she were about to explode, but he pressed ahead. "I confess, you've educated me. I didn't realize sex toys had been added to the internet of things. But anything that's online can be hacked. Can even be a gateway to other devices on the same network."

Kenzi's finger-tapping stopped abruptly. Now she understood where this was going.

"It is an impressive device," Dan continued. "Wi-Fi. Webcam. AI-driven biofeedback. Have you used it?"

Ernie mumbled. "Once or twice."

"With... friends?"

"Not exactly."

"Have you loaned it to anyone?"

"God no."

"So the only person who's ever used it is you."

"Right."

"And here's the interesting thing. This sophisticated little device records all kinds of info about your location, usage, how it's used, who it's used on..." He waved his arms. "Just a cornucopia of data."

He saw a very irritated Kenzi rising. Was his three minutes up? Better get to the point.

"Including time-and-date stamps indicating when it was... in service. Have you ever used it outside your home?"

"Of course not."

"Did you realize those records can be hacked?"

Kenzi rose. "Your honor, is counsel suggesting that he hacked into private records? That's illegal."

"Not necessarily." Dan raised a finger. "There are no proprietary notices on the toy's website. Barely a firewall, I hear, and the password was '8888888.' I mean, come on, these people aren't even trying."

The judge nodded. "I'll allow it. If laws have been broken, Ms. Rivera, you are free to approach the district attorney. Proceed."

Dan returned to his table and withdrew a packet of papers from his backpack. "Your honor, this is a record of the device's use during the month in question. The most notable part is the record for August eighteenth, because it clearly shows that the device was in operation. And since Ernie says he never loaned it out or went anywhere with it, he was at home—at the exact same time that he supposedly witnessed an encounter at his father's house where my client was waving a gun around. An encounter, I might add, that no one else seems to have witnessed or even heard about."

"My dad witnessed it!" Ernie cried.

"Or at any rate, he's not around to deny it. You made the whole thing up, didn't you?"

"No!"

"Look at the printout. You weren't at your father's place at the time you specified."

"Well... maybe I got the dates confused."

"You said you would 'never forget' that day. And now you can't even remember what day it was?"

"No, it happened, but—"

"But you weren't there. You couldn't have been."

"No! I mean, okay, I admit it, I wasn't there, but my dad told me about it."

He gave the jury a long look. "So now you claim you were passing off hearsay as personal experience."

"No, I just—"

"Or to put it more simply, you committed perjury. Your honor, I ask that this witness' testimony be stricken from the record and furthermore, that the jury be instructed to disregard it."

Kenzi lit up like a firecracker. "Your honor, there's no need for that. The witness has gotten confused, and who wouldn't, with counsel throwing things at him he couldn't possibly absorb."

"You're embarrassing yourself. He got caught lying."

"Did it occur to you that he might've confused the dates?"

"Yes, until he confessed that he never saw the alleged event."

"Doesn't mean it didn't happen."

"Nor does it prove that it did. You proffered false testimony. You've got problems, and I won't sit still while—"

The judge held up her hands. "Stop. This is like watching an old married couple bicker. In fact, this whole case feels like that. This is what I'm gonna do. Based upon the new evidence, obtained in the most disgusting way possible, it appears this witness lied. However, I will only strike the portion of his testimony relating to the alleged meeting with Mr. Wu threatening him with a gun. I might add that, had you done this the right way, Ms. Rivera, you might've gotten that in on a hearsay exception. But I can't do that now, because your witness lied and said he was there when he wasn't. So I will strike that part and the jury will be instructed to disregard it. Given the witness' importance to this case, I will not at this time strike the rest of his testimony, though I will be open to a later motion to do that, especially if there are additional indications that his testimony was false in any way. Is my ruling clear?"

They both nodded. The judge did not appear to be in the mood for an extended discussion.

"Anything more for this witness?"

Kenzi shook her head.

"Any more witnesses?"

"No. We rest."

"Good. Then we're done for the day." Judge Parkwood pointed her gavel. "Mr. Pike, you will call your first rebuttal witness tomorrow morning at nine am sharp. Will you be ready?"

He'd better be. This was the last chance they were going to get to turn this case around. "I will."

CHAPTER THIRTY-NINE

THE TIME WAS JUST PAST NINE P.M., DAN'S EYES WERE WIDE OPEN. He wondered if this was the courtroom equivalent of Fitzgerald's dark night of the soul. The endless black before what would likely prove to be the most important day of the case. And the final one.

He'd done all that could be done. He should rest, but he was too tense to slumber. So he paced around the living room, probably trampling a circular hole around the sofa. For some reason, he felt more concerned about this case than he had some of the homicides he'd handled.

Maybe it was the expression he saw every time he looked into Wu's eyes.

Wu knew this was his last shot. Whatever opportunities future laws might yield, he wouldn't be around to enjoy them.

Or maybe it was the expression Dan saw every time he looked into his own eyes. He glanced at a mirror hanging in the entryway over the breakfront. He'd stared into those eyes many times and usually found something wanting. Right now, though, he just looked tired. Okay, he wasn't quite as young as he'd once been... but there was something more. Was it the case? Maria? The imminent arrival of his first child?

He peered deeper into the mirror. Those brown eyes seemed more than just concerned. They seemed... lonely?

He was in the best relationship of his life. He was about to become a father. He was back in the saddle, trying lawsuits again. What was missing?

Dan grabbed his laptop and took it to the most remote part of their home, a garage-adjacent storage room where he kept most of his kitesurfing equipment. He turned on a dim light, sent a text on his phone, then opened a Zoom window.

A few minutes later, Ben Kincaid appeared on the screen.

"Mr. K," Dan said. "Thanks for the last-minute conference. I know how late it is."

"First of all, you don't need to call me 'Mr. K' anymore. My cover is blown." Ben was in his early sixties. His hair was thinner and gray, though he still looked too skinny and baby-faced for his age. Even the wrinkles didn't make him look old. "Second, don't worry about the time. I was awake. Working out a finale for this music show I'm putting together. What's up? The case?"

"Of course." Ben was technically his boss, since he was the head of the entire Last Chance Lawyers network. As Ben had confided during a recent adventure, his mother left him a bundle, but given how it was made by his father, who literally disinherited him—he didn't want to spend it on himself. So he created something wonderful, something the country needed badly and staffed it with people like Dan. The lawyer currently crying on his shoulder. "Not sure what to do. I've got a tough opponent on the other side."

Ben smiled slightly. "Kenzi Rivera. I know. I've had my eye on her for years."

"You gonna recruit her?"

"I would love to. But since she's currently the managing

partner in a huge firm, she doesn't need me." He paused a moment. "Yet. She's very talented."

"And all the evidence seems to be against us."

"Then you need to find some more evidence."

"Easy to say." He sighed. "I'm worried about Wu. This is his last chance. He's been mistreated and unacknowledged his entire life. A loss would devastate him."

To his surprise, Ben smiled.

"Did I say something funny?"

"No. But I remember the punk hotshot lawyer I first brought into this group, the one who thought a win was any case where he got a big fee. Now I see a lawyer who is scared to death—"

"I don't know that I'd go that far . . ."

"Scared not because he has a big fee at stake. But because he loves another human being and doesn't want to disappoint him." His smile grew even bigger. "You've come a long way, Dan."

"Thanks, but that doesn't help me."

"Did I ever tell you about the time I took on the white supremacist group in Arkansas?"

Oh God. Grandpa was going to start telling his stories again. "I think maybe you covered that while we were stuck in the New Mexican snowstorm."

"Heck of a thing. Christina and I were camping and we got dragged into a firestorm. One of the supremacists was accused of murder and no one would represent him. So I did."

Dan went bug-eyed. "You represented a white supremacist?"

"Yes, that was Christina's reaction, too. But everyone is entitled to a fair trial, and this man wasn't going to get one unless I stepped in. So I did."

"What's your point? Your case was worse than my case?"

"No. My point is, I almost bungled the case due to my own blindness. I'd developed an attachment that was . . . distracting me. If Christina hadn't been there, a great injustice might've occurred."

"Still not quite getting the point..."

Ben leaned into the camera. "I was trying to do it all myself. But that's never smart. I had good people." He took a breath. "And so do you."

Yes, of course he had a team. What was he saying?

"Are you saying I should spend more time talking to Jenny? She knows all about comic books."

Ben almost spoke, but before he could, a female voice emerged from the background. "Don't get him started on comic books!"

"That would be my wife." Ben chuckled. "I think she's ready for me to come to bed."

"*Long past!*"

Ben just smiled. "God, I love that woman." He turned back to the camera. "I loved comics when I was a kid. I used to scramble to this place called Down Memory Lane near Nichols Hills. Had my favorite artists and writers. Collected my favorites. *Sugar and Spike.* I loved those silly tykes." He looked up. "Didn't I hear that one of the witnesses mentioned a cover artist?"

Ben was better informed than he let on. "Yes. Neal O'Neill. I was going to send Garrett to interview him, but there seems little point. The trial is about to end and he's signed an NDA with Sidekick. He won't talk to us."

"You need to talk to him immediately."

"Just cold call him?"

"Phone calls never produce anything. He's not far from you."

"Now?"

"OrlandoCon. There's an opening reception for VIPs tonight before the main conference starts tomorrow." He clicked a few more buttons on his laptop, then smiled. "And he's signing at an afterparty till midnight." He looked up again. "How long is the drive to Orlando?"

Dan shrugged. "Hour and a half. Maybe less, this time of night."

Ben smiled like the Cheshire cat. "Go." And then he disconnected the line.

Thus terminating the conversation. Where were his keys?

As if on cue, his very pregnant partner emerged from the hallway wearing adorable loose-fitting flannel maternity pajamas.

"Hey, daddio." Her eyes were dark and heavy-lidded. "Thought you were heading for bed."

"I have to run an errand first."

She came closer and placed her hand on the back of his neck. "You need sleep."

"I'll be fine."

"Dan, Wu's testimony is crucial. You know this already. Are you even planning to call other rebuttal witnesses?"

"No. Assuming there are no more unexpected developments or murders between now and then."

"You might be doing your closing tomorrow too. You need sleep."

"I will sleep. Promise. But about that closing..."

"Yes?"

What was it Ben said? *You have good people.* "I think you should close."

She pulled a face unlike anything he'd seen in the years he'd known her. "Is this a joke? I never even wanted to enter a courtroom."

"But you have. And you were sensational every time."

"Says you. Competent at best, I would've said."

"I think it's a good strategic move."

She gave him a long, penetrating look. "Are you trying to get jury sympathy by parading a very pregnant soon-to-be-momma out there?"

"No, no." Well, that wasn't the whole reason. "But I think

having a woman sum it all up might be good for balance. The judge and eight of the jurors are female. The opposing lawyer and her primary client are female. I know not everyone thinks along sexist lines. But I also know some women are more likely to trust another woman."

"And some women are other women's worst enemies. Especially if the woman seems 'strong.' Which if it's a woman, we call 'strident.'"

"You know how to stay calm and still make your point."

"I won't be generating any courtroom theatrics. I might go into labor."

"That would be dramatic. But a little soap opera. Let's not do that."

"Then why—?" She paused again, and after a moment, she took his hand and they both sat on the sofa. "Dan . . . are you scared?"

He replied, though he did not answer. "I've never handled a case like this. All my instincts are off. I don't know what tone to strike, what . . ."

She squeezed his hand. "What is it really?"

He looked back at her. His voice dropped to a whisper. "I think we're going to lose."

Maria didn't blink. Or argue. "You've lost before."

"Some of them deserved to be lost. This one doesn't."

"You think Wu is telling the truth. That he created King Kaiju?"

"I'm certain of it."

"Then the jury will get that certainty from you. They'll feel the truth. It'll radiate in every word you say."

"Truth? From me? I'm a defense attorney."

"Who is honest to the core. They'll get that."

"No." He tenderly put her hand aside. "They're already tired of me. They'll welcome the change of pace."

"Or they'll wonder why someone who's never spoken to them before is handling the critical summation."

"No, you need to do this. And I want Jenny up front, advising. She should be doing more. For that matter, I don't give Garrett half the credit he deserves. I think . . . maybe . . . I'm not very good at delegating. I need to take better advantage of the fact that . . . I'm not all alone in the universe."

"I don't know . . ."

He exhaled slowly. "Think about it at least, okay?"

"If it helps you." She pressed a hand against his chest. "I'm more interested in what's going on inside your head. Can you explain it to me?"

"Yes. Soon as I figure it out. You'll be the first to know."

CHAPTER FORTY

Cost him a small fortune, but Dan managed to scalp a VIP ticket from a disgruntled fan. He guessed there were maybe two hundred or so people milling about, most in costume. He knew there would be far more tomorrow when the main convention opened, but that didn't matter. He'd come to talk to one person alone.

He threaded his way down Corridor B into the room designated Artists Alley. He brushed past a stunning Wonder Woman, a decent Scarlet Witch, and several beefed up males who interested him considerably less. Some of the costumes left little to the imagination. Some seemed so professional they could've come from a Hollywood set, even though he knew they had been created by talented cosplayers.

He knew some still made fun of people who dressed up for conventions, but Dan thought it was kind of wonderful. Here was another distinct group of people habitually belittled or dismissed because of their interests. But those interests created an empire. Conventions. Collections. Cosplay. Superhero shows. And he admired people who had the courage to wear these costumes, some quite lovely, that they made to transform themselves into fictional characters, not out of need or greed, but out of love.

At the far end of the corridor, he spotted an elderly man sitting behind a six-foot table. His was not as well decorated as the others. No looming posters, no video screen. Simply a tent card revealing his name and some original art scattered across the table.

He did not appear to be in great health. His sweater looked like it came from a different decade and even had a moth hole on the shoulder. The stains on his fingers and teeth told Dan he still smoked. The pallor of his skin and the bags beneath his eyes bespoke the weight of the world. He did not look happy, but given how little attention he was attracting, that was understandable.

"Neal O'Neill?"

The man looked up at him. "That's my name. I think my mother hated me."

"How's the conference going?"

He shrugged. "I shouldn't be here. I let Murray talk me into it. Big mistake."

"These fans love comic creators."

"They love Jim Lee. Brian Michael Bendis. Tom King. They don't know who I am. The only reason I was invited was all this legal hullabaloo surrounding King Kaiju."

Dan stiffened slightly. "You been following that lawsuit?"

"Not at all." Dan breathed a sigh of relief. "This industry is great to some of the people working today, but it treated its founding artists like trash. No one cares about us. Even the collectors. They'll run across the country looking for a Near Mint issue of Baby Kaiju #147. But they're oblivious to the needs of the creators. They pay thousands, even millions, for old comics while the people who made them are barely getting by on Social Security."

"But still, it must be great to see that people still love the character."

"They should bury the character. Seal him in a crypt and bury him beneath the sea."

Dan did a double-take. "What?"

"Think about it. Literally no creator associated with this monster is profiting from it. No one's getting much of anything except corporate execs who couldn't create a good character if their lives depended upon it. It's a dirty business. I can't take any pleasure from it when it's been so hard on so many friends." He glanced up. "Forgive me saying so, but you look a little out of place. This your first comic convention?"

"No. I went to the San Diego Comic-Con."

"The big time. What do they get, like 150,000 people each year?"

"More. I was there for a smaller spring gathering, though it was still huge. But I have to confess—I was there for work."

"Too bad. Did you fall in love with comics?'

"No. But I did learn who Martian Manhunter is."

"That's a start."

Dan browsed through the art on the table, some original boards used to print comics, but also simpler drawings he'd made in advance to sell. And they weren't selling.

Perhaps it was time to play straight with the man. "Look, you know that lawsuit you mentioned? I'm one of the attorneys. Daniel Pike. I represent Kazuhiko Wu."

O'Neill's face brightened. "That's wonderful. I love that man. We worked on comics together. With Joe, of course. Do you think he's going to win?"

"Honestly? It doesn't look good."

All at once, Neal lurched forward and grabbed Dan's jacket. "Don't let that woman control King Kaiju!"

"You mean Delia?"

"I mean that moneygrubbing old bat who played both those boys for a fool."

"I'm sensing you're not her greatest fan."

"Worst thing that ever happened to comics. She thwarted several sensible settlements that could've resolved this a long time ago."

Interesting. "You drew the covers for the first six issues of the original King Kaiju miniseries."

"True."

"I'm no expert, but my friend Jenny thinks you're awesome. For that matter, so does Joe's son. And I just talked to a . . . colleague who mentioned . . ." He thought for a moment. "Did you do any variant covers?"

"No. Wish I had. That particular money grab hadn't been invented yet."

"But you drew the first six."

"Yes. We conceived them all at once. They were already trying to sideline Wu. I always worried about what Wu thought of the final covers because he wasn't allowed to tell me."

"He loves them. Almost as much as he loves King Kaiju."

"I hope so."

"Give it to me straight. Who created King Kaiju?"

"I signed an NDA. I can't answer that question."

"Come on. I could subpoena you."

"That would be a stupid move. I won't break the agreement."

"Then just tell me. Off the record."

"Off the record? Your client created King Kaiju. Hasn't he already told you that?"

"Yes. But others have offered differing opinions."

"Take it from me. He's the guy. Joe made significant contributions, especially to the character's costume. But Wu was the creator."

Dan gave him a firm look. "I need you to come to court tomorrow and say exactly that."

The King Kaiju miniseries issues 1-6

"I can't."

"I'll talk to the people running this convention and—"

"You don't understand me. I can't. Literally. Cannot. Part of my settlement with Sidekick. It not only covers our dispute. It specifically forbids me from talking about King Kaiju's creators."

"They bought you off."

"Yeah, but if they hadn't, I'd be on a street corner somewhere holding a tin cup." He gestured toward the table. "They even gave me back some of my original art. Not all of it, nothing really valuable, but something. I survived." He shook his head. "But I sure as hell can't show up in a courtroom in a highly publicized case saying what I've been forbidden to say. And I don't think the court would force me to violate a prior agreement."

Dan would have to make a showing of extreme need. And even though his case was going down the dumper, he probably couldn't meet that test. He couldn't even argue that Neal's testimony was unique, since he was essentially saying the same thing Wu said. Kenzi would argue that it was cumulative evidence and too late in the game. He would have to argue that Kenzi did something unexpected during her case that only Neal can address. And what exactly would that be? "Do you know anyone else? Still around from the old days?"

"Not many left, I'm afraid. I don't know anyone else who worked on Kaiju."

"Help me."

"I cannot speak."

"Then . . . give me some other way to prove Wu was the creator."

A slow smile spread across his face. "I might be able to help you there. But you have to understand about comic books. Do you?"

"Here's the deal. You tell me what you know. I will not identify you as my source, so you won't appear to have violated your NDA. And as a display of gratitude . . ." He pulled out his wallet. "I'm going to buy every piece of art you have here."

Neill's eyes ballooned. "All of it?"

"Yeah. You can go home early."

"That's a lot of art. It's gonna cost you."

"It's worth it." For the first time tonight, he was starting to feel good. "I know a comics lover who will treasure your art like it should be treasured. What do you say?"

Neal reached under the table and withdrew reproductions of the covers of the first six issues of King Kaiju. "Let me show you something you might not have noticed. Something no one has noticed. Until now."

CHAPTER FORTY-ONE

Dan entered the courtroom feeling as if he were sauntering into the OK Corral. This was the final showdown. Even if the trial didn't conclude, after today's testimony, it would be over. One way or the other.

Kenzi stood at the other end of the nave. Once their eyes locked, she pantomimed a fast-gun shootout.

Yup. Same exact feeling. They both knew this was the last hurrah, one way or the other.

As he scanned the courtroom, he started to feel as if this was the final chapter in an Agatha Christie novel. All the key players appeared to be assembled in the courtroom. Everyone they'd talked to, everyone on the witness lists. Even Bob Lydek and the literary agent. Lydek might feel some obligation, given what happened to his assistant. But some of the others had no reason to be here. He remembered what he thought as a kid, every time he watched an episode of Perry Mason. Why would all those guilty people who end up confessing come to the courtroom in the first place?

Maybe they all had the same feeling. This was the final act.

And they wanted to see what happened before the final curtain fell.

Maria came in with Jenny, both carrying mounds of paperwork. Jenny wore a long brown dress that fit her perfectly. "Jenny, I want you to sit at counsel table with us."

Jenny held up her hands. "I do not feel good about that."

"About what?"

"You know. Me. Looking like...I do."

"I think you look terrific. Your dress brings out the brown in your eyes." He jerked his head toward Maria. "I'm allowed to say that, right?"

Maria grinned. "I'm not threatened."

Jenny shook her head. "Bad enough to be Black. Worse to show up dressed . . . you know."

"I have no problem with it."

Jenny came close and whispered. "This courtroom is in Florida. And I'm trans. If they want to ban books about me, how are they going to feel about me being in the courtroom?"

"If anything, they should admire how well you get around in those heels. God knows I couldn't do it."

"Or me," Maria added. "Dan's converted me. I'm a complete sneakerhead now."

"Our case is precipitous enough," Jenny insisted. "You can't take chances. Those jurors don't post everything about themselves on Facebook. Some may think I'm too 'woke.'"

"Most jurors can put their personal prejudices aside and judge a case on its merits."

"Most. Not all. Why take a risk? There's no good reason why—"

"There is. I need you."

Jenny's face seemed to melt. "You . . . need me?"

"I need your expertise. You know the comics world better than anyone else on earth."

"Well . . . true."

"And now that I've been to two comic cons, I know there's more involved than I will ever understand. Please stay."

"I don't know . . ."

"And I have some great intel for you. Has to do with the first six issues of King Kaiju. If you—"

"You mean the ones with the squiggles? The ornamental design that doesn't relate to anything?"

"Yes." He placed his hand on her shoulder. "You're our ace in the hole."

"Oh, stop."

"It's true. Since we got this case, I've been wondering what made it so important that Ben insisted we handle a civil case. Now I get it. Sure, he wanted to prevent Wu from being ripped off." He paused. "But I think maybe he was also doing it for you."

Jenny raised her hand slowly and placed it against her heart. "For me?"

"He knows what you're going through. I don't just want you sitting at our table. I want you to put Wu back on the stand. You question him. You'll be able to steer him much better than I could."

She started to resist. He squeezed her shoulders. "Will you please do this? For me?"

Her eyes welled up and eventually she shined the sweetest smile he'd ever seen in his life. "Anything for my Aquaman."

DAN WATCHED CAREFULLY AS JENNY REVIEWED THE WITNESS outline (which she had prepared). He knew she was nervous, but everyone was nervous their first time in court, and these circumstances were more difficult than most. He also watched the jury. He detected some curiosity about the staffing changes, but no outrage.

He whispered into Wu's ear. "You okay with this?"

He nodded. "I like her."

He was surprised. "May I ask why?"

Wu thought for a moment. "You and Maria are excellent attorneys. You've taken good care of me. You love your work." He tilted his head toward Jenny. "But she loves comics. She's my kind of people."

THE FIRST FEW MINUTES OF WU'S REBUTTAL TESTIMONY WERE supremely non-controversial, so Jenny was able to ease into it. Find her footing. Her rhythm. Since he had already been on the stand once, they could skip most of the preliminaries and plow into the key question still in dispute: Who created King Kaiju?

"You explained before that you came up with the idea in the late sixties, inspired in part by *The New Apocalypse* and Marvel comics. Since your creator status is now in dispute, can you provide more detail? How did you come up with the idea?"

"I was working about eighteen hours a day, creating content for a small publisher. Marvel was the new kid on the block and absolutely on fire with the Fantastic Four and Spider-Man and such. My company wanted something that would sell as well. I didn't want to do another Superman or Justice League imitation. Because of my heritage, I was more aware of what was happening in Japan, the manga movement, comics written for adults, comics that didn't tell superhero stories. Science fiction. Fantasy. Monsters. I was also aware of the popularity of the Toho movies, Godzilla and the like. I mean, technically, Godzilla is a monster who destroys Japan repeatedly . . . but when you watch those movies, aren't you always kinda rooting for him? I know I was. So I thought, how about if I did some kinda monster hero? Marvel had The Thing and The Hulk. So I put my monster in a costume with a mask, which seems ridiculous since he could hardly masquerade as a mild-mannered reporter in his off hours. But it worked. People loved seeing the monster as the good guy. I deliberately referenced contemporary concerns about pollution in his origin story. And I incorporated themes of prejudice which I knew first-hand. Being othered. Being criticized because you're different. You know what I mean?"

"I have some idea," Jenny said quietly.

"I found out fast that I wasn't the only one who experienced those things. There are so many kinds of prejudice it's practically tearing the country apart. It may yet if we don't learn how to co-exist without demanding that everyone be and act the same. So I started noodling around with this character. And eventually, it came together."

"You created King Kaiju?"

"Yes. 'Kaiju' is a Japanese word. Translates to 'strange beast,' but it's basically used to mean 'big monster.' Originated in ancient Japanese legends. I added the King to show he was the most powerful creature of all and, of course, for the alliteration."

"Just to be clear, you created King Kaiju by yourself."

"One hundred percent. Start to finish. Soup to nuts."

"You are aware that Delia now claims that Joe created the character. Her son Ernie said the same thing."

His voice dropped. "I've been dealing with Delia for many years now."

To the side, Dan saw one of the jurors grin slightly. That had to be a good sign.

"And yes, we dated, if you can call it that. But I didn't have what she wanted."

Take the bait? No. Let the jurors answer the upspoken question themselves. Well played, Jenny. "Was Joe a co-creator?"

"No. Joe was an artist I contacted to bring my vision to life. I'd seen work Joe had done on monster comics for pre-Marvel

Timely Comics and I thought he was the right one for the job. I'd already worked out the character. I'd even rough-sketched Kaiju's costume."

"Wu, today it's traditional to give credit to both the original writer and the original artist, right?"

"Yes, and that's a good thing. We've had decades of comic creators not getting credit. Carl Barks was probably the greatest comics storyteller who ever lived, but he didn't get credit on his Uncle Scrooge comics, despite his distinctive style. Disney didn't allow credits, other than 'Walt Disney Presents.' Fans called him 'The Good Duck Artist' for decades because no one knew his name. We should all give daily thanks to Neal Adams and others who fought for creator rights, for full credit, for the return of original art, and perhaps most importantly, to get rid of the work-for-hire contract."

"You sent King Kaiju to many publishers, right?"

"Yes. People said it looked ridiculous, a giant monster in a mask fighting crime." He took a deep breath. "But of course, before 1938, the dozens of publishers who rejected Superman said the exact same thing. Who would believe a man lifting a car? It's ridiculous. Except, as it turned out, ridiculous or not, people loved it. And they loved Kaiju, too."

"You did eventually sell it, right?"

"Yes. As you know. To Sidekick Comics. And they didn't even really want it. But they had an anthology book that needed an eight-page backup story. So they bought my Kaiju origin and ran it. Basically to fill space."

"What happened next?"

"King Kaiju was an instant hit. People loved that silly, adorable monster. In my stories, the bad guys were usually beautiful and the hero was . . . well, a monster. I was making an obvious statement and many readers picked up on it, even if only subconsciously. I think it's why the character met with such universal acclaim."

"Did you sign a work-for-hire agreement?"

"Never. I endorsed a check. I mean, that's what you do when someone pays you with a check. No one reads the gibberish in faint green ink underneath the signature block."

"What happened next?"

"Sidekick decided to take Kaiju into his own series. Cover feature and everything. They initially committed to a six-issue miniseries. It was a good move. With six issues, I could plot out a more complex, interesting story, and Joe had more work than he'd seen in years."

"Ernie testified that the different cover artist was Joe's idea."

"Maybe. Once Kaiju was a breakout hit, Sidekick put their best artist on the cover. They let Joe remain on the interior for continuity's sake. And because he was cheap. But they spent real money on the covers."

"By Neal O'Neill. Was he a good artist?"

"The best Sidekick had."

"Did you complain?"

"No, I thought the covers were fabulous. I was happy to finally have some money, so I didn't object much. Until the lawsuit."

"That was the Baby Kaiju suit. You testified about that earlier. In the aftermath, you were fired."

"Right. I was a kid and I didn't know anything about lawyers and how people will rip you off. I just wanted to make comics, you know? And then, suddenly, someone else was in charge of my baby." He slowly released his breath. "I had to move to a smaller apartment. Even when I tried to tell people I created this character, they didn't believe me. 'If you created him, why isn't your name on it?'"

Jenny's face evidenced genuine sympathy. "That must've been hard."

"Devastating. I became . . . extremely depressed. Couldn't function. Couldn't write for more than a year. Started to drink.

Finally got my act together, but by then, the comics world had passed me by. No one wanted anything I had to offer. Like the kids would say—I threw away my shot. Now they were doing graphic novels and adding profanity and sex and . . . it wasn't my world any more. I couldn't get work."

Jenny took a strategic pause. Dan knew she was giving that testimony time to sink in with the jurors. She was probably also weighing whether she'd done enough.

"Why do you think Joe claimed to have created King Kaiju?"

"I never heard him do any such thing. With me, he always acknowledged that I was the creator." He paused. "He may have said something different when he was with Delia. God knows he must've, or that woman would never have married him. And she probably passed the story down to her son."

"Speaking of Ernie, did you ever threaten Joe with a gun?"

"Of course not. I don't own a gun. I have never even held a gun. Not in my entire life. I would've been happy to share the royalties with Joe. I knew what he'd been through. What we'd both been through. But of course . . ." His voice trailed. "Not possible now."

Jenny didn't leave it there. "Wu, could you please explain why you want these rights back?"

"It isn't money." Wu took a deep breath. "Money is good to have, but it's no substitute for making your mark in the world. No substitute for happiness. Kaiju was my baby. I can't stand what Sidekick has done with him, having him swear and harm people. Vaping! Tattoos! I even saw a comic where they had him kill someone. That's not my King Kaiju. They not only didn't create the character, they aren't taking good care of him. They're trying to turn him into John Wick so they can get this movie deal with Headmark."

Jenny blinked. "So if you controlled the rights, you wouldn't license the character to Headmark Studios?"

"Not in a million years. Not unless I had complete script

approval and final cut. And they know it. Which is why they're backing Delia."

"That must be frustrating."

Wu shook his head. "She's looking after her son, I assume. Trying to ensure his future." Wu turned and looked right at the jurors. "I have no natural children. King Kaiju is my baby. I made him. And I want him back."

CHAPTER FORTY-TWO

Maybe Dan was imagining it, but in his view, Kenzi approached Wu like a lion might stalk its prey, slowly, poised, waiting for the right moment to pounce.

"For someone who felt he was being cheated, you sure went along with it long enough."

"I loved working in comics. I never expected to get rich. I did it for the joy."

"So you're saying you don't care about the money?"

"Have I brought a claim for past damages? No. I don't want their money. Especially when I know what they did to my character to earn it. All I want is a judicial declaration of rights. Give me Kaiju back so I can start writing him the way he was meant to be written."

"You created King Kaiju and Joe had nothing to do with it."

"Not true. Joe contributed a lot. I think his art on those first issues was exceptional. Best of his career. He was excited." He blinked. "But he did not create the character. He did not co-create the character. He illustrated the stories I wrote. And he was paid for that."

At opposing counsel's table, Dan spotted Delia folding her

arms across her chest. She was not happy. She repeatedly nudged Kenzi's associate, Christopher. As if there was something he could do.

Kenzi shuffled through her note cards. "Joe claimed that he came up with the idea of making the monster's mask purple."

"The mask was originally black, and in the second year, he started adding a purple highlight. That was an improvement. But it did not make him the creator. Did you know that the Hulk was originally gray? In the second issue, he became green. Should the colorist get a co-creator credit? I don't think so."

"But Joe said he was a co-creator."

"Did he? I never heard him say that. Did you?"

Dan thought for a moment. He hadn't, and for that matter, he still hadn't heard anyone but Delia and Ernie say it. Kenzi probably hadn't heard it either.

"Did you ever hear anyone say otherwise?"

"I don't know what people were saying. Frankly, I don't care what people were saying. It isn't relevant."

"Sidekick Comics produced an affidavit during one of the previous legal actions. Signed by over twenty comics creators, many of them your co-workers. And every one of them said Sidekick owned the character, thanks to Joe. Not you."

"They wanted to keep their jobs."

"You're saying they lied. All of them."

"I'm saying they did what they were told. How would they know? They weren't around when I created this character. Probably all they know is what Sidekick told them."

Kenzi did not mask her outrage. "These are your peers. These are the people in the best position to know. I know you're elderly and perhaps suffer from . . . memory problems, but this is too much."

Wu looked weary, almost impatient. "You know what name isn't on that list?"

"Well, I'm sure—"

"I'll give you two. First: Joe. The person in the best position to know. And you know who else isn't on the affadavit?" Wu glanced at Jenny. She smiled back and nodded. "Neal O'Neill. The cover artist for the first six issues. He didn't sign it because he *had* been there when this all started. He knew the truth. He knew I was being cheated, right from the start. Probably before I did. He'd seen it happen before to others." Wu shook his head. "Probably knew there'd be a lawsuit one day. God knows this isn't first one that's sprung from the comics world."

"Is Mr. O'Neill planning to testify?" A question she only asked because she knew he wouldn't.

"No. He can't."

"Then I will instruct you to not give hearsay testimony about what he might say if he were here."

The corner of Wu's lips turned up slightly. "But he left a message behind."

"A message? Nothing he says years after the fact is going to—"

"No, he said this back when it all went down. I didn't know about it until it was recently brought to my attention. May I show you the covers again?"

While Kenzi considered her response, Jenny put the first cover on the overhead screen. "This is the first one." Jenny pushed the clicker. "And here's the second . . . and the third . . ."

"I don't see how this is responsive to my question."

"Patience is a virtue."

"Not in my profession."

"Do you notice how all the covers have the rococo design? The ornamental business? For the first three, it's at the bottom. For the next three, it's at the top. See?"

"Sir, I'm going to stop you right there and move—"

"Just let me finish."

"No, I will not let you—"

The King Kaiju miniseries issues 1-6 (message outlined)

"Win?" Wu leaned forward. "You won't let me win? Regardless of the truth?"

Kenzi fell silent for a moment. Wu seized the opening.

"Remember that Neal knew there would be a six-issue miniseries. He designed all six at once. So they would match."

"Still not seeing the relevance."

"May I see Exhibit 53?" Jenny put it up on the screen. "Look what happens when you arrange the six comic covers, three on the top, three on the bottom. You see how the rococo design seems to . . . flow down or to the side. The covers connect. Now, block out everything else and focus on the flowing lines."

Jenny brought up another slide, same covers, but now focusing in tight on the letters.

"You see it? You may have to squint a little, but it's there. I can't say for sure why Neal did it. But I think he was trying—without losing his job—to give me some ammunition for a future fight. That's why he did it and that's why he finally told my lawyers about it. Do you see?"

Jenny focused in even tighter on the design . . . and it soon became apparent that those lines were not random.

There were letters in that design.

Later, Dan would say it was as if everyone in the packed courtroom spotted it at the same time. The gasp was audible.

Once you focused and blocked out the extraneous lines, the message became clear. It spelled out three simple words.

WU MADE ME.

King Kaiju miniseries issues 1-6 (message in boldface)

CHAPTER FORTY-THREE

After court recessed for the day, Dan grabbed Kenzi's attention. "Could we step outside?"

"Sorry, you're not my type."

"We need to talk."

"Give me fifteen."

"You were planning to step out and do a livestream for the KenziKlan."

Her left eyebrow arched. "On a topic unrelated to this case. You understand me better than I realized."

"I've been watching."

She ran her hand across her side-shave. "Should I be flattered?"

"No. I watch all my opponents. That's how I defeat them."

She grinned. It occurred to him that she was less like a litigator and more like a timber wolf. The smile did not mean she liked you. She was baring her teeth. "Okay, you get one minute."

They walked until they found a vacant conference room, then slid inside. Dan pushed out the OCCUPIED sign.

"Ok, handsome, you got me alone. What can I do you for?"

"We need to settle this case. Before anyone else gets hurt."

Kenzi appeared flabbergasted. "Are you joking? I was the one pushing for settlement and you blew me off, probably because you were hiding this cover artist. Now you're afraid it won't be enough."

"Those comic book covers proved my case. Beyond a doubt."

"Stop trying to gaslight me. Yeah, you had one good moment. But that doesn't mean you automatically win. I'll argue that—"

"But you know it's true."

She stopped short. "I . . . don't . . . and how would you know what I think?"

"I know you're not stupid. Those ornate designs didn't happen by accident. O'Neill was making a contemporaneous record which, if I might remind you of what you learned in law school, is the most compelling kind of evidence. To juries."

"He hid a secret message. How do I know he knew what he was talking about? Maybe he was just messing around. Maybe Wu paid him to do it."

"You know that isn't true."

"If I may remind you, counselor, trials aren't about truth. They're about winning. Absolute truth doesn't exist. Every so-called truth depends upon your personal perspective."

Dan locked eyes with her. "Wu created King Kaiju."

"Look, hotshot, the truth is, it doesn't matter what I think is true. I've been hired to win the lawsuit."

"We can reach an equitable compromise. Like you yourself suggested a few days ago. Wu doesn't object to giving Delia something."

"Table scraps?"

"Well, the one thing we both know for certain is that Delia had no role in creating this character."

"She stands in the shoes of her deceased husband."

He wasn't sure if it was what she said or the way she said it, but something clicked in his brain. "Her deceased husband," he murmured. "You're assuming.." He thought another moment. "Joe murdered a corporate flak, then took his own life . . ."

"I already know this."

"But what neither of know is—why?"

"You can figure that one out. I'm going back in there to win my case. Do you have any more witnesses? Because if not, I'm calling surrebuttal witnesses to—"

"Would you stop?" He took another step closer. "You know Wu created King Kaiju. You've seen the covers. All the man wants is credit for the greatest achievement of his creative life. He isn't even asking for back pay. Let him take credit on future King Kaiju properties, agree to a small percentage of future profits, and we'll give you a generous—"

"No. You had your chance. I wanted to avoid further damage, but now the damage is done. We're riding this one to the final roundup." She turned away.

She opened the door—and to both their surprise, Garrett plunged through.

"Thank God," he said. "You weren't in the courtroom and no one knew where to find you. You were right." He glanced at Kenzi, then modified his tone. "I . . . uh . . . found something."

Kenzi got the drift. "You need to talk to your partner, Dan. I'm going back to—"

"Wait." Dan looked directly at her. "Stay."

Her face scrunched up. "Have you forgotten the whole attorney-client privilege thing? This is work product."

"I don't care. Maybe if we stop keeping secrets, you'll understand that we need to find a resolution that satisfies everyone. Before another tragedy occurs."

Kenzi didn't say anything. But the expression on her face softened.

"What is it, Garrett? I need something big. I need the *Brown v. Board of Education* of intellectual property law."

"Sorry. The most relevant case here—one I know Delia has researched—is *In re Baby M*."

Dan looked puzzled, but Kenzi did not. "Now you're in my wheelhouse. Family law. That's the New Jersey surrogacy case, right? Declared that surrogate contracts were contrary to public policy and thus couldn't be enforced. It's still the law today, at least in New Jersey. But what has that got—"

She didn't finish the sentence. She didn't have to.

"Oh my God."

He exchanged a look with her. "Yeah. Also what I'm thinking."

Garrett passed Dan a sheath of paperwork. A few moments later, Dan passed it to Kenzi.

Kenzi's voice was barely a whisper. "You're thinking what I'm thinking?"

"I fear I may be. And if we're right, we have to get out of here. Garrett, can you drive?"

"Sure but . . . where are we going?"

"We need Wu, but—" His eyes suddenly ballooned. "Wait. I know where he's gone. He hinted about it after he stepped down from the stand."

"Where?"

"Probably the only place on earth he still feels he has friends."

"Which would be?"

He grabbed his backpack and headed toward the door. "Comic Con."

CHAPTER FORTY-FOUR

Dan was glad he'd acquired a VIP pass when he'd been here before. He was able to go straight into the convention center, but the zealous volunteers guarding the doors wouldn't let Maria and Jenny enter until they bought a ticket. And the line was long.

"Is it always this hard to get into a comic book convention?" Maria asked. "I mean, how many nerds collect these things?"

"Millions," Jenny replied, ignoring the shade. "And why are people who love to read always called nerds? I wish we had more nerds reading and fewer non-nerds acquiring their worldviews from social media."

"Yeah, but—"

Jenny continued. "I wish everyone had grown up reading comic books. Reading about Superman—an immigrant who uses his powers to help others, not himself. This would be a very different country."

"Look," Dan said, "I'm gonna go ahead. You two join me when you can."

He checked the schedule. Wu was speaking about the good old days and autographing after. But he wasn't the big draw.

One of the fourteen actors who've played Doctor Who was in the main auditorium, which explained why there was a crowd out front.

Dan made his way to an upstairs room. Wu was up front behind a podium, speaking to maybe fifteen people in the audience. He appeared to be winding down. But what Dan noticed most was the transformation of Wu's character. Before, he had been mostly quiet and unobtrusive, modest to a fault. But here, he appeared ebullient, enthusiastic. Beloved. Several times when people in the audience talked about the difference King Kaiju had made in their lives, he placed his hand over his heart. Once he appeared almost moved to tears.

"I cannot tell you"—his voice choked—"how much this means to me. Some of you may know of the . . . troubles. How I've been severed from my baby. There's a lawsuit pending to determine who created this loveable monster. And I hope . . . I—I almost hate to hope at this point . . . but I hope . . . someday . . . we will see justice and—and—the complete restoration of creator credits to—"

He never got a chance to finish the sentence. Though attendance was sparse, the room erupted with supportive cheers and applause. Wu appeared overwhelmed. He steadied himself against the podium, then eventually raised a hand and waved, which only made the applause grow louder.

"And—And—if I may," he continued, talking over the applause. "Can we have some appreciation for my late partner, Joe Ulrich?"

Again, thunderous applause. Wu beamed.

A few minutes later, he finished his talk and those who wanted autographs lined up to the right of the raised platform. A long table beside the podium allowed Wu to sit and sign.

Dan drank in the autograph seekers. Most had a King Kaiju comic they wanted Wu to sign. Some wanted a selfie. About half sported cosplay. Most were superheroes or monsters. The skinniest Thor he'd ever seen. A Power Girl dressed to kill. A Mickey Mouse with an astoundingly professional head.

And all at once, Dan understood why Wu came here. Why all these artists and writers and fans came. Everywhere else, they might get grief about loving comic books. Anywhere else, Wu might be challenged when he claimed he created this character. But not here. In the safety of this room, amongst the people who loved his creation most, he was a superstar. Or, Dan contemplated, he was the superstar he should've been.

Wu started signing autographs, but the line moved slowly. Wu liked to chat. Dan understood. He was basking in the glow, something everyone should get to do at one time or another. Make it last as long as possible. Enjoy it.

He wondered if he should call security. But what would he tell them? What could happen to Wu when he was surrounded by so many witnesses?

Maria and Jenny appeared behind him.

"Got your tickets?"

"Yes," Jenny said. "Two hundred smackers. And the convention is almost over."

"But you're supporting artists and the arts."

"Now I feel much better about it. Do you see . . . him?"

"No. But he probably wouldn't strike in front of others. When Wu finishes, let's follow from a discreet distance."

"You mean . . . use him as bait?"

"Of course not." He paused. "But let's not let him out of our sight, either."

They waited as Wu continued signing. Ten minutes later, he'd made his way through about half the autograph seekers. "Maybe we should get in line. Jenny, do you have a King—"

He saw that Jenny was not hearing him. "Something wrong?"

Jenny's eyes appeared to be locked on the autograph line. "Yes. Mickey Mouse."

Dan glanced at the mouse in the line. He was wearing the

traditional black tuxedo that Mickey wore in *Fantasia*, if he remembered correctly. "Yeah. So?"

"Look at his shoes."

He did. "Okay, now what?"

Jenny leaned in close and whispered. "They're black."

"Yup. Match the tux. Very sporty."

"It's wrong."

"For a mouse to wear shoes? Technically correct, I suppose, but—"

Jenny grabbed his arm. "Mickey wears yellow shoes."

"Is that a rule?"

"In that outfit? Yes. It's what he does."

"I guess this Mickey left his yellow shoes at home. No biggie."

"Are you joking? That's like Superman showing up in green Spandex."

"I'm sure it's just—" And then he froze. He looked Jenny square in the eyes. "You're saying no real cosplayer would dress that way."

Jenny touched her nose. "Ding, ding, ding."

He whirled. "Maria, get security."

"Don't get rid of me!"

"This is the most important thing you can do right now." And also, he wanted to get rid of her. He did not want his pregnant partner in the firing line. "Tell them we think there's about to be an assassination attempt. Then call Jake at SPPD."

"On it." She bolted outside the room where it was less noisy.

"Jenny. You're with me."

He started moving toward the line, Jenny close behind. He saw that Mickey had made it to the front. Wu was reaching out to shake his hand. Paw? But there was a puzzled expression on his face.

Then he saw Mickey reach inside his tuxedo.

"*Down!*" he shouted. "*Everyone on the floor!*"

Everyone heard but few ducked. He felt confusion and panic circulating around him.

Mickey held a gun. Except, in fairness to the beloved mouse, this was no authorized Mickey.

"Wu! Get out of here!"

The first shot ricocheted off his chair and went wild. Someone screamed, but he couldn't take time to see if anyone was hurt. He had to bring down the mouse before this turned into a massacre.

Jenny tried to help, waiving her hands in the air. "Listen up, panelologists! The cops are on their way. Get out of here before—"

The man in the mouse costume whirled around and fired at Jenny. The bullet sounded like it bounced off something metallic. Wu used the opening to run for the back door.

"Get down!" Dan was closer to the action than Jenny, so he leapt toward the mouse, hoping to tackle him. Unfortunately someone in a Sailor Moon costume got in the way. They both tumbled onto the floor. And Mickey went after Wu.

Dan tried to ditch Sailor Moon, but he was caught up in her necktie.

Jenny offered him a hand up. "Can I help?"

"Of course you can. Now stay here while—"

"The hell I will." Jenny kicked off her heels and raced toward the back curtain.

Damn. Despite her size, she could move. Dan tried to get his bearings and followed. "Be careful. The mouse has a gun!"

"Like I didn't know that."

Backstage it was dark and secluded. He assumed everyone else had fled. But this left them in a dangerous trap. The next gunshot could come from anywhere and he couldn't cover all the possibilities alone. "We need to split up."

"What do you think this is, a Scooby-Doo episode? We're not—"

The next shot rang so close to his head that he could feel the rush of air. He grabbed Jenny by the shoulders. "Stay down."

They both cowered low to the floor, hiding behind a wooden crate that probably would not stop a bullet. His heart raced and his hands were wet with sweat.

It was too dark to see much. Even if he hadn't been the original target, he was now. His appearance told the man in the mouse suit that he'd figured it all out.

Which was another good reason for the mouse to kill him.

Another shot rang out, then another, but not as close as before.

The shooter couldn't see any better than he could. With luck, that might mean Wu was still alive. Otherwise, the mouse would've left the building.

Jenny sounded breathless. "Do you have any idea where Mickey is?"

"Crawled into a mousehole, I assume."

"And Wu?"

"I think he's alive," he whispered. "But don't call out. We don't want to give away his location. Or ours."

He managed to crawl to a long corridor. He couldn't tell how long. This was probably a service conduit for people who worked here. That meant there would be many doors. And the mouse could be lurking behind any of them.

He stood just outside the corridor. If the gunman was in there, he wouldn't have a clean shot. "Listen to me!"

He was answered by the report of a gun. He heard the bullet bounce at least twice. Whether the man had a clean shot or not, firing a weapon in this enclosed space was all kinds of dangerous.

"Listen to me," he repeated. "You don't have to do this. We know who you are. We know why you're here. Don't compound your problems with another murder."

No response. But no gunfire either.

And then he looked down. And saw Jenny on the ground slithering down the hallway like a snake, advancing by her elbows.

He started to say something, but she was exposed. Speaking to her would only make her more of a target.

He needed to end this but fast.

"Look, I'm not going to lie," he shouted. "I can't prevent the cops from bringing charges. But I can make sure you're represented by a good lawyer. In fact . . ." He took a deep breath. "If Wu will waive the conflicts, I'll represent you myself."

"And I will." The voice was faint, but distinctly Wu. Behind him, thank God.

Jenny was still inching down the corridor.

"But if you kill someone today in cold blood . . . there's nothing I can do for you."

He waited. What did he expect? Was the man with the gun going to crater like a computer after a Captain Kirk speech? Probably not.

"We can work this out. I know the DA. She'll listen to me. There are extenuating circumstances. You've been treated wrongly for a long time. But it's not too late to make amends. I will help. That's a promise."

"I don't believe you!" someone shouted. Dan recognized the voice.

"Throw away the gun! Let's talk!"

"Just let me leave. I'll . . . disappear."

"I can't do that. You're trying to kill my client."

"I have no choice!"

Dan tried to keep his voice calm. Jenny was halfway down the corridor. But he wasn't sure which door the gunman lurked behind. Jenny was putting her life on the line. He needed to keep the mouse distracted.

"I get it," Dan said loudly, hoping to cover any small noises

Jenny might make. "You were desperate. You expected a fortune, and now you see it slipping through your fingers."

"It's my fortune!"

"I don't think the trial will come out the way you want and neither do you. If you did, you wouldn't be doing this."

"You don't know anything about it!"

"I may know more than you do. Put down the gun. Let's talk about this like reasonable people."

"No!"

"Security will be here soon. Do you want them to find you holding a weapon?"

"They won't find me." Brief pause. "At least not alive."

Dan felt his heart plummet. "Don't do anything crazy. Let's just—"

He was interrupted by a crashing sound, loud and sharp, like a sudden explosion.

He did not see Jenny on the floor.

Now or never. He ran down the hallway, making a serpentine route just in case someone was firing . . .

About halfway down the hall, he found Jenny. Standing up.

With a big mouse sprawled at her feet.

She was short of breath and heaving. "Had to . . . act . . . quickly." She drew in deep gulps of air. "Clubbed him over the head with a fully loaded Gucci tote. He'll probably be out for hours."

Dan bent down and removed the mouse mask.

Ernie Ulrich. And he wasn't unconscious. Maybe stunned.

"Why?" Dan asked. "Just . . . why?"

His eyelids fluttered. "It's . . . my heritage." And then his eyelids closed.

Jenny shook her head. "That boy really wanted that dinosaur."

Dan shook his head. "He wasn't talking about King Kaiju. He

was talking about his family." He pursed his lips. "Or what he thought was his family."

All at once, he realized Wu stood behind him, gazing down at the figure on the floor.

"Go easy on him. Please." Wu crouched and laid his hand on the boy's forehead, brushing his matted hair away. "Your mother didn't treat any of us very well, did she?"

CHAPTER FORTY-FIVE

Dan shook Kenzi's hand. "Done deal."

They both tumbled into their conference chairs. And began to laugh.

"Can you believe we finally settled this mess?" she asked.

"I knew you'd come around eventually."

"Oh did you now?" She swiveled around. "You figured your mansplaining would eventually persuade me?"

"No. Your obvious intelligence."

She puffed up her shoulders. "Mr. Pike. Did you just compliment me?"

"I'll deny it. I do regret that this negates our bet. I was looking forward to the sunken hollow expression in your eyes when you had to live without your cellphone for a week."

"Yeah. But I don't care about seeing you in a swimsuit again. I was just trying to get Maria's goat."

"I know. When are you returning to Seattle?"

"I don't see why I can't go tonight. I can't wait to get home. This case has completely energized me. I see now how limited I've been."

"You can do anything."

"And I will. There are many ways I can help women. And my firm is going to start doing all of them."

He grabbed a soda from the credenza and popped it open. "Is that why you got into law? To help other women?"

"That's my mission statement."

"But my question was—"

"No. I got into law to prove my sexist father was wrong about me."

Dan chuckled. "I got into law to vindicate mine. Fathers and sons. Or daughters. Parents and their children. That's what it all comes down to, isn't it? Every time. Children and art. Which are much the same thing."

"Certainly in this case. You should try going out on your own, Dan. Why is someone with your talent taking orders?"

Dan shrugged. "I like Ben. He's a good guy."

"Substitute father figure?"

"Maybe. I lost my father. Ben never had a son. It works."

She sighed. "It occurs to me now, Dan, that I . . . may not have treated you all that well. And I apologize."

He waved it away. "We were opposing lawyers. Being tough is our job description. Sometimes I think the adversarial system is . . . not all it's cracked up to be. Dramatic, but possibly not the best way to resolve a dispute. What was it you called this?"

"All-out war?"

"Yeah. Wouldn't it be a better world if we focused less on winning a war and more on . . . making the world a better place?"

"Mr. Rogers Goes to Law School."

"But still. We should be social justice warriors, resolving conflicts rather than intensifying them. I'd like to imagine I left the world in slightly better shape than I found it."

"You go on crusading, Dan, and I'll go on fighting the good fight too. Maybe we'll meet again."

He smiled. "I hope so."

Dan relaxed in the large semi-circular sofa in the living room of the Snell Isle headquarters. It always felt comfortable, but never more so than now, at the end of a long and grueling case.

They were celebrating. Wu was the guest of honor. He was talking excitedly about his plans for King Kaiju, now that he had a seat at the table. He was finding Sidekick considerably easier to work with. Before they had been concerned that if they acknowledged him at all, it would lend credibility to his claims. Now that those claims were resolved, they were listening. And realizing that he understood the character better than anyone. "They say the feature film is basically going to be an adaptation of those critical first six issues." He winked. "With an action scene every six minutes. Gotta compete with those Marvel movies."

Wu appeared happier than Dan had ever seen him. Maybe he should do more civil cases, he mused. Preventing innocents from being railroaded by the government was worthy work. But there were other ways to help people. Maybe it was time he explored some of those.

Jenny prepped most of the snack foods—except "snack foods" made it sound as if she were serving Cheetos, when in fact it was Brussel sprout sliders and baked brie bites. Garrett was noodling on his keyboard, but tonight, instead of the usual jazz, he appeared to be playing triumphant music. One rarely heard John Philip Sousa on a keyboard. But Garrett made it work.

Something caught his eye. He squinted, trying to focus.

Was that a teddy bear in Garrett's lap?

He shook his head, marveling. Seemed like everyone on this team was changing.

And speaking of...

Jenny came racing over to him. "I found your gift. Oh my gosh. I can't believe it. All that original art!"

"From Neal O'Neill himself."

"It's spectacular. But it's too much."

Dan waved her protests away. "He just wanted his work left in good hands. And there are none better than yours."

Jenny wrapped her arms around him and practically squeezed the stuffings out. Maria beamed.

But Garrett continued playing.

Jenny released Dan and grabbed a platter of canapes, hovering in the vicinity of Garrett. They liked to joke that Garrett was the team's "token conservative." No one knew yet how he would react to Jenny's latest choices.

Jenny cleared her throat. "Um, you . . . want a slider? I . . . kinda made them 'cause I know you like them."

Garrett slowly looked up from his keyboard and placed one hand on the teddy bear. "You made them?"

Jenny's forehead creased. Her facial expression reminded him of the last scene in *City Lights*. Maybe . . .

Garrett smiled. "If you made them, I'll take three."

A smile spread from one side of Jenny's face to the other. "Really? I was worried—"

"I feel pretty relaxed these days." Garrett pointed toward the teddy. "Bear-Bear thinks I need to chill. Relax more. Live in the moment."

Jenny's lips parted but froze, as if she wasn't sure what to say. "I couldn't help but notice . . ."

"I got a good deal on him. If you want I could take you to—"

She stopped him. "Thanks. I already have a Dreamer doll, but my husband won't let me bring him to bed." She hesitated. "But . . . maybe we could do something else. Grab dinner."

"I would love to have dinner. What about Beachcombers? Dan loves that joint." Garrett looked straight at her. "And it's always packed." He reached out, pulled her close, and kissed her cheek. "Let's do it soon."

Maria looked at Dan. Dan looked back. Her eyes were wide and watery. And he understood why.

Maria was seated beside Wu, patiently listening to his plans for a comic-book character she knew little about. He recalled once suggesting they watch a Godzilla movie on TV and she laughed out loud. But now, when she was about ten months pregnant, she listened to a detailed account of the time King Kaiju took on the entire Legion of Evil.

"But I want to do more than combat scenes. I want to take Kaiju back to his roots. Fight for the people. That's the root of this entire genre. Go read the earliest Superman stories. There were no supervillains. He fought for the little guy. He took on slumlords. Defended battered women. Prevented innocents from being executed. That's the true work of a hero."

Dan caught her eye and winked. She just smiled. Reminding him how lucky he was.

His iPhone buzzed. "Mr. K" was ready. Maria was occupied and didn't need any unnecessary movement, so he punched the buttons on his laptop and put Ben on the television. He still preferred not to engage the video. He said he didn't like the way he looked on Zoom. Dan suspected it was more about social anxieties, but given how much Ben had done for him, for the entire team, he was more than happy to indulge him.

Ben's voice boomed from the speakers. Everyone drifted back to the living room.

"Hello, team. And congratulations on your success. This turned out even better than I hoped. What a victory!"

"It really wasn't a victory," Dan said. "We settled."

"That's an even better victory. Everyone gets something, by mutual agreement. I wish more lawyers would understand the value of settlement. Before they've spent a year running up the bill with motions practice and discovery."

"I should've figured it out sooner. But when Garrett unearthed that surrogacy case, I finally understood. Much too late."

Jenny cut in. "Could someone please explain the significance of that to me? Because I still don't get it."

"Let me bottom line it for you. Delia researched surrogacy, years ago, because she and Joe were having trouble conceiving. There's a good chance Joe was sterile, not astonishing given how he'd had to live, on the edge of starvation and with no medical care. But that was too complicated and expensive. Much easier to simply have an affair. We've done the DNA tests. Delia held Ernie out as Joe's son. Joe undoubtedly believed Ernie was his son, at least for a time." He paused. "But he wasn't. Delia confirmed it with a DNA test. Then buried all the paperwork."

"Why not burn it?"

"She didn't want to find it…but I don't think she wanted to destroy it, either. She might need it somewhere down the line."

"Like, to keep Ernie in line?"

"Yes. What Delia didn't realize was that Ernie already knew. He stashed an Apple AirTag in his mother's car. He could follow her movements. So not long after she buried the info—he dug it up."

Garrett jumped in. "Joe's will only leaves Delia a third of his estate. The majority, including the Kaiju rights, go to 'his children.' Which Ernie isn't."

"Could he be considered a . . . common law child?" Jenny asked. "He lived with them. They held him out as Joe's son."

"Florida doesn't even recognize common law marriage, much less children. No, a will leaving something to children would include both biological and adopted children—but Ernie was neither. Any grant to Ernie from Joe's will could be challenged. Probably successfully."

"Who would do that?"

Garrett allowed a small smile. "Delia, for starters."

"I'm confused. If Delia only gets a third and Ernie gets nothing—who gets the rest?"

"If there are no children to inherit, the will leaves everything to the Comics Legal Defense Fund, a nonprofit that protects creator rights. Of course, after the Headmark contract went through, Delia's third would be more than enough to live off comfortably. Assuming Joe was declared the creator or co-creator of King Kaiju."

"But if people learned that Ernie wasn't Joe's son, Ernie would get nothing."

"From Joe's will. He could still inherit from Delia."

"Yes." He paused. "Except Delia could live another forty years, plus she doesn't like Ernie very much and she's likely to spend it all and then some before he gets near it. So if he wanted a piece of the action..."

"He had to kill anyone who knew he wasn't Joe's biological son. Delia had no reason to tell—at this time. It wouldn't get her more than her designated third and admitting she cheated on Joe wouldn't help her case. But others might talk."

"Whether Ernie was biologically Joe's child or not," Jenny said, "he loved that boy. A probate judge might still award him something. Joe raised the kid."

"Maybe. But remember that Delia is in the mix. Delia had Joe's power-of-attorney, and if she secured the contract with Headmark, she would've made sure the profits were paid to her or some corporation she created. If Ernie tried to challenge her, she'd reveal the truth and cut him out altogether. Might make her look bad, but if it got her millions—I don't think she'd care that much."

"Who else knew?"

"It happened a long time ago and the records were sealed. Garrett was eventually able to get access, but that's only because he's a skilled researcher and hammered away at the bureaucracy for a long period of time. And his . . . ahem . . ." Dan declined to use the word "hacking." "His computer skills allowed him to unearth documents others might not have found."

"But Wu's first lawyer knew. Kevin Lieber."

"Yeah. And there's a reason for that." He drew in his breath. "He's the one Delia had the affair with."

Jenny's eyes bugged out. "He was Ernie's biological father! He wasn't killed because he represented Wu. He was killed because he had information that could destroy Ernie's plans. That's a wild coincidence."

"Except it isn't a coincidence. There's a reason Wu hired Leiber to represent him. Delia recommended him."

"She recommended her own lover?"

"Probably thought she could control her lover. After all, she didn't want Wu getting anything."

"So Leiber was sleeping with one potential heir and fathered the other. Poor man. No wonder he's dead."

"It's possible Lieber tried to blackmail Ernie. Wanted a bigger slice of the Kaiju prize for himself. In any case, he revealed that he was Ernie's father. The father Ernie never knew. The one who neglected and ignored him his entire life. Ernie lived in poverty while his daddy-lawyer had everything he wanted."

"So Ernie killed his own father?"

"Makes a kind of crazy sense. I mean, think about it. Cutting off someone's head? While they're still alive? That's more than an act of greed. That's an act of personal animosity." He took another deep breath. "That's what you do to someone you hate."

Even though he couldn't see Ben's face, Dan could feel him wincing. "So maybe Ernie hated Leiber. There must be easier ways of venting than decapitation."

"I have some thoughts on that," Jenny said. "Ernie killed Leiber at his home, which remember was in Orlando, close to the airport. He needed Leiber's cellphone, because Leiber had digital copies of the documents that proved he was Ernie's father on his phone. Problem is, the phone was not in Leiber's home. Lieber kept a separate work cell phone in his office. And since Ernie didn't know the passcode, he had to rely on Face ID."

Maria covered her face. "So he cut off Leiber's head?"

"Easier than lugging an adult male corpse around. Ernie severed the head, put it in a suitcase, went to Lieber's office, used the face to open the phone, then deleted the documents. Kept the phone, but later destroyed it, because he knew hackers can recover deleted files."

Maria took a deep breath. "And he almost got away with it."

"Sure," Jenny commented. "White boys commit murder and get away with it. While others can't even put on a dress without being harassed."

"How did he cut off the head?"

"I think he tried several things, and eventually used a bread knife he found in the kitchen. Must've been damn sharp. Turns out the woman at the airport who found the head, Lydia Blankenship, is a seasoned chef and recognized the striation pattern of the bread knife on the bone."

"He cut off a head with a bread knife?"

"I think he started that way. Killed Leiber, but couldn't get all the way through the bone. Finished the job with an axe." He shrugged. "I noted how strong Ernie looked. Told us he lifts weights, remember? And we know he liked hunting. I'm guessing he's gutted deer and other animals. This wouldn't've been pleasant, but he could do it. In the bathtub."

"I can't believe he could clean the tub so well the police couldn't find traces with luminol."

"Why would they examine Ernie's bathtub? He was never considered a suspect."

"And then he dropped the head off at the Lost Luggage office?"

"I guess. I would've buried it ten feet underground. But maybe Ernie didn't think he had time for that. By that point, he was probably anxious to be rid of it. And he didn't think it could be identified. Remember, he didn't ditch the body until much later."

Dan saw the light dawn in Maria's eyes. "Ohmigod. This is so . . . disgusting."

"Yeah." Dan jumped back into the discussion. "He thought he'd wiped the slate clean. Except then he came to the first settlement meeting and heard me talk about how our investigators were digging up the truth. He feared we'd learn he wasn't Joe's son. And panicked."

"And that's why he tried to shoot you!"

"Probably. Jake is running ballistics tests on the bullets to confirm that. While Ernie was going after about me, Elliott Gomez learned about the hidden message on the covers. Probably from Megan Sanderson, who got it from Curtis Swart at Sidekick. She'd been in touch with O'Neill. Remember, she had a secret stake in the Kaiju battle and wanted to make sure it paid off. Gomez contacted Joe to make a deal, cutting himself in for a huge share of the profits. Joe didn't care about the money, but he didn't want his son to lose everything. So he shot Gomez. Making it look as if Lydek was the target."

"Where did he get the gun?"

"Probably from Ernie. the kid wouldn't have lied so boldly about the gun coming from Wu if he thought the true source would ever be tracked down."

"So Joe killed Gomez, then killed himself, trying to end the trail. He knew that after a big dramatic scene and confession, everyone would blame all the murders on him. He must've realized Ernie was the murderer. He was protecting the kid he believed was his son. And no one would be able to get him to crack under pressure. Because he was dead."

Dan snapped his fingers. "That's why he made a public spectacle of it. He wanted everyone to know. To see. To blame him. To save Ernie." He turned his head. "Probably would've worked. If a crack researcher named Garrett Wainwright hadn't been on the case."

"Aw shucks," Garrett said. Dan noticed that as he did, he squeezed his teddy bear.

"Ernie probably thought he'd done all he needed to do," Dan continued. "Until that last day in court. After Jenny's brilliant cover reveal. Once he saw that, he knew there was a strong chance Wu would be declared the creator of King Kaiju. Which meant Ernie would get nothing. At least not until Delia died. And by that time there would be no money left."

"So he dressed up like Mickey Mouse and tried to take Wu out. Thank God you stopped that."

"Yeah. Don't tell Disney. I doubt they would appreciate how he appropriated their IP."

"What matters is that we stopped him," Maria said. She wrapped her arm around Wu and gave him a hug. "And now the whole world knows who created King Kaiju. And you've—you've—" She stopped for a moment. "Excuse me. Pregnant woman. Bathroom break."

Dan smiled. "Ben, do we know who's going to represent Ernie?"

"Well, I do."

"Because you hired them?"

There was a brief pause before Ben answered. "I didn't think it should be you. Nothing personal. Wu may need you to smooth out the various legal matters that will inevitably arise in the aftermath. But I can promise you . . . he will not be abandoned."

"Thank you."

"But here's what I want to say before I sign off. You all did a bang-up job and I'm very pleased."

"Thanks. One more thing before you go. Not to tell you what to do or anything. But I know you've been watching Kenzi Rivera. You should hire her."

Ben laughed. "Already tried. She's not interested. She wants to build her father's firm into something bigger than a divorce shop. And she has the right stuff to do it."

"Understood. Give my best to Christina."

"I will. She wants to know when you're dropping by for another road trip."

"Never. But give her my love."

CHAPTER FORTY-SIX

HE DISCONNECTED THE LINE. WU LEFT A FEW MINUTES LATER.

"Well," Dan said. "That solves all the mysteries. Except one. Jenny."

She looked up and fluttered her eyelids. "Yes?"

"Why Jenny? I mean, why did you choose that name? You said it wasn't a comic book character. Childhood friend? Mother's middle name? I can't remember you ever mentioning a Jenny, but—"

Garrett—the least likely suspect—interrupted. "*Oliver & Company.*"

Jenny clapped her hands together. "You knew!" She tucked in her chin. "I always knew that crusty exterior was a sham. You love me. Deep down."

Dan squinted. "*Oliver & Company?*"

"It's a Disney animated movie."

He pondered a moment. "Is that the one with the dogs?"

"Yes," Jenny replied. "But more importantly, it's the one with the adorable rich girl named Jenny. Who has everything but still feels like something is missing . . . until she adopts Oliver. Or he adopts her, depending on how you look at it." She drew in her breath, fanning herself as if she were suddenly boiling. "That's exactly how I used to feel. Like something was missing. Till I met you people. My new family." She looked up, her eyes watering. "I don't think I'd have had the courage to make this transition without you. You're my Oliver!"

Maria appeared in the kitchen doorway. She leaned against the side of the door with one hand. The other was pressed against her tummy. "Dan. I think I need you."

"Kitchen assistance from a gourmet chef?"

"No, you dunderhead. I need a ride to the hospital. My water broke."

He leaped to his feet. "What? When? Are you sure? How do you feel? Should you be standing up?"

She took a few steps toward him. "Get me to the hospital. As quickly as possible. I'm not an expert, but I don't think this is going to be a long labor."

Jenny and Garrett both started running around in circles.

"What do you need me to do? Hot water bottle? Wheelchair? Popsicle stick?"

"For God's sake," Maria said. "Just take me to the damn hospital."

Garrett emerged from the back office. "Where's the bag? I can't find the hospital bag."

Maria rolled her eyes. "I'm holding it!"

"Okay, okay." Dan patted her on the back. "Let's go to the car."

"Fine. My car."

"But—"

"I'm not going to the hospital in your Bentley. Everyone will hate us."

"Okay, okay." He took her arm and steered her toward the garage. "It'll be fine."

She shrugged him off. "I can still walk, idiot. Just drive the car so I can have this baby of yours."

Even though it was the exact opposite of what she was saying, he stopped. "I'm sorry. I wish we'd gotten married first."

"I don't," she replied, waddling toward the garage. "I'd rather do it later."

He squinted. "You want to get married . . . *after* the baby is born?"

"Exactly. That way . . . we can all do it together." She saw Jenny and Garrett hovering behind her. "Which includes you two. And this about-to-be newborn. All of us together. As a family."

It occurred to Dan that he had never loved anyone more in his entire life. "That's the sweetest . . . silliest thing I ever heard. The baby won't even know what's going on."

She held his face in her hands and looked deeply into his wide watery eyes. "I will."

ABOUT THE AUTHOR

William Bernhardt is the author of over sixty books, including *The Last Chance Lawyer* (#1 National Bestseller), the historical novels *Challengers of the Dust* and *Nemesis*, three books of poetry, and the Red Sneaker books on writing. In addition, Bernhardt founded WriterCon Programs to mentor aspiring authors. He co-hosts an annual writers conference (WriterCon), small-group seminars, a writing cruise, a magazine, and a bi-weekly podcast.

Bernhardt has received the Southern Writers Guild's Gold Medal Award, the Royden B. Davis Distinguished Author Award (University of Pennsylvania) and the H. Louise Cobb Distinguished Author Award (Oklahoma State), which is given "in recognition of an outstanding body of work that has profoundly influenced the way in which we understand ourselves and American society at large." In 2019, he received the Arrell Gibson Lifetime Achievement Award from the Oklahoma Center for the Book.

In addition Bernhardt has written plays, a musical (book and score), humor, children stories, biography, and *New York Times* crossword puzzles. In 2013, he became a *Jeopardy!* champion. He has edited two anthologies (*Legal Briefs* and *Natural Suspect*) as fundraisers for The Nature Conservancy and the Children's Legal Defense Fund. In his spare time, he has enjoyed surfing, skiing, digging for dinosaurs, trekking through the Himalayas, paragliding, scuba diving, caving, zip-lining over the canopy of the Costa Rican rain forest, and jumping out of an airplane at 10,000 feet.

In 2017, when Bernhardt delivered the keynote address at the San Francisco Writers Conference, chairman Michael Larsen noted that in addition to penning novels, Bernhardt can "write a sonnet, play a sonata, plant a garden, try a lawsuit, teach a class, cook a gourmet meal, beat you at Scrabble, and work the *New York Times* crossword in under five minutes."

ALSO BY WILLIAM BERNHARDT

THE DANIEL PIKE NOVELS

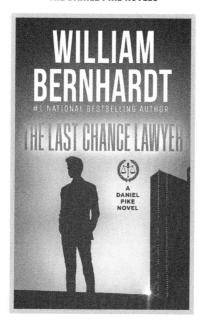

Getting his client off death row could save his career . . . or make him the next victim.

After his courtroom career goes up in smoke, a mysterious job offer from a secretive boss gives Daniel Pike a second chance but lands him an impossible case with multiple lives at stake . . .

- Court of Killers (Book 2)
- Trial by Blood (Book 3)
- Twisted Justice (Book 4)
- Judge and Jury (Book 5)
- Final Verdict (Book 6)
- Partners in Crime (with Ben Kincaid) (Book 7)

THE SPLITSVILLE LEGAL THRILLERS

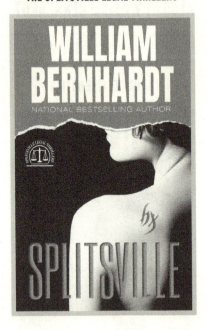

A struggling lawyer. A bitter custody battle. A deadly fire. This case could cost Kenzi her career—and her life.

When a desperate scientist begs for help getting her daughter back, Kenzi can't resist . . . even though this client is involved in Hexitel, a group she calls her religion but others call a cult. After her client is charged with murder, the ambitious attorney knows there is more at stake than a simple custody dispute.

- **Exposed (Book 2)**
- **Shameless (Book 3)**

THE BEN KINCAID NOVELS

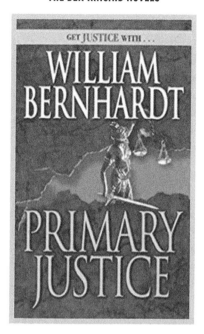

"[William] Bernhardt skillfully combines a cast of richly drawn characters, multiple plots, a damning portrait of a big law firm, and a climax that will take most readers by surprise."—*Chicago Tribune*

Ben Kincaid wants to be a lawyer because he wants to do the right thing. But once he leaves the D.A.'s office for a hotshot spot in Tulsa's most prestigious law firm, Ben discovers that doing the right thing and representing his clients' interests can be mutually exclusive.

- Blind Justice (Book 2)
- Deadly Justice (Book 3)
- Perfect Justice (Book 4)
- Cruel Justice (Book 5)
- Naked Justice (Book 6)
- Extreme Justice (Book 7)
- Dark Justice (Book 8)
- Silent Justice (Book 9)

- Murder One (Book 10)
- Criminal Intent (Book 11)
- Death Row (Book 12)
- Hate Crime (Book 13)
- Capitol Murder (Book 14)
- Capitol Threat (Book 15)
- Capitol Conspiracy (Book 16)
- Capitol Offense (Book 17)
- Capitol Betrayal (Book 18)
- Justice Returns (Book 19)

OTHER NOVELS

- Plot/Counterplot
- Challengers of the Dust
- The Game Master
- Nemesis: The Final Case of Eliot Ness
- Dark Eye
- Strip Search
- Double Jeopardy
- The Midnight Before Christmas
- Final Round
- The Code of Buddyhood

THE RED SNEAKER SERIES ON WRITING

- Story Structure: The Key to Successful Fiction
- Creating Character: Bringing Your Story to Life
- Perfecting Plot: Charting the Hero's Journey
- Dynamic Dialogue: Letting Your Story Speak
- Sizzling Style: Every Word Matters
- Powerful Premise: Writing the Irresistible
- Excellent Editing: The Writing Process
- Thinking Theme: The Heart of the Matter
- What Writers Need to Know: Essential Topics
- Dazzling Description: Painting the Perfect Picture
- The Fundamentals of Fiction (video series)

POETRY

- The White Bird
- The Ocean's Edge
- Traveling Salesman's Son

FOR YOUNG READERS

- Shine
- Princess Alice and the Dreadful Dragon
- Equal Justice: The Courage of Ada Sipuel
- The Black Sentry

EDITED BY WILLIAM BERNHARDT

- Legal Briefs: Short Stories by Today's Best Thriller Writers
- Natural Suspect: A Collaborative Novel of Suspense
- Christmas Tapestry

Made in United States
Orlando, FL
12 February 2025